JUS
BREATHE

Between the Lines Publishing
1769 Lexington Avenue N, Ste 286
Roseville MN 55113
btwnthelines.com

Published October 2022

ISBN: (Paperback) 978-1-958901-03-8
ISBN: (Ebook) 978-1-958901-04-5

JUS BREATHE

B. Lynn Carter

This book is dedicated to Alice.
Alice, who encouraged me, believed in me.
Alice, my ride-n-die, the only one who
could, who would, tell me, "This is the
worst line you've ever written!" . . . and
have me hear it. Alice who doesn't live here
anymore.
I did it Alice!

What's Going On?

I used to sleep. Even when there was nowhere I could call home, I used to lay my head down in any number of shady, frightful places and sleep.

Now, as usual, I am already awake when my little clock radio jumps to life. The DJ announces Marvin Gaye's new release. I like this song. Yesterday morning was the first time I heard it. Marvin's mellow voice had coasted through the air and launched his question into my world: "What's Going On?" I've been thinking about it a lot, that question. But so far, I have no answer. I reach over and shut it off.

I fidget and sit up on my bed. Looking around, I take in my surroundings. Aside from the single bed that my friend Lee and I got from the secondhand shop, there's an unframed full-length mirror with a substantial chunk missing from its lower left corner. This causes it to lean precariously against the wall. It must have been left by the previous tenant. Then there are my milk crates—six of them. Five serve as shelves for textbooks, clothes, and stuff. The other is a makeshift

1

night table. I've placed my new lava lamp on it. In the dorms, lava lamps are the new "in" thing. It's like everyone has one. I had one too, when I was still living there, but I left it for my roommate. Lee gave me this one as a moving-in gift.

Bernadette is sitting prominently on one of the crates. She is the doll I got for Christmas when I was eleven. She's been my constant companion, even during what I've come to think of as my "rootless" years. During those two years when I lived like a nomad, Bernadette was steadfast, always right there with me when "leaving time"—the time to pack-up and tip—rolled around, as it always did.

She is the first colored doll I ever had, the first I ever saw, possibly the first there ever was. Standing eighteen inches tall, she is a fashion doll. Her umber face beautifully formed, her black hair shiny and lush.

But her eyes . . . I can feel them on me. Burnished to a high gloss, those eyes that usually stare straight ahead into nothingness are now clearly filled with judgment and accusation. They target me like a laser. Instinctively, I place one hand on the bulge in my middle and use the other to push myself off the bed. I approach the doll with caution, fearing that look in her eyes could mean she might actually attack me. It's a *Children of the Damned,* spooky eyes, moment. I hesitate for a second. Taking a breath, I grab her and turn her around to face the wall. She offers no resistance.

I don't need shit from her!

This, after all, is my apartment . . . my first. Right here in the Bronx. I did it. I signed Dawn Marie Porter on an actual lease. It's official. It's the first place that is truly my own; no room-mated dorm space, no sofa in a friend's house, no huddling with my dog on a rooftop.

My dog, Siegfried, I think, and something static crackles my chest. I pull in a breath and push away the regret . . . the guilt.

Yes, this is my own space but it's not a home, not yet anyway. This space has no melody. It doesn't sing to me. A home needs a song—a duet. That song will come soon enough. I'll know it when it arrives. I've heard it before . . . in my grandma's house. I think I hear it every time Danny puts his arms around me. It's faint though, very faint.

Mercifully, the being inside me is still. This is new . . . unusual. Ever since it first decided to make itself known it has been in constant motion. At first it was just a little flutter, something easily mistaken for gas. I remember my ambivalence as I thought: *I'm late. I'm actually late. Maybe this is really happening, maybe not. Maybe it's a good thing, or maybe it's a mistake.*

I try to slow my thoughts, to pull in a breath. I need to be careful not to fall into the clutches of "the maybes." The endless maybes entrap me sometimes.

I mean, I know how these things work. It's not like I'm a kid. I just didn't think it could happen so soon. You hear about all these women who struggle, and here before I knew it there were these flutters. Soon the flutters became a rumble, then a twisting—a churning. I think I've felt its tiny body stretching, testing the limits of my narrow rib cage. It's actually alive. And that's a good thing for us, isn't it? Now Danny will be Daddy, and I will be Mommy. We'll be a real family.

Jus Breathe

We'll do it right, a real home. I'll breathe easy, like I used to.
That's what really matters, isn't it? It'll be worth it, worth all
of it. . . maybe.

Seeking the Music

I've been thinking about the music, "the duet," and about Danny. When our music comes it will be magical like the music that always sailed through my grandparent's house. And though everyone always called it "Momma's house," it was actually Momma and Papa's house. It was Momma and Papa's house well before I was born. Momma and Papa had fifty-two years of family and music together. Twenty-two of those years were in their two-family house in the Bronx. Then, Papa passed away, but the music still lingered.

I loved being downstairs in Momma's space. I spent as much time down there as I could get away with. I'd watch Momma play checkers with Papa every evening after he came home from work. There was a subtle rhythm to the sound of the checkers as they hit the board. Their light banter, and even their steady bickering, combined to form chords, themes, and intricate melodies that wove themselves into perfect harmonies.

It's true that Momma's house often rang out with gospel music. If it wasn't the other-earthly sounds of Mahalia Jackson, it was the rocking sounds of The Dixie Hummingbirds or The Mighty Clouds of Joy. But the music didn't come from the radio or from Momma playing her seventy-eights—not the special music. It didn't come from Momma's own church-choir voice that sometimes filled the air. No. They were a duet, she and Papa. The kind of music they made together was ever present.

The music was infused into the carpets, the drapes, the upholstery. It settled down with the dust. It lingered there on the surface, waiting to be released with any touch, lifted up with any step. The mere act of breathing seemed to cause the music to emerge. Once set free it hovered in the air. If I listened hard enough, I could hear it humming through the rooms. Once I knew what to listen for, it could always be heard. Once in-tune with the ripples, it could always be felt.

That was in sharp contrast to the sounds coming from the apartment upstairs where we lived—me, my mother, my father, and my sister, who we called Sista. The shrill discordant sounds that my parents emitted constantly cut through the air and grated on my ears. That's how I have come to think of their sounds: tunes whose notes always fell flat. I'm sure there were words that went with those unsyncopated melodies. I try not to recall them. But there were words—all ugly, out of tune, and off tempo. My father, always missing the downbeat, screamed them at will.

I was five. They were in the middle of yet another of their squealing, high-pitched arias. I had covered my ears. I always covered my ears.

"Look at her!" he screeched to the offbeat tempo of my mother's sobs. "How you gonna fix your mouth to tell me she's mine," he slurred, staggered. "She don't look like me. She don't look like none'a my people. Hell, she don't look like none'a *your* people."

"How can you say that? She's the spitting image of you, only . . ."

Despite my attempt to blot them out—fingers plunging deep into my ears—the drunken lyrics muscled their way into my head, burrowed their way into my chest. They were the last words I ever heard from the first man I ever loved.

"You had the nerve to name her Dawn," my daddy sneered . . . my daddy. "You shudda named her Midnight!"

Then he was gone. Because of me, he was gone. For a long time, I used to wonder if he would've stayed if she had named me Midnight. Maybe.

As it turned out, that was their very last performance together. And instead of screeching music, there was silence. I tried to wrap myself in that silence, tried not to miss Daddy, not to understand the meaning of his words. I tucked those words away—my daddy's words. Occasionally some random thing would push them to the surface, but for the most part I didn't allow myself to hear them. Years passed before their meaning was actually clear, before their toxins were released and became part of me.

But the silence had left a void, and something rushed in to fill that emptiness. On the very day that Daddy stormed away for good, his words still vibrating the walls, there was something. I felt it. It scurried up my spine. It was heavy. It weighed me down. It curved me, rounded my shoulders. I could no longer stand erect. It settled in my chest, took up all the space in my lungs.

I couldn't breathe.

I started gasping, gulping for air, fighting for every breath. A sharp, grating wheeze screeched with each inhalation. My legs turned to rubber. I was falling, collapsing to the linoleumed floor—its edges yellowed, its corners curled and frayed.

I heard my mother cry out. Frantic, she screamed down to Momma. "Call an ambulance! She can't breathe!"

Then, Momma was at my side there in the kitchen, lying by me on the cold, cracked floor, her face so close to mine. "Breathe," she whispered. "Jus breathe."

And I tried. But "It"—whatever it was—had a firm grip on my lungs. It squeezed. I tried to speak, to tell her that I couldn't, that it would not let me breathe.

"Shhh," she cautioned. "Don't try-ta talk lil girl, jus breathe. Ah'll do it wit ya," she said. Then Momma did what she always did, what she did so well. She taught by example. She took a long slow breath and waited for me to do the same. I tried. The breath was strangled. I felt dizzy, my vision blurred, my head filled up with fog. I was drifting through flashes of light and shadow.

"Relax, lil girl," Momma cooed. "Some things is jus in yo mine and dis here is one of em. It gon take yo mine ta deal wit dis. You need ta be da master of yo own mine . . . Jus breathe."

I could barely make out the sound of muffled sobs . . . my mother. And Momma's voice was echoing from some far-off place. My eyes were closing. I could not keep them open. I could no longer see Momma. I was falling away. But I could still hear her, a humming from afar. I tried to relax, struggled to take a breath. Then, I think that "thing" that had a hold on me decided to release a little valve, like a little opening in my chest. Tiny ribbons of air streamed their way into my lungs.

Gradually there was more relaxing, more tiny breaths, more air, and the melody of Momma's voice. "Be da master of yo own mine lil girl . . . Jus breathe."

Then "It" that had possessed me, slowly continued to loosen its grip. It released me. A current of life-giving air flooded my lungs. I gasped and coughed, gulping a deep reviving breath.

That was when I heard the siren wailing out its urgency. It screeched to a halt. Red, white, and blue lights flashed. Searchlights crisscrossed the walls and ceiling sniffing out a victim.

And Momma said, "You can send dat ambulance away. Dis lil girl jus needs ta learn how ta master her own mine. She jus needs ta breathe."

Years passed. And that thing, some kind of creature—or whatever it was that had scurried up my spine that day—

9

settled in, taking up permanent residence in my chest. Although I was never quite able to breathe the same, like deep and easy, I got used to its weight. Even though that thing has lived in my chest since I was five, for the most part it doesn't trouble me. I've made room for it. I had to. Except that now my breathing is not always automatic. There are times, many times, when I have to remind myself to breathe.

When I was sixteen my mother remarried. We were preparing to move in with her new husband—a new start. I thought there might even be music, maybe. I thought maybe I could start to breathe easy, like the way I used to breathe in Momma's house, the way I could breathe whenever I was in the little apartment that Momma called home . . . after the fire. The way I can breathe when I am in Danny's arms.

My mother had said that we could finally "breathe easy." She used those actual words. She said we wouldn't have to worry about money, not anymore. We were going to live in a house again, "our own house," she said. We were going to be a happy family.

All those promises were shot to hell the very first day that we moved in.

Moving in Day

I saw stars! I literally saw stars! Looking back now I guess that was a strange thing to be fixated on at that moment. I recall thinking it was just like in the cartoons. I expected little birdies to materialize and flutter around my head.

Then there was a voice, at least I think it was a voice. Though it was muffled by the cotton forming in my head, it somehow sounded desperate. And there was pain. It shot up from my jaw to my brain and back down again. And there were ghostly figures, moving fast, a blur of white overalls, the smell of wall paint, shuffling feet, a scuffle.

And that voice was rolling through my brain—one word, like an echo from far away.

"Attack . . ."

It's summer. It's always summer when I dream of those childhood days. The boys have hijacked my Spalding ball, again. I am chasing them. I sic Siegfried on them. She is doing her most ferocious growl and a playful tug of war on their shoestrings as I yell, "Attack!! Attack!! Attack!!"

The voice was shrill, shrieking out that word. It occurred to me that it was my own voice guiding my gradual return to the stark reality of the situation; back to what just happened, back to the moment that my mother's new husband's fist made contact with my face; back to Siegfried lunging at his neck, taking him down, to the painters trying to free him from her grip, trying to get me to call her off.

Dazed, I remained in my head a little longer, lingered in the fascination that my big-boned shepherd could take a man down like that, fascinated that she even had it in her. I think I did call her off or maybe she relented of her own accord. That's when "that thing" took possession of my lungs. I gasped for air. I'm pretty sure that all of them—the painters, my mother's husband—were yelling, but it was hard to hear them over the muffled ringing in my brain.

What I do know is this: The moment that meaty fist impacted my face on that momentous moving-in day—the first day of what was to be our "new lives" with my mother's new husband—the world had shifted.

Now, I allow my mind to drift further into that day.

I was completely out of my body. I was some invisible spirit lurking through the rooms. Suddenly there was another "me." A me outside of me. I recognized her as me but somehow light-skinned, pretty, nowhere near as midnight black as me. Right away she started examining scenes, like she was searching for clues. I didn't know where she'd come from, but somehow, I knew she was there to help. It was like she could figure out answers when I couldn't even figure out questions. It was like she wasn't scared, not even a little, like she could handle things. Still, I wasn't sure if I was happy that she'd come to take over. She was only me, right? Why did her light skin make her think that she was "all that?" The very idea got on my last nerve. Still, I have to admit that after a while I did learn to lean on her. That night was the first time she ever appeared, but it wouldn't be the last.

When that "me" appeared that day, I was as weightless and unseen as she was. I had no substance as I haunted through the memory. I let her take my hand, let her anchor me as I watched my sixteen-year-old self stuff things into an oversized pillowcase: my dungarees, my favorite book, my doll.

My mother arrived. Someone must have called her. Where had she been? I turned my back to her. Maybe I was trying to hide the swelling in my jaw; maybe it was the tears running down my face that I was hiding.

I knew this marriage meant so much to Mom. She thought she had found the "good man," a man like Papa. Black women are always looking for the "good man." He was a businessman. He owned a company. Mom would live the American dream. I wanted that for her—for us. I did. But clearly, he was not the one she'd hoped for. We would not be a family. This would not be a home, not *my* home. I had to leave.

Outside Me watched Mom. With her bright and sunny light-skinned take on the situation, it was like she fully ex-

13

pected Mom to go to me, to comfort me. She actually thought Mom could make things better. But that redbone girl turned out to be wrong because Mom just stood in the door. And somehow I felt reassured, because now it was obvious that Outside Me isn't always right. Sometimes things just are . . . what they are.

"What did you say to him?" Mom had asked. For a moment I seriously considered the question. What *did* I say to him? I couldn't recall. But the more I thought about it, the more I realized how absurd the question was.

"What did I say to him!?" I took a halting breath and turned to face her. A gasp escaped her lips when she saw my swollen face. She came for me, then. I rejected her touch.

"What could I possibly have said to him? I don't even know him! Do you? What do you think I could've said to him that would make this okay?"

"I didn't say that it's okay!"

"You didn't say it isn't!"

"Dawny, I just want to know what happened."

"Nothing Ma; nothing happened. I'm just leaving."

I was numb, still free of corporal restrictions outside of myself. I continued to float through the scene. Outside Me lingered, reminded me to breathe. She watched over me as I resumed stuffing things into the pillowcase: my school notebook, my diary, my little clock radio.

"Where do you think you're going?" Mom asked after a while.

"*You* married the asshole; *you* live with him!" Using that language with my mother was unheard of.

"Where are you going?" She ignored my outburst.

"Away from here. Maybe to Momma's."

"The last thing your grandmother needs is a teenager in the house," she said. I dared to roll my eyes. "You're barely sixteen," she said. "You can't leave. I'll report you to the truant officers."

I hovered in the memory, drifting in close, wanting to examine me. Outside Me followed. The two of us peered into my past face. We could see that I was deflated, no appetite for argument. In a voice barely a decibel above a whisper, I heard myself say, "I didn't say I'm leaving school, Mother. I said I'm leaving here."

School. A small inkling—the whisper of a dream, of a future, of college—flittered across my mind, then drifted away. I could not hold on to that dream, certainly not for two more years. College . . . who was I kidding? It was not like something that was ever really anchored in my possibilities anyway.

Suddenly I was earthbound, still feeling unseen. Outside Me stepped back, let me take the lead. I examined the level-headed woman who raised me; the woman who waited tables and worked her way through nursing school, who took a job as a cashier after Daddy left, when the jobs for which she had trained were denied to her. Mom was the woman who made sacrifices, understood survival. I looked into her eyes. I recognized the pragmatism that had sustained us, had seen us through. Her common sense reached out and connected with my own. I could feel it. We were the same. Mom and I both knew that in two years I would certainly leave. I'd be off to start my own life even without college, wouldn't I? Then she would be alone—no good man, no American dream. And if I stayed, they would be two horrendous years. We both knew that. We both knew about resilience. I looked over at Outside Me and somehow her resolve became my own. In that moment I was strong like her, like Mom—a survivor. I only hoped that Mom would continue to survive as well.

I headed for the door. I passed by Siegfried, who whined, begged me not to leave her behind. But I didn't even know where I was going. How could I take her? It was clear that my mother had resolved to let me go, at least for a while. I could see it in her eyes.

"Leave her," Mom said. "I'll look after her. He won't hurt her." I just stared, barely present in the moment. "And he won't hurt me."

Still deep in the memory, I watched myself kneel and hug Siegfried for a long time. I whispered something in her ear, maybe a promise to return for her. Maybe I murmured instructions, gave her permission to protect my mother and try to forgive her husband. If Outside Me heard those whispers, she never let on.

I grabbed my oversized pillowcase. Though something was tugging at my heart, I knew I had to tip. I didn't look back.

Of Wishes and Prayers

The apartment is quiet. That is, it's as quiet as an apartment in the Bronx can possibly be. The music booming from someplace in the building and the intermittent roar of sirens from the streets below fade into the background . . . residential deafness. The only sounds breaking my relative silence are of the rain bouncing off the windowpane, splattering on the fire escape, and the water dribbling from the ceiling. It's the curse of living on the top floor . . . trickle, trickle, little leak.

I watch as each drop ripples the water in the large gumbo pot that I inherited from Momma. I contrast these ripples with the memory of the hot roiling bubbles of Momma's Creole gumbo—the crabs and shrimps churning in the thick savory soup. I can almost smell it, the aroma winging through the air. I sigh and turn away as I promise myself that I will use Momma's pot for its intended purpose . . . one day.

But today, the gumbo pot is actively converting my waterfall into a pond. The water plunking into the pot is rhythmic, like music, each drop sounding its own unique note. I can almost hear the melody in it. My heart hears it too. It reacts to the cadence, matching the slow deliberate rhythm beat for beat. It is lulling me away. My breaths fall into a regular rhythm. I find myself falling into a dream.

Hazy sunlight streams through a soft misty rain that patters gently to the ground. A sun-shower! We walk hand in hand through the park, down the moss-covered lane. The trees, lush and green, form a canopy over our heads. The air is fragrant with spring flowers. I breathe. Danny is with me, and I breathe deep easy breaths. And there is music. The birds are singing a concert. Up ahead a rainbow, its vivid, multicolored bands so spectacular that they illuminate the entire sky with color. We come to an enclave and sit. We wait, expecting the sun to rise.

He places both hands on my belly. I place my hands over his. We wait, expecting some sign of life. The child is still. Suddenly the music is replaced by a thumping, like a bass drum.

Ta-dum, ta-dum.

The beating grows louder.

Ta-dum. A heartbeat.

*Louder it pounds: **Ta-dum**!*

My chest tightens. Where has the music gone? The sound is deafening, throbbing in my head.

Ta-dum, ta-dum!

My belly is a dead weight, a swelling lump! I search for his hands. His eyes are hard, indifferent. He is vanishing, dematerializing. He is being absorbed into the rainbow as its colors run together, morphing into blood-red droplets, then fading to black.

And he is gone.

I jerk myself upright, coughing and gagging. I am alone in the dark, in my single bed. The only hands on my belly are my own. My throat is constricting. I am straining to breathe. I remember to relax . . . *jus breathe.*

I stumble to the bathroom and splash water on my face. I'm standing here, clutching at the sink, staring into the mirror. Its silvery shimmer casts a haze across my face. I think about the part of the dream before it turned into a nightmare. I was so happy. We had the music. But it wasn't real. The bliss dissipated, like mist.

I am left with only that frightening, throbbing beat. I realize now that I can still hear it . . . no . . . *feel* it. I place my hands over my chest. My heart is racing, doing the boogaloo. I hear the sound of water dripping furiously into the gumbo pot that's in the living room, beyond the bathroom door. I realize my heart is marking time with the water's plunking rhythms, beating harder and faster than it should. I pant rapid, shallow breaths. For a moment I feel faint. I close the toilet lid and sit. I try to relax, breathe, "will" my heart to be calm. As my heartbeat slows to a canter, this life inside me finds a rhythm of its own.

I leave the bathroom, pace the short length of the living room—back and forth, forth and back. I've heard somewhere that babies are lulled to sleep by motion. Not this one. Its movements seem to go from restless to angry. I pace for what must be hours, until my back screams for relief. I go into the bedroom and sit on the bed. The baby seems to object to being crunched in. It feels like it's perfecting its boxing skills, delivering unsyncopated, unsteady jabs. Exhausted, I lie flat, stretch out as best as I can, and try to sleep. But tiny staccato kicks to my back nix that idea. I suddenly realize I never gave much thought to the actual "being pregnant" part of pregnancy.

It is morning. I am wide awake when my clock radio jumps to life. There has been no sleep. My head aches. What feels like a small alien being has tumbled and rumbled inside me all night. It's restless, relentless, unbearable. Kicking, stretching, fidgeting; there's been no sleeping, no sitting, no standing, no relief, no peace. I just want some peace, only some peace. That's all.

Something explodes in my pounding head and I jump off the bed. Then, with my arms stretching upward, and seemingly addressing a random crack-line in the ceiling, I propel these words out into the universe, shriek them right out loud. "Will you please stop it! Just be still! I wish, I wish you would just stop! Be still!"

And then, just like that . . . it does.

Another day, I lie in bed watching a ribbon of early morning sunlight meander its way between the tenement buildings. The clock radio comes to life and Marvin is posing the same lyrical question. But on this morning, I am as far from an answer to that question as I've ever been. I don't know what's going on. I place my hands on my belly; no movement . . . still. At least one of us can sleep.

Now my own questions pry their way into my brain. How long has it been? How long since I said those words, made that wish? It was a wish, not a prayer. What if, of all the wishes I've ever wished, this is the one that's granted? Was it two days ago? A week? Was it yesterday that I made that wish?

I sit up in bed between fitful dozing. The baby is quiet, but I still can't sleep. I'm afraid of sleep, afraid of the rapid heartbeat, afraid of the dream, the disappearing hands. But mostly I'm afraid of the wish coming true, the "stopping" I begged for. I'm afraid of joining this baby somewhere suspended, muted, frozen and alone.

I think about making another wish, wondering if it will be granted as well. I think about Danny and I am wishing him here with me to help me sleep, to help me breathe, to help me connect with the baby. But I don't make that wish. I can't, not yet. Things are not ready.

What was it that Momma always said? "Take care Lil Girl, or you might just get what you wish for."

Little Padre

I like to think of the living room as the "sitting room" — funny because there's nowhere to sit. I walk through the living room on my way to the kitchen, smiling as I think about my own little inside joke. I had to choose between furniture or a phone and my music. I opted for the latter. Music is beauty. It will always come first. I reach for the record player that is on the floor and place a forty-five on the turntable. I set it to repeat. The mellow sound of "Rainy Night in Georgia" flows, matching my mood.

In the fridge there are six eggs, half a bottle of apple juice, and six slices of bread, enough for breakfast, lunch, and dinner. I still have half a bottle of vitamins. Ms. Thompson — or as everyone calls her, Ms. T — is my college counselor. She's said that she can hook me up with food stamps. I think I'm okay for now. I may have to do that when this baby comes. I suppress the thought, *If this baby comes.* Still no movement.

I stand in my kitchen, trying to think up yet another way to prepare eggs. I jump at a ringing sound. It's not the phone. It takes me a moment. It's the doorbell. It's the first time I've ever heard it ring. Who could it be? I spoke to Lee this morning. Again, she won't be coming by. Looking through the peephole I can only see pink magnified lips. Sliding aside the heavy steel bar that serves as a second lock, I peek through the chained door to get a better look. Then I hear a familiar voice.

"Dawn, it's me, Ralfie."

Ralfie! A breath catches in my chest. I feel lightheaded. I don't want to see anyone. I don't want anyone to see me. Least of all Ralfie, "the little padre." Rafael Mateo Perez, the nice guy who spent two years in a seminary studying to be a priest. Ralfie with those large brown puppy dog eyes that look like they have things to teach you. Eyes that know your secrets even without a confessional . . . eyes that pity you. Ralfie, my friend. With my hands on my chest, I lean against the door and remind myself to breathe.

"I brought breakfast and some groceries and stuff," he calls through the door. "Can I come in?"

I want to say, "No! Go away!" but "Yes, of course" comes out instead. I open the door. "What are you doing here?"

"Visiting you." His voice as always is soothing, his soft brown eyes smiling.

"I mean, how did you find me? The only ones who know where I live are Ms. T. and . . ."

"Lee." He completes my sentence.

"Oh yeah, Lee. I should've known she wouldn't keep her mouth shut."

"Don't say that. Lee's a good friend to you. She's always lookin' out for you. She told me she hasn't been up here to see you, what, with finals and work. But she's worried about you."

"So she sent you."

"So she sent me."

Ralfie has brought a feast. Working together, we use caramelized onions and cheddar cheese to transform my scrambled eggs into a scrumptious omelet. We serve them with down-home grits steeped in butter, hot croissants, fruit and sweet plantains or—as Ralfie calls them—*platanos maduros*. We sit on the bed and talk between bites. I smear strawberry jam on a croissant, lick my fingers clean, and finish up with a handful of blueberries.

Having eaten until I can't move, I turn my full attention to Ralfie. He's always been such a nice guy. I wonder what I have done to deserve such a good friend, a good guy. Then it occurs to me that Ralfie is more than that. He's a "God-guy," and I'm thinking that maybe I should confess, tell him about the wish and how the baby has stopped moving. Maybe he can put in a word for me with God. I'm not sure that God actually knows me.

Momma always said that I needed to work hard to make myself known to Him. I think she meant that I should go to church. I'm pretty sure such an introduction can only be made in a church. But despite Momma's insistence, my mother never did do baptisms. So, there was something unsettling about being in God's actual house—like I hadn't been invited. I always felt really small there, so small that I doubted he would actually notice me anyway. It was never something I could really get with.

Maybe Ralfie can help me explain to Him that it wasn't a prayer . . . just a silly little wish, not an actual prayer. I'm guessing that God makes a distinction.

"Ralfie?" I ask. "Assuming that He knows you, do you think God deals with wishes and prayers, you know, the same way? Or is one given, like, priority or something?"

"Wow! I'm not sure that I can speak for God, but I'm guessing it depends on the intent of the person who's sending them out, you know, the wishes and the prayers. Why?"

"Just wondering," I say, avoiding those eyes. I'm sure there is another question on the tip of Ralfie's tongue, but he doesn't ask it. Instead, he stares at me for a long moment with those probing eyes, then reaches in his shirt pocket and hands me a piece of paper.

"I almost forgot. This is from Ms. T," he says. "It's the number of a private ob-gyn doctor who's agreed to Medicaid and will see you in the evenings so you can make your classes."

My heart zaps. This may mean I get to stay in school, maybe?

Ms. T is my counselor. She said the rules about taking a leave, even for pregnancy, haven't been laid out yet because it's just the first year of the SEEK college assistance program.

"How did she know?" I struggle to keep the cry out of my voice. "I told her that I was going to a clinic in Bronx Lebanon."

"Hey, she's Ms. T. She knows stuff."

"Like when she's being lied to." I drop my eyes. I hated lying to Ms. T and she knew all along.

"Pretty much," Ralfie says. "She told me that swinging this arrangement with this doctor friend of hers took some doing." The SEEK counselors go all out for their students. But I lucked up with Ms. T. She's the best.

Ralfie grabs some toilet tissue from a roll that I set out to use as napkins. He wipes his hands and mouth. Then he rises, walks into the living room, and shuffles through my forty-fives saying, "I like this song, the rainy Georgia song," he says referring to the record that I have playing on repeat. "But it's a little depressing, don't you think?" He places several records on the turntable's cue and presses play. The forty-five drops into place and The Fifth Dimension's, "Aquarius/Let the Sunshine In" fills the air.

"Now this is more like it," he says. "This is a good song for you."

"I'm an Aries."

"Technicality." He smiles. Then, pointing to the note from Ms. Thompson he says, "Aren't you gonna call and make that appointment?"

"I'll call later."

He picks up the phone and hands it to me, saying, "You'll call now."

Smoke and Mirrors

It has been raining so much lately. Days like this always make me think about Danny. It's that sad kind of rain that happens when a president is assassinated, or when those guys are walking on the moon, or when Danny and I are holed up in his room yearning for the sun—him on one side of the room, me on the other. That's the kind of rain it is— driving, steady, and morose. Looks like there'll be no sun again today.

I check the gumbo pot. The water is nearing the brim. It's heavy as I lift it and water splashes and beads on the floor. Dumping the water into the toilet, I mop up the spill.

I know I should've gone to see a doctor a long time ago. What am I, three, four months gone, or more? Less? I'm not even sure. It's just that, well, going to a doctor at the onset would've confirmed it, made it real. Going to a doctor now might confirm just the opposite.

The doctor that Ms. T hooked me up with can't see me until next week. Guilt about my lack of prenatal care is weighing heavy on my mind. But I did go to the drugstore. I did buy those vitamins. I'm not drinking coffee or smoking grass. Those things can hurt a baby. I am trying to take care. And there is the question of money.

I'm craving coffee, but I settle for chamomile tea. I return to the bedroom and sit on the bed. I sip my tea and push away thoughts of Danny. It's not time yet.

Instead, I think about my counselor, Ms. T. She was the one that helped me get Medicaid. Even though I haven't actually used it yet. I meditate on sending Ms. T a "thank-you" vibe. It was Ms. T who explained the SEEK program to me.

"It's an initiative that followed the racial unrest that erupted in the country several years back," she had said. "It's a real boots on the ground effort to address some of the issues that caused all that strife." She beamed as she continued. "The program offers counseling, financial support, and if you're lucky enough to get in, even housing to top performing, low-income students citywide," she'd said.

As she spoke, I remember thinking how amazed I was to be counted among them . . . me a SEEK student. I've forgotten what it stands for. Thinking about it now though . . . about Danny . . . it's not clear what I've actually been seeking.

It's been almost three years since Ms. T helped me get into the SEEK dormitory, effectively putting an end to the two prior years that I had spent as a nomad. I have so much to thank Ms. T for. She even helped me find the apartment I live in now. It's a fifth-floor walk-up in the southwest Bronx. It's not in the greatest building, but for now it's shelter; a tenement that barely survived a recent fire. The halls are blackened with soot and the smell of smoke pervades. That smell spikes memories of Momma's house—the flames, the blackness, the ice. Those memories threaten every time I step foot into the building.

The super's wife has assured me that they will be cleaning it up as soon as the insurance assessment is done, and that the smell will be washed away. She's also said that before the fire this was one of the nicest buildings on the block.

I think about that, contrasting this row of sad grey tenements with Momma's two-family house that stood in the southern end of the Bronx on the tree-lined street where I grew up. Yes, that was also the Bronx. But that was a different Bronx, in a different time. That was the Bronx before the "pronouncement," before that man on the newscast stood up there and spoke that word: *ghetto*. That was the Bronx before they encircled it with a bright red line, before everything changed . . . before all the infernos. For a long time when I was a child there were actually no blaring fire truck sirens constantly roaring through the streets of the Bronx.

In the tenement building where I now reside, the halls are illuminated with light that comes through the windows located on each landing. In the daytime, you can look out and see the inner courtyard, tattered and in decline. Some people have started tossing garbage through the windows instead of taking it down and placing it in the trashcans below. I've actually considered it. On some level I think I can understand why they do it. In the Bronx, like anywhere else, I guess, large rats run rampant around open garbage. I certainly don't want to be confronted with one either, but I just can't seem to bring myself to toss garbage. So, I keep it in my apartment until I can't deal with the stench and then I drudge it down the five flights. I always make lots of noise in the hope that the rats want to avoid me as much as I do them. I fling the garbage to the top of the pile and run for my life.

When the sun goes down, the hallway is dark and nightmarish. The worn marble steps of the staircase bear the imprints of many past soles. At night, in the sooty blackness of the hall, it feels like your feet are sliding into a stranger's coffin. The slap, slap, slap of each footfall echoes and multiplies, making it unclear if I'm alone or if someone else is stepping right behind me. This is why I try to get out early and be back before it gets dark. With school it's not always possible, so I take care and carry my flashlight.

My stomach is always tense when I'm climbing the dark staircase. I place my hand on my belly as I make my way, trying to relax, and remembering to breathe. My large flashlight beacons the way. Its strong beam banishes all dangers. It is my weapon. With it I am armed and prepared. I make my way up the five flights, flinching and angling my death ray in the direction of any creaky sounds or gaining footsteps. The screech of a door opening, the scratches of something scurrying across the landing, are all revealed and dispelled as I escape into the sanctuary of my apartment.

My flashlight can dispatch the terrors in the dark, but it cannot do anything about that poignant, smoky odor that engulfs me. If I let it, that smell can suck me back into Momma's house, back into the grief. It sends me tumbling into the memory, walking through the aftermath once the flames had been extinguished . . .

I was in abject blackness.

There were shadows, ghostly impressions of familiar items, barely recognizable. Gone was the fragile mirrored music box that once played "Ain't Misbehaving." Missing was that resounding and steady . . . tick . . . tick . . . tick . . . of Papa's wind-up clock that never, ever went un-wound. Absent, the metal-clad telephone, black and heavy. The weighty oversized receiver that used to dwarf my face . . . gone.

The fragrance of loose powder and Tabu had been replaced by the acrid smell of melted plastic, the stench of burnt wood and paper. The actual flames had completely spared Momma's downstairs living quarters, but the intense heat and the firemen had not. They came with sirens howling through the streets of the Bronx. They came to save us. They were an avenging tsunami. They brought a wall of water—a deluge. Then, they proceeded to smash and destroy all that had survived the flames. At least, that's how it seemed to me at the time.

On that mid-winter's night, it was as black as despair and as cold as a crypt. Everything was encased in ice. Everyone was infused with ice. Ice crackled underfoot with every step. That thing, that ever-present thing inside my chest stirred, stretched, expanded in my lungs. My breaths narrowed to a wheeze.

I splintered.

Then my ally, that me, the pretty light-skinned me, the one who stands outside of me, emerged. She took my hand to guide me through the ruins. My mind spaced away that night, just briefly, contemplating the relationship between fire and ice, saviors and . . . interior desecrators.

Or so it seemed.

The glare of flashlights snatched me back, shook me into the moment. Crisscrossing beams cut through the black void, casting sinister shadows as my grief-stricken family picked through the remains, seeking the salvageable.

A beam flashed. In a sooty blue glass mirror, my reflection flickered, split, and straddled a rickety fissure; my face was fractured, cracked, and disjointed. So, on that wretched night this question eased across my mind: Mirror, mirror, who's been shattered most of all?

As always, when I reach the fifth floor, my relief is palpable. I slip the key into the lock and open the door. The smoky smell begins to fade, taking the memory of that awful night along with it. But a subtle grief remains, hanging in the air. I think about Momma, remember how I stared into that fractured blue glass, how I posed that question. How the answer bounced back. It was the loss of her beloved home that shattered her. Yes, it was Momma who was shattered most of all.

As I step through the apartment door, that sad notion flares up, mingles with the smoky stench behind me and fades away.

Sanctuary

My apartment . . . that is the one positive thing about this building that I now try to call home. My apartment is pristine. Miraculously untouched by the fire—an oasis. I'd been afraid of that sooty stench, of those memories. But to my surprise not even the slightest smoky odor invades the space. This is probably because a brand-new solid steel door had been put on the apartment's entrance shortly before the fire occurred. I think of it as my mighty mega door. I shudder to think what happened to the previous door. Also, I used money that I'd saved while still living in the dorms to have the wood floors in the hall and living room scraped and polished. So, whenever I open my mighty steel door, I see a long narrow hallway gleaming the way, leading me to the small square shaped space that is my living room. And although the room is empty, the gumbo pot, my record collection, my record player, and the shiny floors fill the void.

Then there are the two very ornate brass key hooks that are attached to the wall at the end of the hall. I didn't place them there. With their fancy art deco design, they always strike me as somehow out of place here, like something that would've belonged in Momma's house. Still, they're the perfect place to keep the two sets of door keys that I was given— one set for me and soon one set for Danny. When I enter the apartment, I always hang my key there right next to the spare.

The rent for the apartment is as low as one might expect in a half burnt-out building. For now, if I'm careful, I can manage it on my own with my work-study job and the SEEK stipend. Although I'm sure when Danny and I make our plans, he'll want to pool our resources and get the hell out of here. It'll be just a little longer. Things aren't ready yet.

It's raining again. I'm up before dawn, before the alarm sounds, and Marvin sings out the question that I'm still grappling with. I'm no closer to knowing what's going on. Me being awake so early happens a lot. Maybe that's why Mom named me Dawn. Maybe I was born at dawn. I never did ask, and she never did tell me. I never did understand why she named me Dawn.

I take a breath. I reach for my eyeglasses on the night table. Then I go to the milk crates and rummage, looking for something to wear. I retrieve a dashiki, shake it out, and hold it up for inspection. It needs ironing but I left my iron in my old dorm room. I'll have to call my roommate Luanne and tell her I'm coming for it. The dashiki is large and shapeless. I made it myself when I was still living in the dorms. I never really liked it but now it's my favorite. I slide it over my head, the garment fitting tightly across my breasts that are now huge and tender and spilling out of my bra. I sigh and think, *Be careful what you wish for*.

Checking myself in the full-length mirror that leans against the wall, I realize that I look top heavy, like I might tumble forward. The dashiki drapes off my breasts like a tent and hangs mid-thigh, essentially concealing the bulge in my middle. I'm unable to zip my dungarees so I use a belt to bridge the gap.

I step back to take in the overall effect. My bell-bottomed dungarees sweep the floor. They are ragged and worn at the fringes. With all this rain they'll surely get soaked. I fish under the bed and retrieve my platform shoes. I contemplate them as I try to decide whether it's wiser to deal with wet dungarees or to teeter on these elevated shoes in my current state—unbalanced.

Lincoln Hospital

Sirens are constantly screaming their way through the streets of the Bronx. They are the prima contraltos in the chorus of our daily lives, the muted soundtracks of our collective existence. Their howls simply fade into the background. Their requiems go un-noted . . . no matter how loud they blare. That was why, on that day, I took no notice. Yes, on some level I heard those sirens like I always did—distant, dispassionate. I simply doubled my effort to focus on the novel that I was reading for school.

I had just turned sixteen when I left my mother's husband's house and went to live with Momma. That was just before the fire came and snatched our home away, forcing us to move to a small apartment on Fox street. We had only been living there for two months when I was sitting in the front room and overheard Momma and my mother having a loud exchange in the kitchen.

Another argument? I wondered. Then there was silence, one less distraction. I yawned, leaned back in the chair, and turned a page.

Then, a sharp-edged siren screeched to an abrupt halt just outside our building. After all the noise, the sudden, eerie quiet in the Bronx streets snatched at my attention. A flood of déjà vu overtook me as red, white, and blue lights flashed. But this time the searchlights that crisscrossed the walls and ceiling sniffing for a victim, found one.

I dropped the book. It slammed to the floor, the sound reverberating in my head. I ran to the kitchen. Momma was sprawled out on the floor, her hand clutching at her chest, her eyes unfocused, and her mouth open as she labored to breathe. My lungs tightened. My heart jumped into overtime.

My mother, kneeling by Momma's side, was holding her hand, and sobbing. "Mother," she moaned. "Mother, I'm so sorry. I'm so sorry about everything—all of it!"

I slid to Momma's side. "Momma?" I said, my voice soft, tentative.

Her eyelids fluttered and she turned her head. A weak smile graced her lips and travelled to her eyes as she recognized me. "Lil girl . . ." her voice was barely audible.

"Shhh, Momma; don't try to talk. Just breathe. You can't . . . You just have to keep breathing, okay? Just breathe," I said as a river of snot and tears started quietly rolling down my face.

Then there were men, strangers, a gurney. As they prepared to carry Momma away, I thought I felt something hot making its way up from the floor. It raged through me, my legs, my stomach, my crowded chest. It rambled past my heart on to my throat, its pressure building. Seeking release, it forced its way through my open mouth, emerging as a roar.

"What did you do to her!" The ferocity of my words stunned. They were a weapon, sharp and lethal, aimed directly at my mother's heart. They hit their target and she doubled over, sobbing, and gasping for air. I wondered if maybe she too had something heavy living in her chest.

Then she and Momma were swallowed up in the bowels of the ambulance. I wasn't allowed to go. Drained, I could only watch as the ambulance went howling its way through the frigid Bronx streets.

I walked into Lincoln Hospital through the wrong entrance. I had not been back in this hospital since my parents walked out with me the day I was born. I found myself in the emergency room being assailed by the smells of pain and desperation, blood, and body odors. I smelled the sweat of the staff working to triage those most in need; the sharp scent intermingled with the disinfectants that an orderly was using to wash the place clean, as though he could make it sterile, as though there could be a fresh start, a do-over here in this sad place.

I started towards the information desk and was nearly run over by four men, dressed in baby blue, rapidly pushing a boy on a gurney.

"GSW to the chest!" one of them called. The boy looked to be around my age, no more than sixteen. His eyes were fluttering and rolling back in his head. His hands were resting on his stomach like they had been placed there. A hole in his blood-drenched chest was seeping the life from his body, leaving a thick trail of red on the floor. One of the blue suit guys was pressing on the wound, frantically trying to stop the flow.

I cringed, gagged, turned away. I doubled over. The room started to whirl. I staggered and stumbled to a chair.

"You okay kid?" Someone was asking me. I don't know how long it took me to answer. I heard Momma's voice, *"Jus breathe!"*

"Fine," I said. "That boy, will he . . . "

"Only God knows. But there's one thing in his favor. This is the best hospital in the state for gunshot wounds. If you gotta get shot, this is where you wanna be," the nurse said. She started preparing to take my blood pressure.

"No," I said. "I'm not a patient. I'm just here to visit my grandma. She was brought in last night. They said I could see her today."

The tiny space was partitioned off by curtains on both sides. Momma was lying in a hospital bed that looked more like a crib—her eyes closed, my mother sitting by her side. There was an eerie quiet below the sounds of the low steady beeps coming from a machine that looked like a big TV and the soft sniffles coming from my mother. I was encouraged when I saw that three wires from the TV machine were attached to Momma's chest. I thought maybe they were there to make sure her heart kept beating. A needle in Momma's arm was connected to a tube attached to a bottle of clear liquid that hung from a stand next to the bed. Another tube snaked down from under the sheets.

I stood in the doorway. Momma looked so small—not like the same woman who always filled up a room with her presence. Her face had a brown, ashy pallor, and her lips were grey. I sucked in a wheezy breath. My mother turned and looked up at me, her eyes so full of grief that I felt like my heart would deflate. I stumbled to her and took her hands in mine.

"Mom, I'm so sorry. Last night, I knew you didn't . . . I didn't mean . . ."

"Hush," she said, standing and taking me in her arms. "I know. I know."

"How's a body s'posed ta get some rest wit y'all makin' all dat noise," Momma managed, her voice weak and raspy.

"Oh Momma," I said, trying to keep the cry out of my voice. But Momma wasn't looking at me. Her eyes were on my mother. I didn't know what passed between them, but I knew something had.

"I think I'll go get a drink. You want anything, Dawn?"

I just looked at her. The last thing I was thinking about was a drink, and I'm sure it was the last thing she was thinking about too.

"Lil girl," Momma said once we were alone. She reached for my hand, and straining to speak, she went on, "Dhey's somethin' Ah gots ta tell ya fore Ah leaves this body behind. Dis here, dis body, it's just borrowed. It ain't fa-ever. It's just somethin' to keep yo spirit in fa awhile. Ma spirit is bout to go and join the Lord. It's ma time. Ah feels it."

I broke into tears. "Momma don't say that. You're not going anywhere. You can't! I won't know how to breathe without you."

"Course you will. You has to. You's gonna find a way ta master yo own mind. You been workin' on dat since you was little." She paused, breaking into a cough before she continued. "Um worried dat sometimes you lets things, dark noise, all up in yo head and turn you around. Ah sees it. Ah sees how yo eyes be lookin' in, instead of lookin' out. Ah was jus like you fa a spell. Folks said Ah was crazy, fo Ah learned to kill dat noise in ma head." Her voice cracked. I reached for her water glass. I supported her head as she took a sip. "Jus like me," she said. "You needs ta master all dat noise up in yo head. Jus know you's already got all the answers inside ya. And fa-give ma daughter," she said. That was the first time I'd ever heard her call Mom her daughter. "She cain't understand a chil' like you; a chil dat feels things, sees things da rest of us don't see—a special spirited chil'. It's how you's meant ta be," she said. "Fa sho, you's different, special. Don't neva change." She stopped to catch her breath. "Ah was like you, ya know, was on ma own younger than you is now. Just know Ah'll always be wit ya." Her voice trailed off. The effort it took to speak had become too much for her. She looked towards the door and I followed her gaze. My mother, my sister, my sister's husband, and their two-year-old daughter, were standing there. Momma smiled a deep, satisfied smile.

Sista stepped forward, lifted the toddler so that Momma could get a good look at her. With what looked like great effort on her part, Momma lifted her head and reached out her hand to caress the child's face, a weak smile easing into her eyes. Momma looked directly at Sista and said, "Ah'll always be wit ya." It felt like she was placing a blessing on us. I, for my part, felt truly blessed.

I scanned the silent faces in the room. They all wore serene expressions, all accepting of what was about to happen. Clearly, I was the only one who was all turned around up in my head.

Momma dropped back onto the pillow with her eyes wide open, her expression like she was seeing the Lord himself, and she released one last breath. She heaved it like an autumn wind blowing at a fallen leaf. I felt it. It curled around me. I inhaled it deep into my chest. It became part of me. That thing inside me made room for it. And I did not cry.

Then my mother was by my side. She placed a tentative hand on my shoulder and said, "She loved you very much. You should come home now. It's what she would want." But I knew it was not what she would want. She said I was a special spirited chil'. She said I should never change. I looked out to the hallway. My mother's husband was standing out there. I thought I saw him glower at me.

"No. I'll manage, Mom," I say, not at all sure how. Maybe I could stay with Little Gabrielle down the street for a while. I used to stay there overnight when I babysat her. Her father Jonas is such a nice man. Or maybe my aunt Melony. She's always been so welcoming to me.

"Dawn, Momma's gone. You're only sixteen. It's time to come home," Mom says.

I'm thinking, *Seriously? I was only sixteen when I left, and you didn't seem overly concerned then.* I almost say it, but this is no time for an argument.

"I'll be moving in with Little Gabrielle," I lied. "Her father has hired me to take care of her when he's working."

As I walked out of Lincoln Hospital that day, it occurred to me that Momma had ended in the same place where I had begun. I thought maybe there was something significant in that. But I couldn't figure out what it was.

Be . . . longing

Rain again. Ralfie and I are in his car splashing down the West Side Highway. We are sailing through the monsoon, heading to 71st street and Broadway in Manhattan towards the SEEK dormitory. I haven't been back to the dorms since I hinted to Danny that there's a chance there might be a baby. It's been a while. Ralfie says I have to talk to him. He says Danny will probably need time to adjust to the news, wrap his head around it. Ralfie thinks Danny will do the right thing. I wonder about the right thing. Is the right thing loving me back? Can he even do that? Will he let me just love him?

The windshield wipers race to keep up with the pouring rain. The rhythm of their beat is hypnotic. My mind drifts to thoughts of Danny . . .

Danny, when I first laid eyes on him. *Cool*. He was the personification of cool, meticulous in his execution of it. He was the color of caramel candy, like Daddy. He was pensive, a thinker, a person of few words. He had a tight athletic build, a shy easy smile, lips that screamed to be kissed and intense piercing eyes with the slant of a wolf. He was Mister Fine Brown frame, stoic and mysterious.

Yes . . . it was obsession at first sight.

It was a little over three years ago. I was about to enter the student cafeteria on C.C.N.Y.'s north campus for the first time. I hesitated, stood frozen in the entrance. The place was alive with activity, so many different-looking people. Until that very moment the question had not occurred to me. *Where do I fit in?*

I was just getting used to the idea that I was actually there standing in that doorway, that I even belonged on that campus. Despite what my high school counselor had advised—warned, more like—serendipity had intervened and placed me there.

I looked around. To my right were mostly white kids. They made up the largest group in the room. The minorities to my left were truly in the minority. I knew that these were the students from the program, the SEEK students. Upon further observation, it was clear that people had self-segregated. The Spanish speaking kids, who I assumed were mostly Puerto Rican, occupied tables closest to the entrance. Black kids congregated around tables just past them. Further back there was a small contingency of Asians. I imagined that probably even the white kids were grouped off—the Jewish kids with the Jewish kids, the Irish with the Irish, the Italians with the Italians, and the WASPs with the WASPs, and so on. This is what people did.

But I . . . stood frozen.

You'd think that it should've been an easy decision. I should've naturally gravitated to the table with the Black kids. But as I stood there in that doorway, it hit me. Those kids, all of them, were the academic, intellectual cream of the crop. The SEEK program had specifically chosen them, plucked them from poor and minority communities citywide. They had been selected, tested; they had written essays. They had been interviewed and re-interviewed. They were to be the social experiment, the vanguard. But despite my best intentions, my presence there was simply a fluke. I wasn't like the rest of them.

Then I saw him: Danny Barrett. And all those concerns receded back into my chest. He was standing by a table, three girls chatting him up. To my surprise, people at that table actually seemed to have chosen to self-integrate. There were Blacks, Latinos, others whose ethnicity could not easily be determined, and even a few white kids. Some were talking or laughing; some were playing cards, bid whist, or chess, while others looked at a textbook together.

Him . . . I couldn't take my eyes off him. He must have felt it, my stare, because he looked up, targeted me like radar. I smiled. He turned away. I felt assessed. It felt like in those few seconds he had taken the measure of me—mentally, spiritually . . . physically. He had assigned me a number on a scale from one to ten . . . and moved on.

Good Advice

The rainwater continues to drape the windshield of Ralfie's car like a liquid curtain. As we make our way to the dorms, I am going over things in my head. Everything is in place. Still, the very idea that I'm on my way to talk to Danny about the baby spikes a tightening across my chest and a trembling in my hands. I try to relax, and yes, breathe. Will he glare at me with hard cold eyes? Will his voice drop a terrifying octave the way it does? Or will he take me in his warm arms the way he does. Will he let me put my arms around him? Will he say we'll be alright?

I read somewhere that anxiety during pregnancy is bad for the baby. So, I push Danny and his hard eyes and his warm arms aside. I need to think pleasant thoughts. Ms. Thompson . . . Ms. Thompson is pleasant. She found me a doctor who will take Medicaid and see me in the evening. I might actually get to stay in school after all. I might actually get to graduate. I try to meditate, to send out vibes of gratitude to Ms. T, but the car is jostling through potholes. I can't concentrate.

My mind is restless. It floats into the watery world beyond the windshield. It's trying to piece together the events that put me in Danny's orbit. It's like I stumbled into his world, took a random turn and have been stumbling off balance ever since.

A conversation that I had with that other counselor—my high school advisor—muscles its way into my mind. If I'd followed her advice, I might never have met Danny. I might never have been in college at all. But I have proved her wrong, at least partially. Regardless of how it happened, I *am* in college. Whether or not I will get to finish is a-whole-nother thing.

Ralfie's car drones on, rambling through the soggy streets heading for the dorms.

Play Me A Song

I stand outside room 416 while Ralfie waits downstairs. I hesitate, listening. I hear voices inside, along with music. There's always music—loud, rhythmic, rich. The smell of jasmine incense wafts through the door. I'm about to knock when it swings open.

Danny's roommate Raymond hesitates momentarily in the doorway, his eyebrows lifting in surprise. "Excuse me," he mumbles before continuing on his way around me, soon followed by two girls. I recognize one of them. Her name is Angel. Lee told me she's around a lot lately. My heart heads for my stomach at the sight of her. She has pursued Danny forever. I want to slap her . . . or at least say something. I want to make her know that he's mine. Thing is, it has never been clear what we are to each other.

As Angel leaves the room, she turns to place a quick kiss on Danny's lips and touches his face possessively.

I enter the small room, sit on Raymond's bed, and wait for my eyes to adjust. Although it is morning, the room is darkened with heavy drapes and accented with red light-bulbs and loud music. This room with its aromas that used to arouse me, now make me a little queasy. The smell of pot combined with jasmine incense is stifling. Nauseated, I struggle for a scent-free breath.

His eyes find my belly. It's been a while since he's seen me. I needed time to be able to face him. I needed to think about what to tell him. I've been hiding out in my apartment, working on it, trying to make a home for us. I try to read his face, but as usual, his cool demeanor gives no hint as to what he may be thinking. It's clear, however, that he has no trouble reading *me*—never did.

Danny turns off the music, pulls back the drapes, opens the window, and sits on his bed facing me. We are silent. Although I can't read his poker face, I'm sure he knows why I came, what I wish for. If only he would play a song, something to let me know how he feels, to give me a hint. This is what he does. It's his way—our way. It's what we do, what we've always done when the words in our hearts get lost on the way to our mouths.

After a long silence he asks, "So how you been?" His eyes are on my rounded belly.

"Good," I say, nodding my head excessively and lapsing into more silence.

"So, it looks like that situation . . . It's . . ."

"Yeah, yeah it is a situation," I say, placing my hands on my belly.

"I wanted to call," Danny says. "But I don't have a number for you."

"Are you seeing Angel?" I blurt out.

"She's a friend." His tone is flat and his eyes are hard. His voice slips into that dreaded low octave that always frightens me; the tone that says I shouldn't ask questions.

The following silence is piercing. It is closing in on me. It pounds in my ears—or is that my pulse? Suddenly, I'm feeling lightheaded. Something is expanding in my chest, taking up all the space in my lungs, and my heart is doing the boogaloo . . . again. I can't control the trembling in my hands. As a light sweat breaks on my forehead, my mind is filling with fog, and I can't recall why I came here. To ask him about the baby? About us? No . . . no . . . not to ask him, to tell him. I have to tell him. But I can't think.

I need to tell him about the home I've been making for us in the Bronx, in a burnt-out building. Right? No . . . that's not it. I need to tell him something else, but what? Outside Me appears just briefly. I know that disapproving glare. She presses a finger to her lips, shushing me, cautioning me not to speak. But why? It's like she's sure things will be fine if I say nothing. And she fades away.

My heart is pounding. I can't steady my hands. There's that menacing tone in Danny's voice, those angry, indifferent eyes. I'm struggling to breathe.

Then there's a sound. At first I think it's little more than an inkling. But it morphs into a raspy hiss, almost a whisper. It is something alien. I've felt it once before. The hiss—it's coming from inside me. I realize it's not a thought, not *my* thought. It's not Outside Me. As it works its way up through my spine, it resolves itself into mocking words in a jagged grating voice: *Things are not ready, not perfect. You are not perfect! Why would you think there was anything for you to do or say here!* It goes on, *You've got to—need to—get out of here!*

A bolt of fear stabs deep into my chest as I look around, seeking the speaker, my eyes large and wild. There's no one. I jump to my feet; my rubbery legs carry me to the door one tentative step at a time. I hear Danny calling, his voice coming through a wind tunnel.

"Dawn? Dawn!"

My hands find the doorknob. I manage to turn it, open the door, and stagger out of the sweltering room.

Serendipity

Ralfie and I are heading back uptown in silence. The only sounds are the wheels plodding through the potholes that mar the flooded city streets. For a long while Ralfie asks no questions. My mind is slowly clearing. I'm struggling to shake those foreign thoughts out of my head. I concentrate on my breathing, taking slow steady breaths—in through the nose, hold, out through the mouth, relax, just breathe. I'm feeling stupid for having run out of there the way I did. Looking straight ahead, I'm working to slow my heart, breathe, avoid the pity in Ralfie's eyes.

"You okay?"

"I'll be fine."

"Well, I'm starved. Let's get something to eat."

"Seriously? We just had breakfast," I remind him.

"Yeah, but it's *almost* lunch time."

"Ralfie . . . "

"C'mon, I've been dying for one of those Cuban sandwiches from 138th and Amsterdam."

"Okay." I have no fight in me. I have no appetite either. I need to be at work at two o'clock anyway. It makes no sense to go back to the Bronx now.

We sit in a little booth. The restaurant, which is famous for its Cuban sandwiches, is little more than a hole-in-the-wall. Yet the place is jammed, the staff in constant motion, hustling to keep up with the orders. The savory aroma of Caribbean food that usually spikes my appetite does nothing for me now. I decide I might be able to stomach some sweet custard, so I order flan and sit poking at it, still avoiding Ralfie's eyes. But I can feel them, nonetheless, drawing me in like gravity. Slowly, I look up and meet his stare.

"Tell me," he says. It sounds like the eleventh commandment. But I can't tell him. I can't tell him about my pounding heart, my trembling hands, and that frightening whisper; those eerie notions that are somehow thoughts, but not my thoughts.

Instead, I take a breath and say, "Ralfie . . . I don't know how I even got here."

"We came in my car." His eyes smile.

"No seriously, I just feel so . . . "

"Hungry?"

"No."

"Starving?" There's a grin in his tone.

"Lost."

Silence follows the word. Now I seriously consider entering Ralfie's confessional. What could I say? Could I tell him that there's something inside me, something that speaks to me in thought . . . something? He'll think I've lost it. He'll never understand that it's normal, at least for me. I've lived with it for so long. I think I may have inherited it. Instead, I say, "I just . . . I don't know how I got so turned around with him. One minute he's this; the next he's that. If I were never here, I never would have met him. Hell, I don't even know how I got here, to college I mean. It's not like I ever applied."

"Okaaay . . .? I think you're gonna have to explain that— the getting into college without applying part."

"No, really, it started back in high school."

"It usually does."

"There was this teacher, my Spanish teacher, Mr. Anderson," I say, contemplating my napkin, avoiding those probing eyes. "I knew he meant well. He was always pushing me to do things. He said he would be so proud if I were the first colored kid to run for the student counsel. He encouraged me to enter contests, apply for scholarships, awards, stuff like that. He kept telling me about the program, SEEK He always thought I could do those things. Everyone did. I was always smart, you know, good with academics. I actually thought I had the skills needed for some of that stuff, for college. But anyway, I lied and said that I put in the paperwork for SEEK I didn't."

"Why not?"

I stumble into my answer. I can't tell Ralfie that it was a miracle that I even managed to make it to high school on a regular basis. I can't explain about "leaving time," about how I constantly had to tip, moving from friends to relatives and back again, spending hours in the library so I'd have a place to study and get work done. It's too much to tell him about what a struggle it all was. So instead . . .

"Because I had just spoken to the guidance counselor who ruled out college. After all, it was her job to advise me about the direction of my life, about my potential, right?" I say and heave a breath before I continue. "It was the first and only meeting I ever had with my high school counselor," I say. "It was late May in my senior year . . ."

"I see you've been taking an academic program," she had said, staring down at the closed folder that held my very impressive transcripts. "You know that's for college bound kids?"

"Yeah?" I said in a so-what's-your-point kind of tone.

"Was that wise?" She thumbed the ball point pen in her hand, brought it to her mouth and tapped it on her teeth before she said, "You should have been practical and taken a clerical program or at least a general program. That way you'd have something to fall back on when college doesn't work out."

*I stifled a scream, wanted to send her straight to hell. And there was a time when I would have done just that. But for some reason I couldn't locate that indignation. Instead, I shrank into myself. This stranger had somehow gotten a mysterious insight into me, into my life, into who I was becoming. And a whisper, some alien thought, eased into my head and became my own. **She knows about you. She knows that you're a vagrant.***

Momma had said that I was a "free spirit." But I knew it was more than that; I was untethered, a drifter who didn't belong anywhere—a transient. There's a difference. I certainly did not belong in a college, had no right to argue the point.

The fact that I was a survivor, that I persevered, that I managed to stay in school during those past two rootless years did not change the counselor's opinion of me. I could see it in her eyes. I could feel it. And at that moment, those facts didn't change my opinion of me either, nor did they silence those whispers in my head.

She removed the eyeglasses from the tip of her nose and looked directly at me for the first time before she added, "Grace Dodge is running a class in business machines after school. That could work for you. You might want to take that. It's not too late for that . . . "

I've played that meeting in my head time and time again. Wondered why she'd said those things to me. . . things that almost crushed me. I've settled on the conclusion that the counselor probably gave me the best advice she had to offer at the time. I found out later that she gave that "good" advice to all her Black students.

"So I took the after-school business machine course that she told me about," I say to Ralfie, still poking at my flan.

"You're kidding me, right? You've got to be kidding me." My only response is a blank stare. "So then, how did you end up here?"

"Well, I graduated and got a job in an office, running a bookkeeping machine."

"You actually did that?"

"Yeah, at least it was a job."

"Not for very long, I bet. Computers do stuff like that now."

"That's true, but at the time a job was a job. I wasn't living in my mother's house, you know." I struggle to control a hitch in my voice. "I hadn't lived there for quite a while. I was staying with a friend, and I needed to contribute rent."

"Oh, I didn't know." He sounds apologetic.

"Yeah well, that's a-whole-nother story. Anyway, I was making sixty-five dollars a week and after taxes, lunch, and carfare, I was usually left with about thirty-five bucks. But I was okay with it, you know, making do."

"I still don't know how you ended up here," he says.

"So, one day," I continue. "I think it was in December, the phone was ringing . . ."

I caught the phone on the fifth ring.

"Hello,"

"Dawn Porter?"

"Yes, who's this,"

"My name is Anna Chef. I'm a counselor with the SEEK program at C.C.N.Y. You're a hard woman to track down."

I bristled. "Yeah, well I move a lot. What can I do for you?" I say, all business.

"I'm calling because you didn't show up to C.C.N.Y. in September and we need to know if you plan to attend in January or if we can vacate your seat. If you plan to attend, you'll need to swing by the office to sign a letter of intent, ASAP."

"I what?" I said, confused. I never even applied. right? "I can't!" I remembered how just getting through high school took all I had. I was drained. My tank was empty. This woman was pissing me off. She didn't know me, or about my situation, about my . . . deficits. "I have to work," I said. "I have bills, rent. I don't live in my mother's husband's house."

"Then I'll see you tomorrow night. Shepard hall, room 256. I'll be here until 9:00," she said and hung up.

"And you definitely hadn't applied?" Ralfie asks, placing his Cuban sandwich on the plate and wiping his mouth with a napkin.

"No," I say, addressing something unseen on the table. "My head was spinning, you know. And I was thinking, what is this, some kind of joke? I told her I never even applied for college. I tried to make her understand about the counselor and about how I was unsuited for college. I tried to tell her that I'd put that dream to bed and was moving on. But the woman was insistent, annoying."

"Why were you annoyed? It sounds like it was a good thing," he says, ducking his head low to engage my eyes.

"Obviously you went."

"Yeah, I went . . ."

I walked into the office and was greeted by a pleasant looking woman with a close cropped 'fro.

"Miss Porter," she said, extending her hand, flashing a smile like she knew me, or something—like she knew I would show. "Please," she said, gesturing. "Have a seat."

I did not want to have a seat. I had no intention of staying that long. I just wanted to set the record straight, make it clear that I never applied for this so-called program, in case there was any financial obligation involved.

"Thanks, but I'll stand," I say. "I just came here to clear things up. It seems there's been some kind of mis . . ."

"Before you say anything," she said. "I want to tell you a little about the program, SEEK It stands for Search for Education Elevation and Knowledge."

I was thinking, "Oh pleeaassee, spare me" as she went on saying stuff like "political climate," "opportunity," "future," and "success." All the old familiar buzz words.

So I decided to sit, even though I was hardly listening. I was rearing back in the chair, snapping on the wad of gum I was chewing. She just looked at me with this neutral, patient face. It was infuriating. I was chewing, yawning, rearing back in the chair, and thinking, I've made a mistake coming here. *I just wanted to go home and lay out my clothes for the next day.*

"In May, they're opening several new units," she went on. "There'll be space available in the SEEK dorms, which is housed in the first eight floors of the Alamac Hotel on 71st street and Broadway. The top eight floors are still hotel. If you accept, you would be next in line. You can live there at no cost as long as you're in school and you maintain at least a B-minus average. As always, in the city university system, tuition is free. The program covers books and supplies." She paused before she added, *"Oh yes, and there's a weekly stipend of forty dollars."*

Say what? I almost choked on the gum and fell off the chair. Did I hear right? A place for me to live? No rent? College? Me . . . college? My mind was racing. I swallowed the gum.

"You swallowed the gum!" Ralfie laughed.

"Yes, I swallowed it. I needed to think, figure things out."

"So you're saying you can't chew gum and think?" A playful smile lit his eyes.

"Ralfie . . ."

"No, seriously," he says. "You *really* never applied?"

"No!" I say. "I knew there was some kind of mistake, but the woman didn't seem to know . . ."

I avoided her eyes, thinking, maybe I could get into the program. Why not? Would it be a crime if I accepted? Would I be a criminal? I could probably pull it off. And if I do really well before they find out that I'm the wrong girl, maybe they'll just let me stay. They'll have to let me stay, won't they? Or would I be arrested?"

I was in the moment. I wanted to take the chance, reminded myself to breathe, to be cool. I needed to play my cards right.

"Well, Miss Porter?" she said, waiting for my answer, smiling that irksome smile, like she knew something I didn't.

"Can I see my application?" I squeaked out the question.

She handed it to me and I thought I saw my name signed on the bottom line. But my head was whirling, my vision wavering and blurring. It was like trying to look through frosted glass coated with Vaseline. The words, "this is probably a crime" kept knocking around in my head. I was about to be a thief. I was about to steal someone's education, someone who submitted essays, went on interviews.

I could hear my grandmother's voice vibrating through the air and bouncing off the walls. "In this family we don't abide no rogues!"

I struggled to banish Momma back into her permanent residence somewhere in the lower left quadrant of my conscience. I pulled in a breath and made a real effort to focus on that document. It took a moment, but finally I was able to make out the name. It was mine!

"So it *was* your name. You *did* apply," Ralfie says, finishing off his Tamarin Cola.

"Yes, it was my name, middle initial and all. Right there on the signature line. My name was signed in bold and beautiful European letters. It wasn't even an attempt to mimic my chicken scratch signature. I recognized that handwriting immediately. It was Mr. Anderson's."

"What, the Spanish teacher?"

"Yeah, I couldn't believe what he did. I mean, how did he even know?"

"Wow! So, what did he say when you talked to him?"

Now, my eyes drop, and I whisper, "I never saw Mr. Anderson again. I never thanked him."

"Really? That's crazy! That guy actually changed the whole direction of your life."

"I know."

"But it's probably not too late. When was that, over two years ago? You should go back to your old high school and see him soon, before he retires or something."

"Yeah right . . . in my condition?" I say, and Ralfie just looks at me with those eyes. "I guess I could call him. I know I should've, but when I got to school things were, like, moving so fast, so unsettled, you know." Ralfie's stare is unrelenting. "Okay, I'll call him," I say, and I know if there was a phone nearby, a magic phone unattached to wires, Ralfie would pick it up and hand it to me.

Duckling

I stand in front of the full-length mirror that is missing a chunk from its lower left corner. I step closer, remove my eyeglasses, place them on a crate, and examine my face as I apply my ever-present eyeliner and mascara. With glasses back on, I stare at my reflection that, in turn, stares back at me. At least my face still looks like me—the me I have worked so hard to become.

Something I once read in *Raven* or *Shades* or other Black magazines like that, comes to mind. It said, "If one has to be dark skinned, one needs to be smooth," or something to that effect.

My skin, the color of dark ebony wood is now smooth, almost flawless, the result of extreme research on skin care and near religious practice of my skin care routine. I consider my features. I have come to think of them as reasonably proportioned. My eyes are large and shaped like almonds. I've always thought of them as my best asset. I enhance them with makeup so they can be seen behind the thick eyeglasses

64

that I wear. I recall how for so long I avoided mirrors altogether.

I've worked hard at reinventing myself, at being the master of my own mind.

I had decided to go at it scientifically. I was obsessed. I set up case studies, made observations, collected data, studied the secrets of the beautiful Black people, the models, the musical celebrities, the movie stars. I broke down, catalogued, and examined every factor. Then I set out to mimic those factors. I was able to adapt them to myself in one form or another. Granted, I'm still nearsighted, still have my father's chin—nothing I can do about those things.

Growing up, it was common knowledge in my family that I, with my head for academics, was the smart one, and Sista, with her high-yellow skin and hair that grew down her back, was the pretty one.

Momma would take me aside and whisper, "Lil girl, you's jus as pretty as that ol' yella gal."

Momma would take Sista aside and whisper into her ear as well. I can only imagine what pearls were imparted to Sista.

But on my block, when the guy's voices deepened and wispy hairs appeared on their chins, when the girls' hips rounded and soft mounds began to protrude from their blouses, I remained shapeless and flat chested. For me puberty took quite a while longer.

Momma once again took me aside and whispered, "You know lil girl," she said. "Fine fruit take time to ripen. When fruit get ripe too soon, it peak too soon, and fa sho, it fade too soon."

I wasn't sure I understood her meaning, but her words encouraged me anyway. Though I had no idea how to get puberty to find my body, I figured that as a smart girl I should be able to work out how to at least get a pretty face. Luckily, a few events fell in my favor.

Twiggy, the emaciated looking model with large eyes and over-the-top eyelashes, became all the rage. And just like that, I was no longer skinny and flat chested. Like Twiggy, I was model-like slender. Then, James Brown stepped up and declared that I could, "Say It Loud."

I had been a Negro, a Colored Girl. Those were the polite words. Even Nigger, though offensive, struck me as somehow generic. But despite what James Brown said, Black . . . Black was personal. Black was a prelude to a fistfight. Black was that alien thing that grabbed hold to my lungs. Black was . . . "Midnight."

Yes, that's when it happened. It was when the kids on my block started looking at each other differently, at me differently. That's when that entity in my chest made itself known. That's when daddy's words shook loose, when their meaning became clear.

"You shudda named her Midnight!"

Midnight—the word, the timbre, the sound, the memory—it had grown fangs over the years. Daddy spat out that word as though it was some kind of pestilence, some rampant black disease. Suddenly, I knew what had scurried up my spine that day when I was five.

It was like I had this epiphany. I could picture it so clearly in my mind. It was an ugly duckling with midnight-black feathers and evil, freakish eyes. I think they look like my own! Yes, that's the creature that took up residence in my chest. I must have known it all along.

The Ugly Duckling had been my favorite story. I was obsessed with it. I made my mother read it to me over and over. Every time I'd ask her the same question: "What color is the duckling, Mom?"

And every time she'd point out the ugly duckling in the book, its feathers a drab, sickly gray. Somehow its shabby appearance offended me. I'd turn from it, fixate instead on the baby chicks, the pretty ducklings, the ones with the bright yellow feathers. Pointing to them I'd say, "Are they high-yellow, Mom? Everybody says Sista is high-yellow. Is that why Sista's not ugly?"

My mother would sigh, pull me in close, and say. "Color does not make someone pretty or ugly. You are beautiful inside and out. Those ducklings had mean hearts, and that made them the ugly ones. Color is not the point."

Unconvinced, I'd asked, "What is the point, Mom?"

"The point is," she'd said, sounding resigned, "in the end the one they called the ugly duckling turned out to be more beautiful than all of them."

Yes, in the story the duckling turned into a beautiful swan—a white swan. But I knew that this thing inside me was an ugly "Midnight" duckling—a black duckling, a sinister entity with terrifying eyes and fangs . . . Yes, I think it has fangs! It would never be a beautiful white swan.

It had slivered up my spine and settled in my chest. It had threatened to strangle the very breath out of me. It was clear that it was staying. I had to somehow make room for it. And it, in turn, got comfortable and quiet inside me. It was as though we had reached this understanding, this truce. For my part, I had to forget some things—like some ugly words, some ugly feelings—and remember some things, like to breathe. For its part . . . it had to let me.

For the most part, the truce held. I ignored minor infractions. I ignored it as it got progressively stronger. I ignored the static noise that morphed from murmurs to whispers, from whispers to alien thoughts it sent directly into my mind. I ignored that voice in my head mocking me and making demands—sometimes even threats. I tried to keep my end of the bargain. Maybe that was a mistake. Maybe I should have confronted it from the beginning. But I was determined to be the master of my own mind. I thought ignoring it was the only way. So, I just kept breathing. I just kept forgetting. I just kept remembering. I tried to do what Momma said, to keep my focus outward, not inward.

Friends and Secrets

Lee and I have work-study jobs as part time teacher's assistants in the day care center on campus.

I arrive early for my shift. I enter and am mobbed by a cadre of four-year-olds who capture my legs, almost tumbling me. They shriek my name. A rush of emotion overtakes me as I realize how much I've missed these children. I've always had a thing for little kids.

"Hi guys." I stoop low to embrace them, pull their little bodies into a group hug.

"Miss Dawn, where were you? How come you didn't come here for like, a month?" This from Roxanne, her little round face tilting upwards for a kiss, the barrettes that dangle at the ends of her braids brush my cheek. I place a kiss on her forehead and proceed to greet the other four in kind.

There are fifteen children in the class but these five are my posse, the group I always work with. They have attached themselves to me, to my heart, and apparently the feeling is mutual. I often have to remind myself to treat all the children in the room equally. But these five, they are my guys.

"Roxie, I've only been gone a week."

"Is that more than a month?"

"No, it's not more than a month." I smile.

"Why isn't it more than a month?" *Why* is her favorite word. "Why you didn't come here for not more than a month?"

"Well, I wasn't feeling well."

"Why?"

"Sometimes a person just doesn't feel well. You know, like when you have a cold, or a fever and you don't feel well."

"Oh."

"You gettin' a little fat, Miss." Darnell says, his chubby fingers poking, exploring the curve in my middle.

"Dat's not fat stupid! Dat's a baby in dere."

"Joaquin," I say. "We don't call people stupid."

"But dat's a baby in dere, right Miss? Is a very little, tiny baby, right?"

"Yes Joaquin, babies are usually very little-tiny."

"No, but your belly not dat fat, not like my Mama. The baby in dere gotta be really little-tiny."

"Yes Joaquin, there's definitely a baby in there and, I guess, it's really little-tiny."

Then from Luiscita, "¡Ay, Dios mio! How'd it get in there, Miss?" A few wisps of errant hairs have escaped her pigtails. In a familiar gesture, she shakes her head and brushes them off her face. Then she looks at me expectantly awaiting my answer.

"That's not what *I* wanna know," Shaniqua breaks in with a demanding voice. Her head is tilted, mouth in a pout, and her hands are on her slender hips. "I wanna know how it's gonna get outta there."

"We missed you, Miss!" Roxanne jumps in. And I wonder if she's intentionally changing the subject to save me from having to answer the prickly questions. Does she actually know the answer? Though she's a few months younger than the rest, she always seems, I guess, intuitive. I wonder if that's possible. Can a four-year-old not only intuit a situation but also act on those insights? "Since you been gone," she continues, "we haven't played no games; you know, that African game you taught us."

Before I think better of it, I say, "I'm sure Mrs. Clune has played games with you."

All eyes turn to Mrs. Clune, the classroom teacher. She is sitting at her desk fussing with some papers.

"She never wanna play games," says Joaquin. "She never take us to the yard. She jus wanna give us books to color or watch Sesame Street or somethin'."

"She too old," says Darnell.

"She jus lazy," says Shaniqua.

Out of the mouths of babes, I think as Mrs. Clune looks up, checks her watch, and acknowledges me with a nod.

"So, what about Miss Lee? I know she likes to play games with you guys," I say, looking around realizing that Lee isn't in the room.

"Miss Lee? She play games sometimes but not like she used to," says Darnell.

"What's that mean?" I ask. "Like she used to?"

"It's like she's . . . sad," answers Roxanne.

"Sad?"

"Yeah . . . sad," she repeats along with a chorus of little heads nodding in affirmation.

"Where is Miss Lee anyway?"

"She probably in the hall takin' a break," Darnell says.

"Yeah, she take a lotta breaks now," says Shaniqua.

I step outside the classroom and find Lee staring out the window at the end of the hall, her back to me. Something about her posture gives me pause. I hesitate. Then I call, "Yo, Lee!" It is our greeting, our connection. It's the call that was always heard booming down the corridors in the dorms when I still lived there. I'm waiting for her to respond . . . Yo, Dawn! I can almost hear it before it fills the air. But it doesn't. Perhaps she didn't hear. I try again. "Yo, Lee!" Nothing. I approach her, touch her shoulder.

Startled, she turns. "Oh, Dawn!"

"You okay?"

"I didn't see you."

"No kidding, your back was turned."

"Well, I didn't hear you."

"What's wrong?"

"Nothing, I'm fine. Cojelo con take it easy," she says in Spanglish, meaning I should just be cool. But I can't when I see her eyes drift. I follow her gaze through the window to the puzzle of angular brick buildings outside, to the elevated train trestle that straddles the street, to the cars rumbling beneath it.

"Lee . . ."

"I'm just tired. I'll be okay." I hear avoidance in her words and decide not to push it. This is unusual for Lee. She's usually so open, so direct. I contrast the vacant face of the Lee that I'm looking at now with the Lee that I met the day she magically materialized in the dorms. She was the last and only person in her cohort to get into the much-coveted SEEK dorms. She was the one special person admitted into the dorms, admitted into my life that day. It was the very day that I desperately needed someone.

"I'd better get back to the classroom," I say. "Your shift's over. Aren't you going to your next class? It's on north campus, right? If you don't hustle, you'll be late."

"That's right." She sounds like this is a fact that she's just become aware of. It's not sarcasm. Lee doesn't do sarcasm. She avoids my eyes.

I want to update her about the baby, about how it still hasn't moved and about what happened in Danny's room—about how I tried but just couldn't speak to him yet. I might even tell her about the scary notion, that whisper, the reason I couldn't speak. Lee will understand. She'll know I'm not, like, crazy. She'll help me sweep away the boogieman and figure everything out the way she always does. But there's no time right now and it's clear that she has something of her own to deal with. Something of her own? Suddenly I'm annoyed . . . pissed. I share everything with her!

"Roxanne!" I say, stabbing at her with the child's name. It's an accusation. She finally looks directly at me, like she suddenly realized I was there. "Roxanne said that you're sad!"

Jus Breathe

"She's like a little sage . . . isn't she?"

The Creature

I slam my apartment door as I enter, leaving the acrid smell and ghosts of Momma's house outside. The phone is ringing, so I rush down the hall, toss my key onto the hook, and catch the receiver on the fourth ring. It's Ralfie.

"I can come by and take you to the doctor tomorrow if you want. The appointment's in the evening, right? What, like seven-ish?"

"Thanks anyway, Ralfie, but the doctor couldn't see me until Friday."

"Damn, that's four whole days. Ms. T said you needed to get in there right away."

I do know this. I can feel it. A static charge zaps through my chest every time I let myself dwell on the fact that there's still no movement from this baby. Again, I consider telling Ralfie about the "be still" wish. But what would he think of me? What kind of person would wish her baby still? I decide to say nothing. No sense in both of us being freaked out.

"It's only four days," I say. "I'll be fine."

"Let's see . . . I think I can juggle some things and take you on Friday."

"No, that's okay. I can take the bus."

"No, really, I don't have any classes after four and I can cancel that other thing."

"That other thing?"

"Yeah, it was just a play-it-by-ear thing, nothing really firm."

"Ralfie, you have a date?"

"Yeah, I guess it *is* a date. But it's not set in stone," he says. I think I hear a slight swagger in his voice.

"With . . ?"

"Chandra."

"Our Chandra? It's about time! She's been into you for a while. You guys belong together. You know what they say: the best of all possible worlds is when your best friend turns into your lover. She's such a good person and she's really cute."

"Yeah, she is. I guess I am lucky. But we can do it another time. It's taken us this long, a little longer won't hurt. I'm sure she'll understand."

"No! I'll be fine. The bus goes right to the door. It's straight up to the end of the concourse."

"Yeah, but this is the first visit. I don't think you should be alone."

"I won't be. I'll call Lee."

"Oh . . . Lee," he says. And something about the tinge in his voice is alarming.

"You *know* something. What is it?"

"You have to talk to her yourself. I can't say," he says while I think, *The sanctity of the confessional.* "But what I can say is, I need to make sure that you keep your appointment. I kinda promised Ms. T."

"Ralfie . . . I will keep the appointment."

"Okay, if you're sure. I'll call you tomorrow after class."

"You don't have to do that."

"Are you kidding? You're my friend. I care about you. I want to."

"You're the best. Okay, we'll talk tomorrow." I hang up the phone, preoccupied with the notion that Lee is keeping some big scary secret from me. *What's up with her?*

Then I feel it—the sensation. I'm being watched. I turn. There is something . . . a man? It is on the fire escape grinning at me through the locked window. Its bony face is contoured in shadow. Its eyes, set deep in their sockets, are bright with malice. It is missing one tooth in front and the other is chipped, giving the effect of a fang. It is breathing, panting, and grinning as its chest heaves up and down, causing its entire body to quake. There is something eerily familiar about it—some kind of déjà vu—sad and terrifying at the same time. It's like a boogieman that has haunted my dreams . . . many times.

I scream! My heart takes off. My chest tightens. I am suddenly lightheaded. I collapse onto the nearby bed, my heart charging into full gallop. Startled, whatever it was darts away. I am on the bed, catching my breath, letting my heart slow to a canter, gathering my courage. I tiptoe to the window, cautiously look to the left, to the right. No boogieman. For a moment, I let my head rest on the windowpane, watch the fog of my breath come and go. The feel of the cool glass on my forehead is calming as my brain searches for some kind of rational explanation.

Maybe it's the remnants of the boogieman who lived under my bed as a kid, that false creature Mom had dismissed with a simple wave of her hand. Maybe it's something real. That's how it feels, like something horrible I can't quite remember. Maybe it's just a man, an evil man with evil intentions. Maybe. But no matter what it is, I know I need to do something to protect us. I climb on a crate and affix a blanket across the window, blocking the view of unknown entities.

I'm finding some peace in the idea that whatever it is, it can't covet what it can't see. I'm protecting my home, my family. I'm making us safe. Tomorrow, I will use some of my rent money to buy a window-gate and a shade, just in case it's a real man, an evil man.

That's when I feel it—the baby! Or at least I think I do. It is quick and ever so subtle. But I'm pretty sure I felt the being inside me stir, almost like it's pulled itself into a tight defensive ball, like it is preparing for an onslaught.

It's an amazing sensation. It's weird, but it almost feels like a tub of muddy, murky water has been drained out of me and replaced with clear, clean water—pristine and optimistic. I'm feeling something that has evaded me for quite some time . . . relief. The fright I just experienced has drained away. It's replaced by bright, sparkly relief. It's a wonderful, calming feeling. I felt the baby. It moved. The baby . . . it wants to survive!

Suddenly, I'm so very exhausted, feeling the sleepless days and nights taking their toll. I fall across my bed and into a dream.

In the dream I'm in Momma's house. It is light and glistening and as orderly as I remember. Momma is seated on a hassock. I am greasing her head and braiding her hair like I used to. She turns to me and starts to sing:

> *Something in the way life moves*
> *Will have you searching to discover*
> *Something within that you must lose*
> *Leave all the fears behind, master of your own mind*
> > *I'm telling you to search beneath*
> > *Then you'll know, then you will breathe*
> *These answers you must know*
> *What is so? What is not so?*
> *Who is who? Who are you?*
> *Who is who? Who are you?*

Then her ghostly voice trails off and echoes away.

The Kindness of Strangers

Light and shadow play across the surface of the blanket that covers the window. It's stopped raining. I open my eyes and stretch. For the most part, I'm not one who believes in messages from beyond—not even sure there *is* a beyond. But I've had this "Momma" dream before. In fact, I have it quite often. As always, the scene in the dream is so normal, not at all unpleasant. But the strange song that Momma sings . . . maybe she's imparting wisdom like she always did. That's probably why it somehow feels real. Still, her meaning seems almost cryptic. *Search beneath? Beneath what? What is so? What is not so?* I am turning the dream over and over in my mind, trying to grasp it's meaning. For now, I resolve to put it aside, again.

Despite the dream, or possibly because of it, I've actually slept through the night. Maybe it's because I felt so relieved that the baby moved. Whatever the reason, I can't remember the last time that's happened. I sit up, my first instinct to snatch aside the blanket and enjoy what little sunshine finds its way between the buildings. But the specter of that thing on the fire escape looms to mind and puts me in check. Instead, I cautiously push aside the blanket and peek. No monster. Light clouds drift in the sky, alternately veiling and revealing the sun.

I'm up and heading for the shower. Suppressing a strong urge for coffee, I dress, eat a quick breakfast, take the vitamin, grab my key off the hook, and head out the door.

I enter the hardware store on the corner to find a pleasant looking man, mid-forty-ish. He is medium height with a barrel chest and thick muscular arms. His light brown hair is cut short and blunt, covering his ears and stopping just above his chin. He is wearing bell-bottom dungarees and a short-sleeved button-down shirt. The first two buttons are undone, revealing a small gold crucifix nestled in a tangle of curly brown chest hair. He greets me with a jolly, "Guud-morning." His voice is booming. He speaks with what sounds to me like some sort of Eastern European accent. "And what I can do for you this fine morning?"

"I need to buy a gate, you know, for the window."

"Ah yes, this I have, sturdy, strong." I can feel him not-so-subtly eyeing my belly.

"You have husband . . . to install?" It takes me a beat too long to come up with an answer. "I also do install," he says, "very cheap."

"Husband? No, no husband," I say. "I just thought I'd do it myself."

81

Now something shifts in him, in his eyes. It's something I sense but can't name. There's only the feeling that he is forming some conclusions, making some judgments about me . . . about my life.

"You have tools?" he asks.

I hadn't thought about tools. I only have ninety dollars and my rent is seventy-two. I begin to fidget, shifting my weight from left to right. "No," I say. "No tools." There's an uneasy silence.

"Come, I show you gate."

I follow him down a cluttered aisle. There are sliding window screens, assortments of light fixtures and several pipes and gadgets that I can't identify. It's dusty and my nose is starting to itch.

"How much?" I ask.

He looks at me. His gaze is intense, and one of those alien thoughts drifts through my mind. *You know about merchants like this. He's trying to decide how much he thinks he can get out of you. They size you up—your clothes, your demeanor.* Then warming to those sentiments, I look around the store. It's true. I don't notice price tags on anything. But I need this gate. I don't know how long a window blanket can protect us.

"Forty dolla," he says and my heart deflates. That's almost half of what I've got. The rent is due, and I still need to buy a shade, and now, some tools. I get paid on Friday, but I need this gate today.

"How much for the tools?"

"That depend; you need make screw?"

"Excuse me?"

"Hole, make hole for screw to go."

"Oh, holes. Damn, I don't know."

"If you not need make hole, you need only screwdriver," he says, rolling his Rs. "What building you live?"

"Twelve twenty-nine, on this block."

"Ah yes, this burnt building."

"That's the one."

"I know this building. Window for sure have hole for screw."

Back at the register I notice a small white tag swinging on the gate. It reads: $59.99.

"Hey, I thought you said forty dollars?" I accuse.

"Is sale," he says, ripping off the tag and discarding it. *Sale*? I've never known one of these little shops to run sales. I don't know what to think. He reaches onto a shelf and pulls down a box of screws.

"How much are the screws?"

"Come with gate."

"I also need a window shade," I say. "Does that come with the gate too?" Again, it comes out sounding like an accusation. What is wrong with me? I can't believe I am actually accusing him of trying to give me a break on the price. Why would he do this? On the one hand I need it, on the other hand I'm no charity case. Am I?

"No, two dolla." He ignores my tone and routinely begins to ring up the items. "Gate is heavy," he says. "After close, I bring, I install. You pay when you can. You have name?"

83

Now I feel a loosening in my chest. My defenses are slipping away. "I'm Dawn, and you?" I ask, thinking I can probably call Ralfie and he'll come and install the gate for me. But a feeling coming from my gut, not my chest, is telling me that this is not a ploy to get into my pants. Remembering the Momma dream, I'm deciding who is who. I'm thinking that this is one of the good guys, a man with compassion. Compassion, after all, is not as offensive as pity.

I am absorbed in these thoughts when I hear, "Eli."

"Huh?"

"My name."

Now I ask him the question he probably hears every day. "Where you from, Eli?"

"Rou-sha!" he bellows, his tongue vibrating the R. It takes me a second to understand that he's saying Russia. "And you?" he asks.

"The South Bronx."

Stranger Strangers

I am snatched from a solid sleep by the ringing of the phone. It's Ms. Thompson. She sounds both frantic and relieved that I haven't been to the doctor yet, despite the fact that I lied to her. It seems the Medicaid card has to be activated. To do this, I have to go down to 14th street, to the welfare office with a valid ID, a work-study check stub and the SEEK stipend award letter. And today is the deadline.

A cat bath, a quick meal, and I'm dressed in twenty minutes. I grab my keys off the hook, and I'm headed for the door when the phone rings. I'm in a hurry, thinking that if I get there early, I may be able to be in and out. My first inclination is not to answer, but the whine of the phone tugs at me. I pick up the receiver.

"Yo, Dawn." It's Lee, but if it weren't for our greeting, I wouldn't have recognized her voice—so subdued, so un-Lee.

"Yo, Lee. What's wrong?"

"I need to talk to you."

"Yes, of course," I say, feeling something heavy settle on my chest. She sounds so desperate. I heave a sigh and say, "But I was just leaving. I have to go downtown and do stuff for the Medicaid card."

"So, can you come by later?"

I'm hustling down the smoky stairway, going to join the rush hour crowd in the subway. I am surprised at my chagrin when a man on the subway actually gets up to give me his seat.

Arriving at my destination, I open the door and feel this wave like a mixture of tension and despair. It rushes at me like a gust of wind that threatens to blow me over as I enter.

I'm standing just inside the office looking around. There are all these people in various states of activity and inactivity. Along one wall there are small glass encasements, partitioned offices, just large enough for a desk and two chairs. Along two other walls there are counters where people have lined up in silence, for the most part, as they shift their respective weights from one foot to the other. I notice the fourth wall. It has large windows with mustard-colored shades slumping in various states of in-utility. The windows are so dirty that at first glance I think they are frosted. Still, they do let in a good amount of natural light, which is clearly better than the artificial rays and white noise coming from the rows of fluorescents overhead.

The rest of the office is a sprawling open floor. Despite the size of the room, I am feeling claustrophobic. In one large section there are all these chairs arranged in close rows, people squeezed in tight. I don't even see one empty chair.

Some of the "chair-people" are talking loudly, others are silent, their eyes turned inward. Harried mothers fuss with small children while people doze in seats, their heads slumping. A tiny woman in filthy clothes stands on a chair, ranting, protesting, venting her frustrations. Her voice is shrill and dissonant compared to the general compliant tone of the place. Her protests are powerless and futile. No one stirs. Two security guards come and unceremoniously escort her, kicking and screaming, out the door. Some watch, grumble under their breaths. Others just sit, relatively subdued, their eyes dull and blank with the patient acceptance of the routine.

Confronting the chair people head-on are the desk people: cramped rows of tight elbows and haggard faces; slack jaws and crooked collars; heavy eye bags beneath their hollow gazes. I touch my face, wondering if I mirror their expressions. Knowing that Momma would call this place "one big bowl of pitiful," I take some comfort in the fact that at least she's not around to see that I'm here, all up in the mix.

I take a few steps further into the room. My heart is working its way into double-time. I don't know where to start. Then I spot a counter labeled "Information" and a long line of people who are waiting there. The weight of my belly is taking a toll on my lower back, and even though I'm wearing my Converse, my feet are starting to ache.

Mercifully, the line moves pretty fast and within fifteen minutes or so, I reach the uninterested clerk at the counter. I hand her the paperwork that they gave me to fill out.

"Miss, you skipped a section. You didn't say what kind of assistance you're applying for. You need to go fill this out and get back in the line when you're done." She shoves the papers at me.

"No, I'm not here to apply for welfare."

"Well lady, in case you didn't notice the sign on the door when you came in, this is the Welfare Office." She rolls her impatient eyes, snaps her gum.

"My college counselor referred me. I have to get this Medicaid card activated. There's no place on this application to indicate this."

Again, her eyes roll before she says, "You must have us mixed up with the Board of Ed. We ain't got nothin' to do with no college."

"No, you don't understand."

"That's for sure. Now either you tell me how I can direct you, or I have-ta move on to the next person in line."

"Can you direct me to a supervisor . . . please," I add, hearing Momma's voice in my head—something about flies and sugar.

"Fine, go have a seat over there. Someone will call you." She points to the chair people section.

My shoulders slump, my breath ekes from my chest. I am to join the ranks of the chair people and I'm not even sure if there's an empty chair. I watch as she tosses my paperwork into an unmarked basket just before another worker comes by to spirit it away. I'm obsessed with knowing where it might end up. I imagine it sitting on the desk of some bored, underpaid bureaucrat who's only interested in running out the clock until quitting time.

I manage to find a seat. I wish I had brought a book and a sandwich. It's beginning to feel like I'm on the subway. I keep my eyes on my hands, folded on my lap. I decide to pass the time worrying about Lee instead of dwelling on my current situation here in the middle of this "great big bowl of pitiful." But after about five minutes, I am seriously considering climbing on this chair and venting my frustration.

I'm more than a little surprised when a petite woman approaches the chair section and calls my name. I haven't even been here ten minutes. Ignoring the suspicious glares of the people who have probably been sitting here for hours, I rise and follow her into one of the glass partitions.

"Hi," she says, extending her hand. "I'm Maryann Porter." She is white, youngish, with a mass of sandy brown hair that cascades down her back in unregulated ringlets.

"Porter?" I say.

"Yes, and I understand your name is Porter too." She sounds cheerier than seems warranted, and blinks at me with her large eyes as she gestures for me to have a seat. I detect a little southern bell in her accent. I'm wondering where she's from but have no intention of asking. I am wound tight. This, after all, is not some social occasion.

"Yes," is all I say.

"For all we know, we could be related," she says, all smiles, sounding like Pollyanna. I am taken aback and trying not to show it. "I hail from North Carolina, Wake County, just outside of Durham. Where are your people from?"

Now I am stunned. A subdued memory shakes loose, assaults me. *She ain't mine! She don't look like none'a my people!* A spike of irritation flares. Not that it's any of this woman's damn business, but Daddy is, in fact, a Porter from Durham, North Carolina. I have worked hard at blunting the rough edges off those memories, off the mixed feelings that I have for my father. He, after all, has not been an actual "thing" in my life. When I think of my people, I think only of New Orleans. That's where my mother is from and Momma, Papa, and all the uncles, aunts, and cousins that have been in my life. That's where I spent summers as a child. So, as far as I'm concerned, I have no people in North Carolina.

Anger is creeping up my spine, and I'm starting to feel really pissed. If I *were* somehow related to this woman, it could only mean one thing: that her family owned mine, enslaved them, raped them, broke them up, and sold them like cattle. The last thing I want to do is sit here and reminisce about Daddy and make chitchat with this silly bitch.

"New Orleans," I say.

"Well, you never know," she says. "You actually look a lot like some of my cousins."

"Fro and all?" It comes out more sarcastic than I intended, but I don't regret it. Still, I'm quite aware of the power dynamic here. I need that Medicaid card. Where is she going with all this? Is our shared last name the reason why she pulled me out of the crowd?"

"Yep, some of 'em," she says. "Fro and all."

After the awkward silence that followed, I finally find the words to say, "About my Medicaid card . . . My SEEK counselor said it had to be activated or validated or something before I can use it. Can you do that?"

"Sure can," she chimes. "I have your paperwork right here. I understand you're only interested in activating the card. Now why's that?"

"Excuse me?"

"Well, from where I stand, you easily qualify for cash benefits. Why wouldn't you take advantage of it?"

There's an angry response growing in my head but it's scrambled, disorganized. I'm having trouble arranging the words in order to launch it. "I'm okay for now," is all I can manage.

"Are you sure? Y'know, there's nothing wrong with accepting a little help. Everyone needs a little help now and then."

I'm not sure what I imagined, but I certainly didn't imagine an interview like this. Clearly this woman, my "distant cousin," doesn't get it. I'm not some pitiful unwed mother. Well, I am . . . but not for long. She doesn't understand that Danny and I will be together soon—as soon as he has time to wrap his head around it. Then we'll be a family. There'll be music. And once things settle in, I may even find a way to finish school.

The pressure of my stifled response is building. I feel like I might explode. I need to get out of here before I erupt, say something I shouldn't, and blow the whole Medicaid thing sky high. I imagine the security guards grabbing me kicking and screaming as they toss me out the door.

"If you would please just do the Medicaid card so I can get out of here."

"Okie dokie, but I think you're making a mistake."

Okie? Dokie? The alien thought flies through my head. *What the hell does she mean, okie dokie?!* I don't know why but that's all it takes to set me off. I let loose. "How many of your *white* relatives do you push like this?"

"What do you mean?" she says, her tone suddenly sober, her eyes direct.

"I mean I'll bet you would discourage *them* from getting tangled up in the system. Bet you would tell *them* to tough it out because you're sure *they* can handle it. Well, I know how this goes. I don't want these people all up in my business, inspecting my home, making sure my baby's father is nowhere around, summonsing me to come down and prostrate myself before the temple of face to face. My grandma always said, 'nothing's free.' If you take something, you have to give something. She warned me about you people!"

"You people?" Those two words cut me short. That's supposed to be my line. I feel justified about the anger that just pulsed through my body. I believe every word that I said. But I'm suddenly not certain that my tirade actually had anything to do with this woman or this place. It's like something old and prickly has been itching in the back of my throat for quite some time, something that I haven't managed to cough up. I'm beginning to regret my outburst, thinking it must be hormones.

That's when Pollyanna disappears. "Are you kidding me?" she says. "Do you think I don't know how fucked up this system is? I didn't go to school to be a case worker. I'm a social worker. And I didn't become a social worker to be a paper-pusher, or even worse, an overseer. I came up north thinking that things could be different, that *I* could be different. And I've tried, but I can't do anything for anybody working here in this hellhole! So for now, I do what I can. I give away their money. I give money to anyone and everyone who comes across my desk! And I'll keep doing it until they catch me and kick me outta here. So . . . can I give you some money, or what?"

Embarrassed and flustered, I have to close my mouth and take a beat before I'm able to answer. "I . . . I just don't want a case in my name," I say, concerned about how receiving welfare will affect the situation after Danny moves in.

"Fine, have it your way. But I hope you do know that through this SEEK program of yours, Medicaid automatically comes with food stamps—not negotiable. And don't worry, it's not like a cash benefits case. No one will come knocking on your door."

She leaves the office and returns shortly. She hands me a permanent Medicaid card, a food stamps booklet, a business card . . . and a white envelope.

"What's this?" I open the sealed envelope to find a NYC Social Services check for five hundred dollars.

"It's an emergency allotment. I'm authorized to issue it at my discretion. In fact, if you come here every day, I'll cut you one every day until they catch me. You have my card. You

93

have to call my direct line and let me know if you're coming in. It's the only way I'll know that you're here. It's important that you call, never go through the desk," she says. I nod my ascent although I have no intention of ever coming back here. "And don't worry," she says. "They can't come after you for it. I'll just get fired, and I plan to quit anyway."

My first instinct had been to hand the envelop back to her. Now, I start to extend it over the desk, except she reaches out and touches me. She actually touches my hand using both of hers; her grip is firm, determined. She folds the check into my palm and presses it there. With her touch feeling vaguely familiar, she says, "Good luck . . . cuz."

Baby . . . Maybe

I stare at Lee. I'm sure my mouth must be wide open, but I can't seem to close it. I'm trying to wrap my head around what she just told me, and I'm having trouble figuring out exactly how to feel about it.

"Apparently pills don't always work," she says. I look down at my belly and she adds, "Apparently neither does the diaphragm."

I study my feet. A slight wheeze issues from my throat. My hands begin to tremble. I clasp them together, avoid her eyes and ask, "Well, what did Jamal say?"

"You know him. He's great," Lee says. "He said he'd be there for me no matter what I decide. He really wants me to have it. He thinks we'd make great parents. But he made it clear that he knows it's my body and my decision."

I came here anxious to tell Lee about my case worker "cousin," the money festering in my bookbag, about the baby who's opted for life, the creature on the fire escape, the good man in the hardware store, about missing her—all of it. I was even thinking of telling her about that creepy voice—The Duckling's voice—that's been messing with my head more and more lately. But at this moment, I'm consumed with thoughts about Lee and Jamal, about their relationship . . . and now her decision.

I am struck by the notion of how one thing leads to another, which then leads to another, and events fall neatly into place like the pieces of a puzzle . . . for some people.

Jamal Jefferson was the first person to speak to me on campus. I remember I was standing in the doorway of the student cafeteria at C.C.N.Y., probably looking like a lost puppy. Jamal walked over, his smiling eyes, large and dark, shining like black onyx below black, wavy hair. I have to admit that I was kind of disappointed when I realized that he was being kind, not flirting. He had deep olive skin and stood at least six feet tall. He probably would have been a little taller if it wasn't for the slight bowing in his legs. I found myself trying to guess at his ethnicity, just something I do.

Although my eyes were all but glued on Danny, it was Jamal who welcomed me. Over time Jamal and I grew close. As often happens with me and attractive men, he started calling me "little sister." I have to admit that I might've had ulterior motives for introducing Lee to him.

Here was this beautiful new girl in the dorms—a single girl. And there was my friend Jamal, my beautiful friend Jamal. The timing was perfect. Jamal, who didn't live in the dorms, was newly single. His girlfriend Gina had dumped him for a guy she met at a red light, a guy who drove a better car. Actually, I think Jamal was relieved. I never thought she was a good match for him anyway.

I'd like to think that introducing Lee to Jamal was a brilliant move on my part, but the truth is they were meant to be together. It was destiny, not me, that was brilliant.

"I feel bad, you know," Lee is saying. "But we talked, and I think he's finally okay with it. He agrees that we have time. We can think about kids in the future. I think he's just worried, you know, about me, about finding a safe way to get it done."

My mind drifts, my eyes follow. I look around, take in their living space—the apartment Jamal's parents left to him when they retired to Savannah, Georgia. The room is bright and airy, sun streaming through a picture window, no brick wall. It seems spacious probably because it's so sparsely furnished: a small futon, two beanbags, and a component set for music mounted on a milk crate. There is a kitchenette, a small dining area, and a cozy bedroom just large enough to accommodate a double bed and two night tables. It is a home. A place to breathe easy. And I am having trouble understanding why Lee doesn't want a family to go with it.

"So, you're seriously thinking about getting rid of it?" I ask.

"Dawn, what can I say? There's my future to consider. I have my dreams, my plans."

"Of course. But you know what they say, 'the best-laid plans . . .'"

"I just can't do this, not now."

"Why?" I ask. The question is a judgment. It slips out before I have a chance to collar it. A thought zaps across my mind like an ungrounded current. Plans: what has become of my plans? Did I ever have any? Has this been my plan all along? And my future? What has happened to my dream of graduating college? Still, I just can't see a future without Danny. Then it occurs to me that this may be a case of misery loves company—or worse. Envy. Lee, with her perfect guy who loves her, who doesn't need time to wrap his head around things. I find myself needing to suppress a touch of jealousy. Am I this devious? Lee runs her hand through her hair and turns away.

"You're taking this on without even knowing where Danny stands. You know how erratic he is. You're actually going to end up doing it alone," she says.

"That's not true! Danny's not always erratic, and he hasn't said he's not going to be with me."

"He hasn't said he *is*," she reminds. "Have you even been back to the dorms to talk to him?" I ignore her question. We fall silent. There's only the sound of a low wheeze in my chest and my heart beating in my throat. "What about school?" she asks. "If you get kicked out of the program, what then?"

I know Lee is speaking well-meaning words, but I can't seem to hear them, don't want to hear them. Pressure builds in my chest, pushing out my own words before I realize I've spoken them aloud. "It's not like this was ever meant for me anyway."

"What the hell are you talking about?" she asks.

"What the hell do you think?" I shoot back, anger rising. I think maybe The Duckling is orchestrating. "This! School! College! It's one big fluke! I was never meant to be here. This was never going to be my life!" I say, the fact that I can't keep the cry out of my voice is making me even angrier.

"So what ever happened to striving to be the master of your own mind? Huh?" she asks. "Isn't that what your grandmother always said?"

"What the hell does that have to do with any of this?" I sputter, the wheeze in my throat becoming more pronounced. I turn my back to Lee. I'm struggling to take a breath, struggling to suppress the words rumbling up from my chest, trying to bust their way out. *Oh Lee, fuck-off!* I turn to face her and am relieved, when I see by the look on her face, that I haven't said those words aloud.

"I'm pretty sure that being the master of your own mind includes being the master of your own future, your own life," she says. I bat away an unruly tear. I drop my gaze and turn away from her, remembering to breathe. "Look," she says after a while, placing her hand on my shoulder. "I don't want to get into this with you again. There's just no reasoning with you where he's concerned. But me . . . I'm just not ready. I'm not like you, not strong. Can't do it. Don't want to do it."

Me? Strong?

"Listen," she says. "I need your help. Will you help me?"

"Of course, of course I'll help you," I say turning back to meet her eyes, grateful for the change of subject. "What do you need?"

"You told me once about a woman who takes care of stuff like this, someone from your old block. Who was it? Louise? Luann?"

"Luella," I say. "Miss Luella. But I don't really know her, not like that. Not like she would trust me. The word is, she doesn't help strangers. You have to be referred by someone she trusts, and she doesn't come cheap. But if you're going to go through with it, I've got money. You can have it." The image of Maryann Porter's face looms to mind and I am suddenly feeling like fate has sent her, or Momma, or maybe even God.

"Say what? You have money?"

"Yeah, I've got a five-hundred-dollar check with me right now and if you need it, you can have it."

Lee raises one eyebrow at me. I know that look.

"Don't look at me like that," I say. "I didn't do anything, like, illegal. It's a long story. I'll tell you later. But about Miss Luella . . . Gabrielle said she's very careful about who she takes on. Supposedly she's pretty good. Gabrielle said she helped her friend Maria and that turned out alright."

"Gabrielle?"

"Yeah, you remember I told you about Little Gabrielle from the block. Her father Jonas is a friend of Miss Luella's. I told you about him—Haitian, single parent, good guy. I used to take care of Gabrielle when he worked. That was one of the places I lived for a while after Momma died."

"Yes, I remember," she says. "When you were sixteen, right? And you didn't actually leave Gabrielle's on the best terms."

"Yeah, sixteen," I say, feeling like it was a million years ago. "And no, I didn't leave on the best of terms. But I had to leave, you know. It was time to tip."

"So then, do you think they'll help—I mean with Miss Luella?"

"Maybe. I know that Gabrielle's still mad because of how I left. She hardly talks to me when I call, just gives the phone right to Jonas. Even he sounds strange—like tight—when I call. I guess I really incinerated that bridge. It's going to be hard to go back and try to cross it now," I say, remembering what went down on the day I left four years ago.

Burnt Bridges

"Why?"

I could barely hear the question over the stereo blasting Latin salsa music, not to mention the noisy voices coming from the living room. I remember how the song's refrain was booming off the walls: *Chicharron, hog maws and pig's feet!*

Still, I knew what she was asking. Ignoring the question, I continued to stuff my belongings into my oversized pillow-case.

"Why are you leaving?" Gabrielle had asked again, this time louder and more insistent.

"It's time," I'd said without meeting her eyes. It was true. It was time. Eventually leaving time always came around. Yes, "tipping time" was dependable, inevitable. I'd gotten good at recognizing the signs. I knew when it was time to tip. I opened a dresser drawer, pretending to search for my non-existent clothing.

"What do you mean it's time? Time for what? To just walk out on us with no explanation? I'd think you'd be tired of constantly moving around from place to place like some kind of gypsy. My dad has always said that you could stay here with us as long as you like."

Chicharron, hog maws and pig's feet!

"I *have* stayed here as long as I like."

"What's that supposed to mean?"

"Nothing." My tone was flat. For some reason, I continued the pretense of searching, wanting to, and not wanting to, have that conversation.

"Nothing? Then what do you call yourself doing?"

"I'm leaving!" I said, my voice rising over the music.

"You still haven't told me why."

"I'm good at it," I snapped, resuming the pretense of searching for my belongings.

"That's no reason. I think I deserve a reason. You owe me that much."

"Okay, you want a reason? How about I can't be responsible for what's going on here anymore. This place has become, like, hangout central. What would Jonas say if he knew what goes on here when he is out driving a cab all night?"

"That's it? You're upset because once in a while I have a party?"

"Once in a while? Really?"

"So what? You feeling left out?"

"Left out?! What, from partying with you and your little friends? No, that's not it," I said. But what I didn't say is that I was sure I couldn't stay there and keep up with my schoolwork. Not with all the noise, all the distractions; not with being laughed at for being a "brainiac."

"So, what then?" she asked.

Deciding not to say anything about school, I placed my pillowcase on the floor and faced her for the first time. "Jonas expects me to take care of you," I said, an angry tremor rising in my voice. "He expects me to be responsible. He expects me to be the grown-up. But I can't handle this. It's out of control. And I'm so tired of being the killjoy, the bad guy, the geek around here," I said. "And I'll be blamed. Jonas will blame me, just like before when you snuck out and ended up in the hospital after falling off that fire escape that you had no business playing on in the first place, remember?"

This too was true. I thought about how Jonas's words stung. *"How did you let this happen?"* But it wasn't so much his words as his eyes, that disappointed look. I was overcome, then, with a sudden pang of guilt about walking out, not on Gabrielle, but on Jonas. Jonas the single dad, the Haitian American cab driver, intellect and scholar, a good decent man. Jonas, a father figure who had been nothing but good to me, a brilliant man who had taught me much of what little I knew of the world. But things here were off the hook. It was no longer a home. And I couldn't stand for Jonas to look at me that way, not again.

"You're abandoning me," she said, her voice shaky, near tears. I didn't respond, avoiding her eyes. "Well fuck you, then!" she screamed.

Chicharron, hog maws and pig's feet!

Something furious and indignant ignited in my head and flared out from my chest. "I am not abandoning you," I said, my voice harsh and low. "It was your mother who abandoned you! *I* am just leaving!" I knew that the subject was taboo, but I could not stop myself from going there. As soon as the words left my lips, I regretted them. And all the ambient noise fell away as a long uneasy silence closed in between us. Injured, she dropped her eyes and turned away from me.

"Gabrielle . . . it's just," I said, reaching for her shoulder. She flinched away and turned to face me, steel in her eyes. I could see that it would take some time for her to unhear, not only what I just said, but also the way I'd said it. I was suddenly contrite and confused, angry and sad, but most of all exhausted. There would be no talking things out . . . not now anyway.

"Y'know what, never mind. I'm outta here," I said. I retrieved my pillowcase and started making my way down the hallway to the door. The hall felt like it was stretching, growing longer as I went, the door moving further away. My resolve began to waver. Did I really want to leave like this, this time for good? Or did I just want Gabrielle to give me a reason to stay, cut the music, throw everyone out, say things would be different, go back to how it used to be when there was sanity, when this was a home? Would Gabrielle even want me to stay now after what I'd said? Maybe, just maybe. We only needed some time to cool down.

I was about to stop and try to talk to her when I smelled the cigarette smoke. I turned to see Gabrielle leaning against the wall, cigarette in hand, blowing smoke ringlets towards the ceiling.

"Oh, so you smoke now?"

"Everybody smokes now."

"Everybody is not twelve years old!"

"Oh, here we go again with the age thing. I'm twelve; you're not that much older."

"*I* don't smoke!"

"Age is just a number. Whaddaya care anyway. You're outta here, remember?!"

Then I did remember . . . Bernadette. "Where's Bernadette?"

"She's in the little room where she always is. Why don't you just leave her? It's not like I won't take care of her."

I shot Gabrielle a look that said, *Have you lost your mind? There **is** no leaving without Bernadette.*

"What is it with you and that doll anyway?"

I ignored the question, went to the little bedroom and opened the door. I was assailed by the distinct smell of grass. Two figures, startled, sat up in bed. It was Gabrielle's thirteen-year-old friend Maria and some older-looking boy I didn't know, who was holding a joint.

"What's this?"

"Dawny cool out, we're just having a little fun," Maria said. "Really man, you're like, such a killjoy. It's like having my mother around."

"Not anymore!" I grabbed Bernadette and headed for the door.

"Where will you stay this time? How can I reach you?" Gabrielle said, suddenly sounding genuinely concerned.

I had no answer. I actually didn't know exactly where I'd be staying—probably in my aunt's house. Although she'd sounded tentative, she said I was welcome there. I figured it would be good, at least for a while. Momma's house was no more. Momma was no more. In that moment I resolved that, at some point in the future, I would go to my mother's husband's house and get my dog. She was *my* dog and I planned to take her, to save her from that man. I'd find a way to provide for her.

"I'll call you," I had said, opening the door, ignoring that familiar tug on my heart as I left. Trying not to acknowledge that there was something satisfying about that closure.

Doctor . . . Doctor

Today, I step into the doctor's office and lose my feet in the carpet. Relief sweeps over me. I'm finally seeing a doctor, finally going to get prenatal care. The waiting room is unnaturally quiet, like there's this *husssh* in the space. Looking around, I think that the ceiling tiles and wall paneling are probably designed to absorb sound. Instead of fluorescents, there are elegant fixtures that emit soft white light. In one wall there is a large picture window, its peach pleated drapes drawn shut. The walls are painted a pale ocean-spray green and hung with several complimentary-colored paintings which I think are oils.

Although this is the fanciest doctor's office I have ever been in, it is clearly a small, one-doctor operation.

I hand my Medicaid card to the receptionist behind the dark wood desk. She stares at it, then at me with a question in her eyes. She doesn't ask anything, instead standing and walking briskly into an inner office. She returns, walking slower now. She gives me a smile that looks like her face has been cast in plastic.

"Please fill out these forms and have a seat." She gestures to the plush sofas flanked by matching dark-wood end tables. "The doctor will be with you shortly."

I take a seat not too far from a well-dressed woman who must be a patient, while Ralfie, who has been parking the car, enters.

"Wow, this place is something else," he says, settling in next to me.

"You really didn't need to bring me. I would've been fine on the bus."

"I know but Chandra said she understands. We're going on our date tomorrow instead."

A nurse emerges, calls my name. I follow her into the inner office, where she gives me a gown to change into. After a while an olive-complected man enters. With his white coat swinging open around a stocky frame, and his sleeves rolled up to reveal extremely hairy arms, he looks more like a truck driver than a doctor.

He is fortyish, medium height. His dark, curly hair is thinning and slightly receding. His dark eyes are set deep under bushy brows with lashes that any woman would kill for.

"Max Dimitrious," he says, looking over the top of a pair of wire framed glasses that balance on the tip of his nose.

He extends a hand which dwarfs my own. His grip is firm. There is something about his demeanor—about his eyes. It feels like I've met him before, like he's an old friend. "So, you're Yolie's student."

"Yolie?"

"Yolonda . . . Yolonda Thompson."

"Oh, Ms. T. Yes, she's my counselor."

"Great lady, that Yolonda . . . very persuasive." There's a definite accent to his tone, but I can't place it—not Spanish, not Italian.

"Yes and thank you for seeing me. It really means a lot to me."

"I can see that you're as charming as she said you were." I drop my eyes, not used to compliments from anyone, especially doctors.

"Thank you."

"Okay, so let's take a look." He shows me to a chair and places his stethoscope on my chest. I'm feeling a little anxious, a little lightheaded. I've never had a GYN exam before, never had a strange man touch me the way I know he's about to.

"Deep breath," he says, and my heart moves from a trot to a canter. "Umm . . ." He moves the stethoscope from place to place.

"What?"

"Just breathe, we'll talk later." He continues to listen to my heart. It continues to boogie. "How far along are you?"

"I'm not sure."

"When was your last period?"

"February . . . maybe. It might have been March." My voice drops as I say, "Could have been April."

He just looks at me, and I feel like a complete idiot. Time has been a blur. I know I was late; I just can't remember when.

The silent nurse helps me onto the examining table. She drapes me with a sheet and shows me how to put my feet in the stirrups. The doctor snaps on rubber gloves and begins the examination. His hands come near, and I tense.

"Try to relax." He pushes and probes with a gentle and experienced touch. I feel something, then—a movement. The baby repositions itself, then settles, and is once again still.

"It moved!"

"Hmm," he says, withdrawing his hand. He removes the gloves and tosses them into a receptacle. "You can get dressed now," he says, and leaves the room I dress and sit-up on the side of the examination table. When he returns, he stands by my side and says, "Now, what were you saying about movement?"

"The baby it hasn't been moving. It used to move—like a lot—but then I made the wish and, don't get me wrong, it wasn't a prayer, just a wish, and I didn't really mean it, never thought it would be granted . . . " I babble, my gaze towards the ceiling.

"Slow down," he says. "What are you talking about?"

"The baby . . . it had stopped moving altogether because of the wish."

"Are you saying that the baby has been active?"

"Yes . . . turning, stretching."

"When did that begin?"

Again I feel so damn ditzy. "I'm not really sure. A month ago?"

"And when do you think it stopped?"

"Two or three days ago, I think. Maybe the beginning of the week."

"I see. And you're sure it was very active before?"

"Oh Lord, yes!"

"Okay, let's just see what's happening here." He places the stethoscope on my belly, moving and repositioning it as he listens intently. "The baby's heart sounds fine—strong and steady. Now your heart, on the other hand, seems a little problematic."

"Problematic?"

He looks at my paperwork. "Says here you don't have any kind of heart condition."

"I don't. Do I?"

"You have an irregular rhythm. How often do you feel palpitations? When did they start?"

There's a name for it?

"Well mostly when I get nervous, but that happens to everyone, right?"

When did this start? I think back. It never happened when I was growing up. There was the night of the MLK uprising on 125th street, but that was extreme. And despite trying to push the memory and the grief of that *other* night away, I think about what happened to my dog Siegfried on the roof. For sure my heart was pumping hard that night. For *sure*.

"Actually, I think it started with the pregnancy," I say.

"It may be related to stress." He taps the end of the stethoscope against his giant palm. "That doesn't mean it shouldn't concern us. For starters, you need to try to find ways to deal with your stress. I try not to prescribe medication during a pregnancy. Maybe yoga or meditation. I'd like to run some tests."

"But what about the baby? It hardly moves."

"That's not unusual. Most babies aren't active this early in the pregnancy."

"Early? I thought I was, like, coming to the finish line. How far along do you think I am?"

"I think you're just going into your third month."

"What? How could that be? I'm huge!"

"Actually, the baby is quite small. There's a lot of fluid. It's probably why you look further along than you are. This happens in some pregnancies."

"But what about how active it was before? I felt body parts and everything."

There's a worried look in his eyes. He squinches-up his brow and stares at me for a while, like he's weighing his next words carefully.

"Perhaps those were phantom movements that you felt."

"You mean like all in my head? Like I'm nuts?" *What is so? What is not so?*

"No, like you were experiencing phantom movements," he says matter-of-factly. "It's uncommon but not unheard of. You may have suffered what is known as a hysterical pregnancy. You may have believed you were pregnant well before you actually were.

113

"How is that possible?" I ask. He blows out a breath, pulls up a chair and sits facing me.

"It's caused by something they call a mind-body feedback loop." I give him a blank stare. "It's when an intense emotion effects hormone levels resulting in physical symptoms that mimic a true pregnancy."

"But the kicking . . ."

"Actually, several normal movements of a woman's stomach can mimic a baby's kick."

"Normal movements?"

"Yes, like muscle movements or gas, for instance. Even peristalsis, the wave-like motions of intestinal digestion, can be interpreted as kicks to a woman who's stressed and convinced she's pregnant," he says, pushing up the eyeglasses that threaten to slide down the slope of his nose. "I don't think we should dwell on it now. Now, you are quite pregnant, just not as far along as you thought. You'll be fine. Nurse Smith will take a history and make arrangements for the tests. I'll see you next week."

I'm drifting in and out of my head. Hysterical pregnancy? Phantom movements? A heart condition?

"Thank you, Dr. Dimitrious," I manage.

"Please, call me Max. Everyone calls me Max."

"Okay, Max. Thank you . . . Dr. Max."

"Just Max."

Clouds are filling up my head. What was all this about a hysterical pregnancy? One of those ridiculous notions, which isn't my own, pushes its way through the fog and into my brain.

114

There was no hysterical pregnancy. Ralfie probably put in a good word. "He" forgave you for that wish you made.

The more I think about it, the more I agree. Maybe I was granted a do-over and that's why I'm only in my first trimester. Ridiculous or not, this theory snuggles up inside me and gets comfortable, somehow seeming feasible. Yes! That's probably what happened.

The nurse is asking me questions about the history of my health. A small ache is working its way behind my left eye. *A do-over!* In my brain the questions, "what is so?" and "what's not so?" are making their rounds.

On autopilot, I'm answering the nurse to the best of my ability. Then she asks, "Is the young man in the waiting room the father?"

The clouds part; my focus snaps back. This cannot be part of the required clinical information. "No. He's a friend."

"Will the father be coming in with you in the future?"

"Why are you asking me this?"

"Just routine. It's possible that a test may leave you slightly impaired. We need to make sure someone will be here to help you get home."

I don't believe this for a minute. "Yes," I say. "He couldn't make it tonight, but he will be with me for the next appointment." The lie becomes the truth the moment the words stumble off my tongue. Of course Danny will come with me if I ask him.

This is it. This will be our do-over. It's just what we need. This will be what gets our little ball rolling again. It's not like we were never a "thing." We had beautiful, intimate moments and not just sex. We had something. We *have* something. Our "something" started almost three years ago. It was bittersweet, how we started. It's not something anyone would ever forget . . . not that day.

Burn Baby
ΩΩΩ

It was three years ago—just another day that started out like any other. Classes had ended, and as usual, the plan was to meet up with my friends. I had found my place. I hung out with what I came to think of as the "progressive posse"—the ones who collectively had no specific ethnic identities. That was where I met Ralfie, Jamal, Chandra, Gina, and many others. It was no coincidence that Danny was in with this crowd.

Though we ran with the same crowd, I barely had any interactions with him. He rarely spoke to me. And when he did, I always managed to say something asinine. I was a clique member. He was clique royalty. I settled on admiring him from afar.

And then there was Gina. Everyone knew she wasn't the sharpest tool in the box, but somehow she managed to make that fact beside the point. She had medium brown skin and medium brown hair, medium brown eyes, and routinely wore medium brown clothing. My first impression of her was that she was monotone and mediocre.

Although I never thought of her as classically pretty, she was attractive in a strange, animal sexy kind of way. To me her body looked squat and shapeless, yet she exuded a kind of confidence that made her irresistibly attractive to guys. She believed it. She sold it. I actually made a case study of her, but I could never quite tease out the unique factors that she had going for herself. Some things just can't be quantified.

Luckily, she had her sights set on Jamal. I think every clique has someone like Gina, the popular one. Someone who talks the loudest, dominates the conversation, is able to exert influence . . . has a car. I think about this. When I was a little kid, I was that girl. Now, that little take-charge girl is long gone, having retreated to places unknown.

On that unremarkable day three years ago, one that had started out like any other, I was steadily falling in line. I was fast becoming a Gina groupie.

It was several weeks before Lee materialized and moved into the dorms. I know it was a Thursday because that was the day that we SEEK students always got together to dance. The weekly dance on campus was called "Coattails." I never knew why. But every Thursday evening, the student lounge on south campus was magically transformed into the Coattails lounge. Getting all dressed up and going to Coattails was something I looked forward to every Thursday. We all did. It was a blast. Although I didn't recall ever seeing him dance, Danny was always there.

I usually got dressed in my friend Chandra's house because she lived in Harlem, close to campus. Chandra was trying on her new halter-top while I was fussing with my 'fro. I pushed it into an upsweep and secured it with a large wooden barrette and stylus. I was putting on the second coat of mascara when the words screamed from the radio on her dresser:

"This just in: ABC news is reporting that Dr. Martin Luther King has been shot in Memphis!"

Chandra and I froze as dread's icy fingers reached in to squeeze my stomach.

"What?" she gasped.

"Turn that up," I ordered.

We sank onto her bed, glued to the radio. A small voice inside me was whispering, assuring me: This too will pass. He had survived attempts on his life before, and he could do it again. He's Dr. King. He's bulletproof. He stood up, spoke truth to power, showed us that we could overcome.

Then the white man on the radio said, "ABC news has confirmed that Dr. Martin Luther King has expired." Expired? What, like some library card? Like there was a predetermined date beyond which he would be no more? Then this eased across my mind; don't we all have that date?

A slow burn worked its way up my spine but extinguished itself into a dull grief that settled in my heart. I broke into tears. Chandra broke into tears. We tried comforting each other but there was no comfort to be found. This was actually happening . . . again.

I was younger when President Kennedy was assassinated. I had no idea how the world worked. Not that I was much better informed the night when Dr. King died. I did know a little something about him. I knew he was a man of peace, a leader—our leader. I knew there would be a big wide void where he had stood.

Assassinations teach sobering lessons. This one taught me about expiration dates. Dates you never think about, aren't ready for. So I cried. I cried that night for the loss of that good man. I cried for the loss of my world, the world where good men aren't assassinated, and we only expire when nature intends it.

Chandra and I headed to Coattails to meet up with our friends. They were there on the street, milling around, looking lost, crying, keening. I don't know who it was, but someone stepped up and took the reins. Someone made a decision. We would march. A peaceful protest march like the ones that Dr. King himself had led . . . this, to honor him. We would march across 125th Street. I never knew what the final destination was to be, nor did I know what we would do once we got there. I just knew that it felt right to march. We would march, raise our voices, sing and chant away our grief, like somehow it would make us feel better . . . or be better.

We started down Convent Avenue, heading to 125th Street. Danny, Jamal, and Gina were up there in the forefront. I hung back with Chandra and Ralfie. At first, we were all silent. Then a female voice filled the air with a chorus of: "We Shall Overcome." Very few people joined in. It petered out. It was clear that at that moment no one felt like we would ever overcome.

Another voice rang out: "We Shall Not, We Shall Not Be Moved!" One or two people joined in. Then Gina raised her throaty voice, and the rest followed suit. We sang. We marched. Windows opened. People gawked.

Calls went up. "Come down, join us. Brothers, Sisters, join us!"

And they did. They came aggrieved. They came agitated, incensed, burning. They came in hordes.

"We Shall Not, We Shall Not Be Moved!"

The first crash took me by surprise. I had imagined passive people coming together in the streets, the whole world raising their collective voices, protesting this tragic injustice. I didn't understand that this was not an injustice at all . . . It was an outrage.

There was rage.

A furnace of well-stoked fury had been smoldering just below the surface for some time. Once ignited, it would not be contained. So yes, for me, that first crash was a hard lesson to learn. The smashing that followed . . . not really.

"Brother, we're not about that!" A male voice—a student—shouted to no avail. The place erupted. The only thing that was missing was the mushroom cloud. And I stood glued to one spot, my eyes gaping. Time slowed down. It was inching by as if the action had actually split from reality. Fixed on my axis point, I listened to the shatter coming from all directions. Slowly I circled, tracked the clatter as each glass display exploded. Jagged shards sparkled, reflected streetlights as they descended and crashed to the sidewalk. I listened to distorted screams, slurred whoops, and someone singing over the din. It was a woman's voice, rich and resonant: **"We Shall Not, We Shall Not Be Moved!"**

People jostled me as they hustled by, knocking me from my reverie.

Then things started moving fast, real fast . . . too fast. I was running. I looked around but didn't see any of my friends, didn't know where to go, which way to move. I was being pulled along in the wake of the crowd. It was run or be run over. I spotted a building and managed to ease and elbow my way to it. I pulled on the door, but it didn't give. The doorway itself offered some shelter from the wave of people running past carrying their spoils. Did that make them the winners? Deciding to stay put, I flattened myself against the doorway as best as I could and almost fell backwards when the door swung open. A tall, muscular young man emerged. Despite his size, his baby face said that he was about fifteen years old, maybe younger.

"You live here?" he asked.

"Yes, yes," I said. "I . . . um, forgot my key."

"You don't live here."

"No," I confessed. "I actually live . . ." I paused. Where did I live? I'd been staying with Chandra here in Harlem, but "leaving time" was fast approaching. "In the Bronx," I said.

"That's okay cause neither do I. I just needed to stash some stuff, you know." I looked into the vestibule. There were several large items sitting there. "So, listen here," he

122

said. "I think we can help each other, you know, work to-gether."

I tilted my head back to look up at him. He towered over me. He was massive. At that moment I was thinking I'd rather take my chances with the chaos outside. He must have seen it in my eyes because he said, "No, no, I'm a nice person. And I think you're a nice person. I just need to take advantage of the situation, you know, with the King-dead-thing and all. My mom is sick; I been really trying but I can't find no job. Look, you don't need to hear all this. All you need to do is stay in here and watch for me. Don't open the door to nobody else. If you do this for me, you can have your choice of anything I bring back." I looked at the huge boxes in the hall. "I'll get something small and valuable just for you. Deal?"

Then he was gone and just like that I was a partner in crime thinking: Is this a crime? What would Momma say? After all, I reasoned that there are many terrible acts committed by many terrible people who are never labeled criminals, right?

So, I stood behind the door and watched through the glass. I watched the running and screaming, some people carrying off anything they could get their hands on. A woman, her face distraught, seemed to be looking for a safe way out. I thought to call to her, but I hesitated and then she was gone, swept away with the crowd. So I watched.

Then the crowd parted, and I saw her—a child, a toddler. She couldn't have been more than three. She was standing in the middle of all that craziness just wailing, tears and snot running down her face. As the crowd closed around her, she was blocked from view. I questioned the sighting, like maybe it was some sort of illusion. But the crowd parted again, and she was still there standing tiny and alone. It was clear that others saw her too, but no one stopped to help. It was as though she existed in some kind of invisible protective bubble. In the middle of all that turmoil, people just ran around her. She had not been trampled, at least not yet. Again, I hesitated, waiting for someone to come and claim her. Where had she come from? I was frozen with indecision. A woman rushing past bumped her ever so slightly and she howled, teetered, barely keeping her balance.

Then my body reacted, took off before my brain had a chance to catch up. I knew if I left the building, the door would lock behind me. I wouldn't be able to get us back to safety. My fingers found the wooden barrette in my hair and used it as a door jam. Elbowing my way, I started towards her, but just before I got there a woman appeared and scooped her up. The child wrapped her chubby arms around the woman's neck, placed her thumb in her mouth, and rested her head on the woman's shoulder. I felt a tinge of relief, as well as a jab of disappointment. It was like I'd been cheated . . . or something. I watched as the woman disappeared in the crowd, child in one arm, toaster in the other.

That's when I looked up to see the Four Horsemen of the Apocalypse riding large snorting animals, bearing down on me. I swiveled and dodged; everyone swiveled and dodged. It took a moment for me to understand that they were mounted police, clearing the streets, herding folks like cattle.

A collective shriek went up as the horseman headed into the crowd, continuing past me up 125th Street then turning and heading back in my direction. Overhead, the thunder of a helicopter rumbled the air. Its blinding floodlights swept the crowd.

Suddenly the police were everywhere, chasing down the panicking mob. I turned to run. Being pulled along with the crowd, I could not muscle my way back to the building. Clearly unreliable, Outside Me didn't step in to take my hand and show me the way. That's when I felt the impact. Someone had shoved me from behind and I was falling forward, unbalanced, out of control, arms flailing and grasping as though thin air could somehow support me.

I went down hard. Pain shot through my wrists and knees. There was a low ache in my ankle, which had twisted underneath me. People were running past me, jumping over me. I couldn't get up. I tried to hunker down, covering my head with my arms. I felt kicks and blows as panicked people fled, trying not to trip over me. I heard the sound of hoof beats in the distance, closing in fast. My lungs contracted. *Jus breathe.* My blood burst from my heart. It shot up into my head and settled in my ears. Someone was yelling at me, but I couldn't make out what was being said over the roar from the sky and the liquid in my ears. It sounded like I was submerged in ten feet of water.

Then the ground was falling away. I was escaping gravity—moving upward, lifted by some benevolent force. There were hands and arms—strong arms—embracing me. My partner in crime had returned to save me. I turned to look up at him, to thank him. Instead, I found myself looking into the "he's so fine" face of a caramel-colored guy. Danny? His sexy lips set in a pout. His wolf-like eyes, so close to my own, were hard and angry and confusing. Something electric shot through my chest. My brain reeled. Something was squeezing the air from my lungs; my head was filling with fog and the world went fuzzy just before everything faded to black.

Gone Baby

An eyeball squints suspiciously through the door's peephole. There's the sound of a turning lock and an unlatching chain. A tiny woman peers from behind the partially opened door. Then she moves the heavy steel bar aside and motions us to enter. Lee, Jamal, and I hesitate before we follow Jonas in.

"These are the people I told you about, Luella," Jonas says to the woman.

Her eyes skim from Jamal to Lee to me. They settle on me.

"You's too far along. Ah don't do shit like dat."

"No, Luella," Jonas says. "This is Dawny. You remember her. She used to take care of Gabrielle. This young lady is Leelia; she's the one who is in need of your . . . services."

"Dey gots da money?"

"Right here," I say, handing her an envelope containing most of the money that I got from Maryann.

127

She takes it, and licking her thumb, she proceeds to count. Then she turns to Jonas and asks, "Dey knows da rules?"

"Yes." Lee's voice is barely audible. "If anything goes wrong, I tell the authorities that I did it to myself. I never mention your name. No refunds."

"Datz right. And Ah gots me some big strappin' grandsons who knows how to deal wit folks dat don't follow dem dere rules."

Sounding agitated, Jamal says, "Okay. You have the money. We know the rules. Can we just get this over with?"

"Good luck," Jonas says. He nods at Luella, shakes all our hands, and looking harried, he makes a hasty exit.

We follow Miss Luella down to the basement. The wooden stairs groan under our feet. It is dark. It is damp. It is dusty. The smell of stale blood lingers in the dank air. I shiver and wrap my arms around Lee, and Jamal wraps his arms around both of us.

"Y'all gon stand dere cuddlin' o she plannin' on gettin' up on dis here table." As my eyes adjust, I see two wooden tables. Thick ropes bond them together at the legs to form one long platform. There is a sheet that looks fairly white draped over them and another folded on top. Luella flicks a switch, turning on a shop light that hangs low over the tables. She flips another and two florescent lights react as though they have been in hibernation, flickering and crackling like they're protesting this rude awakening. Gradually gaining strength, they come to life. But the light they emit is not enough to overcome the basement's blackness, so the atmosphere feels muddy and dull. The crude lighting casts eerie shadows across Miss Luella's face.

I watch her as she goes about making preparations, her movements slow and labored. She is older than I remember. Deep wrinkles define her eyes and forehead. The lines on her narrow face look like someone has crinkled up a brown paper bag and tried to flatten it out again. The skin sinks into the hollows of her cheeks, then sags and jiggles off her chin and neck. Her hair is rusty brownish and very thin—the results of over-processing, no doubt. She looks like her body might snap in two if she were hugged too tight. But her eyes are alert and intense. It's like they never miss a thing, like they see right through you straight into your essence. When she turns her stare on me, I bristle and look away.

A metal cabinet with narrow drawers stands near the wooden tables and serves as a surface for her tools. There are several long, pointed rods of various thicknesses resting in size order on a whiteish bath towel. *Knitting needles?* A can of Sterno and a small saucer sit to the left of the rods. To the right, more towels are uniformly folded and stacked high. The entire set up strikes me as surprisingly neat.

A folding room divider is positioned just behind the tables and against the wall there is a wash sink next to an old refrigerator. Under it, a large metal pail sits with an oversized mop resting against it.

Miss Luella hands Lee the sheet that is folded on the table and points to the room divider, indicating that Lee should step behind it and disrobe. She puts a lit match to the Sterno and blue flames jump to life. Then she gestures impatiently for Lee to mount the tables.

"Give us a minute," Jamal says, lighting a thick joint and handing it to Lee. "Maui Wowie should do the trick," he says.

Lee takes several long drags and tries to hold the smoke deep in her chest.

"Ah don't like y'all bringing dat shit up in my house. It ain't legal." We all turn and stare at her. "What!?" she says. "Um doin' God's work up in here. Bible say He gave folks free will. Folks needs to pick what dey gon do wit dey life and dey chil's life. Worst life a chil' could have is being raised by a momma who ain't never wanted it in da first place." Her eyes sweep past Lee and Jamal and settle on me. "O jus' as bad," she says. "A momma who don't have da means to raise it proper."

My breath catches in my chest, emitting a slight wheeze. My hands find their way to my belly. It takes a moment before I am able to tease out what, if any part of that applies to me. I set my jaw. Free will . . . Despite the law, Lee has made her choice. I have made mine.

Lee's shoulders slump, her eyes tear up, and her chin drops. Jamal lifts her chin with his finger, kisses her gently and says, "It's okay babe. We'll be okay." The way that they look at each other almost brings tears to my eyes. It kicks up a vision: Danny and I looking at each other like that, me laying my head on his chest, listening to his heart . . . and breathing.

Lee climbs onto the platform; the tables sway slightly, the wooden legs creak and cry out. It's like they're protesting the extra weight. Miss Luella is at the sink washing her hands and I can smell the Ivory soap. She dries her hands on a towel positioned near the sink and retrieves a mayonnaise jar of cloudy liquid from the fridge and rests it on the metal cabinet. She places one of the rods, the thinnest one, on the Sterno fire. Then she retrieves a neatly folded apron from one of the metal drawers and puts it on.

"Here, drink dis," she says, handing the jar to Lee.

Jamal grabs it, smells it, and looks at Luella with "*What the hell is this?*" in his eyes.

"Dis here is whas gon help her get through dis thing. She don't drink it, Ah don't do it. Ah cain't have her jumpin' round on dis here table. Dis'll keep her still, won't hurt her none. She don't stay still, Ah might end up poking a hole in her where no hole got no business to be. Dat would not be good."

Staring at Luella, Jamal is frozen in place holding the concoction. Lee pries it from his hand and downs it in one draft. She screws up her face and her body shudders. I get the impression that it tasted as bad as it looked. Soon her eyes float away, and she sinks back on the table. Luella bends Lee's knees and spreads her legs. Then, lifting the sheet, she uses ropes to fasten her feet to metal rings stationed there for this purpose. It puts me to mind of a torture chamber or some kind of S&M thing.

The knitting needle is glowing red-hot when Luella removes it from the fire. She rests it on the saucer and puts the next one in the flame.

"You're not going to put that hot thing in her!" Jamal and I erupt in unison.

Luella fixes us with those eyes, effectively putting the brakes on us. "Course not. Ah waits til it cools. Ah needs to wait fo' the medicine ta take her proper. Ah knows what Um doin'. Y'all gots ta go sit ova dere. Dere's chairs backa dere." She motions to yet another room divider that suddenly appears in the shadows at the far end of the basement. It is taller and wider than the one that stands behind the tables, four sections of thin white paper-like fabric. "Ah don't works wit folks standin' ova me," she says. "Dis ain't neva pretty."

I know we have to comply. Jamal resists, but I pull on him gently and he finally relents. From where we are sitting off in the shadows, our view is obstructed by the partition. And I'm thinking that maybe it's better this way. I don't want to see. I can feel the phantom baby inside me pull itself into a taunt defensive ball, like it fears it may be next. But this is probably all in my mind.

We sit for days, or so it seems, with our eyes glued to the muddy shadows floating across the thin paper wall. Miss Luella is a silhouette in black outlined against the quiver and glow of the Sterno flame. Her fuzzy form looms large, then small. Suddenly, she is moving faster than I thought her rickety body capable of. She is a series of wispy disjointed stills, a distorted ghostly figure defined by the flickering strobe light as the fluorescent fixtures crackle overhead. Like a kung fu abortionist, her shadowy arms are rippling, flying, her feet shuffling, her head bobbing up and down. A beam from what must be a flashlight appears, illuminates the papered wall, then alternately casts rays on the ceiling and floor. I even think I hear a martial arts howl. But it's a scream . . . Lee's scream.

Jamal is on his feet and there is no restraining him. He knocks the partition to the floor. It slams, bangs, resounds, flares up a wall of dust. I follow as Jamal sprints towards the table. We stop when we see all the blood. There is so much blood—white towels now crimson. Scarlet droplets dribble down the sheet and puddle on the floor.

I let out a shriek with one hand covering my open mouth, the other holding my belly. My heart takes off, my lungs spaz, my head spins, and I double over trying to breathe. Jamal rushes to Lee. She is awake. She cries into his chest with wrenching, hiccupping sobs. He holds her close, running his hand through her sweaty hair. Then he turns and glares at Miss Luella. If there is such a thing as murder in the eyes, I see it now in Jamal's eyes.

Luella sees it too and she takes several tentative steps backward. Then in a voice much higher than her usual, she says, "She awright. It went good. She gon be fine. Dis blood, dis's awl natural. Look, look she don stopped bleeding. She gon be fine. Gon have babies when she ready an' everythin'."

Lee sits up. The towel between her legs is still white. She's stopped bleeding. That's the most important thing, isn't it?

Heat!

"She's running a fever." Jamal's voice blasts through the phone receiver. "It started last night. At first, I didn't think much about it, thought it was probably natural. It wasn't that high. I gave her an aspirin. But this morning . . . she's burning up. It's like I can feel the heat coming off her."

"What's her temperature?"

"I dunno, high."

"What, you didn't take her temperature?"

"I don't have a thermometer. But I know too high when I see it."

"You need to get one."

"I can't leave her."

"Okay, okay, I'll bring one. I'll be there as soon as I can, but I think I have to go downtown first to see my new cousin. I have no choice. We may need money."

"Your what?"

"Never mind, I'll explain later. Meantime, give her more aspirin and put her in the tub with warm water and make it cooler little by little."

"How do you know to do this?"

"I learned it from Jonas. Gabrielle was always getting fevers and stuff."

I hang up the phone. I am groping through the bottom of my bag looking for the business card that Cousin Maryann gave me. I don't feel it. I'm sure I threw it in here. Panicking, I start pulling everything from the bag, which is really just a big sack-like thing. I am throwing things on the bed—a pack of tissues, my make-up pouch, a little change purse holding some cash and my student ID, a deck of cards, a ballpoint pen, my copy of "Soul on Ice." I turn the bag upside down and inside out . . . nothing. I'm about to freak out when I remember the small, zipped compartment sewn into the lining.

I pick up the phone and dial Maryann's number.

I'm on the express train heading back uptown to Lee's, an illicit social services check folded snugly in the zip-up compartment of my bag. Maryann has proved to be as good as her word. I never expected to be going back down there, never expected to see her again. But this is an emergency. I am in need, just like all the other "chair people," I guess. Shit happens.

I tried to explain it to Maryann, but she wasn't interested. It's clear that she didn't care why I was there, didn't require any explanations or ass kissing. She just handed it to me, used two hands, folded it into my palm. She nodded. I nodded. I left.

The uptown train I'm on is supposed to be an express train but it feels like it is slowly chugging along. I decide to pass the time practicing the visualization techniques that Nurse Smith, Max's nurse, has been teaching me. I clear my mind, trying to contact my inner self or Outside Me, either one will do. Nurse Smith's lessons were all about my heart. She taught me to visualize warm, positive energy moving into and around my heart, to slow it down.

Instead, I focus on what's really important. I focus on the murderous antibodies in my blood.

It was my second visit to Max's office. Max was already in the examining room when I walked in. I looked around for Nurse Smith but she wasn't there. I eyed the paper gown folded on the examining table.

"I won't be doing an internal today," Max said, and something in his tone sent a ripple of concern through me. "Please," he said, motioning to a chair that sat by a desk. "Have a seat." I sat, concern edging towards alarm.

"There's no need for alarm," he said, and alarm headed for panic.

"Dr. Max . . ."

"Just Max."

"Max, is there something wrong with the baby?"

"No, no, nothing like that."

"What then?"

"Your blood test shows that your blood has the Rh negative factor."

"My blood has what?"

"Rh negative. Normally, this is nothing to be concerned about. Millions of people have Rh negative blood. But in a pregnancy, it can be a little tricky if the fetus has Rh positive blood. Then, the body will create antibodies that will attack the fetus as a foreign invader."

"Oh God!" I said and cradled my head in my hands.

"Let's not get ahead of ourselves. Even if the baby's blood is positive, it's not usually a problem with a first pregnancy. The body doesn't have enough time to build enough of a defense to harm the fetus," Max said, and the breath trapped in my chest broke through. *"So you're here today to have blood drawn. We'll need to draw blood every week in order to keep an eye on the antibody levels."*

"Will you be doing it?"

"Well, me or Nurse Smith."

"Oh," I say, dropping my eyes and trying to keep the pout out of my voice.

"If you prefer," he says with those caring, doting father eyes of his. *"I don't see why I can't do it myself."*

The trained jostles to a stop. Its jerky motions prevent me from really getting into my meditation. I can't seem to connect with the antibodies, to sooth them, calm them, get them to relax, to be cool. I double my efforts to concentrate, trying to visualize them embracing the baby, surrounding it with warmth and love . . . no attacking. But the train is moving in fits and starts. My mind won't cooperate. I'm having trouble keeping my focus on antibodies. My thoughts swing back to Lee.

I think about how, when we first met, Lee rescued me from becoming a Gina minion. Gina was the girl with the big car and big personality, who simply took over every situation on campus, who was surely taking over me.

"You know, it's insidious," Lee had said. "It can happen so gradually that you never even notice." I have to admit that it was easy to let myself ebb away. Minor slights became routine condescension. I was shrinking into myself.

On some level I felt like I should be able to take some credit. I had been the clever girl who managed to survive on her own for two years and was still standing. I actually got through high school without a reliable roof over my head— no easy feat. But being around Gina made me feel like I was grasping at myself through fine-grained sand. I kept slipping through my own fingers. I couldn't quite get a hold on "me." I was forgetting who I was.

The train screeches to a stop and the doors slide open. Four giggling girls get on. I watch them. It's subtle but certain if you know what to look for. One girl holds herself apart from, or more like above, the others. Clearly, they look to follow her lead, seek her approval.

That used to be me. I used to be the "Gina" of my block. It's true. When I was a little kid, I was the one who held court, listened to suggestions from *my* underlings and made the final decision as to what games would be played, how we would spend the day. Whether it was ringoleevio, double Dutch or football, two-hand touch, sewer to sewer down the middle of the street on roller skates—the decision was mine. I was a leader of men (or at least of little kids.) The train rolls to a halt. The "Gina" girl rises. The others follow. It's their stop.

I think about how Lee always says that the Gina and Danny situations are the same. She says Danny is chipping away at who I am just like Gina did.

"People like them, like Gina and Danny, they consume you, drain you of your spirit until you have nothing left inside. Trust me. I know," she says. But Lee just doesn't understand that it's Danny who loses his way. He does. But he always finds his way back, back to me. She doesn't really understand him the way that I do. She's never seen how he looks at me when we're alone behind closed doors, like I'm pretty, desirable. He doesn't see The Duckling. It doesn't dare show its face when I'm with Danny. Lee doesn't know that with Danny I'm beautiful.

Still, she's always here to support me, come what may. She always has a shoulder that I can cry on. She actually gave me back "myself." I owe her. I think that introducing her to Jamal has kind of evened the score, maybe.

I enter Lee's apartment and my heart drops into my stomach. She is shivering, drenched in sweat and barely conscious.

"She was a little better after the bath," Jamal says. "But now she's even worse. We have to take her to the hospital." I know Jamal is right but I'm afraid. I'm afraid of what will happen if we take her to the hospital. I'm afraid of what will happen if we don't. Jamal is actually looking at me for an answer. I don't know what to do. I can't think. An idea is trying to organize itself in my head. It is fragmented and won't seem to come together. This happens to me sometimes. *Think.* Lee needs medical help but not in the hospital . . . medical help . . . a doctor . . . Lee needs a doctor. Max! I have no choice. I have to take a chance. I have to call Max.

"Jamal, I need the phone."

Moments later a wave of relief rushes through me. Max is coming! He's actually agreed to help. He said he'll be right over. Max with his doting eyes, hairy arms, and skillful hands, is coming. And he'll fix Lee. He'll put her back together and she'll be alright. My next call is to Ralfie, just in case. We definitely need someone with a direct line to God.

It's been three months since I first stepped into Max's office, but it feels a lot longer. Because I have Rh negative blood, once a week Max checks the level of the antibodies. He always does it himself. During this time, I've come to know him, to respect him. We've actually gotten close. I think about the concern on his face as he listens to my heart doing the boogaloo or looks at the results of the blood tests. And there's something about the patience in his eyes as he helps me work through the insanity of the baby's phantom activity, the hysterical pregnancy that he says I was having. I guess I believe him. Yes, now I believe him. And then there's our talks on the phone. Max gave me his private phone number. He said I could call and talk to him if I was having one of my bouts of the "maybes." Maybe I'm hysterical, still imagining the entire pregnancy. I think about my uterus, a battleground, mother and child locked in mortal combat. Maybe my blood is attacking the baby, a sneak attack that will end it right there in my womb . . . maybe. Maybe The Duckling will expand, puff itself up, take up what little space exists in my body and press the life out of the baby.

I try and take care not to overdo it with the calls to Max's house. For the most part I don't call more than once or twice a week. Sometimes Max is not home. Then his wife takes a message. She sounds really nice. Max always calls me back when he gets in. I guess he's indulging me. He really doesn't seem to mind. He puts up with me. It's true that he's always busy, but he manages to give me a few minutes anyway. Lately, the "maybes" have subsided, but I still call Max mostly in the evening to talk, say hello, even if it's for just a little while. It warms my heart when I think about how hardily he laughed that time on the phone when I suggested that maybe I wasn't experiencing a hysterical pregnancy at all.

"Maybe," I said. "Maybe my baby is just a prodigy and that explains its early activity." I didn't mention The Duckling's theory, about how I'd been granted a do-over. I didn't think that Max would laugh.

I am so happy to see Max walk through the door at Lee's house that I forget all protocol and fling my arms around his neck.

"Max! I'm so glad you came." He does not respond in kind. He holds his body stiff and I drop my embrace and step back.

"Max I . . . "

"Where's the patient?" He asks, his voice harsh; a voice that I never imagined him capable of. He walks into the bed-

room and stops short when he sees Lee. He rolls his eyes upward in a gesture that I think is exasperation, but I can't be
sure. I feel like I'm shrinking. Like I'm very small and somehow very guilty. He turns to Jamal and asks, "Is this your doing?"

"I . . . I mean, not the procedure, but yes, I guess it is. It's
not like I wanted her to do it. I wanted us to keep it." Then
pulling himself up to full stature, Jamal says, "So you gonna
help us or what?" Max doesn't reply. He places his black bag
on the night table, pulls out a thermometer, prepares it with
alcohol and places it in Lee's mouth. Then he checks her eye
response and blood pressure. He snaps on rubber gloves and
asks me to wait outside while he does an internal. Jamal can
stay.

I am in the living room pacing the floor when the doorbell rings. Ralfie enters, his eyes so full of angst that it makes
me want to cry. Then I hear Lee holler in pain, and I do cry. I
cry right into Ralfie's chest. His arms find their way around
me. It feels like his arms are holding me together, like if he
lets me go, I'll break into all these little pieces. I look up, then,
into his eyes and for a moment it feels like we are two planets
on a collision course, being drawn together by gravity, closer
and closer.

Then, "I think she's going to be okay," Max is saying to
Jamal as they step out of the bedroom. Abruptly, I turn away
from Ralfie, confused and embarrassed. *What just happened?*
"Luckily there's no perforation to the uterus. The shot I gave
her should start knocking down the infection. Be sure to give
her the pills every four hours—that's day and night for the

next forty-eight hours. This is very important. Can you handle it?"

"I'll manage," Jamal says.

"I'll help," I say.

"Me too," from Ralfie. "We can take shifts."

Max nods an affirmation at Ralfie. His eyes move right past *me*. "Good then," he says. "Keep an eye on her tonight. If her fever doesn't break by morning she may have to be hospitalized." Max is pointedly addressing his comments to Jamal, freezing me out. Then he turns to me and in a very business-like manner says, "I'll see you for your regular appointment next week."

"Max . . . What did I do?"

"Why wouldn't you come to me first!?" he barks.

"You're a doctor. There are laws. I didn't think . . . I didn't know."

"*That's* what you did."

"What? Because I didn't know? Max, I'm sorry." He is heading for the door. "Okay . . . okay," I say. I'm near tears again. "What do we owe you? I have money."

"Keep it. I have a feeling you're going to need it." He looks back at me just before he exits. "How could you not know that I hate these filthy underground abortions, hate that women are suffering? I thought that you . . . that we . . . " he falters before he goes on to say, "This girl could have died! I'm a physician! I'm sworn to healing. That's why I agreed to treat *you*. How could you not know that I'd never look the other way while women die? How could you not know that about me? How could you not trust me?" His words assault me. My heart is jogging. I'm feeling lightheaded. I stumble, back away. His eyes are hard and angry . . . hard angry eyes . . . like Danny's eyes that day three years ago, the day of the King riot . . . the day that started "us."

Partners?

The world was gradually returning to focus. I could hear the commotion still raging outside. I was back in the safety of the building with the locked door. I was on the floor. I was lying on cold filthy tiles. Horrified, I attempted to get up but the pain that shot up my arm when I put weight on my wrist nixed that idea. My wrist was swollen. A knot as large as a plum clung to it. There was another even larger knot gracing my right ankle. There were bruises on both my knees, blood oozing from one of them.

I groaned. A figure that had been rambling through the boxes in the vestibule came to my side.

"You're awake," he had said, his face so close to mine that I thought I might black out again. "Can you sit up?" He placed his arm around my back and helped me to sit up against the wall. He was touching me. In that moment I felt no pain. Then, what had looked like concern in his eyes quickly dissolved into irritation.

"What the hell did you think you were doing?!"

"Excuse me?"

"Running out in the middle of all that shit. What were you thinking? I saw you go in the building. Why didn't you just stay in here?"

"You were watching me?"

"I . . . just happened to be looking in your direction."

"Then you must have seen the baby."

"What baby?"

"The baby. That's why I went out. She was standing there in the middle of the street, just wailing. How could you miss her? People left a wide space around her. Guess no one wanted to run her down. But no one wanted to help her either."

"I dunno. I didn't see any baby."

"Well, I did. She was so small. And I couldn't just do nothing. I had no choice. I had to go get her before she got trampled."

"So that's your story. You ran out to save a baby?"

"My story?"

"Okay, say I believe you. So, where's the baby now?"

"Her mother, or at least I think it was her mother. It was definitely someone she knew. Anyway, this woman grabbed her up just before I got to her."

"If you say so."

"Well why else would I have run out there!?"

"Relax," he said, placing his hand on my shoulder, his touch warm on my skin. "I believe you." But I knew he didn't.

I ran the whole thing back through my mind. I saw the kid. Didn't I? I ran out to get her, right? Suddenly Momma's dream advice was playing in my head. She said I should see things as they really are. What is so? What is not so? Is that possible? Do I not see things as they really are? Is that what the dream means?

Following an awkward silence, I managed to ask, "What were you doing over there?" He gave me a blank stare. "With the boxes," I said.

"Oh, I was looking for something that I could use to maybe bind your ankle and wrist or at least clean up your knees."

My heart was starting to do a jitter and my ears felt like they were on fire. I was actually talking to him. He was actually talking to me. He was so close. The smell of sweat and Life Buoy soap wafted off him. And there I was, broken and bloody . . . not cute. My Fro, having been unceremoniously liberated from the barrette, was wild and asymmetric. This is not how I imagined it would happen. And I did imagine it. I imagined it all the time.

"I went all through the building knocking on doors trying to get some help," he said. "But either no one in the entire building is home or they're just not answering for a stranger."

He walked to the door and looked out.

"Things are calming down now, since the cops went away."

"What? They went away?"

"Well, they're still out there but they're not messing with the crowd. They're just kinda standing around and some folks are still carrying stuff off."

"How is that possible? Why would the cops even do that?"

"A while ago, a man with a megaphone—I think it was mayor Lindsay—ordered them to stand down. Looks like they have. Do you think you can walk?"

"I don't know. My ankle might be broken."

"It's not broken, just a bad sprain."

"How can you be so sure?"

"Years of basketball injuries. Trust me." I did trust him.

That's when the muscular young man appeared at the door, carrying packages, and tapping on the window.

"Oh, it's my partner. Let him in."

"Your what?"

"Open the door. It's okay. He's okay." Reluctantly, Danny complied.

"Hey, who the hell are you!? What the hell did you do to her?" The kid asked.

Danny stepped up to him. "No, who the hell are you?!" Danny was his equal in height but not in girth. They were standing there nose to nose, and I realized that I didn't know my partner's name.

"Yo!" I called. Responding to the universal handle, they turned to me. "He didn't do anything to me," I said, addressing the young man. "He's my . . . friend. I fell when I ran out to get the baby . . . Hey, I don't even know your name."

"Jordan. What now? A baby?"

"It's a long story," I said.

"Well, regardless, looks like you basically kept up your end of the bargain."

"What bargain?" Danny addressed his question to me, but Jordan answered.

"She stayed. She opened the door, or had you open the door, and my stuff is still here," he said, looking over at the unopened though somewhat disheveled boxes.

"You were working with this guy?" Danny asked. I just shrugged my shoulders.

"Well, I kept my part of the bargain too. Here . . ." Jordan held out something that looked like an oversized transistor radio.

"What is it?" Danny asked, taking it from his hand.

"This, my man, is El Diablo. It's the latest state of the art. You can actually record music straight off the radio with it. I took it from the locked display case. The sign said, 'Coming Soon.' They ain't even selling them here in the states yet. I had my eye on it for the longest. I got it just for her like I promised cause it's small enough to carry."

Danny's face came alive as he examined the radio. "That's some speaker. How do you record music on it?" he asked.

"With this here." Jordan handed him something that resembled a miniature reel-to-reel tape.

"A cassette, right?"

"It's a blank cassette. It goes right in this compartment. This is the future, my man. With El Diablo you can play pre-

149

recorded albums or record music right off the radio and play it anytime—free."

"Hello!" I called from where I was stuck, sitting down on the grimy tiled floor. "Remember me? I want to get out of here. Is it safe to leave?" Jordan went to check. Mesmerized, Danny continued to explore the radio.

"It looks like there was a war out there, but I think it's safe to leave now. Can you walk?" Jordan knelt by my side. "Here, let me help you up. I'll take you to my house. I only live around the corner. My mom is really good at patching people up. She always wanted to be a nurse. Then you can call someone if you want."

I was standing, leaning heavily on Jordan, my arm around his neck. Then Danny was there with his sweaty Life Buoy smell, pushing his shoulder under my other arm. He placed his arm around me and pulled me in. He glared at Jordan and said, "That's okay, 'my man.' I'll see that she gets home. Don't you have some booty to deal with?"

"What? Some booty?"

"Your stuff," Danny said. Jerking his head in the direction of the boxes. "Here you go." He held the radio out to Jordan.

"Nah man, I got that for her. She can keep that. In fact, I'm gonna go get you guys a cab, on me. It's a long way to the Bronx with that ankle. I'll be right back."*

"Where to?" the cabbie asked. Danny waited for me to give him my address in the Bronx. Only I didn't have an address in the Bronx or anywhere else. In three weeks, I would be moving into the dorms . . . where Danny lived. That thought brought invisible heat to my cheeks.

"I think I'll go to Chandra's house," I said. "It's closer and I was supposed to stay with her tonight anyway."

Danny asked the cabbie to wait while he helped me up-stairs. But there was no answer when I rang the bell. I rang over and over . . . nothing. No one was home. I started to worry. What if something happened to Chandra? What if she got swept up by the cops or trampled bloody and was lying in a hospital bed somewhere? Then panic and guilt set in when my concerns swung back to myself. Where can I go now? What do I tell Danny? Do I tell him that I'm some kind of tramp, living from one place to the other? It's the truth, isn't it? Guess I'm about to find out if it will set me free.

"Guess we have to go to the Bronx after all," he said.

"Okay," I said, my voice tentative. "So, here's the thing . . ."

Something

I am in Momma's house. It is bright and sparkly and as orderly as I remember. Momma is seated on a hassock. I am greasing her head and braiding her hair like I used to. She turns to me and sings . . .

Something in the way life moves
Will have you searching to discover
Something within that you must lose
Leave all the fears behind
Master of your own mind
I'm telling you to search beneath
Then you'll know, then you will breathe
These answers you must know
What is so?
What is not so?
Who is who?
Who are you?
Who is who?

Who are you?

Then her ghostly voice trails off and echoes away.

With a sharp intake of air, I had startled myself awake. This might've been the fifteenth night in a row that I had the dream. And this time was not unlike any of the others. I shot up, tried to catch my breath, thought about the dream, tried to understand it. Momma was singing a song that wasn't a hymn. That fact alone made it weird. And she sung in this alien, haunting voice. It was so eerie.

Then disoriented, I looked around. As always, it took a moment to get my bearings. I was on the floor entangled in a scramble of bedclothes. I sat up and looked over at the figure sleeping in one of the two twin beds. It was Gina, the bed sheet pulled up over her head. On the other side, her roommate Millie and her boyfriend Jarred were curved into each other, his arms securing her. She was barely visible on that tiny bed. They looked like one person. Something green spoke to me. *That will never be you!* They were asleep so I could stare openly at them, imagining how that might feel, being held like that, being loved. In a few days, I'd be official. I'd be moving into the dorms, into my own space. Maybe then . . .

There was a tap on the door and something electric zapped through my chest. I knew who it was. I smiled. He was literally up before Dawn. Like me, he was an early riser. Or at least he was since I'd been staying here with Gina. He was since that night, a little over two weeks ago, that one amazing night, the night of the riot, when I stayed in his room . . . with him.

"I . . . um, I'm going down for breakfast and wondered if you . . . or anyone, wants anything." That's what he always said. He'd said exactly the same thing every morning for the last fifteen mornings . . . but who was counting.

"I don't know about anyone," I said. " But I'm starving. Give me a moment and I'll go down with you." That's what *I* always said.

"You know what?" he asked. "I have a better idea. Grab that blanket." This was different, something new. As usual he had the El Diablo radio with him. I'd left it with him, seeing as he was so enamored with it.

We went into the deli and bought breakfast. I got tea and an egg-n-cheese croissant. He got coffee and a BLT on a roll. I also picked up some blueberries. Then we walked the few blocks to Central Park. It was early, just a little past six. The sky was getting lighter though the sun hadn't come up yet. A wispy purple cloud, looking like water paint, drifted across the pale palette that was the sky. The morning breeze was nippy, and I wished that I had remembered a sweater. I followed him to a spot that was relatively wooded, almost private. The grass was full and uncut. Clearly there was not much foot traffic here. He knew exactly where to go. I wondered how often he came here and with whom. I spread the blanket. We sat. For a long while we were quiet. We didn't talk or eat or even move. We just sat. Usually, it took all my will power to refrain from fidgeting and babbling on. It was what I did when I was nervous. Strangely, I wasn't feeling particularly nervous that morning.

Having breakfast with him the past two weeks had taught me the virtue of silence. After our first night together, there was so much more I wanted to know, so many unanswered questions. But he was reserved . . . mysterious. It was what made him cool. And there was this understated shyness about him. It was surprising. So, I knew better than to probe. He would tell me things—more things than he revealed that night—when he was ready.

He pushed a button on the El Diablo and the Beatles' "Here Comes the Sun" filled the air. It was the song that he played for me that first night in his room. His eyes were cast skyward. Gradually, the sun eased its way to the horizon. Ribbons of dazzling white light erupted, flared out through the branches of the trees as bands of gold and amber traversed the sky. It was beautiful. It was breathtaking. It was romantic. He actually planned for us to watch the sunrise together! My heart did a little happy hop, and I didn't have to remind myself to breathe. I was breathing deep and easy.

Though we'd spent all these mornings together, nothing he ever did or said gave me any indication that he had any romantic interest in me. We had become friends. I felt myself rapidly slipping into the "little sister" category, especially when we were around other people. But in the mornings— our mornings—we'd eat in the diner across the street and then we'd sit together in the lounge and he'd put music on the radio box. If we spoke at all we'd speak about random things—school, sports, meticulously avoiding the things we had confided to each other that first night in his room, acting as though nothing had ever been said. I knew it was strange. He was strange. Together, we were strange. But at least I was close to him, got to orbit in his universe. Hell, he came for me—for *me*—each morning. And there was something in his eyes. It was something that I needed to figure out. He was playing "Here Comes the Sun." He was playing it for *me*. Maybe it was a hint. He had played it for me that night, the night of the riot, our first night together.

Here Comes the Sun

"Say what? You don't live anywhere in particular? What's that even mean?" Danny had asked the night of the riot. We were sitting in the cab that Jordan had called for us. My ankle was throbbing and I was feeling stifled. I rolled down the window, looking up the street, hoping for Chandra to come and save me from having to explain.

"I'm just sort of between places right now. In a few days I'll be moving into the dorms. I was planning to make some arrangements for the interim. I didn't expect to be in a riot."

"I'm not sure I understand."

"Listen, it's been a long day and I'm tired. I don't want to talk about it. Just help me sit on the stoop and I'll wait here for Chandra to get home. Her mother's not happy. I know it's leaving time, but I think she'll let me stay one more night."

Now the cab driver who had apparently been listening to our exchange cleared his throat and said, "So . . . where to folks?"

And Danny said, "Seventy-first and Broadway."

With one arm over Danny's shoulder, I limp into the Alamac hotel. The lobby is a wide, sprawling space. Its worn red carpet and dusty, low-hanging chandeliers with several crystals missing, give the impression of a place whose best days were behind it.

There's a white guy working behind the lobby's front desk; at first glance I think it's Paul McCarthy. Of course it's not. The Paul look-alike smiles weakly. His eyes follow us as we make our way into the elevator.

There's the faint, lingering smell of incense as we enter Danny's room. The rectangular room is small and tidy with two single beds on opposite walls. A small desk in front of a window is situated in the limited space between them.

"You can take my bed," Danny said. "Raymond, that's my roommate, he's not big on doing laundry."

He helped me limp into the room and lowered me onto his bed. Then he began to strip the sheets from Raymond's bed.

"Won't Raymond be coming in?"

"Nah, he went home for spring break. He'll be gone all week." He folded the sheets, neatly placed them in a hamper, retrieved a set of crisp clean ones from a closet and began putting them on the bed. "Actually, he's gone most of the time—stays in his girlfriend's room a lot." A suggestive silence fell between us. My ears began to feel hot as both angst and possibility filled my head. Searching for something to say, I spotted a photograph in a silver toned frame sitting on the desk. It was the picture of a couple. A dark-skinned woman, petite, and pretty, with a tall light-skinned man, who wore no smile below his intense, wolfish eyes. His arm was hooked around her neck possessively while her arms hung limp, down at her sides. She was staring straight into the camera, looking as though she had been ordered to do so. Her smile was neutral, her eyes uncertain.

"Are these your folks?" He took the picture from my hand and placed it into a desk drawer that had orderly sectioned-off compartments for all the items it held.

"Yeah, it's an old photo. Raymond must've left it out when he was searching through the drawer. He's always doing stuff like that," he said. He went to a dresser and then back to the closet and returned with a clean, neatly folded white T-shirt, some Ace bandages, and a pair of crutches. Then answering the question I had not yet posed, he said, "Like I said, lots of basketball injuries." Then his beautiful lips formed a slow, perfect smile and I relaxed and. . . breathed. "My boy C-Jay, he has a kitchenette in his room. I'll go get some ice. You probably want to clean up a bit," he said as he readjusted the crutches to my height. "Do you need help? I mean, do you think you can handle the shower, you know, alone?" I'm sure we shared the same mental image because his eyes found one wall and mine found the other.

"I think I can manage."

"Good. I'll go get us some food and the ice. You like burgers?"

"Burgers sound good."

"Maybe you should wait 'til I get back. You know, to wash-up. In case you fall or something."

"I'll be fine."

159

"Just wait. Okay?"

"Okay."

But the minute he was gone I heaved myself onto the crutches, grabbed the oversized T-shirt and made my way to the bathroom. I knew some of the rooms only had shower stalls. I was relieved to find that this one had a tub as well as a shower. My body ached for a hot bath. On the sink there was a small bottle of dish washing liquid. Apparently, the sink did double duty. I ran the water hard and hot, infusing it with the liquid soap. I stripped and lowered myself into the tub as fluffy white suds bloomed around me. I exhaled a long, deep breath and let go, releasing the grief and insanity of the day's events from my bones. I leaned back and rested my head on the wall behind me. After a while I found myself crooning softly.

"Something in the way he smiles, makes me want to be his lover . . ."

"You like the Beatles?"

Stunned, I splashed water all over the floor and almost sat up before I realized that the suds offered some cover. My heart was thumping, and my face was hot. I wanted to slip under the water and never come back up. "I didn't mean to startle you. I just wanted to make sure that you were okay. You are, aren't you—okay?"

"Was my caterwauling that bad?"

"No. Actually, you have a very nice voice. So, the Beatles huh?"

"Not really, just that song."

"It's a pretty good song. You know of course, that's not how it goes."

"Excuse me?"

"The song lyrics; that's not how it goes. You weren't singing the actual lyrics."

"Oh, lyrics," I say, embarrassed by what my song may have revealed. "I never pay much mind to the actual lyrics. I just kinda make up my own. It's just something that I do," I said, hoping I didn't sound like a complete ditz.

He just stared at me for a while, like he was forming some opinions. Then he said, "You're pretty stubborn, huh?"

I shrugged my shoulders.

"Your own lyrics—sure why not?" he said. "And it's good that you're soaking the sprains in hot water. It makes it easier to loosen them up before we ice them. It should've been done right after the injury, but I guess it's better late than never. He left the bathroom and returned with a lit joint and the mellow sound of the Beatles' "Here Comes the Sun" floating in the air.

"So, you like the Beatles, huh?" I smiled, mimicry in my voice.

"Not really, just this song." He smiled back. Those lips, that smile . . . I thought I might melt.

He took a drag and handed the joint to me. I hesitated. For the most part, I didn't indulge. When squatting on the floor with my friends, I always just passed the joint along. In a room lit with candles and dim red lightbulbs, no one ever noticed. I guess it was something about Momma's eyes in my head.

161

"It'll take the edge off," he said, apparently sensing my reluctance. "It's like a muscle relaxer."

Following that logic, how could I say no? Not to mention, the idea of putting something to my lips that had just been on those lips of his was not entirely unpleasant. I took a puff and he smiled.

"No, you have to inhale it; take it into your chest and try to hold it."

I took a long drag and inhaled deeply. The smoke cut sharp into my lungs. It felt like it had gone down the wrong pipe and I choked into a coughing fit.

He waited until I was able to compose myself before asking, "You okay?"

I nodded, still coughing a bit.

"One more," he said.

I took another drag, this time cautiously, and managed to hold it for a while before coughing it out.

"I think that should just about do it," he said, amusement in his voice. Then reaching a hand towards me he asked, "May I?"

It took a moment for me to understand that I was supposed to give him my foot so he could loosen the sprain. Something in my brain was busy expanding. My mind was liquid overheating, transforming itself into steam. Propelled by the richness of the music. A Beatles' song announcing the majestic advent of the sun, flared out like tiny droplets of consciousness. The flourish was lighter than air. The music was one with everything, with the whole universe.

Danny stood, his outstretched hand summoning. My leg rippled upward as I offered my swollen ankle. He took possession of it in his strong grip. His hands felt hotter than the water. Slowly, he rotated the ankle, lathering his hands with soap and applying gentle pressure. He slid his hot hands over the sprain, moving halfway up my calf, and down . . . and up again . . . and down again. The song's lyrics were muffled through the closed bathroom door and filtered through the smoke haze in my head. In my mind, I filled in the music with words of my own.

"Little lover, looks like the ice is surely melting."

Dual sensations shot up my leg, through my spine, on into my brain and back down again, settling ultimately somewhere between my legs. The pain was intense . . . the pleasure exquisite. Delirious, my eyes closed. I let my head fall back and rest on the wall as I immerse myself in those sensations.

Twenty-four hours earlier he didn't even know that I was alive. I wasn't even sure he knew my name yet. As I sat there on his bed wrapped in the scent of his T-shirt, all of this suddenly struck me as hilarious. The laughter that bubbled up from somewhere inside me could not be controlled. I laughed tears down my cheeks. I laughed pain into my sides. I laughed until I coughed, until I couldn't catch my breath, until I almost cried . . . until I did cry. Then he was there by my side on the bed, his arm around my shoulder. I buried my face in his chest, inhaled his scent. I was too embarrassed to face him. I couldn't control the laughing-crying thing.

"Hey, it's okay. You're okay. It's the giggles, happens to everyone."

"It isn't happening to you," I sobbed-laughed into his chest.

"Yeah, well, it used to. It doesn't affect me like that anymore. I wish it did."

I looked up at him and said, "You do?" We were sitting on his bed, and he was actually holding me, both arms around me. Those lips were inches from mine. I tilted my face upward, closed my eyes. And although it felt surreal, I knew what was about to happen.

Except . . . he let go of me and turned away.

"Yep, I do. But it affects me in different ways now—still good ways," he said. "Why don't we eat? The food is getting cold, and the toaster oven isn't working."

Heat rose in my face as I tried to play it off like I wasn't actually expecting to be kissed. It was a ridiculous notion anyway, followed by an alien thought that eased its way into my mind: *Why would Danny Barrett want to kiss you anyway?*

He opened a TV table and placed the food on it. He shuffled through some forty-fives and placed several on the automatic turntable. He lit another joint and took a toke. I reached for it. Appearing somewhat surprised, he handed it to me. I inhaled and held it until I thought my lungs would burst. Music touched with cow bells and images of grassy fields filled my head. Then I took two more and felt better, felt like giggling again. The music and food were magical. The flavors and textures slid across my tongue startling my

164

taste buds. I'd never had a burger so delicious—the pickles, the ketchup . . . unbelievable.

We ate without speaking, the rich, pounding music filling the void. I could actually feel the song. It embraced me, made everything beautiful—made me beautiful. Aretha was singing "Chain of Fools," her voice so soulful it felt exotic. It felt like she was this third person in the room with us, alternately singing out warnings and encouragements. I wanted to dance. I love dancing. If it weren't for my ankle, I would have. Instead, I sat bobbing my head and swaying to the rhythms. My body was rippling to the melodies, my shoulder touching his ever so slightly. Then I'd sway away and back again for another electric touch. He was smiling that broad, beautiful smile.

A thought was trying to occur to me, then. I think that duckling was sending it. It was circling the room, looking for a way to get into my head. It was trying to say that he was not smiling with me but laughing at me. I didn't engage, deciding I didn't care one way or the other. I was amazed that I managed to dismiss it—that thought.

Martin Luther King was dead. Though that made me sad, I truly believed that I too had come close that day. And something had shifted. I was still there. I had not expired. I was there eating magical food and swaying to exotic music and sitting on Danny's bed . . . next to Danny. I reached for the joint and took another toke.

"Your stereo is something else," I said, breaking our silence.

"It's a component set. The speakers are kinda cool. They're Yamaha, the largest on the market, with the best sound."

"Yama-wha?"

"Yama*ha*." He smiled out the word. Then, with his expression suddenly changing, he said, "Where will you stay tomorrow? Will you go back to Chandra's?"

"Maybe. I'm not sure. I have to make some calls."

"You can stay here, I mean for a while, if you want. Like I said, Raymond is definitely gone for at least a week."

I was actually more shocked by my response than by his offer. I was surprised that the last thing I wanted at that moment was to stay with him, alone in his room, pursing my lips for a kiss that would never come. No. Gina also lived in the dorms. I never asked her because I knew that her roommate's boyfriend Jarred was all but living there too. Still, I was sure I could probably stay with her, on the floor or something. It would just be for a couple of weeks, just until I could move into my own dorm room. Gina would be okay with that.

"That's very nice of you but it's okay. I'll manage. I always do," I said, suddenly captivated by the maroon and black pattern in the worn carpet. The colors seemed to be vibrating with the music.

"Exactly *how* have you been managing?" he asked.

I looked up at him. In his eyes I thought I saw what might've been genuine interest, if not concern. He didn't strike me as nosey, someone who just wanted to get in my business.

"May I?" I asked and he handed me the joint. I took a quick drag, releasing a sigh along with the pungent smoke. "It's like I said. I've been staying with Chandra for a while and before that with my friend Little Gabrielle, my aunt's house, her cousin's house, back to Gabrielle's, and so on and so on. Momma's house is gone." I suddenly needed to steady my voice.

"Momma? You mean you mother's house?"

"No. Momma was my grandmother. She passed shortly after her house—the house I grew up in—burned down."

"That's rough. I'm sorry." I shrugged and dropped my eyes. "So why aren't you living in your house? I mean, with your parents?"

"It's a long story. There was this evil stepfather thing going on. I had to tip. I couldn't live there."

"And your mother? She was cool with that?"

For a second my response hitched in my throat. I wasn't sure that I wanted to tell him all of this. "Well . . . at first I think she agreed to let me leave until things calmed down. I'm pretty sure she never thought it would be, like, forever. She probably thought that I'd lose my resolve, that I'd be back, and we'd work things out. You know, one big happy family, in one big happy home. But I knew that wasn't happening. I could never live with that man."

"He wasn't trying to . . . "

"No . . . nothing like that. Actually, I didn't stick around long enough for anything like that," I said, the hitch in my throat having found its way into my voice. My eyes went vacant. My mind skipped to the memory. My words felt involuntary. "He hit me," I said. "The very first day we were supposed to move in with him . . . almost dislocated my jaw. I had to leave." I was suddenly aware that I had never told this to anyone, not in so many words. There were people who already knew—Little Gabrielle, some of my relatives. But I had never actually said those words out loud. I couldn't believe I was actually telling Danny Barrett, of all people.

Unable to face his eyes, his pity, I turned my attention to the stereo. I watched as another record shimmied down and dropped into place. I watched the jerky motion of the mechanical arm. I marveled at how it placed the needle in precisely the right groove for Smokey Robinson's song, "Ooo Baby Baby" to fill the air."

"I do call my mother to make sure she's okay," I said. "And to let her know I'm okay. After a while, I guess she finally accepted that I wasn't going back. We started meeting in restaurants or museums, movies, places like that. You know, spending time together. She'd give me some money. I always sidestepped her questions when she tried to find out details about how and where I was living. That would put too much pressure on her. It's better for both of us this way. As it turns out, he doesn't hurt *her*. He's never laid a finger on her. So now that she knows I'll be moving into the dorms soon, she and her husband are moving to Arizona. She said it's because of his business. She asked me, but there's no way I'm moving there with them." What I didn't tell Danny was that I didn't want to mess up Mom's life . . . again.

"Damn, how old were you when you left?"

"Sixteen." He got up and changed the forty-fives on the turntable. The Impressions sang, "Gypsy Woman" and just like that, I knew that song was me—my song. It was an oldie, one of my all-time favorites. I was impressed by the depth of his collection.

"So," he said. "You're a bit of a badass, huh?"

Time

The question, if it *was* a question, took me by surprise. *Me . . . a badass?*

"No," I said. "I'm just treading water." That fact was dawning on me as I spoke the words. "Just trying to stay afloat."

"Seems to me that you do a lot more than just tread water. Someone who's just trying to stay afloat doesn't run out in the middle of a riot to save a baby."

"So, you *do* believe me that there was a baby?"

"I believe that *you* believe it."

"Oh, so you think I'm delusional."

"Hey, even if you ran out there tilting at windmills, it was a badass thing to do."

"Did you say, tilting at windmills?" I asked, infatuation merging with obsession. *Damn, he's gorgeous and schooled too.*

He smiled but didn't respond. Instead, he got up to light a candle and a stick of jasmine incense. He switched the ceiling light off and turned on a black light and a red-bulbed lamp. The space dimmed, mellowed. The psychedelic posters on the walls and ceiling and the white T-shirt that I was wearing jumped to life, glowing neon white.

Danny went into the bathroom. The sound of the water running in the shower piqued my imagination. I envisioned him lathering up his fine brown frame, the hard spray of the shower hitting his naked body. My heart sped up just a bit as I could almost see the sudsy water caressing the strong noble features of his face and those lips, slowly rolling over his broad shoulders, past his chest, his tight abs, dripping off his shaft, flowing down his long legs, down his muscular thighs and calves before easing down into the drain.

When he returned, he was wearing pull-string pj bottoms and a sleeveless undershirt that clung to his body, accentuating his broad basketball shoulders and tight abs. Shamelessly, I eyed him as he shuffled through his forty-fives and placed a few of them on the stereo.

Then, using the candle to light an unfinished joint, he flopped onto Raymond's bed. He lay there staring at the ceiling, the joint's flame flaring amber in the dimly lit room. The aromas of Danny wafted throughout; their intermingled scents were even more intoxicating than the grass I'd been ingesting. He leaned over, offered me the joint. I was in my own private high. I waved it away. On the turntable, a throbbing song dropped. The song featured the driving sound of a clock counting down time. It infused itself into the psychedelic posters on the walls, causing them to vibrate. It rumbled into the air . . . into my head.

I was floating in and out of vibrant posters, their radiant colors set afire by the black light. The driving *tick, tick, tick* of the song's musical clock counting down propelled me back in time to Momma's house, to the old wind-up clock that never, ever went unwound, to the scent of loose powder, of Taboo, of jasmine incense, of Lifebuoy soap . . . of him. *Tick, tick, tick.* I was drifting in and out, back and forth between two lifetimes. At first, it was not at all unpleasant. I'd allowed myself to relax, breathe, let my thoughts go where they would. The music was throbbing. Its heady beat was forcing itself into my brain. My mind got caught on the sound of the base drum. Maybe it was the grass, because suddenly the rhythms morphed. They were the sound of a ticking clock. The clock's psychedelic beats were counting down to . . . tipping time.

My heart zapped electric with the memory. I had overstayed my welcome. I had no place. I had to leave! I had no choice! The music's countdown clock had pried open some shrouded crevice inside me. It released thoughts that I'd long since wrapped in fog. And events that I had securely packed away, someplace just below consciousness, came bleeding out. I cringed as the memory broke through. Tipping time had caught me off guard. Yes, I had slept on a rooftop.

The last record in the cue dropped off, and a quiet broke out. The sudden silence was jolting. It pulled me back into Danny's room. After a while, speaking in a whisper I said, "I'm no badass."

"What? Did you say something?"

"Badass? I'm no badass."

He remained silent. It was as though he knew I had more that I wanted to say. He was giving me the space to say it.

"I had a dog," I said.

"A dog. Okaay? I like dogs."

"Siegfried. She was a really good dog: beautiful, fearless, smart . . . so smart."

"Those are the best kind."

"I went to get her, you know, from my mother's house. I shouldn't have. I should've left her there, but I couldn't stand the thought of her living with that man, my mother's husband." I was sure I was sounding like a complete ditz. I wasn't making any sense. But he just laid there listening. I went on. "So yeah, I went to get her. I don't know what I was thinking. People were always good to me, you know. They welcomed me into their homes, at least for a while. But with a dog? No matter how great Siegfried was, a big boned Shepherd was the deal breaker." I took a breath before I continued. "I was determined to keep her with me, you know, one way or another. I thought I'd, like, figure something out eventually. But that very first night is when it dawned on me. I literally had nowhere to sleep. That had never happened before."

Danny rolled onto his side and faced me. "So what did you do?" His casual tone encouraged me to continue.

I took a beat and a breath. I had to give the scene time to settle into my chest. Siegfried and I had been sitting on a bench in Crotona Park, sharing a sandwich. The sun was shining. There was a chill in the air. I think it must have been late August. I knew it would get cold once the sun went down. For the first time since I left home, I had to worry about shelter. But I knew I didn't have to worry about safety. No one ever messed with me if Siegfried was there.

"I decided that the safest place for us to sleep, at least until I was able to make other arrangements, was on the top staircase landing of the building across the street from the park." As I spoke, the memory was shaking itself loose. Soon it ballooned large. I could hear the sound . . . *footsteps*. . . like they were right there in Danny's room.

Dog Daze.

I told Danny about the night on the roof, remembering how Siegfried's ears flew up, how she was on her feet before I even knew what was happening. She'd emitted a low growl that came from somewhere deep in her chest. Someone was coming. I cautioned Siegfried to silence. She quieted, bared her teeth. Then the sounds stopped.

"So that's where you slept? On the top landing?" Danny crushed the joint in an ashtray. He sat up in the bed across the room, his back against the wall, his knees bent, his unfocused eyes trained straight ahead.

"That was the plan," I said. "But the constant sound of people coming and going on the staircase kept Siegfried on high alert. There was no way to sleep. I was so exhausted. Even though it was cold, I decided it would be just as safe and a lot quieter if we slept out on the roof."

Danny lit a joint, and from way over there on the other side of the tiny room, he listened.

175

The image of Siegfried and I huddled together on the rooftop bloomed in my mind. Siegfried . . . she was my blanket. She was my pillow. Her fur was my comfort and reassurance; the warmth of her body, the whisper of her heartbeat, all lulled me to sleep. I slept. I slept well.

"How long did you sleep on the roof?" he asked, smoke veiling his beautiful face.

"That one night. It was okay that one night," I said, trying to keep the tremor out of my voice. "I knew then I couldn't keep Siegfried, couldn't provide for her. The next day I called my mother to tell her that although I would never go back home, I needed to bring Siegfried back. But it was her husband who answered the phone. He said that the dog was no longer welcome in his house." I didn't tell Danny the effect that those words had on me. That once I heard what he said, I had trouble hearing much else over that grating roar that went rushing through my brain. I didn't mention what else my mother's husband had said. Or at least, what I think he may have said that day. Something about a dog only having one master; that *he* was not that master. I think maybe he said something about it being dangerous to have such a large animal who didn't respect his authority. I'm sure he said he wasn't my father and didn't care to be. Yes, that's what he said. But I didn't tell Danny any of this. What would he think? How did we even get on this subject?

"So what did you do?" he asked with his eyes straight ahead, speaking to something unseen on the opposite wall.

I sighed and plunged on. "I spent that day trying to find a place for her . . . for us. I thought about asking my friend

Gabrielle, but I knew her father had developed an allergy. So when night fell, we went back to the roof."

The memories, having been resurrected so abruptly, came flooding through. I clasped my hands together and tightly interlocked my fingers, as though I could somehow slow the mental images down, squeeze them away.

I took a beat, pulled in a breath and tried to tell the story in the most coherent way that I could manage. But the fractured images came pouring out in disjointed spikes and shocks, in strobe-like tangles and distorted flashbacks . . .

Siegfried and I enveloped in our cocoon. Me asleep. Siegfried on her feet . . . a creaking sound. Siegfried baring her teeth . . . roaring out a warning. The screech of the roof's door opening. Two dark figures silhouetted against the bright full moon. Two shadows, one female scantily dressed, staggering. One male, tall, lanky, sure footed. They halted. Siegfried, ferocious, snarling, snapping, a wild beast. Me holding her collar. Them standing, staring. The man, a creature, stepped into view—bony face contoured in shadow, eyes bright with malice set deep in their sockets, one front tooth missing, the other a chipped fang.

"Now looky what we got here," he said, and flashed a ragged grin—breathing, panting, his chest heaving up and down, his body quaking. Bile was rising in my mouth. I was clinging to Siegfried's collar. Siegfried was snapping, snarling out threats, clambering for release.

"I'll bet that sweet young mouth of hers can give a real good blow job—much better than yours, bitch," he said addressing the woman.

For some reason, she ventured a smile that was really just a gummy, toothless grimace. She was gaunt, skin swinging off her skeletal frame. Her vacant eyes saw nothing. She staggered, said nothing. "Now why don't you save us all a lot of time and trouble and tell your little puppy there to calm down."

Cold fear shot through my spine. My heart took off. I had to get away, get to the door. The skeleton woman teetered directly in my path. If I made a run for it, she would be no obstacle. The man stood slightly off to one side. He was old, probably forty, thin, not in good shape. Based on where he stood, I was sure I could out sprint him. He took a step towards us. Siegfried went crazy. It was all I could do to restrain her. Something metal glinted in the moonlight, something ominous that he held in his hand. I knew I had to go for the door. Get away, get away, go! Go! Go! was running through my head. I dropped my gaze so as not to telegraph my intent.

Releasing Siegfried, I yelled, "Let's go!" I charged forward, tackled the woman head on. Her body, like a sack of butterfly wings, gave way easily. She crumbled and fell. But Siegfried was not by my side. Once released she had charged the man, taken him down, protecting me just like she'd done with my mother's husband. The hollow-eyed creature's screams cut through the night air. At the door, I stopped and turned. "Siegfried, c'mon girl, let's go!"

My dog looked up, headed towards me. I was halfway down the first landing when I heard Siegfried's howl. It was not a victory howl, but one of pain, then a whimper, and then silence. Siegfried! Conflict and indecision shot through me. Get away, get away! Go! Go! Go! replayed in my head like a needle stuck in a record's groove. Get away, go! Fear was in control, adrenaline was pushing me forward, my feet flying down the stairs, out of the building, into the frigid Bronx night . . . my eyes never looking back.

This, or some version of this, is what I told Danny as he sat up on his roommate's bed, on the other side of the world, in the low-lit room with the psychedelic posters glowing.

After a long awkward silence, without looking at me, he said, "Did you ever find out what happened to your dog?"

"I woke up the next morning in Gabrielle's house," I said. "I don't even remember how I got there. Anyway, I called my mother's house praying that she would be the one to pick up the phone. She was." Then never looking at him, I told him about that phone conversation.

"Mommy . . . Siegfried," I sobbed into the phone, tears streaming down my face.

"Dawny, thank God! Siegfried's here. What happened? Are you okay?"

"She's what? She's there?"

"Yes, she showed up late last night, limping, looking like she'd been in a fight with a wild animal or something. I was worried sick about you! What happened? Why isn't she with you?"

"She's hurt? How bad is it?" I asked.

"Yes! Like I said, she's hurt. She's very badly hurt. She has some kind of a wound on her left side and there's blood coming out of her ear. She can barely stand up. Are you okay? What the hell happened?"

"I'm fine. It's a long story. I . . . um, I couldn't find a place to stay—not with the dog. Well, the thing is, she was defending me."

"What?! Why didn't you just bring her home? Why don't you just come home? It's time!" Obviously, she didn't know. Her husband didn't tell her about the phone call, about how he didn't want the dog in his house, or how it was clear he didn't want me either. I thought about telling her what he said but for some reason I decided against it.

"It's complicated, Mom."

"Well, I patched her up as best as I could, but she's not looking good. We're getting ready to take her to the vet. Where are you?"

"I'm at Gabrielle's."

"You should come. We'll pick you up."

"We? Meaning you and your husband?" A specter emerged then, his ghostly fist impacting my face, bringing on the dread, the grief . . . the guilt.

"I wish you'd stop calling him that," she said.

"I keep forgetting his name," I said, not even trying to hide the sarcasm in my voice. "Anyway, I'll pass on going. I'll call you later to see what the vet said. If it's okay, I'd like to come by and see her later. He'll be going to his factory, right?"

"Of course it's okay. This is your home."

"Right. Anyway, you can reach me at Gabrielle's. I think I'll be staying here for a while."

In Danny's room there was a long silence . . . a time-out. It felt like the story was just hanging there in the air, like it needed a moment to settle in, to nestle its way into all the room's darkened nooks, to ease its way across the chasm, to reach out for Danny.

"So your dog . . . she was okay?"

"No," I whispered. "They put her down."

Dad Daze

"So that's why you're no badass? Because you didn't try to save your dog?"

"Please, I don't want to talk about it anymore."

"Yeah, I get that, but I'm jus sayin'. There was nothing you could've done for her. That dog was probably a bigger badass than anyone we know. Anyway, none of that, not saving a baby or a dog, none of that is what makes you a bona fide badass."

"Oh?" I said, somewhat intrigued. "So tell me, what exactly makes me a bona fide badass?"

He retrieved the joint, lit it, took one long drag and offered it to me. I waved it away. He crushed the bud in the ashtray. Then, resuming his previous position, he opened his mouth as if to speak but said nothing. It was as though he was rethinking it, deciding. I realized then that I had been doing all the talking and he had been doing all the listening. This time I waited. When he finally spoke, his voice was strange. It sounded like it was coming through a tunnel. "You're a badass because . . . you left," he said, never making eye contact. "Damn girl, you were sixteen years old! You picked yourself up and left. You saved . . . *you*." Although he was speaking softly, his words resonated through my head. A long silence congealed in the space between us. After a while he said, "My mother . . . she had a husband too. And when we were little, he used to have his—let's call it his moods."

"We?"

"Yeah, I have an older brother. What about you?"

"I have an older sister."

"Did she leave too?"

"She was already married and out of the house when he materialized. That's a-whole-nother story. But please go on. You were telling me about your mother's husband—his moods?"

"Yeah, his moods. Well, sometimes he was great, you know. He put us in the basketball league, came to all the games. He paid for us to study martial arts. We studied for years. Tommy—that's my brother—he took karate. I took judo. But then there were these other times, the times when he'd come home with this look on his face. I could tell just by looking at him what kind of mood he was in, usually because he felt guilty after being with other women. Mom knew. She could always tell—we all could. He'd have this defiant look . . . angry. Like he ruled and could not be questioned. He looked like a different person altogether. He was like Jekyll and Hyde. And she never dared question him either."

"He was your stepfather?"

183

"He was my father. People say that I look like he spit me out." Danny heaved a sigh into the dim room and continued. "It was like there was this demon that lived inside him, you know. Like it would just jump out on any random day for any random reason. I never knew what would set him off. I never knew what to expect. When he was in one of his moods, he'd find any little reason to beat us. I mean anything. I got clocked once for leaving the cap off the toothpaste. Tommy was almost knocked out cold for being ten minutes late for dinner. And if my mother tried to interfere, she'd get the worst of it. Once he dislocated her shoulder. Another time he broke her eye socket. I can't even remember the reasons. She always told the hospital that she fell."

"He drank?" *She ain't mine*, a voice slurred in my memory.

"Never touched the stuff. No booze. No drugs. Just craziness, mean and hateful. He excelled at meanness. Sometimes he was mean just for the sake of being mean. I never understood it. For a long time, I didn't even know that other kid's fathers didn't do shit like that. I actually thought that shit was normal."

"And he stayed?" I asked, the question ringing strange the moment it left my lips.

Danny turned his look on me, then.

"I mean he never, like, abandoned you guys?"

He took a moment and a drag from his joint, turned away. With his eyes unfocused he addressed the wall before him. "Dad leave us? I wish. No. I dunno why, but I do know that for him, that was never an option. I guess it just wasn't in his DNA."

Then he smiled a skewed little smile, his perfect teeth glowing in the black light. I sensed hesitation, like he was about to reveal a truth but might change his mind.

"And my mother, she wouldn't leave either. It was like they were condemned to live miserably ever after," he said. "She didn't have the sense or the courage to do what *you* did at sixteen. She didn't try to save herself and she certainly didn't try to save us." He let out a laugh that was devoid of humor. It was a sad laugh, one that made me want to cry. "But those martial arts lessons," he sneered. "Those martial arts lessons were his undoing." His words were followed by another grating, humorless laugh. "Yeah, martial arts were *all* our undoing—the whole family."

Suddenly, it wasn't just his good looks and sexy body that I coveted. I coveted him. I wanted to explore all the deep, distorted crevices that he kept beneath that beautiful veneer. I needed to know more. I needed to know about the martial arts. Why did he call it "the undoing?" It was as though we now had this connection . . . secrets and pain. It felt like, in time maybe, I could tell him about my father, about The Duckling, about Midnight. Like maybe in time, he wouldn't laugh and call me a ditz. It felt like maybe together we could find each other's dark and twisty wounds and heal them. Like, I'd show him mine, if he'd show me his.

Then his eyes went vacant, and I wondered where his mind had drifted to. He reached out and turned off the red lamp and the black light. Darkness closed around us. It felt like he had shut the door, like he regretted what he had just shared.

"It's 3:00 am," he said and turned away from me. Way over there on Raymond's bed he made good his escape, finding sanctuary under the sheet.

Roomy

It was exactly fifteen days after the Martin Luther King riot, fifteen days since that crazy night in Danny's room. My breath got lost in my chest the first time I entered the tiny dorm room that was to be my home. My little room was beautiful! It was smaller than either Gina's or Danny's rooms but that didn't matter. It was cute, shaped like an equilateral triangle that had been blunted at its tip. Technically, it was a trapezoid, but I didn't want to think of my cute little room as a "trap." Bright, with two windows facing south and one facing west, I was already thinking about plants.

The bathroom just to the left of the entrance had a shower stall but no tub. I smiled to myself thinking, *Guess I'll just have to use Danny's.*

One of the single beds lined the wall in front of the double windows and the other was on the opposite wall. Identical chest of drawers stood adjacent to each bed. There was a small desk positioned along the short wall of the "trap" in front of the single window.

Being a sun lover, I decided to claim the bed near the double windows. I sat Bernadette on my chest of drawers. Then, I tossed my bookbag and the oversized pillowcase containing all my worldly belongings onto the bed.

I was suddenly filled with an overwhelming feeling of euphoria. This is home! I can live here! No more gypsy days, going from one place to another. No more internal clock counting down to tipping time. And although I tried to block it, the thought of no more rooftops pried its way into my mind. *Siegfried.* I swept the thoughts aside, replacing it with no more sleeping on the floor in Gina's room trying not to listen when Millie and her boyfriend Jared did "it."

I was effervescent. A bubbly giggle made it's way up through my gut, on to my throat, to my open mouth. I had this urge to throw back my head, spread out my arms and twirl and spin and spin. I was mid-pirouette, arms outstretched, head flung backwards, mouth open, when he pushed on the door that I'd left slightly ajar.

I caught a glimpse of him from the corner of my eye as I spun. I wasn't sure. I thought maybe that my rotational high was playing tricks on me.

"Careful, you already have a reputation for being dizzy." I tried to stop spinning but the room went on without me. I stumbled. He caught me. "I think you better cool it," he said, his eyes smiling as he directed me to the bed.

"Who says I'm dizzy?" I asked, a hint of false indignation in my voice, the spinning room slowly coming to a stop.

He smiled that smile with those lips, and said, "I wouldn't worry about it." And so, I didn't. "So you all moved in?"

"Yep," I said, directing my gaze to my empty, oversized pillowcase.

"Nice doll." I thought I heard a hint of mockery in his voice.

"That's Bernadette, and she's not just a doll. She's practically human."

"Hence, the 'dizzy' thing."

That's when my body went on autopilot. I stood, grabbed a pillow, and playfully swung it at his head. He ducked, a testament to his quick reflexes. I was coming around for another shot when he tackled me onto the bed.

I felt like I was outside of myself, then. Outside Me was standing there guiding the action. This, after all, might've been a pivotal moment—a happy moment, possibly one of many to come.

His body lay halfway across mine, his chest trapping me. I reveled in the physicality of our horseplay. I wriggled under his weight, laughing, trying to free myself. He pinned my hands over my head, looked into my eyes. Our faces were close . . . so close. Outside Me appeared, issuing instructions and warnings: *"Remember last time. Turn away. Don't look into his eyes."*

But I ignored her and her light-skinned privilege, ignored how casually she could rebuff someone as beautiful as Danny. I wasn't going to blow this moment, so I did look up. I looked into his eyes, and I thought maybe, just maybe, I saw something there. But that outside me kept urging: *Turn away!*

Releasing my hands, he said, "Oh yeah? You think you're bad? You gonna hit somebody with a pillow? Let's see if you're ticklish."

I was not ticklish. Or at least I had never been ticklish. But his hands found their way to my midriff, under my T-shirt, onto my bare skin. His touch was a current that ran through me.

Turn away! Turn from him before he turns from you! I wasn't sure if it was Outside Me or The Duckling that spoke. But I heard the warnings. Fighting every instinct in my body, I did turn my face away from him. And wriggling, I managed to turn my body as well. But he held fast, his arms around my middle. His breath warmed my ear and the back of my neck. He pulled me in closer, his breaths coming faster. I stiffened . . . then let go. I relaxed into his embrace and was amazed at how easily I could breathe—deep satisfying breaths. Every point of contact was supercharged. I could feel his heart beating against my back. I could feel his urgency. We folded into each other, then. We were one—a single fetus assuming the position. I felt dizzy. We were floating together, whirling in some primordial stew, waiting to be born again.

Then I heard it, a single word . . . a name. It was uttered ever so softly into my ear, a raw longing in its timber. "Daawn . . ."

It was like a sound that had been carried in on the wind. I realized I had never heard him speak my name. I turned my head to face him then. The look in his eyes was jarring. Then those lips were on mine, soft and tentative at first, then with more urgency. I turned my body towards him, and he pulled me in even closer. The only sounds coming from the universe at that moment were those of our hot, ragged breaths and our hot beating hearts.

That is, until . . .

"You must be Dawn." Those four words snatched me from a beautiful dream. Then addressing Danny, she said, "I dunno who you are, but whoever you are, you two need to get a room. And I don't mean this one."

I looked up to see a pretty, brown waif of a girl standing in the doorway with a suitcase. If I was petite, she was miniature. She was wearing fashionable high-calf boots that had to have been altered to fit her slender calves.

Danny shoved me away, freed himself of our embrace. The spell was broken. And without a word or even a glance backwards—not so much as a goodbye—he was on his feet and out the door. But I could still feel the imprint of his body pressed against mine . . . and I missed him.

I looked up and was confronted with the questioning eyes of my new roommate Luanne.

"What the hell was that?" It was clear that subtlety was not her strong suit. The thing was, I had no answer. I had no idea what "that" was. I had no idea what any of it was. I ignored the question.

"You must be Luanne. Hello," I said, shaking off the spell I was just under. Luanne and I had already gotten off on the wrong foot and I desperately wanted this—my new home to be a comfortable place. I needed to make nice. She just gave me this blank stare, threw her suitcase on her bed, and began to unpack. In an attempt to start over I said, "Hope

191

you don't mind I took the bed near the double windows. Love the light, but I'm open if you have a preference."

"Yeah, I'd prefer not to sleep by two drafty windows in the winter and we definitely gotta talk about getting some shades," she said, rolling her eyes before she added, "and about some ground rules."

"Yeah, shades—good idea," I said, ignoring the ground rules part. I wasn't ready to have that conversation. I had no explanations for what she just saw. And for that matter, I was not at all inclined to explain myself to her. There's all kinds of stuff going on in this dorm, all the time. Instead, I said, "You know, I was thinking about cafe curtains. I sew a little and there's a sewing machine in the student lounge."

"I knew this would happen. Why me?" she asked, throwing her hands in the air, addressing no one in particular.

"The curtains, they're really easy to put up on tension rods."

"Nice doll," she smirked. "Why do I have to get stuck with the weirdo roommate?"

"Cafe curtains will let in light when we want it, and we can get the shades for when we don't."

"We're really gonna have to put down some ground rules," Luanne repeated.

"I think plants would really make the place feel like home."

"They all said you were a nerd," she said, but it was clear she still wasn't addressing me.

"I'll buy the plants and I'll take care of them. Not too many, you know—a few."

"They warned me. They said Dawn Porter, she don't smoke, she don't drink and she don't screw! Looks like they got it wrong."

"I what!? I don't!"

"Which one? Smoke, drink, or screw?" she asked, hands on her tiny hips, suddenly staring directly at me.

"I have wine at parties."

"*You* get invited to parties?"

"Oh no you didn't!"

"What about smoking grass and screwing?" she pressed, doubling down on the fact that: Oh *yes* she did!

"Not that it's any of your damn business but I've recently been introduced to the pleasures of marijuana and I'm working up to . . . the other thing," I said, bristling, beginning to feel like I was being stalked.

"That's not how it looked to me. Was that guy even your man? Or was he just supposed to throw the money on the bed," she said, advancing her attack.

"What?! No. It's not like that!"

"Which one?" she asked, backing me into a corner.

"I'm not like that. There's no money-on-the-bed business going on. And no, technically he's not my man. I . . . I don't have a man." The words stung my ears as I said them.

"Well, I do. And sometimes he will be spending the night, and when that happens you need to be elsewhere," she pronounced, sounding all large and in charge.

Suddenly I was conflicted, embarrassed . . . pissed! Over the past two years, I had spent too many nights "elsewhere." And on that day, there had been too many mixed-up emotions in too short a period. It felt like I was spinning again, like my arms were spread, like my mouth was open and my head about to implode. *Oh hell no!* I was finally in a place that I could call home—at least for the next four years—and that tiny bitch thought that she could dictate when I could be in my own room? I started to tell her about herself, but something stopped me. I pictured what the coming years would be like warring with my roommate. I took a deep breath, counted to ten. That was it. That was the moment that will set the tone for our relationship from here on out. I knew I needed to choose my words and actions carefully.

I think she may have seen it in my eyes, or sensed it, or felt the same way or something, because before I could speak, she said, "Okay, maybe we need to back this up." She paused, let out a breath, her eyes softening. "This is what I think; check this out," she said. "Boyfriends, assuming you get one, can only stay on Friday or Saturday."

"But not both," I said.

"And never on the weekdays. Agreed?"

"Agreed," I said. "But it has to be arranged in advance. So there's no misunderstandings. Agreed?"

"Cool," she said. "But no Johns."

"What!?" Then she broke into a dimple-faced smile and said, "Kidding!" We laughed then. But I laughed longer and harder than was warranted. I laughed myself into hiccups, into tears. And Luanne just stared at me looking puzzled.

"What color should we get for the curtains?" I asked, still laughing, wiping my eyes.

"Whatever," she snapped and turned away. "But the shades need to be black." Then she turned back, looked me directly in the eyes and said, "And if he isn't your man, who was that fine looking guy who was all over you when I came in?"

It was a good question. Who was that guy? I had no idea.

Turn About

I startled myself awake. I only had an inkling as to why. I looked around. It was quiet except for a soft murmur coming from Luanne as she slept. I sat up on my bed and tried to slow my breathing. The room was dark. The black shades that Luanne and I bought proved to be very effective. I peeked past the shade towards the sky. It was light and clear; no clouds, but the sun was not up yet.

My first impulse was to get dressed so that I'd be ready when he came for me. But that was short lived because I knew he hadn't come yesterday. He hadn't come the day before or the days before that. He hadn't come for me since the day I moved into my own room—since Luanne had walked in on us.

Yesterday I saw him on campus. A group of SEEK students were visiting from Queens College. People were greeting each other as I entered the cafeteria. I saw Danny and smiled. He averted his eyes and I wondered what I had done wrong. Still, I walked over and stood next to him, awkwardly. There were introductions going around—handshakes, people giving each other a pound, high fives. Jamal introduced Gina as his woman. Danny glossed right over me. I stood there trying not to shrink into myself as I was being ignored. I considered extending my hand and introducing myself as his woman, but I didn't. What would he have said if I had?

"This is 'Lil Sis,'" Jamal introduced me, somehow sensing the tension.

Even though it had never been spoken, it was understood that we weren't supposed to make our "thing" obvious in mixed company. In the beginning I thought it was odd, our covert breakfast meetings, the sharing in his room on that first night—the night of the riot. We hadn't discussed anything like that since. Instead, he started calling for me early in the morning. That was before my own room was ready, when I was still sleeping on the floor in Gina's room. We'd started having breakfast together in silence, sometimes watching the sunrise in the park. After a while, I came to think of it as a good thing . . . sweet. It was our private little secret, "our thing," something that we didn't share with anyone else. Even though I'm sure my friends knew there was something going on between us, I never spoke about it to Ralfie or Chandra or Gina or anyone. Something about it felt fragile like "our thing" needed to be nurtured and carefully tended to in order for it to grow. On the other hand, I wasn't really sure we even had a "thing."

In the song, in the Momma dream, she sang, *What is so? What is not so? The answer is what you must know.*

What is so? That kiss, the way he held me, the way he pulled me into his hollow places, the way he said my name . . . that was real.

I'd startled myself out of sleep and I think it was because in that cloudy place between asleep and awake, I'd made a decision. I decided to take the initiative, turn the tables on him. I'd knock on his door. I'd invite him to breakfast.

I hesitated in front of room 416. I put my ear to the door and listened. I could hear movement inside. He was up. I tapped before I lost my courage. I knocked as it occurred to me that he might not be alone. I pounded before I thought it through and was taken aback when he yanked the door open just wide enough for a face, with "yes?" in his eyes. I wanted to kick myself.

"I . . . um, I'm going down for breakfast and wondered if you . . . or anyone, wants anything."

"I dunno about anyone," he said, smiling, playing out our mantra. "But I'm starving. Give me a moment and I'll go down with you." My relief was palpable and probably quite obvious. "Actually," he said. "Why don't you come in? I'll only be a minute."

As I entered the room, the lingering smells of pot, jasmine, Life Buoy soap, and Danny assailed me. I had not been in this room since the night of the riots. It had only been a little over a month before, but it felt like years. I sat on his bed while he went into the bathroom.

There was a knock on the door that seemed unique; it had a pattern, and it caught my attention. *Knock-knock, pause, knock-knock-knock*. Then there was silence before it repeated. *Knock-knock, pause, knock-knock-knock.*

Danny swung out of the bathroom, shirtless. He went to the desk and retrieved something I couldn't see. It was small and fit in the palm of his hand.

"Who else is up this time of the morning?" I asked as I thought, *Who knows? It might be the coded knock of some mysterious lover that he has.*

"No one," he said. But it was obvious to me that "no one" wouldn't be knocking on a door. He stepped out of the room for five seconds and returned saying, "I'll slip on a shirt, and we can go."

"But who was that?"

"You ask a lot of questions," he said.

"It's just . . . It's so early. I just wonder who it was."

"Drop it."

"But . . ." Something in his demeanor had shifted, his eyes hardening. He was standing over me, shirtless, as I sat on the bed, his fingers slowly curling into fists. Instead of me thinking how sexy his body was, it felt menacing. It made me feel vulnerable. So, I dropped it.

I stood up. "Fine, whatever," I said. "Let's just go."

"No. You go." His voice was flat. Its tone, at least an octave lower than usual, sent a shiver through me. His words echoed through my head. *No. You go . . . You go . . . You go.* What just happened? I tried to run the last few minutes through my brain. Did I miss something?

"Danny I . . . I didn't mean to . . ."

"Leave!" he raged, punching things off the dresser for emphasis.

Startled, I flinched, stumbled back a step. As things plummeted, rolled across the floor, an incandescent threat lit up his face. He was a stranger, his beautiful face no longer recognizable. My heart took off.

He flopped himself on his bed, reached over, grabbed a roach from the ashtray, lit it, patted the bed, and sneered, "Unless you want to strip, come over here and lie down."

I was stunned.

On a different day, using different words, in a different tone—a very different tone—I might have jumped at the chance to lie down next to him, inhale him, let nature take its course. I actually had to take a moment to sort out the conflicting impulses that were racing through me. My head was abuzz, and I wasn't sure that I'd even heard him right. Then he laughed a sardonic laugh, and I knew that I had, in fact, heard him. It was clear that my confusion gave him some kind of callous satisfaction. I was injured in my heart. I was humiliated—terrified. But mostly I was sad, so very sad. I staggered from his room as these words floated through my mind: *What did you expect? You should've known better*.

Lee

One month after I moved in, the SEEK dorm was capped. There wasn't supposed to be any new intakes until further notice. But on the afternoon of the very morning that I stumbled from Danny's room—dazed and bereaved, my vision impaired by tears, a cryptic voice pursuing me—the sole exception to that declaration moved in.

Momma always said that just when a body is in need, "He" will provide. I never really connected to Him the way that she did, but I do believe He's out there. And even though I never really made myself known to Him, I think He may actually know my name.

Lee's arrival sent a small ripple through the place, especially on the guy's floor. Luanne dragged me down to the lobby for the occasion. Everyone wanted to get a look at this one new girl. And then she appeared as though she were blown in on a breeze of expectation that somehow swept her directly to me. Like she, or maybe He, knew that I was in need of someone right then.

She was sunshine. And though she was slender, there was a roundness to her—a softness. She seemed to be all arcs and curves, no sharp angles or rough edges. Her eyes were large and round and always seemed animated. Deep round dimples defined her broad open smile. Her sandy brown hair rested on her shoulders . . . She was light skinned.

Just when I was ready to work myself into a deep green hate, she walked directly over to me . . . me of all the people standing there gawking at her. It was as though she could feel my sadness, as though it attracted her. She extended her hand and said, "Leelia Marionette, hola."

I took her hand, mimicked her firm, confident grasp and the deal was sealed. "So you'll be attending City?" I asked.

"Yeah, I registered yesterday."

"I'm in City too," I told her. "Not everyone who lives in the dorms goes to City."

"Oh," was all she said.

Faltering, suffering a loss of words, I said, "So, Marion-ette . . . that's unusual."

"So I've heard."

"What kind of name is it?"

"You mean, what am I?

"Yeah, I guess. I'm sorry I didn't mean to . . ."

"No, it's fine. It's the essential question these days, right? What are you? Either you're part of the solution or part of the problem. I get it. The name's French but I'm Puerto Rican."

In time, Lee and I curled into each other like a fragile hand in a boxing glove. Together we could form a fist. At first there wasn't much talk. The silence was comfortable, healing—I think maybe for the both of us. For the most part we just hung out. I'd place forty-fives on the record player and dance, losing myself in the music. Lee would sit with her sketching pad, scratching out intricate entities in black charcoal. After a while there was chatter, laughter, gossip. I felt a slight touch of betrayal as we laughed about Gina and her limited intellect, her monotone boxy body, her big car, her absolute personality.

Then one day Lee looked up and said, "You know, I come from a family of artists." This unsolicited offering was not surprising. Lee was an artist. That, I knew. I could tell by just looking at her and the unique way she presented herself—all loose and free and colorful. "Both my mother and sister are artists," she said.

"You have a sister?"

"My twin. We're identical." The idea that there was someone in this world exactly like Lee was mind blowing. "She lives in Ohio with her husband and baby."

"She's married?"

"Yeah. She got pregnant pretty young and kinda had no choice."

I took a moment, let that settle-in before I said, "Same here. My sister, she's older than me. She got pregnant really young and had to get married too."

Lee took a breath and simply said, "Oh."

Then a soft silence found its way between us, a silence that seemed to wrap around us and draw us into each other. After a while she said, "So anyway, I'd been going to Western State in Connecticut. I was living there with my boyfriend.

203

He was a real shit, you know. Not at first . . . at first, he was wonderful, exciting. I thought I loved him. I probably did. I thought he loved me. He didn't."

"Oh," was all I said, but I felt her, understood her feelings. And although I'm sure that heartache is universal, it somehow felt like these sorrows were uniquely our own.

It was clear she wanted to talk—like *really* talk. It was time, so I cut the music and sat down facing her.

"He screwed everything with a skirt," she said. After a while he didn't even bother to try and lie about it. Then he started chipping away at me, at who I am, and then pushing me around—physically. I knew I had to leave."

I thought about my mother's husband, about how I've been "leaving" happily ever after for quite some time. I said nothing.

Then there was something, an idea, a solution. It sparked its way around the room, around my head. It was electric. Jamal! Of course, they would be perfect together. *This is why Lee is here, why her sadness gravitated to mine!* Momma always said there are no coincidences. I'd wait though, until she was ready. It was not the time.

I thought to ask her how she managed to be the one person admitted into this much-coveted dorm, especially after it had been officially capped. But I didn't. Momma also said, "Take your blessings as they come."

"There's this guy," I heard myself say because it was clearly my turn. "Danny. He's gorgeous and popular and ever since the riot . . ."

"The riot?"

"Yeah, the King riot on 125th. I was there. And he saved me from being trampled by the horsemen. So ever since then, we've been kind of seeing each other. You know, for breakfast and watching the sun rise and stuff."

"I'm not sure I follow."

"Actually, neither am I. So anyway, I finally got my own room here and he came up and he kissed me, this like amazing kiss and it felt like we had something." I struggled to keep the quiver out of my voice. "But that morning—it was the same day you moved in—I had gone to his room, and everything was fine for a while. We were about to go for breakfast when something happened. I'm not sure what. But he turned on me, yelled at me, told me to leave. He was like this evil entity—like scary, intimidating, or something. I didn't recognize him." My voice cracked. "He hurt me, my feelings. He really hurt me. I felt so stupid," I sobbed.

Lee was by my side then, wrapping her arms around me. Her touch felt safe. I cried onto her shoulder, leaving fluids on her blouse.

"The yo-yo game," she said.

I didn't understand the reference, wasn't sure I even heard her right. I used my forearm to wipe my nose. Recovering, I wanted to change the subject. I thought about telling her what Danny had shared about his father but decided that would be wrong. Instead, I blurted, "So anyway, before I moved in here, I didn't really live anywhere for, like, two years."

"You were homeless?"

Homeless? Strangely, I never really thought of myself as homeless. Technically there existed a home, the home of my mother's husband, that I could go to. I just chose not to. Home took on many meanings. Home was wherever I was welcome, wherever there was a place to set Bernadette.

"I wouldn't put it like that," I said.

"So you ran away?"

"It's more like I walked away," I said, fractured memories of the day I left surging into my mind. "My mother married herself a husband. It's like the tale of the evil stepfather, I guess." The words were spilling out. "On the first day that we moved in with him, he almost broke my jaw. So I left. She had to let me; you know—the survival thing. She knew. We both knew." My mind rambled on. My mouth followed. "But I made a mistake, a bad mistake with Siegfried."

"Who's Siegfried?"

"She was my dog. I took her with me, and I shouldn't have. Then on the roof I didn't save her and . . ." I struggled to keep the water out of my voice. "They put her down."

Lee just looked at me with those large, patient eyes and waited. I was sure she didn't know what I was talking about, probably didn't have a clue, but she didn't probe.

It was months before I was able to explain that stuff coherently. I toyed with the idea of telling Lee about Daddy. His words would pry their way into my mind. *"You shudda named her Midnight!"* But I couldn't bring myself to do it. I didn't tell Lee about Daddy. I didn't tell anyone about Daddy.

206

Instead, I told her how my mother's husband literally took my mother away from me when, right after I moved into the dorms, he moved her to Arizona for business—or so he said. Lee just let that settle in. I guess she felt like I did. There were no words.

"You know," Lee said, one day. "My mother got herself a husband too. That is, several years after my father died." Although her tone was casual, my ears perked-up. "Qui-que, that's his name. It's short for Enrique. Actually, he's not so bad."

A tinge of disappointment rippled through me. I guess it's true about misery and company.

A few weeks later, Lee and I got work-study jobs at the daycare center located on south campus.

"I've got a meeting with my chem prof," Lee had said to me, one day. "It's North campus. I know it's my turn but, can we switch? I'll put out the snacks. Can you read them the story?"

"Of course! Go, go," I said, with a wave of my hand.

"Thanks, you're the best." She placed the "Little Golden Book" on the little brown table and I froze. "Dawn, what is it?" she said, in a whisper. "You okay?"

My vision blurred. I felt lightheaded and slightly nauseous. There on the cover of the glossy book, the ugly gray duckling stood large and offensive. Its image blurred and wavered. I rubbed my eyes. I watched in horror as that clumsy thing morphed from drab gray to morbid black. Then it was the Ugly Midnight Duckling. It glared up at me, mocking, as a shrill, grating cackle cut through my brain. I couldn't block the noise and the pain in my head was unbearable. Gasping to breathe, I stumbled out of the classroom, fingers plunging deep into my ears.

Back in the dorms, the pain had subsided. I was lying on my bed, a cold compress over my eyes, when Lee tapped on my door. She peeked in, entered, and sat next to me on the bed. She didn't say anything, didn't pepper me with questions like Luanne had done before she left for dinner. She just placed her hand on my shoulder and sat.

I don't know how long we were there in silence—me lying, her sitting, both breathing. After a while, I removed the compress from my eyes and asked, "Your meeting with the chem prof?"

"It's fine. I rescheduled," she said, and we fell silent again.

Finally, I sat up. "You know," I said, needing to find a way to ease into an explanation for what happened to me earlier—for why I slammed out of there like I did. "I haven't always been the vision of loveliness that you've come to know and love." I was going for humor, but Lee just stared at me, her eyes sober and patient. "No, honestly," I said, working up the courage to share what I was about to. "I've worked really hard on myself."

"Okaay?"

"I was like the ugly duckling, you know, in the fable. The ugly black duckling."

"So this had something to do with the story book?"

"But I worked on it—my looks," I said, ignoring her question. "And I got fixed, like, for the most part anyway." Lee listened. I hesitated, took a breath, steeled myself. "Lee, I think I have this, well, this Duckling inside me—like literally inside me. Sometimes it still haunts me. It's always there. I can feel it in my chest. It doesn't let me breathe—not like easy, you know, like normal."

Suddenly, I was talking fast, my mouth rapidly shoving out words before I lost the courage. "But it's okay, for the most part," I said. "I just have to remember to take a deep breath every now and then." Lee's expression was neutral, unreadable. I went on, "So anyway, it kind of talks to me, you know. Not at first. At first there were just noises like the sound of wind blowing through my head. After a while there were murmurs, then whispers, like it was growing, getting stronger or something. Now there's this voice, or more like these thoughts. Yeah, more like thoughts. It sends thoughts, you know, directly into my head."

Lee waited, her eyes patient. She said nothing.

"Sometimes it pushes its way through, like —literally," I said. "It used to be just a flicker across my face in the mirror. Now it actually shows up there in the reflection, that ugly black duckling! But when it does show up, it's silent. It never speaks, not in the mirror. It just watches."

I waited for Lee's reaction, feeling drained but somehow relieved, like I literally just got that "thing" off my chest. But something about the look in her eyes sent my heart into a trot; sweat beaded on my forehead and my windpipe was starting to close.

Then . . . Lee laughed. She burst into a hardy guffaw, holding her sides, and rolling on the bed. My heart zapped electric. My lungs spazzed. I didn't know if I was supposed to be amused or incensed, disappointed or terrified. Would Lee think I'm a schizo? Would she even want to be around someone so crazy? I had shared my ridiculous secret and immediately regretted it.

Then, Lee chuckled out one word: "Misgivings."

"Wha?"

"Misgivings. You have so many misgivings. This is the worst of them."

"My misgivings?"

"Yep, your misgivings." And with that one word she debunked the entire concept of a duckling. Her laughter swept it away so casually, so convincingly, that I almost believed her.

"If that ugly black duckling ever actually existed," she said, "it's certainly long gone now. You need to relax. Cojelo con take it easy," she said in her native Spanglish. "Look at you." She grabbed my shoulders and directed me to the mirror. "That ugly black duckling has turned into a beautiful black swan," she smiled out the words. "Listen," she said like she was just hit with an epiphany. "They're giving an African dance class down in the lounge. I know how much you love music and dancing. I think that organized exercise would be good for you—maybe even therapeutic. It would certainly help you work off some of those misgivings, help you relax. Why don't you take it?"

"Why don't we both take it?"

"Me dance? No thanks. I'd trip over my own feet. But you . . . I've watched you. What I really want to do is photograph you as you dance. Your dancing is so beautiful."

Beautiful? Dance therapy? Yes. I believed her . . . for the most part.

Dance Skin

The drum's beat was pulsing, compelling in its regularity. Each downbeat tugged at something inside me—something old, ancient even. I began to move to the rhythm, thrusting my pelvis and arms forward the way Gus had·instructed. All the other girls in the dance class did the same. It came naturally.

To provide cultural enrichment to the students, the program had contracted with Gus Dinizulu. Gus was the West African percussionist who headed up a professional troupe of African dancers and founded the center for African Culture and Research. The class was held in the dorm's ballroom just off the lobby. Lee was right. The class provided a distraction—something other than Danny to torment my mind.

I'd concentrate hard. My moves had to be perfect. Sweating, I tried to follow Gus's demonstrations with extreme precision. I was always amazed at the way Gus could gyrate that pelvis despite that tire around his middle. Gus looked to me like the West African version of Fats Domino—four feet tall and four feet wide—but the man could move. And as it turned out . . . so could I.

I watched a girl in the mirrored wall. She was petite, slender but shapely, with a small waist, full breasts, and firm round booty. She was graceful, precise, enraptured with the beats.

She sang along with the words to the traditional African folksong, "Funga alafia, ashay, ashay." She was me. Me in my black Danskin top and leotards that clung to every curve in my body. Shamelessly, I couldn't take my eyes off me.

I had never been one who dressed to show off my body. I had never thought that I had a body worth showing off. My outfits usually ranged from a pair of penny loafers, some Wrangler dungarees, and either a man-tailored shirt, a sweat-shirt, or a T-shirt—any of which draped me like a tent.

I danced. I watched. I was mesmerized by the pretty girl looking back at me. I didn't recognize her. I didn't know when she'd arrived. It felt like I was in someone else's body. But there she . . . I . . . was. I guess puberty had snuck up on me.

I wasn't sure how to react to the looks I was suddenly getting from the guys hanging out in the lobby as the class let out, my Danskins clinging tight to my sweaty body. But I knew how to react to Danny as I passed by him there. His eyes followed me. I could feel them. They pursued me as I made my way to the elevator. I never looked in his direction. Ever since that morning in his room, this was how I dealt with that mixture of anger, desire, humiliation, and fear that grabbed at me whenever I saw him. I took Lee's advice.

"Cojelo con take it easy," she'd told me. "Just don't look at him."

I was about to push the elevator button when a deep voice from close behind me said, "Allow me."

I looked around to find myself assaulted by the intensity of Ahmod James's stare. Ahmod didn't hang with our crowd, and he had never spoken to me before. But the dorm was a small community. He was a fine brown brother with his meticulously manicured goatee and stately 'fro. I was flattered by the attention. "After you." He motioned as the elevator door slid open. "You live on the eighth floor, right?"

"Yes, as a matter of fact, I do," I said, stepping into the elevator, sounding coy and realizing that I was flirting. I slid my gaze over to Danny and smiled. His wolf eyes never left my face as the elevator door slid closed.

Yo-Yo

The knock on the door was faint, unsure. If I hadn't been lying there awake listening to Luanne breathe, I might not have even heard it. I looked at the clock. It was 6:40 a.m. I knew who it was. I didn't move. Frozen, I just lay there hoping that he'd go away . . . praying that he wouldn't. Lee was right. She said he'd come around. She said he was just like her ex.

"They're all alike," she'd said. "They throw you away, and then when they're afraid that you're really gone, they pull you back in. It's like you're a yo-yo. Well, I decided that I wasn't going to be a yo-yo anymore. So I cut that string and you need to do the same. Make a clean cut. You don't need that shit."

There was a second knock on the door, this time louder, more insistent. I reasoned that if I didn't answer, his knocking would wake Luanne. I opened the door, stepped out, closed it behind me and turned to face him with "yes?" in my eyes.

He hesitated before he smiled that smile, those lips. Then he said, "I . . . um, I'm going down for breakfast and wondered if you . . . or anyone, wants anything."

Channeling my inner Lee, I heard myself say, "No. Thank you for asking but I'm not really hungry."

It was the wrong answer. A flash of surprise followed by a hint of irritation skimmed across his face before he was able to regain his usual reserve.

"On second thought, since you're going," I said, wavering, unable to let go so easily. "Can you bring me back a small coffee, three sugars, no milk?"

"You usually drink tea."

"I'm not doing the usual these days."

He returned carrying two cups of uncovered coffee in a cardboard tray and tapped on the door. I hesitated, took a breath, and opened the door. He handed me a cup.

"Dark and sweet," he said. And I thought that maybe I heard a double meaning in those words. He took the other cup in his hand and placed the tray on the floor. "I'm gonna drink mine in the lounge," he said. "Wanna come?"

I felt my heart gearing up for a run. He was standing there at my door pursuing me, really pursuing me, wasn't he? He wouldn't do this if I didn't mean anything to him, if we didn't have a "thing," right? *Maybe that day in his room was a fluke*, I thought.

Outside Me appeared, her face glowing with indignation. *"Remember that scream? Leave!"* she said, mimicking Danny. Then she fell silent, leaving me to think about her meaning.

Maybe he was just having a bad day, I reasoned.

"And what about that scary tone in his voice, that sneer? You don't need that shit," Outside Me said and I agreed. I had enough shit in my life, didn't I?.

"It was all your fault. You pressed him," came the Duckling's caustic voice. The accusation searing my brain.

My mind was swinging back and forth between my two inner tormentors.

"And that angry outburst when he punched stuff off the dresser; what about that?" Outside Me countered, distain on her pale face as she turned from me and disappeared into nothingness. It was true, I thought. That scary outburst, it came out of nowhere. I was so shocked. And he was actually enjoying my distress. How could he?

Danny was standing there waiting for my answer to his invitation. I looked up into his eyes, like I could somehow glimpse a hint of what he was thinking. But his "cool" was solidly in place. I couldn't get past that wall. I thought about what Outside Me said and about that lewd sexual remark he had made that morning. There was that. But that wasn't what prompted my answer. It was the uneasy feeling that I got when his face morphed and the tone in his voice dropped an octave. He sounded like a different person. He looked like a different person. There was his menacing body language as he stood over me. There were his fingers slowly curling into fists, one at a time. And it was true, about that rage as he punched at things on the dresser . . . Yes, there was fear.

I contemplated the coffee swirling in the cup. I couldn't say what I was about to say while looking into those eyes.

"No. But thanks anyway. I'll just drink mine in my room." I was pretty sure that would be the end of it, our conversation . . . our "thing."

Then I heard him say, "Daawn . . . " I thought maybe it sounded like a plead. It was only the second time I ever heard him say my name. Memories of the first time brought heat to my face. He placed his finger under my chin and lifted my gaze out of the coffee and into his eyes. Gently taking the coffee from my hand, he placed both of them on the floor. Then he said something that made it clear that even though I couldn't read him well, he very easily read me. "I would never hurt you." I wondered whether he meant emotionally . . . or physically. I could feel a tremor building inside me. The pressure was growing, testing my resolve. "I'm sorry," he said.

I lost it, then. I let go. My breath hiccupped and released in my chest as tears burst from my eyes and streamed down my face.

"I'm sorry. I'm so sorry," he kept saying as he pulled me into him. With his arms around me, I sobbed into his chest and inhaled him. "I dunno what came over me. Let me make it up to you. Have dinner with me."

"Dinner? Not Breakfast?"

In reply, he smiled out the word. "Dinner."

The door hit Luanne in the head as I entered the room.

"Damn," she said, rubbing the bruise. "Dude actually loves you."

The Candle

I was freezing. Outside, it was eighty degrees but the air conditioner in Victor's Restaurant was set to full tilt arctic. I wrapped my hands around the warm belly of the glass-encased candle in front of me. The small square table between us served as a barrier. I realized that we had never really sat facing each other. We'd sat side by side at the breakfast counter or facing east in the park waiting for the sun to rise. Here, it felt like we were two people trapped in frost. I was trying to think of something to say, something to break the spell, but no magic words came to me.

Releasing the candle, I turned to stare through the picture window at the people passing by. I could almost swear that some of them were glancing my way with knowing little smiles. I thought I saw them nod and wink. It felt like some of them were reading my thoughts, gleaning my secrets, while others actually seemed to look concerned. I could almost hear them pushing warnings into my head.

Flustered, I tried to shake off those ridiculous thoughts, tried to keep my head clear. *What is so? What is not so?* I turned back to the table, to the stoic eyes watching me from the other side to the candle, now cradled in his hands.

The waitress brought our drinks. The Margarita was frosty to the touch. I actually wished I had ordered something hot. I took two sips. Then craving warmth, I yearned to resume my embrace of the glowing orb that was now in his possession.

"You look nice," he said, and at least my ears got hot. I had pushed my Afro into an upsweep atop my head, wore my new contact lenses and the red paisley blouse that I bought from GrabBag, a local boutique that specialized in form fitting clothing. I thought about saying that he looked nice too, but he always looked nice and I was sure all those girls I've seen pursuing him have told him as much.

"Thanks."

I wondered, then, if he was as awkward with all of them as he seemed to be with me. I would think that someone with his looks would have his game down by now. Again, those abrasive thoughts forced their way into my mind. A wheeze escaped my chest because I knew they were coming straight from that Duckling.

Maybe he isn't interested in running a game on you. Maybe he just doesn't want to lose his friend—possibly his best friend. After all, who else is up early enough to hang out with him in the morning. Maybe that kiss was a mistake. Maybe you imagined the rest, the feelings. Maybe you even

imagined the kiss. You've been known to do things like that.
You know it's true. You imagine things. You forget things.

He was staring at me. I smiled a shaky smile and struggled to sweep those thoughts aside. No Duckling tonight.
They were just "misgivings," that's all they were.

"It's chilly in here," he said, removing his hands from
the candle.

"Yeah," I agreed.

Then he stood. Suddenly, he was on my side of the table.
He cloaked his jacket around my shoulders. I felt the warmth
of his body radiating through mine. Melanin hid the heat that
rose in my cheeks. I avoided his eyes, slipped my hands
around the candle, and turned back to the window, prefer-
ring the knowing smirks of conspiring passersby.

"That better?" he asked, rubbing his hands together.

A thought occurred to me. I wasn't sure if it was mine. I
wondered if he was just playing with me, with my feelings.
Maybe this was his thing, playing with feelings.

"Here, why don't you warm your hands on the candle,"
was all I could think of to say. He accepted my offering and
reached for the flickering bulb where my hands were resting.
I watched as his hands slowly approached. They were sturdy,
a smattering of hair, barely visible, long lean fingers for
"palming the basketball," he'd said. His nails were trimmed
neatly to the skin line. Just above a right knuckle, an angry
red scar had the shape of a crescent moon. I'd never noticed it
before. I found it beautiful and captivating, and I wanted to
stroke it and kiss it and make it better. I let my hands linger
on the shimmering ball for a moment, fantasizing. I dared to

think that the kiss, the feelings, were all real, that he actually wanted to touch me in that way. I dared to imagine the sensation, my hands captured under his, strong and ardent, the candle warm and round and smooth.

As casually as I could manage, I withdrew my hands just before his reached the candle. Not sure what to do with them, I grabbed my drink, took several long greedy gulps, and regretted it two seconds later. The frigid liquid rushed cold fury up through my head as the alcohol raged hot, ignited sparks, and pulsed heat throughout my body. I fell deeper into the comfort of his jacket, deeper into his scent.

"It's really cold in here," he said, dropping his hands from the candle. "Wanna get outta here? We can take the food to go."

I did. I wanted to leave that cold place and go with him to someplace warm and secluded. The alcohol had infused its way into my brain. It turned the candle into a radiating globe. I was suddenly mesmerized by its flames. They were undulating—a spastic dance. They fluttered and wavered, throwing off spears of gold, blue, and amber. Their quivering spasms were compelling. I reached out to capture them, encircle them in my palms. I felt it then—I was sure. It wasn't my imagination. I felt his desire as he wrapped his hot hands over mine.

Other Ways

We entered his room holding hands. He had held my hand as we walked from the restaurant. He held it as we walked through the lobby, as we passed by all the curious onlookers who were hanging out there. For all the world to see, he held my hand.

The room was dark. He flicked on the black light and the red lamp, lit a candle and a joint, and gestured for me to have a seat on his bed as he went about selecting music to place on his machine. His movements seemed practiced and polished, and I wondered whether he had some game after all.

Suffering a lukewarm bout of insecurity, I was afraid to indulge in the expectation of what was about to happen. Or maybe, I was just afraid. This wouldn't be my first time. My first time had been awkward and messy. I had resisted, but it happened anyway. So, I wrapped it in fog and locked it neatly away in the back of my mind. And all the times after that was with the same boy, Jackson. He was the boy I went out with in high school. After all, it was expected. I was actually someone's girlfriend. It was what girlfriends were supposed to do. Those encounters had not been unpleasant, nor had they been enjoyable. They had simply been endured. I concluded, then, that I must have been doing it wrong or maybe that there was something wrong with me altogether. I just didn't get what all the shouting was about.

After high school, Jackson married someone else—someone who didn't have my issues, someone who got pregnant. With mixed feelings, I think about him sometimes. I wonder if I dodged a bullet or missed out on something good. But I never did breathe easy around Jackson, never did hear the music.

The mechanical arm of the turntable placed the needle in the groove. A voice sang out. The singer was decrying his reluctant love, a love he never wanted, tried to resist, but was trapped into by some unwelcome attraction, some alien desire.

But not in *my* head, not in that moment. In *my* head the lyrics sounded like this:

> *I do love you, cause I am meant to*
> *All of my thoughts are only of you*
> *Oh, little girl I want you madly*
> *I'd have you gladly*
> *You really got a grip on me*

The song played on. Then Danny was standing over me with his hand outstretched. I wondered if the lyrics that I was hearing were the actual lyrics. I could never be sure. And if so, was this Danny's way of saying how he felt about me?

224

"May I?" To my surprise he was inviting me to dance. I'd like to say we danced cheek to cheek, but he stood at least a head over me. My cheek only reached to his chest, to his heart. His right arm around my waist pulled me in. His left hand held my right. The music played on. My mind, or maybe my heart, steady pumping out personal lyrics.

Oh, how I need you. Oh, how I want you
I want to kiss you, hope that you do too

I swooned to the melody and embraced the lyrics. We were two bodies caught in a gravitational ellipse. I leaned my head on his chest and listened to his heartbeat. He released my hand, wrapped both arms around me and pulled me in closer. I reached up, wrapping my arms around his neck and tilted my face upward. This time I was not disappointed. He placed his mouth on mine. A blue mist filled my head. I parted my lips and our tongues met. He was delicious. The song, my song, wafted through the room, through my head.

You really got a grip on me
It's true you got a grip on me, lil girl
So into you, so what I need you to do
Is just hold me, touch me, squeeze me
You really got a grip on me

We were rolling around on his bed, fully entangled, when a bothersome thought grabbed at me. It muscled its way in despite the heavy breathing. Ignoring our frantic discarding of clothing, that troublesome thought would not be denied. It forced its way into my mind. *Protection.* It put the brakes on me. I looked up to see the sallow face of Outside

Me standing there looking like she disapproved. I bristled, dismissing her with a wave of my hand.

"What?" he asked, breathing heavy but clearly in touch with me, with my feelings.

"Do you have something? You know, protection?"

He took a deep breath and let out a sigh before he said, "Raymond."

"Raymond?"

"Yeah, Raymond. He took them from my drawer yesterday, said he'd replace them, never did."

"Oh," I said, my eyes falling on my blouse rumpled up to my neck and my pants down around my knees. The moment had passed. I sat up, tried to straighten my clothes.

"There are other ways," he said. I gave him a blank look. "Other things . . . you know."

I did know. But at the same time, I didn't know. I had never been involved with "other ways." I was barely familiar with the main way.

"It's okay," he said. "We don't have to do anything you're not comfortable with. We don't have to do anything at all." And I was thinking, *Just like that he no longer desires me.*

"Not that I don't want to. I want to. I really want to, trust me." I was beginning to think he could actually read my mind.

"Stay the night . . . please."

I nodded my assent. He took a neatly folded white T-shirt out of his drawer. It looked like it had been pressed. He handed it to me. "You'll be more comfortable in this. Then let's just play it by ear. Okay?"

226

When I came out of the bathroom in the T-shirt, The Temptations "Can't Get Next to You" was playing. I smiled. He was in loose pull-string pants, no shirt. He sat on the bed next to me, lit a joint, and handed it to me. I took it and just looked at it. Part of me wanted to be fully sober for this sleepover. Retrieving the joint from my hand, he took a long drag and inhaled deeply. He placed the joint in the ashtray. Then holding the smoke in his mouth, he motioned for me to come close. I leaned in, and placing his lips on mine, he released the smoke into my mouth. I took it in. It felt sensual, like he was sharing his essence with me. Then his lips were pressing. I parted mine to receive his tongue, his smoky kiss. He pushed me back on the bed.

My heart was racing. There was a tightness, an ache growing deep in my stomach. He was kissing me all down my neck, down my breasts, down my stomach . . . down further. Then he was the professor, the master instructor teaching me about "other ways." My body responded like an ocean rising and falling, wave after wave of pleasure washing over me. My breath was stabbing sharp into my chest. A furnace in my stomach was steadily pumping heat.

The sensation was luscious, exquisite.

"Oh Danny! Oooh!" I wanted to savor it, hold on to it for as long as I could . . . a little longer . . . just a little longer . . . just . . . It would not be denied. I let go. The furnace erupted, spewed fervor all through my limbs, on past my heart, up into my head. A raspy trembling shriek ripped from my throat. "Dann-eee!"

He was by my side then, kissing my neck, my face, petting me, easing me back down to earth. He was smiling at me, this broad triumphant smile. "First time?"

"Oh my God, Danny." I had not yet caught my breath when he took my hand in his and guided it to where it mattered. I had never touched a man like this. With Jackson, I never actually touched it. I don't even recall looking at it. It was a faceless, nameless, invader. Now I was getting acquainted with it . . . its girth, its length, its warmth, it's rigidness. He placed his hand over mine and slowly, deliberately, he gave me yet another expert lesson in "other ways."

Tell Me About It

We lay there in the dimly lit room, on the narrow single bed that was suddenly big enough for two. We lay staring at the psychedelic posters on the ceiling and breathing, so deep and easy. At that moment there was no obstruction in my chest. My head was resting on his arm, and he pulled me in. I turned, rested my head on his heart. He held me. There was a comfortable silence. There was no record spinning, only the sounds of long languid breaths and hearts slowing to a trot.

After a while he sat up, reached for my hand, led me to the bathroom and into the shower. I thought my heart would boogaloo right out of my body. I was so happy. We lathered each other with what, for me, had become the essence of Danny: his spicy Life Buoy soap. I felt vibrations with every touch. When the shower was over, he wrapped me in a towel and patted me dry. I was surprised that I didn't cringe with shyness. I allowed him to possess me, to take care of me. It felt like that was what he wanted to do. But when we exited the bathroom, he retreated to Raymond's bed, leaving me alone on his.

I didn't understand. He sat there smoking a joint, his knees bent, his back leaning against the wall, his eyes straight ahead. He was a remote silhouette in a darkened room. It was silent, but this silence was not comfortable—not at all. This silence was blasting through my head, hurting my brain. I wished he would put on a record, a song to give me a hint as to what he might be thinking.

Then it hit me. Once again, my inexperience was my undoing. I had naively thought that we'd had a beautiful thing. But clearly, I had somehow fallen short, done something wrong. I looked around for Outside Me, but she was nowhere to be seen. An onslaught of maybes that originated from that alien source, soon became my own. Maybe Outside Me was disappointed, maybe even offended, and that's why she didn't show. Maybe my body's reaction to Danny's touch was not cool enough. Maybe that was not how things were supposed to go. Maybe I was supposed to control myself. Maybe my touch was unsatisfactory. Maybe I shouldn't have insisted on protection. But I thought about Sista, and I had to. Maybe he was just disgusted by what he did to please me. Maybe . . .

All those maybes were multiplying exponentially, arresting my brain. I felt like I might scream. I decided to gather my clothes and go back to my own room, or better still, find Lee. Even though she'd probably say, "I told you so," at least she'd put her arms around me and let me cry.

I wanted to leave . . . I didn't want to leave. I didn't want what I thought was our beautiful evening to end like this, with maybes gripping at me.

Danny was complicated. I knew that. I'd learned that the night of the riot. The night that I'd told myself I'd find my way into his deep, distorted places and draw him out—that I'd let him into mine. But the opportunity never presented itself.

I wanted to say something, but the words kept slipping away. What could I say to try and reach him? I got up and went over to his record collection, expecting to shuffle through forty-fives arranged in random order. Instead, I found them meticulously categorized in record bins, each individual disc preserved in a record sleeve. They were grouped by year, by genre, by artist. It was impressive . . . and a little scary. I searched through the oldies bin and was actually not surprised to find the record I was looking for, a song that might explain my shortcomings. I removed it from its jacket and placed it on the turntable. And though I wanted to push my way into bed with him, to worm myself under his arm and snuggle into his chest, my feet brought me back to the empty bed across the room. The song's lyrics filled the air.

> *I'm not even sure how to hold you*
> *In the way I ought to do*
> *But I'm eager to learn*
> *Yes, I'm ready . . . to love*

Mimicking his pose, I sat up in bed on my side of the world. My legs were bent, my back against the wall, my eyes staring straight ahead as the song lyrics spoke the words that I couldn't manage.

Then I thought I heard him say, "That's not true."

"Excuse me?"

"That song . . . that's not the case," he said, smoke rising from his lips. "This wasn't your first . . . I mean, you're not . . ."

"No! I'm not."

"Oh, I wasn't sure, not that it matters."

There was silence as I thought, *What does matter?*

"It was amazing," I said, giving in to impulse. "The way you made me feel—*that* was my first." My mouth kept pushing out words. "I never felt anything like that . . . with anyone. I had no idea it could be like that. So, I wasn't prepared, you know, and I'm sorry if I . . . "

"Sorry? Sorry was not exactly what I was going for."

"What *were* you going for?"

"I guess I wanted to make you feel good, share something with you."

I wasn't sure how I was supposed to respond to that. The word "share" resonated in my head. It occurred to me that this might be an opportunity knocking. This is what couples do, right? They share. Normal couples, they tell each other about their previous relationships.

"There was a boy in high school . . . Jackson. He was the only one." My words flowed, seemingly on autopilot. Danny leaned over, reached across the chasm, and offered me the joint. Maybe he thought I would need it for courage or something. I took it. "He wasn't from my block. He was, like, from a different world." I waited for him to respond. He didn't. He just sat there with his eyes straight ahead. "I mean, he seemed special, you know."

I fell silent for a while, thinking about the day I met Jackson. I was at a cousin's wedding on Long Island. I remembered that I had been smiling at a guy who was playing in the band when I felt these eyes on me, checking me out. It felt intense. I wasn't used to being looked at like that.

Jackson wasn't in Danny's league insofar as looks were concerned, but he was fine . . . and he knew it. He was over six feet tall and ripped. He had a cheeky smile, and over-the-top swag; he looked a lot like that boxer, Cassius Clay. I remember how people would actually approach us in the street and ask if he was Clay. And as strange as it may seem, I truly loved how arrogant he was.

"He lived on Long Island," I said. "It was like a world away from the South Bronx." But I didn't tell Danny everything. That my transformation from The Duckling only seemed to work on people who didn't know me from before, who didn't know what might still hover just under my facade. And I was well aware that it was, in fact, a facade. I didn't tell Danny that I was sure if Jackson had been from my block, he would never have been interested in me. If he had been from my block, he would've known that I was everybody's good friend, everybody's little sis, but nobody's girl. I didn't tell Danny that I was sure that was why a guy with Jackson's looks would pursue me—because he didn't know. Danny didn't know either, and I had no intention of telling him.

So I went on, "It was during my gypsy days. Every other week he'd send money to my friend Gabrielle's house for me to take the Long Island Railroad to Freeport. He used to complain a lot about not knowing where I'd be from one week to the next. He lived in a house with a white picket fence, a garage for two cars, and a master bedroom for two parents—his own parents. I would stay in the guest room. They had a real guest room. Like I said, a-whole-nother world." I took a drag of the joint that had been smoldering in my hand. "Anyway, even though he never dared to try and sneak into the room at night, there were times during the day when we were the only ones home," I said. As I spoke, I felt pressure growing in my head. The memory that I had pushed down so deep was getting a foothold in my mind and was climbing its way out.

I remembered that Jackson's parents had gone to church. I was getting dressed. He came into the room, started kissing my neck. He did that a lot, but this felt different. His hands found my breasts. This too felt different. It was not like we hadn't done any heavy petting before, and I knew that eventually it would lead to sex. I thought I was ready. I thought I wanted it. Then he was on top of me, and though at first I was willing, an image of Sista barged into my head.

She had gotten pregnant before finishing high school. I remembered her lumbering around looking like she'd swallowed a basketball. For me, at twelve, the entire business with the pregnancy was disturbing and scary. Then she got married. I think she was okay with that. In fact, whenever they came to visit, I was impressed that she actually looked happy. And although I didn't hear any music when I went to her place, it was cozy and warm. It seemed like she had gotten want she always wanted: a loving husband, a baby, and a real home of her own. Then she and her husband moved to his native Puerto Rico, and she was gone from my life. It was like she could be a wife or a sister, but not both.

"First time, you know, I was nervous," I said to Danny, who just listened, giving me space.

I remember Jackson on top of me when another image filled my head. It was my face. My face had replaced my sister's. My face was there on Sista's bloated body. I don't know why but I freaked out. I couldn't breathe. I wanted to say *protection* or *wait* or *no* or something but his mouth on mine stifled the words. I struggled. At least I think I struggled. I think I said no. *No!* I must have yelled it. But I was never really sure if all the yelling was only in my head.

Suddenly, Jackson's face oozed out of a psychedelic poster. It was there in Danny's room, just hanging in the air and grinning at me. Words came tumbling out despite the cautions coming from my brain. I was addressing Jackson but talking to Danny. I think I spoke out loud. I think it was a whisper, a hiss. "I said no! No! But you didn't stop! Why didn't you stop!"

And there was silence. It moved in to absorb the impact of the words I had just muttered. Danny was a statue. If he heard me at all, he didn't react. His stoic form was a flickering shadow outlined in candlelight. Then . . .

"There was this woman," he said without preamble, his voice sounding to me like it was coming from somewhere far away, "in the building in Brooklyn where I grew up. She was a friend of my mother. She had no kids. She and her husband lived in the apartment next door. She used to take care of us on and off when my mother was working. Sometimes my mother sent us to her when my father was having one of his moods." He paused for a long, awkward moment. I began to wonder if he was going to say anything else, but then he spoke, "It's funny but like you said, her place was like a-whole-nother world, even though it was just across the hall. Her place was extremely, like, disheveled . . . a wreck. There were clothes laying on the bed, the sofa, sometimes even the floor. There were books and magazines and letters scattered on every flat surface in the place. There was even dust." He took a drag from a joint. The black light revealed his perfect teeth as his lips curled into a wry smile, his eyes peering deep into a scene from his past. "There were usually dishes in the sink although there weren't that many, you know. It wasn't like they were piled up. But compared to my house where one fork might mean someone was in for a beating, it was chaos. But I really liked being there, you know, in that place. It felt like real people lived there. It felt relaxed, I dunno . . . like freedom?" I wasn't sure if that was a question. I wondered where he was going with this. I was intrigued with what he was saying but a little disappointed. I wanted to hear about his first time. I decided to just give him some space. "My brother Tommy was never comfortable there. But for some reason I was drawn to her chaos . . . I was drawn to her. She was pretty, you know, very pretty for someone that old." I wanted to ask how old she was. "I think she was older than

236

my mother, like early forties, but she looked a lot younger. I guess I had a crush. So anyway, one day when Tommy was watching TV, she called me into her bedroom. She said something like 'you're a beautiful child' or something to that effect. And she put her hand on the side of my face and kissed me on the lips. I'm pretty sure I fell in love that day. Or at least I fell in what generally passes for love. After that, I found every excuse to go over there.

"She started placing my hand under her blouse, into her bra. After a while she'd unzip my pants. She'd touch me, you know, manipulate me. I was crazy with lust for her. One day when I was supposed to be playing outside, I decided to knock on her door. It was the first time I went there without it being arranged ahead of time. She opened the door without even looking through the peephole." He stopped to take a drag. "She was only wearing this little lacy bra and panty thing. And she had this look in her eyes, you know, like she knew it was me, was expecting me to show up there."

I was thinking, *Oh, my God! This was his Mrs. Robinson.*

"That was the first time I had intercourse. I have to admit that first time was not exactly what I'd imagined. But being with her was a hell of a lot better than what I did under the sheets in my own bed. As time went on, she taught me things. It got better. I got better. I just knew that we were in love. I was young, you know. I actually believed that eventually she would leave her husband for me." I wanted to ask how old he was, but I decided against it. "I was fourteen," he said. He seemed to know my thoughts before I could formulate them. It was a little unnerving. "But I have to say, I

learned a lot from her. She taught me a lot about other ways."
He drifted off and it was silent again until, "So one day, I
went to her place, as usual, expecting to be with her. When
she answered the door, she seemed different, like she was
surprised to see me, or more like she was annoyed that I was
there. She had this kind of smirk on her face as she opened
the door wider. I could see someone standing there, half
dressed. It was a boy. Dude looked like he was younger than
me, maybe eleven or twelve. It took a minute before I recognized him. It was this kid, Mikey. We used to play basketball
together. I remember her pitying grin as she told me that
maybe in the future I should call before just showing up." He
took a breath before he said, "I never went back, never." He
dragged on the joint and let the smoke travel up past his nose
and dissipate into the murky room. "Yep, I learned a lot."

"You were just a kid," I said. "That was sexual abuse. She
was a predator. In effect . . . you were raped!"

He turned then, and for the first time since we started
talking, he looked directly at me. I could see his eyes. I saw
something there that looked like resignation or maybe just
sadness when he said, "So were you."

Perfection

It was early morning when he came to call for me. Two days had passed since our sleepover. Because of the residual maybes that lingered in my head, I wasn't sure that he would. I wasn't sure he would ever call for me again. But he did. We ate breakfast in the park and watched the sun rise. He played "Here comes the Sun" on the boom box and held my hand. We didn't speak much—not that we ever spoke much—but sunrise watching was never the place for chatter. I sat there, my hand in his, feeling warm and sure. It was settled. We were a "thing." That evening we were going to have dinner together in his room. I was all set. It would be a perfect evening.

Lee and I had gone to the Planned Parenthood office earlier. We wore our Woolworth's wedding bands and attested to the lie that we were lawfully married women. They didn't ask many questions. Lee got her monthly supply of the pills. I opted for a diaphragm. I remember I was more than a little concerned when I saw the size of that thing in the display case, but the nurse, Miss Parker, assured me that size was relative.

She did an exam and chose the size that she said was right for me. She gave me some literature and she showed me how to use the spermicidal gel. Then she gave me some privacy while I practiced inserting it.

When I thought I had the hang of it, I asked, "How well does it work?"

"Generally, between ninety-four and eighty-eight percent effective depending on how well you follow the instructions. In any case, it works a lot better than using nothing," she said, busying herself with packing it up for me. Then she turned, looked me in the eye, and in a sober voice she said, "It's very important that you check it before each use. Hold it up to the light to make absolutely sure there are no holes or ruptures in it. The smallest pinhole could render it useless."

The door to room 416 swung open even before I got a chance to knock. Smiling, Danny ushered me in with a flourish.

"Right this way, mademoiselle," he said as he took my hand. The usual dim lighting had been enhanced by several glass-encased candles he had placed around the room. The sweet smell of jasmine incense intermingled with a spicy, pungent odor that I couldn't quite identify. Three TV tables were arranged end to end, down the middle of the room between the two beds. Two folding chairs, apparently borrowed from the student lounge, were positioned at opposite sides of the middle table. Clusters of candles adorned the

centers of each outside table. It was beautiful. It was thoughtful. It was so romantic. I felt like I was in the middle of a fairytale. And this fairytale was not entitled *The Prince and the
Duckling*. No. He had done all of this for *me*. It was clear this
was his way of letting me know how he felt about me—about
us. I honestly feared that I might break out in song, but I
managed to contain myself.

Instead, I smiled at him demurely and eased my way to
the bathroom. "Protection," I said. "Remember, I told you? I
took care of it."

"You're sure," he said. "Cause there's always *other* ways."

"I'm sure."

"Cause I have rubbers." There was a touch of doubt in
his voice.

"Danny, I'm sure." Then he relaxed, nodded approving-
ly, and smiled that smile.

Emerging from the bathroom, I went directly to his record collection. I shuffled through the forty-fives and way
back in the 1960 bin I found The Shirelles' "Will You Still
Love Me Tomorrow." He threw back his head in a full belly
laugh. I had never heard him laugh before. The sound filled
the room; it swept over me, and though I had actually wanted an answer to that question . . . I relaxed. I breathed.

"Come here, you." He took my hand, and still laughing,
he led me to the table. We smoked grass. Something special,
he said. He cautioned me to go easy, saying it was powerful. I
didn't ask any questions. We ate burgers dressed with toma-
toes, lettuce, and crisp, savory pickles along with French fries
garnished with amazing ketchup. We drank spring wine and

sat facing each other; the flickering candles danced shadows across the contours of his face. He placed records on the stereo and the magical music played.

The first song to drop was Smokey Robinson's "You've Really Got a Hold on Me." I wasn't sure if the song was speaking something to me or if it was just one of his favorites. I wasn't sure I understood the meaning in the actual lyrics. The song was followed by a number of classic oldies as well as some latest hits. The Four Tops' "Can't Help Myself," Solomon Burkes' "Got to Get you Off my Mind," and Percy Sledge's "When a Man Loves a Woman." Then the Beatles' "Something" came on and he extended his hand.

"Just this song," he said.

There was just enough space at the end of the TV tables for us to hold each other. He pulled me in close. I placed my arms up around his neck. My head rested on his heart. We swayed. Suddenly we were rippling, vibrating into the music. I tilted my head upward, my eyes inviting a kiss. Gently placing his lips on mine, he accepted my invitation.

We made love, then. And it truly felt like love. It was different from just pleasuring each other the way we did before, although there was lots of pleasure involved. I inhaled him, breathing deep satisfying breaths. The alien entity in my chest had been banished. There were only his lips—those lips—on mine. Our tongues met. Our bodies fused. But it was not just our bodies. Perhaps it was the grass. It felt like our minds had melded. My mind meandered through his, through tunnels and passageways, some bright and glowing, others dark and twisty. There were no words or thoughts, just feelings. I felt them, his feelings, his joy, his terror, his desire. Some emotions were warm and rounded and tranquil, others rough and jagged and cold. I wanted to touch them, his feelings. I pursued them on through the passageways. I reached out. With my touch, I wanted to blunt the razor-sharp edges of dread. I wanted to wallow in the sleek, smooth warmth of his desire.

Through all of this, I could feel him as well. He was inside my head meandering through my tunnels, exploring my feelings. He was inside my body, exploring me. And for one anxious moment, I worried that he might come across that ugly black duckling inside me, that he might withdraw in horror. But that moment passed. It ebbed away and was forgotten. Neither one of us had anything to hide. We were no longer individuals. Together we had surrendered. We had opened up and revealed ourselves. We were something new, something better. Gradually, we began to feel it, this delicious sensation. It was encroaching, like a tide, teasing, lapping at the shore, and retreating. It would surge forward and retreat, surge, and retreat, gaining strength with each roiling incursion. Each time it pushed its way further onto the shore. We teetered on the edge. Then it rushed in. A large rambling wave that took us by surprise, washed over us, could not be contained. Our simultaneous release was powerful, intense. Our cries were guttural. They burst out in a singularity. We had   achieved   .   .   .   perfection. We lay on his bed breathing hard and bathed in sweat. Slowly, our bodies disentangled but our minds were still engaged. I could feel him withdrawing. I felt like he was seeking a secure crevice where he could shove his feelings, shield them from my prying. Though I tried, I couldn't pursue him through those passageways. An acute attack of the maybes was coming on. I wondered if he could feel my angst the way I could feel his. I wondered if it was always going to be like this for us . . . afterwards.

Just as we had done before, we took a shower, slowly lathering each other's bodies. It was sensuous. It was intimate. Then I dressed in his clean white, well-pressed T-shirt. When I exited the bathroom, I found him clearing away the remnants of our meal and putting away the TV tables and chairs. I feared that he would head for Raymond's bed the way he did last time. I couldn't let that happen. I'd miss him too much. Working to slow my heartbeat, I took a breath for courage and grabbed him by the hand. I could feel his hesitation. There was a touch of resistance before he allowed me to lead him to the bed. When I was sure he wouldn't run away, I went to place some music on the stereo. I returned to the bed to find him in his familiar pose, smoking a joint. I snuggled my way in, wormed myself under his arm, rested my head on his chest, wrapped my arm around him. I wasn't going to let him drift away, not this time. The Four Tops' "Still Waters Run Deep" filled the air. He placed a kiss on the top of my head and pulled me in closer.

I don't know how long we sat there caught up in song lyrics. Me with my head on his chest, listening to his heartbeat and breathing easy, the smell of pot and Life Buoy filling my brain, the candles flicking light and shadow across the psychedelic posters. Him with his eyes straight ahead, his head bobbing to the music, marijuana smoke rising, veiling his face.

He offered me the joint. I took a drag and suddenly dared to have questions. There was so much I wanted to know from this guy who practiced this economy of words.

"So, you studied karate?" I said, not really sure how to start the conversation. I felt him tense. I thought he might pull away, but I held tight, and after a while, he relaxed.

"Judo."

I waited to see if he would add to his one-word response. He didn't. I tried again. "So, you used to compete?"

"Tournaments."

"Were you any good? Did you win?"

"Some." I heard a smile in that last word.

"So, you going to play this one-word answer game?

"Maybe."

Spontaneously, playfully, I lashed-out to hit him. He caught my wrist mid-strike. His grip was like steel. He pushed me back on the bed. I struggled. We were laughing. It felt almost normal.

"Why don't you just ask me what you want to know?"

"Okay then," I said. "What did you mean when you said the martial arts was the undoing of your whole family? What happened?" I thought he would be taken aback by the question, but he just looked down at me, his lips so close to mine, a thoughtful expression on that handsome face. He opened his mouth and was about to speak when we heard it. It was that tapping on the door. *Tap, tap,* pause *tap, tap, tap.* He jumped up so fast that he almost pulled me off the bed. He went to his desk and got something. I couldn't make out what it was. But whatever it was, it seemed much larger than the thing he got last time. He stepped out of the room and closed the door. He was gone longer this time too, maybe five minutes. I could hear voices. But as hard as I tried, I couldn't make out what was said. When he returned, he went directly to his desk to put something in. He turned and looked at me like he expected me to ask about what just happened. Remembering last time, I had no intention of asking, although there were questions and conclusions slamming up against my brain. There was a clear, common-sense explanation for what I just saw. I knew that. But I pushed it aside. *What is so? What is not so?* It was a thought for another time. I watched as he retreated to Raymond's bed.

He had retreated from me . . . again. After what we just shared, he retreated from me. It felt like rejection. I sighed. I looked at him way over there on his side of the world and suddenly I understood that I would never be able to forge that gap. It suddenly struck me as hopeless. In that moment, I knew I couldn't do it anymore. How could I? Rejection . . . drug dealing? Leaving time was looming. Yes, it was time to tip. I felt it. I got up, gathered my clothes, and started getting dressed.

"What are you doing?" he asked.

"I'm going back to my room," I said, my voice low, steady, and resolved.

"Don't," he said, his voice an echo from across a canyon. "Stay."

It sounded like a request, a simple request. But it was more than that. It froze me as I headed for the door. It was a rope tugging at me, trying to tether me, to keep me stable, to prevent me from drifting the way that I do. But there was that other tug too. It was that tug on my heart that I always felt when I left. I realized, then, that there was something satisfying about that old tug, something that would save me. It was familiar, comfortable. It was something that I understood, something that somehow made sense. It was a sad sense of closure, but I craved it. I needed it. I don't know how long I stood there facing the door, teetering, competing impulses pulling at me, playing tug of war with my emotions.

There was quiet. The silence was daunting. Finally, remembering to breathe, I inhaled, managed to place one foot in front of the other. I continued to the door without looking back; I had no intention of looking back.

Behind me, the room erupted with sound, a soulful melody was working its way into all the room's darkened spaces. I think I actually heard him sing,

Stay, honey
Please won't you stay
Please won't you stay
Stay, darling, stay

Dirty Dealings

"So let me get this straight. You were deciding whether or not to stay or leave? And what did you do? You left, right?" Lee said.

"I stayed," I said, trying to sound matter of fact, repositioning Bernadette on my bureau, brushing the hair away from her face.

"You? Really? Why?" She sounded incredulous.

I thought about that. I needed a moment. I needed to explore my reasons and put together an answer. I wasn't sure there were words to explain it. Some things are just feelings, impulses. I was about to speak when I was saved by a knock on the door.

A neutral voice called, "Dawn, phone call for you."

I went out to the hall and answered the communal phone that hung on the wall. "Hello?"

"Dawn, it's Ralfie."

"Hey Ralfie, wassup?"

"A few of us are planning to go to Coattails this Thursday. You should come."

Coattails. The word alone sent a little jolt through me . . . the march, the riot, Danny. I hadn't been back to that Thursday night party since Dr. King's expiration day—none of us had. I guess it took some time for us to get back to our lives, to try to feel normal again.

"Yeah, sure I will," I said, trying not to sound tentative. "Of course I'll go, sounds good."

"Great, it starts the same time as usual, six-thirty. Can you tell the others? Let's see, who else in our crowd lives in the dorms? Oh yeah, Gina, Lee, Luanne—and I know you'll tell Danny."

"And why would you think that I'd especially tell Danny?"

"C'mon Dawn, really?"

"Touché, Ralfie." I laughed. "I'll let everyone know. We'll be there."

I returned to the room to find myself confronted with Lee's accusing eyes. "Well?" she asked.

"Well, what?"

"Well, why did you stay? Hell, even I would have tipped if I were treated like that. And you, you're famous for walking out. How about all those times that you mentioned? You left with little or no provocation."

"That's not true. I left when I had to, when it was leaving time."

"And . . . ?"

"And I guess it wasn't leaving time."

"It must have been the sex. Was it the sex? You guys did do it, right? Please tell me it wasn't just about the sex. No one is that good."

"I beg to differ," I said, a coy smile playing on my lips.

"That good?! So, it was the sex?"

"Oh my God, Lee, it was amazing! It was, like, religious. And it wasn't just sex. I'm sure it was love; we made love. He loves me, Lee. And he's trying, you know, to make things between us better." What I didn't tell Lee was that for a moment, a real moment, I wasn't sure that was enough to make me stay.

Looking exasperated and unconvinced, Lee said, "So, if things between you guys was so great, why were you about to leave?"

"Afterwards, he went to sleep on Raymond's bed. You remember, I told you about how he did that before. Hell, at the time, I figured if I'm going to sleep alone, I might as well be in my own bed."

"He is so strange," she said. "So that's it? You were about to leave because he went to Raymond's bed, but then you didn't?"

I thought about it. That was not the only reason. Clearly Lee sensed there was something I wasn't saying, something I hadn't quite come to terms with. The thought shot through my mind. "Danny's a drug dealer." I heard myself say. It was a lie. It was a truth. I lowered my voice, spoke the words in a whisper. It was a truth that was raw and naked. I felt like I needed to cover it up, drape it, protect it from lurking eavesdroppers.

"Say wha?"

"It's the only thing that makes any sense. I mean, he's a real pothead. I know that. Hell, he's turning me into a real pothead. But I dunno, I never thought he was dealing. That makes things different somehow, right? My grandma would snatch me into her grave if she thought I was in love with a drug dealer. Am I crazy?"

"Well, that depends."

"What? My being crazy depends?"

"No, his dealing. I think it depends on what he's dealing and how much."

I hadn't thought about that. My mind drifted back to last night, the dim lighting, the pattern of the knock on the door, the package that Danny retrieved from the desk. It was dark. I couldn't actually see how big the package was. The harder I tried to concentrate on it, the smaller it got.

"Okay," I said to Lee. "Maybe Danny's selling, like, small bags of pot. What do they call them?"

"Nickel bags."

"Yeah, nickel bags or maybe even dime bags. Is there such a thing?"

"Yeah, I think. Jamal is the one who buys the pot."

"Does he buy it from Danny?"

"Not sure. I can find out."

I fell silent then. My mind floated away, back to the block in the Bronx where I grew up.

"I remember the drug addicts," I said, my eyes looking into the past. "Those junkies would appear on the street corners, you know. I remember how they looked like the walking dead, the way they used to stagger and lean forward. Their bodies would bend so low that I actually thought they were, like, about to kiss the sidewalk. Me and my friends used to watch them, laughing, waiting for them to tumble over, but they never did."

I turned to face the mirror that hung on the bathroom door. I was startled by Outside Me, who had appeared suddenly, the way she does. She was standing in front of the mirror, her hands on her hips, judging. "Okay," I said, addressing her. "It's true. I never thought about it at the time, but I know now that it was sad. They were sad. They were sad, lost people and it wasn't right that someone was getting rich off their misery." Outside Me just waited, expecting me to say more. "I know, I know," I offered "It wasn't right for me to make fun of them." Then she dematerialized, the way she does.

Lee followed my gaze into the mirror. I ignored her confused expression.

"I'm still not clear," she said. "You were about to leave but then you stayed. Why were you about to leave? Was it because of him dealing pot?"

I realized I wasn't really sure. Was it just a reflex, survival, that familiar urge to run? Was it the pot thing? I decided, then, that Lee was probably right. Lots of people sell small amounts of grass. It was no big deal. They did it so they'd have some for their own personal use. That didn't make him, like, an actual drug dealer, right? Hell, one day they might even make it legal.

"That was part of it," I said.

"So, after the pot selling thing, he returned to the bed with you?"

"No."

"So why the hell would you stay?"

"It was the song," I uttered, an alien realization emerging with the words.

"What?"

"Because he asked me to."

Coattails

We watched the sun making its slow and graceful ascent in the sky. Danny pushed the button and the music box played "Here Comes the Sun" to accompany the sun's majestic performance.

We'd been sitting in our spot in the park. Breathing deep, unobstructed breaths, I reached over and took possession of his hand. I rested my head on his shoulder and he'd let me.

I wasn't sure how long we were supposed to sit there silently holding hands and breathing. I was never sure. Danny was the decider. He decided when sun gazing time was over, and I'd let him.

We had folded into a comfortable fit. We had a rhythm. I was sure that our melody would follow soon. It was only a matter of time. We were a "thing."

Danny extracted his hand from mine and started unwrapping his breakfast. I did the same. Then remembering

Ralfie's phone call, I said, "Oh Danny, I almost forgot. It's Thursday."

"Yes, it is," he said, his eyes still trained on the sky.

"Ralfie called. He said some people are going to Coattails tonight."

"Why'd he call *you*?"

"What do you mean?"

"You. He called *you*. He calls you a lot."

"Yeah?" I said, my mind doing a slow roll before arriving at his point. "Ralfie does call me. He calls me all the time. He's my friend."

"Humph!" Was all Danny said, his eyes skyward, those lips in a pout. "Um jus sayin. You spend a lot of time with that guy."

Something warm spread through me. I couldn't believe it. He was actually jealous. It was so cute. I smiled and explained, "Ralfie called because he wanted me to spread the word to people in the dorms, you know, about tonight. It sounds like fun. It's time. I told him that we would be there."

He responded with an uneasy silence.

"Danny? We're going, right?" I asked, taking his hand, trying to engage his eyes.

Then turning those wolf eyes on me he said, "We'll see," and I winced as he squeezed my hand much harder than was comfortable.

I was in my room getting dressed, putting on my final coat of mascara and wondering where Danny was. He said he'd call for me at 6:00 p.m. It was 6:15. A touch of worry was trying to worm its way into my head. Danny was rarely late. A thought that was probably not my own, managed to break through. **What makes you think that he wants to go public with this "thing" that you imagine you have?**

In the mirror, something was flickering across my face. In my chest, something was stretching out, taking up all the space in my lungs. I bent over, trying to breathe. Over time, I had learned how to deal with The Duckling—to be the master of my own mind. Rule number one: don't engage. I stumbled away from the mirror, stood upright, closed my eyes, and forced a breath into my lungs, then another, and another. I grabbed my bag and headed for Danny's room, thinking that The Duckling wouldn't dare try to threaten me when I was with him.

I stood in front of room 416 trying to compose myself before I knocked. No music played and the smell of jasmine was conspicuously missing. There was a stillness inside the room. I knocked again . . . no answer. Then I saw the note wedged between the door and its frame. It read: *Dawn, sorry, something came up. You should stay. Don't go without me. You need to study for your midterms, anyway. We'll go together next time.*

My head was about to explode, conflicting thoughts doing battle. Really? Something came up? And he couldn't come upstairs and let me know?! What if it was an emergency? But he didn't use that word—emergency. And since when does he care about my study habits?! What if it was something about his father, or his mother, or even his brother who is in 'Nam? What if it's just some fucking drug deal?!

256

So, despite what *Danny* thought I should do, I decided I needed to go to Coattails. I needed to dance and drink wine and be with friends. I needed to stop my mind from swinging back and forth with thoughts of Danny. What I didn't need was to go back to my room and face that duckling.

Double Dealing

Many days passed, and I hadn't seen or heard from Danny. Since the day I went to Coattails, I had been staying in my own room. And he hadn't come for me in the mornings. That's what he always did if I slept in my own room. He'd come for me, pull me back. I didn't run into him on campus, and he wasn't even standing in the lobby when the dance class let out. I found myself alternating between pissed, confused, and terrified. Why hadn't he come for me? Why hadn't he apologized for standing me up. After all, it wasn't that big a deal, right? Still, I was afraid to go down to his room uninvited. I couldn't believe he was avoiding me just because I went to Coattails when he told me not to. Maybe I shouldn't have. Maybe I should have just stayed home and studied like he said. What was going to happen with our thing, assuming we still had one? Maybe he had moved on. Maybe . . .

"You really have to stop with the maybes," Lee said as she watched me pace the floor. Then she said again what she'd said so many times before. "This is all just part of the yo-yo game that guys like him like to play. You need to cut that string and move on." She looked into my eyes. I think she actually felt my angst then because her tone softened. "Okay." She said and touched my shoulder. "He'll come around soon enough. He will. It's part of the game. I know that's what you want. But think. Is that what's best, I mean, for you?"

"That's easy for you to say."

"Actually, it's not. It's very hard for me to say these things to you. I know they upset you and that's not what I'm trying to do."

Deciding to drop the subject, I turned from her. Lee just didn't understand. I couldn't breathe. His scent, that sensuous combination of Danny and his favorite soap, curled through the air. It assailed me with every labored breath I took. He had taken over my mind. Ever since that night when I ignored my instinct to leave, every other thought I had was of Danny. It was like I was engulfed in this blue, misty grief. I just had to do something. I had to reach out to him.

So, despite admonitions from Lee, I made a plan. Danny still had the boom box—technically *my* boom box. I'd never given it to him. I'd never taken it from him either. I'd take a chance, go down to his room, and pretend that I wanted to use it for a while. I was sure that when we were alone face to face, he'd play "something" and take me in his arms. We would dance and he would kiss me and apologize. And we would listen to music and smoke pot and work it all out.

Just as I got to room 416, someone was opening the door to exit. My first inclination was to slip away before I was seen, but no one came out. The person turned back into the room, leaving the door slightly ajar. I could hear a guy's voice. Struggling with indecision, I wasn't sure if I should knock on the open door, wait for the guy to exit . . . or listen. I opted for the latter.

"Say, yo man. I wanted to ask you, and if Um outta line just tell me and forget I even asked . . ."

"Wassup, man?" I heard Danny ask.

"That sister, wha's her name—Dana? I seen you around with her lately. Like I said, if Um outta line just say so, but are you hittin' that? I mean no offense if she's your lady."

Then, Danny's voice dropped at least two octaves and a chill trickled down my spine. "You . . . talking about that little dark chick?"

"Yeah, she's dark but she's fine, gotta bod on her that won't quit. Have you seen the booty on that girl?"

"Yeah, I've, ah, seen it. Impressive, if you like the type."

"Hey man, you know what they say, 'the darker the berry, the sweeter the wine.' I think the sister is beautiful. So, are you saying you haven't been gettin' with that?"

"Nah man. She's just a friend. She's not my type. I can do much better than that. You've seen some of the sisters I deal with."

"Well, I think she's fine. There's something about her, you know, those eyes."

"Hey man, if that's your speed, go for it. She don't mean nothing to me."

I froze. I was too numb to react. My heart was beating in my throat and my bowels were turning to water.

Ahmod James practically ran over me as he exited. "Oh Dana, what a coincidence. I was . . ." he stopped short. It must have been my open mouth and tear-filled eyes that put a halt to him. He followed my gaze as I stared at Danny through the open door. He must've seen Danny's open mouth as well and his wide-eyed, shocked expression as he stared back at me. In that moment everything stood still. There was only this sound, this whistling noise in my head, like steam escaping a pressure cooker, the pressure building, approaching unbearable. Then Ahmod looked from me to Danny, from Danny to me, and back again. And he quietly eased himself away.

I don't know how long I stood there trying to get my mouth to close, my body to turn, my legs to carry me away. My brain was issuing orders that my body couldn't process. The impulses were crossed. They were confused and conflicted. I wanted to hurt him, slap his face and claw at his eyes. I wanted to run away, to run and run and keep on running, to find a hole, crawl into it and never come out. I wanted to cry, to throw back my head and wail like a baby. I wanted to go to him, let him wrap his arms around me, run his fingers through my hair and say that I misunderstood, that he would never say those things.

In the end he spoke one word that released me. "Dawn . . ."

I turned then, slowly, and started my retreat, putting one foot in front of the other as best as I could manage, one step at a time, one breath at a time.

Then he was by my side. "Dawn," he said again. He placed his hand on my arm. His touched seared my skin. I glared from his hand to his face. I wasn't sure what he saw in my eyes, but his mouth flew open as he hastily withdrew his hand and took a step back. I continued to my room.

Of Dreams and Nightmares

I was in a dream. It was one of those dreams when I was aware that I was dreaming. I wanted to stay right there in that dream, safe and loved. I was in Momma's house. Everything was bright and sparkly. Rainbow colors shimmered across the walls. I was greasing Momma's scalp and braiding her hair. There was music. She was singing.

Then Momma rose, her eyes unseeing. She turned and walked into the shadows. I tried to follow. A duckling appeared in a liquid mirror, signifying, its voice raking razors across my brain. I was walking through abject blackness, seeking Momma, coughing, the acrid smell of burnt wood and plastic choking me. The Duckling cackled. My hands flew to my ears. Caustic sirens screeched. Searchlights streaked the ceiling. I looked up, squinted. There was a creature, its eyes bright with malice. I opened my mouth to scream, but the sharp keen of a wolf's howl emerged instead. It pursued me as I stumbled down endless flights of stairs. I faltered, fell, saw stars as pain shot through my jaw. The

263

Duckling's cackle split the air. I was trapped in the night-mare, struggling to wake up. I was running, then . . . running. The sound of hoof beats pounding, closing fast. I tripped, and a faceless stranger was on top of me, his mouth on mine, smothering me. I couldn't breathe. He was pushing himself into me. His face kept morphing. I didn't know him. Who was he?

"No!" I shrieked. "No! No! No!"

Luanne was by my side. "You okay? I've been trying to wake you. You must've been having some hell of a night-mare."

I was sobbing, the pillow moist with tears. Covered in sweat and gasping for air, my head was throbbing, my heart pounding.

"You kinda over did it last night with the wine. It was a special bottle I was saving for me and Ronnie. But that's okay, I don't mind."

"Oh my God, Luanne. Did I drink some of your special wine?"

"More like *all* of my special wine. But it's okay. Um jus sayin'. It seemed like you needed it."

My heart did a sharp contraction as it all came back to me—Danny, Ahmod, me being offered around like some common trick. I burst into tears.

"Come here," Luanne said. Tentatively, she wrapped her arms around me. "I would think that you should be all cried out by now."

Then embarrassment was edging out pain. I must have told Luanne everything last night. I must have blubbered it all out in a drunken stupor. I wanted to go under the covers and stay there. Luanne must have sensed my chagrin, or seen it in my eyes or something, because she said, "You didn't say much of anything that made any sense. But it was clear that you were hurt and pissed. It takes a man to put a woman in a state like that. Men are dogs, and fine-looking men are were-wolves. So anytime you care to tell me about it, I'm all ears. Meantime, take Lil Momma's advice and give it some space. Stay away from the asshole for a while."

I sat up on the bed. It felt like someone hit me in the head with a hammer. I grabbed my head and groaned.

Luanne brought me a glass of water and two aspirin. "Drink all of the water. Water's your friend right now." The concern in her eyes was heartening.

I sipped the water, but it went down the wrong pipe. Luanne patted me on the back while I coughed.

There was a soft tap on the door. I glanced at the clock. It was a little after six in the morning. "I got this," Luanne said. She opened the door just wide enough to accommodate her tiny face and said, "She don't wanna see you. Fuck off!" Then she slammed the door.

Rehab

The new semester brought in a fresh crop of SEEK students—new friends, a fresh start, deepening relationships with old friends. I busied myself with work-study and classes. I was running a 3.6 GPA and aiming for better. I had picked my major: creative writing. I buried myself in the work, the diversion was lifesaving.

Danny had dismantled me. I was a collection of fragmented puzzle pieces whose cuts and grooves had been altered. They no longer fit together. And The Duckling loomed constantly. My only shot at defeating it was to find a new configuration, some way to get the pieces to fit together and make sense or some sort of glue to bond the fragments in place until I could be me again.

"You need to come into the sixties," Luanne had said. So, we went shopping. Little hot pants, low cut blouses, midriff bells that revealed my abs, and halter tops that revealed the smooth brown skin on my back became the basics of my wardrobe.

Lee disapproved. "You're out of control," she said.

I brushed her words aside. I tried to assure her that I was fine and in complete control. After that, she never said another word, but I could see it in her eyes.

Despite Lee's objection, I was feeling better. It was a do-over, and I was enjoying all the attention I was getting from guys. I'd gotten fairly skilled at flirting, though I didn't tease. I didn't want to start something I had no intention of finishing. I wasn't ready to go there, not yet. I wasn't sure I ever would be. I started wearing my contacts all the time. It took some doing for me to get skilled at putting the tiny glass lenses into my eyes. And taking a page from Twiggy's book, heavy eye makeup finished off my mask.

And there were the white boys. They seemed to have come out of nowhere. I think I was more than a little shocked when white boys started pursuing me. There was this one on campus—tall, blonde, nice looking. He hung out with the brothers playing basketball mostly. He kept asking to walk me home.

"I live in the dorms way downtown," I said.

"Hey, I like walking. Do you?"

I'd just smile and play it off. There were others. The guy who worked the front desk for the Alamac hotel where the dorm was housed used to call to me every time I walked through the lobby.

"Hey, smiley," he would call. "What's your name?"

He was cute, had this Paul McCartney thing going on. I'd give him a flick of my head, a flirtatious smile, and kept it moving. One day Luanne witnessed our little exchange. After that, I never heard the end of it. She kept trying to get me to take him up on his offer. I have to say that I was flattered, but I never really knew how serious to take them, the white boys.

In fact, I was leery of any guy who showed interest in me, no matter what color they were. I didn't trust their motives and I certainly couldn't trust my own instincts. My track record proved that I had the worst judgment when it came to guys. I always got the signals wrong. Despite Momma's advice from beyond, I couldn't trust myself to know *who is who* and *what is so* or *what is not so.*

All of this is not to say that I was comfortable with my new look, my new me. It was a disguise. I was playing a part, ignoring the Ugly Black Duckling, ignoring its weight in my chest. I managed to accommodate the narrowing of my windpipe, to pretend that The Duckling no longer existed, that it had never existed.

The upside to my performance was this heady sense of power that I never knew I had. Guys who never gave me a second glance were suddenly interested in me. It was amazing what a girl in hot pants could get them to do—sit up, roll over. I knew it was because of the disguise. It was like my looks and my sexuality were all I had to offer, like without the disguise I was invisible; I had no value at all . . . no power.

But despite all this—the guys, the grades, the disguise, my newfound power—inside I mourned for Danny, missed him.

Lee could see it in my face. "It's either you or him," she'd say. "Somebody's going to be sacrificed. Some relationships are just plain toxic. Trust me. I know." I did trust her. That didn't mean I wouldn't wake up every morning before sunrise listening for a tap on the door . . . dreading that it might actually come. I often thought about going to our spot in the park to watch the sunrise. But I knew it was his spot . . . not mine.

Although I tried my best to avoid him, it was like Danny was everywhere. I'd run into him in the dorms or on campus, in the lecture halls, or the student cafeteria. I cringe as I remember that time when I ran into him, quite literally, in Shepard Hall.

"Shit! I'm so sorry," I had said, looking down at the books and papers that had scattered around my feet, instead of looking up to see who I'd almost run over. On some days I was like a drunk driver. It was a struggle to focus on anything, let alone where I was going. Then I added insult to injury when, bending down, I butted heads with my victim.

"Not at all. I got this," he said, and his familiar voice cut right through me.

"No, I can manage," I said, hating the tremor in my voice. I looked up and got caught in his eyes. I reached for the papers he held in his hand. I was having trouble keeping my heart in line, re-living the riot of humiliations I'd endured that night. He seemed to be the master of "cool." Suddenly I was angry.

"I said I can manage," I repeated, ice in my tone. I snatched the papers from him and suffered some kind of current as our fingers brushed. Our eyes locked. There was something in his expression. I thought maybe his cool was melting away. He faltered, suddenly appeared to be as rad-dled as I was.

Outside Me appeared then and grabbed my hand.

"Dawn, wait!" I heard him call, as "we" turned and sprinted down the corridor.

Afterwards, I felt so dumb, running away like that. And The Duckling made it worse. It tortured me, peppering my mind with thoughts.

You know this was all your fault. What did you do? Things had been perfect. Why couldn't you just stay home and study like he said?

So, I had regrets—or misgivings, as Lee would call them. She didn't understand why I was grieving, that I missed how genuinely beautiful he made me feel. I missed being Danny Barrett's beautiful lady. I missed his arms around me, missed inhaling him and . . . breathing easy. I had lost him. Without him, I had to fight for every breath. It was exhausting. And Outside Me was no real help. Although she meant well, she'd sashay in and out, offering useless advice that only someone who thinks they're "all that" could possibly pull-off.

Lee said all of this would pass in time.

"How could I have been so wrong?" I'd said to Lee after telling her about the embarrassment of running into Danny and then running away like an idiot. "I actually believed he cared about me."

Of course I had told Lee the actual detailed account of the hideous exchange between Danny and Ahmod. Lee never repeated it. She wouldn't. But I couldn't bring myself to tell her about the regrets, the grieving, about how I brought this all on myself. Although I'm pretty sure she knew. My other friends—Jamal, Ralfie, Chandra and even Luanne—probably ended up hearing some blubbering version directly from me, as I went through various stages of tearful wine-hazed rantings. If I did blurt out what actually happened, they were discreet and never brought it up.

For a time, they never left me alone. One or all of them were always by my side. Sometimes, I resented their interference. Especially with The Duckling's constant screaming in my head, *This was all your doing. You should apologize. Plus, you never even let him explain!* Despite me, they ran interference. Any time Danny tried to talk to me, they'd gather around, crowd him out, and whisk me away. I do have to admit that those days, the days when my friends shielded me, served as a sort of rehab period. It gave me some space, some time to detox, deal with The Duckling, fit my pieces back together. After a while, when he'd approach me wanting to talk, Outside Me would emerge, and with her nose in the air and a fling of her long ponytail, she'd take me by the hand and lead me away.

Eventually he stopped trying. Gradually, it got easier being around him, easier to mask my feelings. We were cordial. We, after all, still hung out in the same crowd. Of course, there were the usual stable of girls vying for his attention. There didn't seem to be anyone in particular that he spent time with. But he was so secretive, I could never be sure. There were times, quite a few times, when I felt those wolf eyes on me. When that happened, I would initiate some sort of playful flirting with a guy in the group, any guy. It was part of my rehabilitation. It made me feel very un-duckling.

But despite my personal drama, there was real turmoil brewing on campus, turmoil that would eventually ensnare all of us.

The Takeover

I had signed up for the nightshift. Ralfie and I were standing guard together at the southernmost entrance to the campus. The newly formed Black and Puerto Rican Student Coalition, of which I was a member, had taken over C.C.N.Y.'s entire south campus—eight buildings in all.

Ralfie enjoyed explaining college trivia to me. "This used to be a convent," he said. "So, it's completely gated in. It's like a little fortress. That's why it was so easy to take over." This was why I liked doing guard duty with Ralfie. He was so knowledgeable about the history and the politics of any given topic. Also, he was my friend, and he wasn't Danny. "There should be open admissions to college," he'd said. "It's one of the things we're fighting for."

I'd never thought about it like that. If it weren't for the SEEK program, I wouldn't have even been there. After all, I was told that I didn't qualify. How many others had been kept out due to a few points lower on their GPA?

"The Vietnam war is raging," Ralfie had been saying. "Nixon is illegally bombing Cambodia. Young men, poor young men of color, are being drafted into the army to fight other poor young men of color in some jungle somewhere." He was always so animated when he spoke about the injustices in the world. I wondered if that was why he left the ministry, to fight for justice. "People don't know that most of the Americans that are sent to the frontline are men of color," he said. "We only make up, like, twelve percent of the population but we're seventeen percent of the draftees! How's that fair?"

I studied Ralfie as he spoke. It was like he was transformed—no "Little Padre," no puppy dog eyes. I was looking at a crusader, a revolutionary, someone to admire. The fire in his eyes made him quite attractive. "Not to mention . . ." He suddenly stopped short. I think it was because he caught the intense, approving way I was looking at him. He flushed crimson. My cheeks burned. Luckily for me, *my* reaction was not apparent. For a moment we stood staring at each other. Then we both turned away.

"So, is this why you left the ministry? You wanted to crusade for justice?" I asked, hoping to get back to the subject.

"Not exactly. I could've been a priest and still crusaded for justice, as you say."

"So, why?"

"Girls," he said, color returning to his cheeks. "I like girls."

"Ralfie, I didn't mean to pry."

"Not at all," he said, his stare direct. "I actually wanted *you* to know that I like girls."

The issues that Ralfie spoke about had been widely debated around campus for some time. A sense of unrest prevailed, like static rippling through the air. Before the actual takeover there had been general assemblies and cell meetings to plan strategy. There had been sit-downs with the administration where demands had been presented and rejected. Smart people who had obviously thought things through were calling the shots. Those folks were focused and serious. I, on the other hand, had been too caught up in my own little drama to participate in any meaningful way. It was all I could do to keep up with what was going on.

It was decided that we would take action. We were going to try and close down south campus for a day to call attention to our grievances. The plan was that we'd leave when they sent in the cavalry. But four days in, no cavalry came to dispossess us. It was decided that we'd stay until they did. Then we'd leave peacefully. People actually started setting up encampments. Sleeping quarters were assigned. A kitchen was established in the cafeteria. There were plans for general assemblies and cell meetings. A schedule for guard duty was set up. I signed up, wanting to make sure I wasn't anywhere near Danny. I wasn't sure how I'd react to his touch if he even tried to give me a casual five. I could just see it: up high, down low . . . my heart on the floor.

Helicopters flew low, buzzing the compound. I wrapped myself in the excitement of it all. Instead of fear, I felt exhilarated. I was a cog in a well-oiled machine—a rebel. On some level I knew that I wasn't dealing with the gravity of the situation; still, I was intrigued.

And there was music; songs reminiscent of the old civil rights anthems yet uniquely our own. One of my favorites was the one that was sung about the back gate on St. Nicholas Terrace.

> *I got a feelin', I got a feelin' brothers*
> *I got a feelin' somebody's tryin' to sneak in the back*
> *There ain't gonna be no shit like that!*

We were revolutionaries fighting for a cause. It was fun . . . for a while. We were into the second week of the takeover. Ralfie and I were at our post at the south gate on Convent Avenue. Despite the helicopters hovering above, tall metal bars encased the entire south campus. It was like a fortress. Somehow, it made me feel safe.

I bristled as I watched Ahmod James approach our post. He hadn't spoken to me since that time that I heard him commenting on my ass in Danny's room. He was actually one of the brothers who convened meetings and made decisions for the rest of us.

"Yo brother," he said to Ralfie. "I'm gonna take over here; you need to go get some sleep."

"What? Who's this coming from?"

"It's coming from me, my man. I checked the schedule and you been on for three nights straight. You know two nights is the limit." It was true. I was off last night but Ralfie volunteered to do guard duty with Chandra. Still, this was unusual. Ahmod James didn't do guard duty. He was one of the H.N.I.C.'s He and Enrique Cruz were basically large and in charge. Reluctantly, Ralfie left and Ahmod turned his gaze on me.

"So, I haven't spoken to you for a while," he said. "How you been?"

I avoided his eyes, peered past the metal gate, focused on cars as they rumbled through the Harlem night. Then, I resolved to push thoughts of his and Danny's obscene exchange from my mind. After all, it was not Ahmod who hurt me, who betrayed me. I rolled my eyes, tilted my head to the side, pouted my lips and gave him a long sideways glance. It was a flirtatious gesture, but I couldn't help myself. I liked exercising my new power. I liked being desired. Ahmod was fine and powerful, and he desired *me*.

"Me and my booty are just fine. Thank you for asking."

"Hey Sis, I'm sorry about that. It was just talk, you know. It's how us guys talk. I didn't mean no disrespect."

"Apology accepted," I cooed.

"So, listen here," he said. "I've carved out a little spot for myself in Gallagher's house. Maybe you'd like to come by and have a drink with me." Gallagher was the President of the college. Unfortunately for him, his home was located within the gates of south campus.

"Maybe, it depends on . . ." Before I could finish my sentence, a sister ran up to us. She was out of breath as she handed Ahmod a note.

"Looks like we have to rain check that drink for now," he said after reading it. "Listen, I gotta go. But I'm definitely having a party to celebrate this victory. It'll be in my room back at the dorms. I'll let you know. Please come as my special guest. For now, you need to go pack up. They just issued an injunction. We're leaving."

As was always the plan, we left quietly with no resistance. The next day there were at least a thousand police on campus. They stood single file, shoulder to shoulder, down the middle of Convent Avenue. With shields held in front of them, they formed what looked to me like a human wall. Their black helmets with clear masks shielding their faces gave them the look of some kind of alien extraterrestrial creatures.

The speeches were heated on either side of the street. On their side, the group that called themselves the "engineering students" were taunting us about having been kicked off the campus and shouting about their right to an education. On our side, the "Black and Puerto Rican Student Coalition," as we called ourselves, decried the Vietnamese war, the lack of open admissions to college, racism, and any number of weighty grievances. Insults and racial epithets were hurled from both sides, flying across the divide. For two weeks the engineering students had threatened to come down to south campus to throw us out. In the end it was the police who were called onto campus that ended our siege.

With the police in the middle of the street separating the competing rallies, I was feeling safe because they were there to act as a buffer and to keep the two factions apart. I had always been taught that the police were my friends. Not to mention that they were facing *them*, not us. Their scary shields and scowling faces were aimed in their direction.

I felt safe until I heard that sound. That sound sent a jolt throughout my body. I didn't know that human beings could emit such a roar. Shouting in unison, it sounded like the howl of a large fearsome animal. *"About face!"* I realized it was some sort of military chant and with that they turned.

With no provocation whatsoever, they attacked . . . us. Collectively, it took us a moment to take in what was happening. And then, we were running. We were running like prey up 138th street. I was overcome with a flash of déjà vu. I couldn't believe that this was happening again. It was just about a year ago that I had been running for my life with a panicked mob down 125th street. But instead of the four horsemen of the apocalypse bearing down on me, when I looked up, I saw a battalion of cops coming from the opposite direction. They were coming down 138th in full charge. It was an ambush! There was no way around them. With that realization, I saw the members of the Black and Puerto Rican Student Coalition take a stand and prepare for battle. It took me a second to digest the fact that they were actually going to fight the cops. It was insane. I think I was in shock as I scanned the crowd. I think I was looking for my friends. I know I was looking for Danny—for him to come and save me, to carry me off back to his room where we would reconcile and make love. These were the thoughts that flowed through my mind in the middle of all that upheaval.

Battles broke out. All around me there were scrimmages. The cops would grab a sister and slam her into the wall. Then they would taunt the brothers to try and do something about it. When they did, they were pounced upon and thrown into a paddy wagon. A paddy wagon? Where had it come from? All around me, this went on. Everything seemed to slow down. Arms were twisted, heads bashed, all occurring in slow motion as I pivoted on my axis, my focus drawn to the hideous sounds of the battles being waged around me.

A collective shriek cut through the air, cut through me. All at once there was not so much a silence as a hush. The cries, the taunts, the screaming resolved themselves into one single sound: a human chorus of high-pitched soprano voices like a howling wind that came whooshing through my head. The sound rocked me. I felt off balance. My heart sprouted legs and took off in full gallop. My windpipe spazzed, fluctuated. I struggled to breathe. This time *I* was the passive baby in the bubble, waiting to be engaged. Then I would have no choice. I would have to stay inside myself. I knew there would be no perfect Outside Me to safely lead me away. I would have to fight as best as I could. I tried to prepare myself mentally. I would claw and bite and kick. I would fight what I knew would be a losing battle. I imagined myself bloodied and broken, being thrown into the paddy wagon with the other brothers and sisters.

Seconds were ticking off like hours when I sensed his eyes on me from across what felt like a raging storm. Seconds moved even slower when I saw the cop behind him. The cop must have been running but to me it looked like he was moving ever so slowly. His ample body bounded and bounced heavily with every footfall. The meaty cheeks on his flushed face flounced with every step. His eyes were wild. A billy club in his hand was raised over Danny's head.

"Behind you!" I shouted as the cop bought the club down hard. Danny shifted to his left, the blow glancing off his shoulder. The cop raised the club again but in some kind of martial arts move Danny flipped him and sent him flying. Seeing what happened, another cop charged. Danny parried, causing the cop to lose his balance, trip, and plummet to the ground, hard. Then Danny took off running in my direction.

The police line that had been blocking the exit up 138th street had broken. Taking advantage of the opening, those who could were running again. I snapped out of it and joined them, running for all I was worth, the cops in urgent pursuit. We were cattle stampeding up 138th Street.

Suddenly I felt myself being grabbed from behind. An arm around my waist practically lifted me off my feet. My first thought was that a cop had caught me. My second thought was that Danny was saving me like before, that saving me was just something he did, like it was his job or something. I was swung off to the left and found myself facing a chain-link fence with no outlet. My savior, whoever it was, bent himself over me, covering me with his body. I hunkered down, folded myself into the curve of him. Then I realized we were not safe, and my heart dropped into my stomach. We were about to be apprehended. He was shielding me from the blows that he knew were coming. I braced myself.

Nothing happened.

We held our position like statues. Then everything was still, quiet. We were alone. It was surreal. The crowd, cops, and all, had run right past us, down 138th street towards Amsterdam Avenue. After what seemed like a very long

time, I turned and looked up into the playful grinning face of
Ahmod James.

Paartey!

The music in Ahmod's room was pumping. The atmosphere was dusky—candlelight, black light, shaded lamps, and blue bulbs. The familiar smells of pot and incense wafted through the air. It took a moment for my eyes to adjust. The room was bigger than any of the dorm rooms I'd seen before. It was actually a suite. There was a separate space off to the left with a sofa and another little nook with a kitchenette, a small table, and two chairs. There was only one bed and I wondered how Ahmod had managed to get a room all to himself. People were sitting on the sofa, squatting on the floor, and clustered on Ahmod's bed. There was enough floor space for dancing and there were shadowed figures doing just that. Their bodies bounded in sync with the music's pounding rhythm. Ahmod rushed over to greet me as I arrived.

"Dana," he said. "I'm so glad you came."

"It's Dawn."

"Yeah, that's right. Forgive me, Sis. I'm bad with names but I'd never forget that face," he said as he took my hand and pressed it to his lips. His stare was intense. An involuntary little spark zipped across my chest and my ears felt hot as I was thinking, *Or that booty*. I almost said it out loud, but a bashful little thank-you smile was all I could manage. He kept possession of my hand as he led me in. "You look nice," he said. Again, I smiled in reply as I thought about all it took to accomplish looking "nice."

I had used every tool in my arsenal to perfect the disguise and pull off the daring transformation. This included but was not limited to, brow plucking, leg shaving, and hair wrapping. I went to the GrabBag boutique on 98th Street and bought an A-line mini dress that stopped halfway up my thighs. It was mauve velvet and extremely low cut. I also got a push-up bra because what's a low-cut dress without one? A pair of sparkly silver tights to go with my platform shoes finished off the look. The entire ensemble cost me more than a week's salary. Looking in the mirror, I put in my little glass contacts, meticulously applied my eye makeup, pushed my hair into an upsweep, and put on my dangling hoop earrings. I was set.

Just before I turned away from the mirror, my inner Duckling loomed. My heart jumped at the sight of that hideous hybrid, that unnatural entity—part creature, part me . . . yes me. It glared. I was horrified when I realized that it was true. It actually had my eyes. With dull midnight feathers in a constant state of ruffled, it puffed itself up and spread satanic pterodactyl wings and bared its fanged teeth—its rendition of a grin, I think. Then it flickered and flashed across my face and was gone. It took a while before I was able to slow my breathing and calm my heart. I lifted my chin, pulled in a hard wheezy breath. Refusing to engage, I dismissed it . . . no Ugly Black Duckling tonight.

"Make yourself at home, Sis."

"Thanks, *Bro*."

"I'm sorry . . . Dawn. What can I get you to drink, Dawn? If you like the hard stuff, there's my famous Ahmod's secret punch. The secret is that folks are free to add any hard liquor they want as long as they don't mix in wine. That could be deadly. Needless to say, it does pack quite a punch."

I looked over to see someone pouring something into the punch bowl. "I'll take wine, if you have."

"Oh yeah, I have." He went in pursuit of my wine as I looked around. Lee and Jamal were away for the weekend so I was happy to spot Ralfie and Chandra's familiar faces standing by the wall across the room.

"Hey guys." We greeted one another with our usual hugs and cheek kisses.

"You look great," Chandra said.

"So do you."

"Hey, doesn't anyone think *I* look great?" Ralfie said, and we laughed.

Ahmod returned with a lit joint and a large paper cup filled to the brim with Catawba wine. He offered the joint to Ralfie who waved it away, but Chandra reached for it and took a deep drag before passing it to me. I had only smoked grass with Danny. The distinct aroma of the burning herb sent my mind tumbling into his murky world, into his arms.

"Dawn?" Chandra said. "You want some of this?"

Ahmod looked at me expectantly.

"Maybe later," I said.

Ahmod took my hand and led me to the sofa. Its occupants promptly vacated to make space for us to sit. The music was loud. Still holding my hand, Ahmod leaned in to whisper in my ear.

"So, tell me about yourself," he said. "You've lived here for a while, right?"

"Since they opened the new units."

"Damn! You been here all this time. Why haven't I noticed you before?" I was thinking: *That was the pre-disguise era.* I just smiled and shrugged. "Well," he said. "I'd like to get to know you, make up for lost time." His eyes were on my breasts. *Why should it offend me?* I thought. *It's the reason I pushed them up there in the first place, isn't it?* My head was working overtime. Ahmod James was one of the most desirable guys on campus. He was smart and powerful and fine. And he was sitting here whispering in *my* ear. Still, I was having trouble figuring out *who is who, what is so,* and *what is not so.* And why should I have cared anyway? What did it matter?

I felt a rush of air as the door opened and Danny walked in. He stood for a while scanning the room. His eyes rested on Ahmod and me but only for a moment. He seemed to be looking for someone. Across the room a girl raised her hand, signaling to him. I recognized her from the takeover. Her name was Angel.

She was one of those sisters who didn't use a disguise. She was a natural beauty. She wore her beauty confidently. It was a cloak that wrapped around her and draped carelessly off her shoulders. Her tan skin was smooth and glowing, her large eyes cleverly unadorned. She was tall. The silky loose garment she wore flowed over her breast, offering just a glimpse of their fullness; it teased as it cascaded around her hips. The promise of a tight, shapely body hinted with every graceful move she made. Angel seemed a fitting name for her because her Afro—Momma would call it "that good hair"— flared out like a halo, light and airy around her head.

She was with Danny. I was with Ahmod. It made me sad. But I was determined not to sit there and slip into a deep green grief that everyone around me would easily see on my face and pity me. Instead, I regarded her with a detached clinical interest. She would be the subject of my next case study. I tucked the lessons that she taught away in the back of my mind. I would dissect and catalog them later. Spotting her, Danny smiled that smile, and headed in *her* direction.

I took the joint from Ahmod's hand and inhaled its magic deep into my lungs. It was powerful and, right away, my head felt like it had lifted off my shoulders. I took a gulp of the wine and passed the cup to Ralfie. I turned and smiled at Ahmod, who smiled back at me—a hungry smile. My hand was captured in his as he led me to the dance floor. He pulled me in close, both of his arms around my waist, my arms around his neck as he sang, channeling sensuous lyrics into my ear, urging me to light his fire. His voice was deep and husky. I looked up into his eyes. His lips came down on mine. He was a good kisser, and I could feel my own fire being lit.

Suddenly Chandra was by my side. Her eyes were glassy, and she slurred her words when she spoke. "Sorry but can you come with me to the bathroom? It's my damned bra strap again." It seemed a strange request, in the middle of a dance.

"I was wrong," she said once we were in the bathroom.

"What?"

"I was wrong. We all were. I can see that now."

"Chandra, you're not making any sense. Wrong about what?"

"About running interference, you know, between you and Danny."

"Wha?"

"You guys had something. And you still have something. Anyone with eyes can see it. But you'll never know what it could be if you don't deal with it, see it through. You guys have to talk, see if there's anything there. You don't just give up and walk away because of one mistake. You fight."

"Chandra, where is all this coming from?" I asked, momentarily entertaining the terrifying notion that The Duckling had somehow invaded *her* head as well.

"I'm gonna do it. I'm gonna fight. I just want to let you know up front. I intend to fight."

Satisfied that there had been no Duckling cross contamination, I was at a complete loss. I had no idea what she was talking about. I just assumed she was high and a little outside of herself. "Is this about Ralfie?" I asked.

"Ralfie? He doesn't even know I'm a female. I'm his 'good buddy.' I'm pretty sure he's hung up on someone who doesn't even know he's a male. You . . . He's hung up on you."

"Me? What are you talking about? Ralfie and I are just friends."

"Yeah, he and I are just friends too. That's the problem. It's always like that, isn't it?"

"Chandra I . . . "

"I dunno if you're into him, like secretly or something. I can't be thinking about whether or not you're into him. I just know that you're my friend, so I want to tell you up front that I'm going for it. I'm gonna fight. I'm gonna tell him how I feel," she said as she began to cry.

I pulled her in, held her until she had cried her fill. I was confused, but I brushed it aside. Clearly, it was the pot and booze talking. "I would say you should go up to my room and sleep it off but it's Luanne's night. She has company," I said. "I'm supposed to stay at Lee's tonight. They're away on another one of their scuba diving trips. I have the key if you want. We can figure something out."

"No, that's okay. Ralfie will drive me home. You know how he is, everybody's best friend. I'm jus' sayin' fight for what you want, or you'll never know if you could've won."

Ralfie was waiting as we exited the bathroom. "Everything okay?" he asked.

"Yeah, but I think you should take her home."

"Fight!" she called to me as they left.

I returned to find Ahmod awaiting me with a glass pipe and a shot cup in his hand. There was something brown and sticky-looking in the pipe. He lit it and handed it to me. The smell was sickly sweet and spicy.

"What is it?"

"Hashish."

"I don't do drugs. I mean, grass is my limit."

"But this *is* grass. It's just a more concentrated form of cannabis."

"Cannabis?"

He smiled. He had a nice smile. "It's the name of the plant that you've been smoking; grass is cannabis. It's not habit forming. It's not like you'll get hooked or anything like that. Trust me. It'll just send you a little further into your head. Don't you want to know what's in there?"

I sat there trying to decide whether or not I dared to explore what was inside my head. I didn't have to look up to know that those wolf eyes were watching me. I could feel it. But I did look up. I looked up to see that Angel was sitting on Danny's lap. She placed her hand on the side of his face, bringing his gaze back to her. Then she looked at me and smiled.

I took the pipe from Ahmod and puffed as he lit it, releasing the intoxicating fumes. The fumes traveled through my mouth and nose, up into my head, then down again past my chest and lungs, stopped to caress my heart and continued downward. The fumes settled somewhere between my legs where they rippled and tickled and made me laugh out loud. Ahmod let out a little chuckle of his own before his mouth was on mine, stifling my laughs. Then his tongue was in my mouth. He tasted delicious and I wanted more. He broke off the kiss and encouraged me to drink from the little cup. I took a sip. It was strong but it was sweet, and I thought that maybe I liked it. I drank some more. Ahmod stood and took my hand. Yes, I did want to dance. Standing up was a ripple-like experience. Everything was moving in billows and waves. The music pulsed through me. The music and I were one and the same. I was a beautiful sound wave. I could float on the air or travel through any conductor that caught my fancy. I wanted to dance and to twirl and to fly through my waves. Instead, I staggered and stumbled awkwardly. Ahmod caught me, stabilized me so I wouldn't fall.

"I had my bed moved next door so there'd be room to dance. I think I should take you there—next door. Maybe you should lie down a bit."

"No, Ahmod," I slurred. "I don't wanna lie down. I wanna dance. Let's dance!" I stumbled again.

"It's okay, Sis. We can dance later. Don't worry. I won't leave you alone. I'll be right there lying down with you."

"No, Ahmod, I wanna dance."

"We'll lie down together. It'll feel so good. I can make you feel so good." He was leading me to the door, pulling me.

"No. I don't want to. Ahmod, no!" Then I heard a thud. Actually, I felt the thud. Angel was on the floor. Danny was by my side.

"Yo dude, she said no."

Ahmod looked confused. I looked confused.

"You said she was just a friend." Ahmod's words tripped a memory. *Yes, I heard him. That **is** what he said. It made me so sad.*

"She *is* a friend. Friends don't let shit like this happen to friends."

Danny's my friend! I love that shit! It's so nice to have friends!

"I don't get it, man. You told me to go for it."

"Not like this."

That's right! Regular dancing. No horizontal mambo!

"Aren't you the one who told me she wasn't your type. Like you didn't give a damn about her one way or the other?"

"Yeah man, I said all that. I guess I lied," he said with a shrug, his eyes intense, his tone deadly.

He lied! He's a fucking liar! This is so great!

Danny scooped me up into his arms and headed for the door. I looked over at Angel who was still on the floor looking flabbergasted. I heard Chandra's voice in my head, "fight!" Possessively, I placed my hand on the side of Danny's face and smiled at her.

The Gremlin

It was 7:00 a.m. We were sitting in the park waiting for the sun to rise, listening to "Here Comes the Sun." He was holding my hand. Everything was back to normal, our version of normal.

It had been months since the night of Ahmod's party, but we never discussed any of it. We never talked about why he said those hurtful things about me to Ahmod. He never apologized, not with words. We never talked about that night at the party. Why did he stop Ahmod? Was it because he loved me? He did love me, didn't he? I guess I just had to accept that he was the kind of guy who could only show love with actions.

So, we made love. He had rocked my world almost every night since the party. For a while, I was practically living in his room. But I was missing too many classes, smoking too much pot. My grades were suffering. I was beginning to think that I should be sleeping in my own room, at least on weekdays.

293

And there was that other reason that I wanted to sleep in my own room. The constant, coded knocking on the door was disturbing. The handshakes that passed subversive substances back and forth worked on my last nerve. I had come to accept that this was not something that I should question, so I didn't. I calmed my nerves with the thought that dealing a little pot didn't make him a drug dealer, not really. On the nights when he conducted business, I'd busy myself with his record collection.

And on occasion when his eyes drifted away, and for no reason that I ever understood he retreated to his roommate's bed, I'd nudge my way in with him and hold tight. And he'd let me.

Although I was pleased with our new rhythm, I knew I needed to spend more time in my own space.

"Danny," I said with my head resting on his shoulder as we waited for the sun to appear. "I'm thinking about going back to my own room." I felt him tense. "At least on weekdays."

"Why?"

"You know," I said. I straightened up, slipped my hand from his. "My schoolwork is falling off. I need to turn in a first draft and I'm nowhere near finished," I said, wishing for the sun to appear and save me from having to say anymore.

"So that's it, your schoolwork? You can't do that in my room?"

A small wheeze escaped my chest as I realized that I had to tell him the rest. "Well, not that I'm judging, but I'm, like, not really comfortable when you're busy with customers."

"Oh, so it's my little enterprise that's bugging you, huh? Are you sure? Are you sure it's not that you want to do some entertaining of your own, in your own room? Maybe invite Ahmod?"

And there it was, the little green-eyed gremlin that had only shown itself once before. I couldn't believe Danny Barrett was insecure, unsure of *me*. It was sweet, endearing and . . . slightly unsettling. Maybe he had his own version of a duckling. Maybe everyone did.

So, there we were, sitting in our spot in the park waiting for the sun that was obviously late. I slipped my hand back into his, rested my head on his shoulder. I was overwhelmed with affection for him. I never wanted to be the source of his angst. I knew very well how that felt. I didn't want him to suffer the maybes. I placed my free hand on the side of his face, turned him towards me, and kissed those lips—a warm, reassuring kiss.

"If you want me to stay," I said. "I guess I can manage to work in your room."

Love?

I was deeply, hopelessly in love with Danny. But aside from knowing that he wanted to keep me in his room, close to him, I had no idea how he felt. Was that love? I wanted to tell him. I wanted to say "Danny, I love you." I needed to hear him say those words to me as well.

That evening in his room, I was determined to tell him how I felt. I was sure that he loved me. I was sure he'd tell me.

I was sitting at his desk, typing on the electric typewriter that I had signed out of the student resources office. I needed to get some chapters done before he touched me. He was playing his music. It was loud and I was having trouble concentrating. Then he came for me, placed his hot hands on my shoulders and all concerns about schoolwork melted away.

In accordance with our ritual, I sequestered myself in the bathroom and inserted the diaphragm. We made love, showered, and lay on his bed in each other's arms. Smokey Robinson was singing his song, "You've Really Got a Hold on Me."

I snuggled into his armpit, my head on his chest, listening to his heartbeat. Breathing easy, I inhaled him. I looked up. He looked down. He placed a gentle kiss on my lips and smiled that smile.

The words, "Danny, I love you," had gotten lost on the way to my mouth. I couldn't force them out. Desperate, I turned to the record collection. I placed the forty-five on the player and scrambled back into his arms. The record dropped, the mechanical arm placed the needle in the groove and Billy Steward's mellow song, "I Do Love You" rang out. I felt Danny cringe. It was not the reaction I was hoping for. Then he turned to face me, his eyes searching, his lips so close to mine.

"Danny, I think I love you." The reticent words eased themselves out on an exhaled breath. They emerged low and husky. He just stared. My heart slowed to half time as it counted off the seconds of silence that became minutes of silence and what seemed like hours of silence.

Just when I was sure that he had no intention of saying anything at all, he turned away from me and said, "I never did get to tell you why the martial arts training was the un-doing, you know, of my family." He was changing the sub-ject, substituting something that he knew I wanted to hear for something else that he knew I wanted to hear.

I said nothing.

He got up, lit a joint, went to Raymond's bed and as-sumed the position—knees bent, back against the wall, empty eyes staring straight ahead. I stayed put. The last record on the stereo dropped and silence broke out, giving him space to speak. He took a toke on the joint, its embers flaring amber in the murky space. Smoke rose from his mouth and nose and vanished into the shadows. I waited.

"There was this day," he said. "I think I must've been, like, sixteen—that would make Tommy eighteen. Tommy and I had competed in a tournament. Actually, it was a tournament and a show, you know, for the parents, to show them what they were paying their money for. Anyway, Tommy took first place in karate. I came in third in judo. We both got trophies. All the way home Dad was going on about how proud he was . . . of Tommy. I was nervous, you know, when he said nothing about me. I didn't know what to expect, but I knew it wasn't going to be good. When we got home my mother had the table set for dinner. Tommy and I ran to show her our trophies while Dad inspected the table setting. We knew that one of his moods was coming on. Tommy was going on about getting first place. I didn't really say anything 'cause I could feel Dad staring at me. My mother kissed Tommy on the forehead and said she was proud of him. Then she hesitated for a while before she kissed my forehead and said she was proud of me too. Dad went crazy. He attacked her, backhanded her across the face. I remember seeing the look in her eyes—hurt and surprise. Hurt and surprise? Really? Like that was not who he was, not what he did; like she expected some sanity from him? Blood was running from her nose, from her mouth. I guess that's when I went crazy too. I grabbed him and flipped him clear across the room. It's funny because I was thinking that it was a perfectly executed judo move and he should've been proud. He wasn't. I think he was more shocked than anything else. But then he was mad, really mad." Danny paused, took a drag on the joint. "It was in that moment I decided I was never going to take another beating from him. He came at me again. I used his momentum to send him flying just the way I was taught. Then he grabbed a carving knife from the table and charged at me. There was this rage in his eyes. I thought I was going to die. That's when Tommy flew across the room and delivered a textbook flying side kick." He paused, staring into the darkness before he sighed and went on, "Caught him in the lower back. I still remember that sound this, like, sick cracking thud. And Dad went down like a rock." He paused again, took a breath, a drag, and started to say something but stopped. After a painful silence, he finally said, "I kicked him." He took another deep drag on the joint and slowly released the smoke that veiled his face, drifted upward, and disappeared. "He was down on the floor, and I kicked him." His voice was low and intense. "I kicked and kicked and kicked." He heaved a breath. I thought I heard a quiver in his voice. "I was kicking, kicking and screaming. I kicked him in his head, in his face, in his stomach; I couldn't stop. If Tommy and my mother hadn't pulled me off, I might still be kicking." He swung his feet off the bed and began rolling another joint. "His spine was severed," he said.

I was speechless. What could I possibly say?

"Dad told the people in the emergency room that he slipped in the bathroom and fell on the sharp edge of the vanity. These people knew us. They were the same people who repeatedly stitched me, Mom, and Tommy up when we suffered our various inexplicable mishaps. They dealt with the situation just like they always did in the past. They didn't ask many questions. The weird thing was that if it wasn't for his 'accident,' they would never have diagnosed that he had this heart condition, had it all along." Letting out a little humorless chuckle he said, "I just always thought that his heart was missing altogether." He pulled on the joint. "So later, Dad told us that he lied to the authorities about what happened to protect his family. He said that he had to protect us because he loved us, that he would always protect us. Love. Funny, it's what he always said to Mom too, after he betrayed her time and time again with other women, after he almost beat her into unconsciousness. It's what he would say to convince her to stay. It always worked. Those magic words. 'Oh, baby I love you.' He was so full of shit, you know. He'd use love to manipulate her, to get her to stay with him. He threatened her with losing her kids. Love again. He knew she loved her kids. I think she was so afraid of not having that love that she'd put up with anything he dished out.

"So anyway, that's how the martial arts were our undoing. After that, we were never a family. Not like before. We were un-did. Tommy enlisted. Like I told you, he's in 'Nam. I spent all of my time at school or at the center. Then I found out about SEEK and moved into the dorms."

I wanted to know what happened with his parents but couldn't find the words to ask. "My dad is paralyzed from the waist down," he said, answering the question I never posed. "He still tries to be a tyrant, but now he's just a paper tiger. I'd like to think that my mom would slap him around now and then. But I know she'd never do that. She loves him." Sarcasm dripped off those last three words. "I think my mom got the worst of it, you know. She refuses to put him in a home. She has to put up with him all day. She's more a slave to him now than she was before. His heart medications are costly. So, she can't even afford to hire help or even to put him in one of those daycare facilities where they take him for a few hours during the day so she can get a break. That's why I have to . . . " He stopped short, pulled on the joint, and said, "I send her money, you know, to help out."

I did know. I hadn't known before, but I knew then. I understood so much more about what was going on with him. On some level, I wanted to push my way into bed with him, but I also knew—sensed—that he would not be receptive.

Embedded somewhere in his story there was a touch of rejection . . . again. So, my instinct was to pick myself up and leave, walk away, back to my own room, to my own life. But that instinct faltered. I knew, then, that Danny didn't believe in love. Danny would never love me. Maybe he would never love anyone. Maybe I could just love him . . . Maybe he would let me.

I also knew I couldn't leave, not after what he just shared; how could I? Instead, I lay there staring at the psychedelic posters on the ceiling, feeling conflicted . . . and lonely.

Getting to the point

I was in Danny's room, staring into the mirror that was mounted over the bathroom sink. The sound of Smokey's "You've Really Got a Hold on Me" filled the airways in the room beyond the closed bathroom door. He was out there waiting for me. It was our routine.

"Are you sure?" he had asked. "'Cause I have rubbers." It's what he always asked.

I used to wonder why because he would know if the diaphragm wasn't in place. He could feel it, he'd said as much. He mentioned it that first time. He said it was fine, no big deal. Still, it always made me sad, another barrier between us.

"Danny, I'm sure." That's what I always said—every time. It was our diaphragm mantra.

But standing there in the bathroom, I couldn't steady my quaking hands. My mind was rambling through thoughts, through impulses—my heart gearing up for a run. I couldn't slow it down. And there was that Ugly Black Duckling. It was in the mirror staring back at me. I tried to dismiss it, tried not to engage, but it wouldn't be denied, not that time. It stood its ground. Speaking aloud for the first time, it had found its hideous voice. It was not merely sending thoughts into my mind. No. Instead of a silent, mocking stare, for the first time it croaked actual words at me.

"Do it! Do it!" Duckling egged me on.

I wheezed and closed the toilet lid. I sat, placed my head in my hands, and tried to think. How long had it been since I understood that Danny didn't believe in love? How long since that night when Danny told me about the martial arts, about how it undid his family? It seemed like years.

That was the night that something changed. It was a subtle shift at first, barely perceptible.

"You know," he had said as casually as he could manage. "Maybe you *do* need to spend more time in your own room." My breath hitched in my chest. It was what I needed. It was not what I wanted, not anymore. I wanted to stay right there. Like a satellite, I wanted to orbit in Danny's universe. I wanted to breathe deep fulfilling breaths flavored with essence of Danny and Lifebuoy soap.

But as time passed, it became clear. He was drifting away from me, or more like he was shedding me, ever so gradually, one piece at a time. Our early mornings in the park became fewer and fewer until they stopped altogether. He said that he was up late doing "business" and needed his rest. I started spending more nights in my own room. The funny thing was that instead of my schoolwork improving, it declined steadily. I couldn't concentrate, couldn't breathe when

303

I wasn't near him. I spent a lot of time forcing myself to inhale and exhale.

Then the change between us went from gradual to abrupt. After a while, instead of me just assuming that we'd spend time together, I sensed that I needed to wait until I was invited. Things were different, awkward. I'd been burned before when I showed up uninvited. I didn't want to show up to find the unthinkable. So, I didn't allow myself to think it.

Then there was that day. The African dance class had just let out. The lobby was bustling with the dancers and the students who normally hung out there. It was not unusual for Danny to meet me after the class. We would get some dinner and go back to his room. But that too, had changed. So, I was pleasantly surprised when I saw him there waiting for me. Or at least I assumed he was waiting for me.

I walked over to him "Hi," I said. "Give me a minute to change and we can go to Victor's, my treat." As I followed his gaze, I hastened to add, "That is, if you like."

Across the room, he and Angel were locked in a stare that was so intimate it seemed obscene right out there in public. The lobby was hot and stuffy, but I felt like an ice cube had been slipped down my back.

"Can't tonight," he said. "I've got something I need to do."

Or someone you need to do.

In that moment my inner gypsy flashed. The impulse to turn on my heels, hold my head high, walk away and never look back, flared . . . and petered out. I couldn't connect with my inner survivor. It was something I should've had, something I think I used to have, but I couldn't tap into it. Or maybe I had. Maybe Danny *was* survival. Maybe the only way I could ever survive would be in his arms. Maybe I would never find a way to breathe freely without him.

So, I ignored that prideful Outside Me when she appeared, reaching out with her pale-yellow hand to lead me away. I ignored the pity in her eyes as I refused her guidance. I was willing, then, to get in line and vie for my share of his time, his affections. After all, there was nothing that proclaimed we were an "us." There was no glue. We needed to be an "us."

Just because you screwed someone doesn't mean he's yours. He never said he loved you. The Duckling's voice was in my brain, grating on my ears. That was when a realization, an idea, hit me like a slap upside my head. I could sense The Duckling. It was smiling.

"That's okay," I said to Danny, suppressing the quiver in my voice. "Can we do it tomorrow?" His attention was elsewhere. "Danny? Tomorrow?"

"Yeah, yeah, tomorrow."

Tomorrow morphed into the next day . . . . that decisive day. And there I was, sitting on the toilet's closed lid in his bathroom with my head in my trembling hands, listening to that damned duckling squawking in the mirror. *"Do it! Do it!"*

Then The Duckling fell silent and Outside Me appeared. I was so relieved to see her. She was the light-skinned "me" who guarded my survival, kept things from spinning out of control, helped me to banish The Duckling. The "me" that always took my hand and led me away from danger. Although she wasn't perfect, wasn't always reliable, at least she never suffered the maybes. She'd decide what needed doing and wasn't afraid to do it. I watched her. Her hands were trembling, her eyes were sad. She went into my bag and took out the diaphragm. She held it up to the light. It was sound, flawless. Then she took a needle from my bag. I had no idea how it got there.

And Momma's voice broke the silence. I think she was trying to warn me. But her voice sounded so far away. I could barely hear her, something about a man's heart and his stomach and the only way. Then Momma was gone. Outside Me raised the needle to the diaphragm. She hesitated, looked at me, seeking permission. I just stared.

The Duckling shrieked, *"Do it! Do it!"* And she did; she did it. She jabbed the sharp point right through the very middle of the diaphragm. I felt it. I winced as the needle violated the smooth rubber surface. The tiny pop echoed and bounced, shimmied across the walls, the floor, the ceiling.

Once the deed was done, I never wanted to see that Outside Me, that red-boned me, again.

PART TWO

Growing Home

Finally, the living room in my little apartment is truly a sitting room. There's actually a place to sit. I've put some of the Maryann Porter money to good use. I went to Piser's discount furniture store and bought a futon. Yesterday, I called Maryann to thank her, but they told me that she doesn't work there anymore. The man who answered her extension wanted to know my name. I told him that I was Maryann's cousin and that I'd call her at home. Then I hung up. Strange, I kind-of wish I *could* call her at home. I wish I knew how to contact her. Not that I want anything from her. I just want to know that she's okay, like, not in jail. I think we could've been friends.

I am sitting on my futon, my hands resting on my belly as I look around the room. There is music coming from the small speakers attached to my record player that is no longer on the floor. It sits on one of two end tables that I got secondhand and refinished myself—that is, with the help of my friend Eli who owns the hardware store. Actually, Eli helped me redo both the end tables and the little coffee table that stands on the throw rug in front of the futon. His wife Natasha helped me pick out curtains. It's like they've adopted me, and I've adopted them.

I'm thinking about what's needed to finish off my living room. There are these beanbags that I've had my eye on for a while and this cool lamp that would float over the futon on a long arching pole. And maybe a plant—a snake plant—they don't need much light. I think that's all I would need to complete the living room. The bedroom will take some time.

I've retired the gumbo pot because the leak in the roof has actually been patched. The lighting on the staircase has been repaired. And there are men in the hall working to wash away the smoky stench that always spirals me back to Momma's house. All of these things have happened. All of these things are good.

But this is not a home.

This morning I walked through the rooms listening. I sauntered through the bedroom, the living room, the kitchen, and up and down the long narrow hallway . . . nothing. There is no song. Despite all that I've done to make this a home, it doesn't sing to me, not like Momma's house did. It's because there is no duet . . . not yet.

I still can't breathe easy here, despite the qigong classes down in the village that Lee drags me to. Actually, I have come to enjoy going there to hang out with Lee's artsy friends, all of whom apparently need to be the masters of their own minds, as well. We're all practicing qigong, learning to breathe together. I am not alone.

The mechanical arm of my stereo jerks into position and drops another forty-five into place. The harmonious sound of four male voices takes to the air. I place my hands on my belly and wait. I croon my rendition of the song, swaying to the melody,

Like a flower growing in the heat of a summer day . . . It's thriving

It's a little more than just a rumbling, a little less than protruding limbs expanding my rib cage, but it's there and it's real. Even Max said so. The baby is moving and it's not in my mind. I get up and put the song on repeat. I'm about to go into the kitchen and prepare some lunch when the phone rings. It's Danny.

"So, about that doctor's appointment tonight," he says. I wait to hear him say that he can't make it . . . again. "I can meet you there or I can swing by the apartment, and we can take a cab together."

"That sounds good," I say, trying to sound casual, to catch my breath as his words settle in. Danny's actually coming here. He's actually going to the doctor with me.

"Which one?"

"Whatever you think is most convenient."

"I'll be at the . . . your place at six."

I call Ralfie to tell him, "Danny called. He's coming here! We're going to take a cab. So I don't need a ride."

"Oh that's . . . that's great," he says. Something in his tone is off.

"Ralfie, I can't tell you how much I appreciate your friendship. I really love you for all you do for me."

"Hey, that's what friends are for. I'll call you tomorrow." He hangs up before I get to say goodbye.

I call Lee next and tell her how excited I am that Danny is coming to the doctor's appointment with me. I tell her that she is wrong, that Danny does love me, and we are going to be together, that this is just the beginning. I communicate all this to her, only without words. I'm sure she hears it in my tone. I don't need to gloat.

The doorbell rings. It's exactly six o'clock. Punctuality is something I have yet to master but Danny is always on time. I'm feeling a little anxious because this is the first time he's been here. I realize that it's been quite a while since I've seen him. He walks down the hall into the living room and looks around. The smell of Life Buoy soap follows him in. His presence fills up the space, making it feel much smaller. I don't know if I am supposed to greet him with a hug, a kiss, or a handshake. We end up doing an awkward hug-shake thing. I'm surprised to see that he seems just as nervous as I am.

"Nice place." And I'm thinking, *This can be our place. We can be like Momma and Papa. You only need to want it.*

"Thanks, have a seat," I say. "Can I get you something? A soda?"

"You did this all by yourself?"

"Well yeah . . . with a little help from my friends."

"You really do like the Beatles."

"Just that song." He smiles. And I smile. And we both relax a bit.

We are silent in the cab on the way to Max's. I'm trying to think of something to say, some conversation that would be easy and normal. But there has not been much about our relationship that has ever been easy or normal. This is the first time we've been in a cab together since the night of the King riots a little over three years ago. For me, that night will forever be etched in my mind. And I wonder if he is also remembering that night.

Bad Blood

We walk into Max's office. With Danny at my side, I'm feeling less like a duckling and more like a peacock. I beam at Nurse Smith. "This is Danny," I say to her. "He's my . . . the baby's father."

Danny nods.

"Mister . . ?"

"Barrett," he says.

"Yes. You can wait out here, Mr. Barrett."

Max enters the office. Acknowledging me with a curt nod, he continues into the examining room. His back is turned to me as I enter. Nurse Smith prepares to draw blood. Max won't be doing an internal today. He did that last week. He only does that once a month. Today is just taking blood and checking antibodies.

"I'm concerned about the level of your antibodies," he says.

"Hello Max," I say.

"Oh yes, hello. So, about the antibodies," he says, not looking at me, plunging ahead. Then he stops, finds my eyes. His face relaxes. "Hello Dawn," he says again.

It's been like this with us ever since the Lee debacle. It takes a moment for us to fold into our old rhythm. I've apologized profusely. Max had almost become like a godfather to me. I don't think he's still mad. No. It's more like he's hurt. We both are. Ralfie says things will be back to normal eventually. I hope it happens soon. I miss the Max who used to look at me with fatherly concern and laugh at my corny jokes. I miss how he'd talk sense to me when thoughts of a phantom baby plagued my mind. I miss our talks.

"Is that your young man out in the waiting room? You might want to have him join us. This concerns his child as well." A shot of angst runs through me. Something's wrong. Danny enters the room and nurse Smith shows him to a seat.

"I was just explaining to Dawn that I have some concerns about the levels of antibodies in her blood. I'm sure she's told you about the issues involved because her blood is Rh negative."

Danny and I just look at each other. Talking about the pregnancy would be something that regular couples do. We haven't gotten there yet.

"What about them . . . my antibodies?" I ask.

"The levels are higher than expected. Usually in a first pregnancy the body doesn't have enough time to produce sufficient antibodies to do any harm to the fetus. The body then continues to build antibodies after the birth. It's usually the second pregnancy that we have to worry about."

"But . . ?"

"But your levels are slightly higher than expected at this stage."

"Oh," I say, thinking that I haven't been meditating long enough or hard enough to keep my baby safe.

"So, what does this mean? You know, for the baby?" Danny's voice, spoken here in Max's office, sounds so out of place.

"Well, it depends on a few variables. For now, I think it's safe to continue to monitor the situation. Sometimes the rate of progression will slow. On rare occasions it doesn't."

"Then what?" Danny asks.

"Then, depending on how far along she is and how big the baby is, we may have to induce and deliver the child early."

"Induce?" I hear myself say, realizing that I've said it out loud.

"Yes, give you something to bring on your contractions. That, or I would schedule a C-section."

"What's the bottom line?" Danny asks. "You know, worst case scenario."

Max takes a breath, and removing the wire framed glasses from the tip of his nose, he says, "Worst case, it could be a very sick child, perhaps even death. Best case it stays in the hospital awhile, in an incubator, and grows to be a strong, healthy human being."

A shiver is making its way down my spine. I place my head in my hands and try to shake it off. My own blood is poised to attack the baby like it's some alien invader. And all of my visualization, qigong breathing, and meditation has not put the brakes on it. A caustic voice scrapes across my brain. *What were you thinking? Did you think that you'd just effortlessly pop out a perfect healthy child?* Did I? Did I think that I could just make us a family? I look up at Danny. His expression is empty. As always when he doesn't want to be read, he cannot be read.

If the cab ride going was awkward, the return trip is stifling. The silence is throbbing. Despite the chill in the air, I roll the window all the way down. My heart is trotting and I'm having trouble catching my breath. If Danny notices, he doesn't say anything. He doesn't react at all. The cabbie drops me off at home. I exit the car and Danny continues on his way. We never speak. I try to figure out how we ended up here, in this place, unable to talk . . . unable to touch.

Going in Circles

Entering the Alamac hotel, which houses the SEEK dorms, I try not to waddle. I avoid the eyes of the Paul McCartney look-alike behind the desk. He doesn't call to me.

Lee says it's crazy that Danny and I haven't even spoken about the baby. I want to tell her that I couldn't bring myself to see him, to talk to him; that any time I thought about talking to him my hands would tremble. I'd like to say that I don't know where all this angst is coming from, that it's something I can't explain, something hiding someplace inside me. But that would be a lie. I know what it is. I know it's about guilt, about my plotting.

I had listened to that black duckling, that ugly thing.

Isn't your sister happily married? It had shot a thought at me. The shrill pitch of its horrid voice blazed across my brain, causing me to wince.

I remember considering its question. I wasn't sure about the happily part, but Sista is married, has been for several years now, no complaints. She has a family and a home and probably the music.

And what about Jackson? Remember? Didn't he marry that girl, the one who got pregnant? The Duckling shot. *Didn't she steal him from right under our nose? How else will we hold on to him?* It continued to shoot thoughts at me, suddenly using first person plural. "We," like *It* wasn't the opposition? Like "we" were one and the same, on the same side, or something?

This is the only way! The sound had screeched through my brain. *This is how it's done. Why else would he even stay with us? He is the only one. We love him. We need him. Only he can bring the music, the beauty, the breath. There is no other way.*

I believed it. I may still believe it.

And we need something in our life, a baby, a baby who will love us! It had blasted into my brain. Yes, that part was true. Of course, it made sense. My baby would love me, even if Danny couldn't. But I'm sure that I didn't do it, couldn't have made myself do it. I don't think . . . I didn't actually carry it out. I couldn't. But I was there. I didn't stop her. The Duckling . . . it issued commands, a clear threat in its voice. *Do it!* So, I let it happen.

I'm standing outside of room 416 . . . again. But this time I called ahead. I raise my hand to knock when the door swings open.

"Hey," he says.

"Hey." The room is unusually bright, almost airy. The drapes are pulled back, the window is open and there is a white bulb in the overhead light fixture. There is only a hint of pot and incense lingering in the air. I'm relieved because lately even the slightest whiff of either makes me want to hurl. I can't shake the feeling that he actually knows about the nausea, that he always seems to know what I'm thinking. He motions for me to have a seat on his bed. He sits on Raymond's bed. We are facing each other, and I feel a hint of déjà vu. He has set his face to neutral. I have no idea what he is thinking so I decide to just ask. "So, what do you think?"

"About?"

"About the situation, about the baby, about . . . me."

"I think it's a lot to think about."

I take a beat, place my hands on my belly before I say, "Don't do that." He gives me a puzzled look. "Don't give me answers that don't answer anything."

"Oh, you want answers. Well so do I."

A current zaps through my chest. My eyes are glued to the hands resting on my belly as they begin to tremble. He knows what I did! He knows just like he always knows what's in my head. I swallow hard and manage to ask, "What kind of answers?"

"Why'd you do it?"

My heart crumbles into a heap and settles, quivering somewhere down in my gut. "I didn't . . . I did . . . It wasn't me . . . You don't understand. It was for us!"

"For us? That's why you keep disappearing?"

"What? Disappearing?"

"Yeah, one minute you were here, living upstairs. That was when I agreed . . . we agreed, you needed to sleep in your own space, remember? I thought we were getting along pretty well. The next thing I know you moved out, never said a word. None of your friends would tell me anything. Even Ms. T wouldn't tell me anything. You were just gone—no address, no phone. You never showed up at school. What was I supposed to think? Then I hear rumors. You're pregnant. Rumors! That's how I found out! You never came back to tell me one way or the other. Weeks passed, maybe months. Then you showed up that day out of the blue, sat here for like two seconds and ran out of here like the place was on fire. That was the last time I heard from you until you started calling and asking me to go to the doctor with you, after all that time. By then I was at a complete loss. So you tell me what I'm supposed to think. How do I even know it's mine?" I look up. Our eyes lock. Something congeals between us, an understanding, a truth. "Okay," he says, taking a breath and turning away. "Okay, I know it's mine."

I can't reply, can't prompt any words from my mouth. My mind is filling up with fluffy white fuzz. But I know I can't let myself spin away, drift up into my head—not now, not this time. I have to hold it together . . . breathe. I have to stay right here in this room and talk to Danny. I have to do this. I drop my gaze. I'm staring at my hands. They have slipped down to my lap. My fingers are clasped so tightly together that they are beginning to throb. I never thought of it that way, the way he put it, that *I* disappeared, that *I* abandoned him. *What is so? What is not so?*

He is waiting for me to speak. The silence is growing. It's pressing down on me. I get up, go for the forty-fives. I need something to fill my wordless void. There on top of the stack is a song that can speak for me. I remove it from its jacket. I place it on the stereo. The mechanical arm jerks and the record drops. The song jumps to life. The lyrics are spinning, mirroring the fog that is swirling around in my head. A deep baritone croons . . .

I'm a whirling, whirling top.

Maybe I *am* the one who pulled away. Why *did* I do it? I needed to prepare. Things needed to be right—perfect—so he could bring the music. That's why I did it, right?

Throw me a little hope.

Something to sing to

I'm feeling woozy, all twisted around, jumbled lyrics circling in my mind. How did I end up on defense? Isn't he the one who pulled away from me just because I love him? Isn't he the one that shed me like yesterday's used paper plates? And there was Angel with her hypnotic grace and her light-skinned beauty. She was confusing him, leading him astray. He was making a mistake. He does that sometimes. Like when he withdraws to Raymond's bed. Yes, it's like that. Then I would do something. I would go to him, hold him, bring him back. It's like that. I just had to do something.

It was what I had to do

I had to bring him back. I couldn't let him slip away, drift off with someone else.

My head was in a whirlwind

321

He was making a mistake. Then she appeared, Outside Me. She allied with The Duckling, said it was the right thing, said it had to be done. She wanted to do it so . . . I let her.

"That's no kind of answer," he says, referring to the song as though, he too, is affected by lyrics rotating in my head. His voice slips into that low timbre. "It's true. You are one dizzy broad. I know that. I've always known that. Maybe that's why . . . I guess there's just something about dizzy broads."

You have me spinning and spinning
Ooh all around I go

He pauses, takes a beat. Then in a stunning roar, says, "But this, this shit is no kind of answer!" He slaps at the turntable, smacking the needle hard. I flinch, jumping as my heart flies into a gallop. The needle rips across the record, scratching and screeching into its grooves. The mechanical arm reacts, jerks up then down, swings to the left, jerks to the right and back again. Like me, it's confused—disoriented . . . and terrified. "And now a sick baby?!" His roaring hits me like a punch in the gut. "How the hell did this even happen?! You said you took care of it! You said you were sure!"

"I did! I was!" I say, my voice strained and shaky. "But The Duckling." I am grasping for words, for air. "Then that other me was there," I screech. "She always knew what was best. She always knew! I know now that I was wrong to let her do it. But I couldn't do it myself. Then I couldn't face you. That's why I stayed away, the way you always read me. I wasn't ready."

"She? She who? A duck? What the hell are you talking about?" he bellows. He is on his feet standing over me as I sit on the bed. I am fixated on his fingers as they tense and slowly curl into fists, his voice dropping another octave. My heart is in my throat, beating hard. Liquid is flooding into my ears. The baby has pulled itself into a tight, defensive ball . . . ready. I get to my feet, manage to push past him. As I rush for the door, I hear what sounds like a wolf's howl, "What the hell is wrong with yoou?!"

I don't remember how I get to Lee's house. I just know that she opens the door and I practically stumble into her arms.

"Dawn? What's happened? Are you okay?"

"Lee," I blubber. "Lee, what the hell is wrong with me?"

Then, it's like a dam inside me has failed. I'm stunned as a deluge comes gushing from my body and splashes to the floor.

323

Happy Birthday

It's a Sunday morning. I am in the Neonatal Intensive Care Unit (NICU) at Bronx Lebanon Hospital, looking into a glass incubator at the tiniest living being I've ever seen. He— a boy—is literally in his birthday suit. His eyes are taped closed and there is what looks to me like fluorescent light bathing his tiny form. The nurse said that at five pounds six ounces he's not that small and isn't technically premature. But I'm sure I could hold him in one hand if they'd actually let me hold him at all.

The hospital pediatrician, an impatient man with a puffy red face and fingers that look like sausages, tells me that the baby will need a blood exchange transfusion.

"That's when we replace all the baby's blood with better blood," he says, clearly dumbing down his words, using simple terms that he thinks I can understand.

My baby needs better blood. Even my blood has something wrong with it.

"The baby's condition is called hyperbilirubinemia," he says. Even though I have no idea what that means, I feel like someone has grabbed a hold of my stomach from the inside and is squeezing hard.

That's when I call Max. "Hello, Max, hello," I say, trying not to sound like I'm pleading.

"Hello, Dawn," he sighs.

"Max, I know you're not a pediatrician," I sob, knowing he wouldn't hang up on me. "And I know I was wrong not to trust you, but I do trust you, and I need your help, your advice." He is silent on the other end. I take a breath and continue. "Max? Are you there?"

"I'm here," he says. "Never mind all that. It's in the past. What's happened? Are you okay?"

"The baby's sick."

"What? You gave birth? When? Why wasn't I called?"

"This morning. They looked at my Medicaid card and said you weren't on call. I don't think they believed that you were really my doctor. I was in no shape to argue. Anyway, they put me out. I don't even know who delivered the baby. Forceps . . . they used forceps, Max! And now they're saying that they have to take out all the baby's blood and put in new blood, better blood."

"What! This is outrageous! Who's the doctor?"

"I don't know his name. He has a red face, doctor Redface."

"Yes, I know exactly who he is. Is there a phone in your room?"

"Yes, there's a phone on the wall. I share it with the two other women in the room."

"Okay. I'm going to make some calls. I'll take care of it. Don't worry. Stay by the phone. I'll call you back."

So, I wait. The lying clock on the wall only registers twenty minutes, but I am sure it's been hours when the phone finally rings. Max tells me that a nurse friend of his checked the chart. He says that once he questioned it, they changed the plan for treatment. There is no longer any plan to transfuse the baby with better blood. Apparently, the baby's own blood will do just fine. Max says the baby only needs to be under the lights for a few days, and then I can take him home.

The Home Coming

Ten days after I gave birth, Ralfie and I enter my apartment. I am bringing my new son Daniel home. I had called Danny several times from the hospital, but no one picked up the common phone that hangs on the wall in the fourth-floor lounge. It just rang and rang. As I make my way down the long hallway, the tiny apartment suddenly feels cavernous, empty, and so quiet. Until . . .

"Welcome home!!" A cacophony of familiar voices ring out. I look around to see the smiling, loving faces of my friends, Lee and Jamal, Eli and Natasha, Chandra, and of course Ralfie, who picked me up from the hospital. I am mobbed with hugs and kisses. Lee takes possession of Daniel, her eyes full of awe. I think I see a wisp of sadness, a longing. It momentarily shades her face like a cloud. Then, it passes over, floats away, and is gone.

The smell of roasted chicken accents the air. And there is a bassinet, it's lacy skirt sweeping the living room floor. It is filled to capacity with gifts—some wrapped, some un-wrapped.

I burst into tears and collapse onto the futon. A collective "Awww" fills the air as they all rush to me. Ralfie is the closest. He wraps his arms around me, and I weep on his shoulder. Smiling faintly, Chandra takes a step back.

Everyone waits for my tears to subside, but they keep coming. Weeping becomes sobbing, sobbing becomes whining. Except for my bawling, there is an awkward silence in the room. I go from whimpering to wailing and back again. Try as I might, I'm not able to stop my hiccupping heart-wrenching cries. Looking concerned, Lee hands Daniel to Chandra. She sits beside me and places her hand on my shoulder.

"Dawn?" I turn from Ralfie to Lee and cry even harder.

"I'm sorry. I'm so sorry," I am blubbering into Lee's chest, my tears dressing the front of her blouse. "It's hormones," I wail. "It must be hormones."

"Guys," Lee says. "I think Dawn is tired. Maybe we can celebrate another time."

The fact that I have ruined the celebration only adds fuel to my angst. What is wrong with me? I obsess over the question. What the hell is wrong with me? I continue to whimper long after everyone has left. Only Lee remains. She is in the kitchen putting the food away. She sterilizes the baby bottles and prepares the formula with Carnation evaporated milk according to the instructions they gave me in the hospital, just after they gave me that shot to stop my own milk from flowing. I wasn't sure I wanted that shot but the nurse assured me it was for the best.

"I can stay the night," Lee says. "I guess I'll just have to wear the same clothes to work tomorrow, not that anyone will notice. I'm on early shift and that temp they got to replace you is absolutely useless. The kids miss you."

"I miss them too!" I break into a fresh round of tears.

"That settles it. I'm staying the night."

"No, no. You should go home. Jamal will be waiting for you. I'm fine. It's just hormones. You've done so much already. You've set everything up for me. And look how good Daniel is. He's slept through all of this. Go home. I'm fine. I'll call you tomorrow."

As Lee leaves, I am haunted by the sound of the door as it shuts behind her. I can't shake the feeling that it sounds like the solid slam of a jail cell. Not that I've ever heard that sound — so final, so trapped.

Mini Milestones

At ten days old, Daniel looks more like a little old man than anything else. I stare down at him as he sleeps. His eyes are puffy. There are wrinkles on his forehead. He is bald and has no teeth. And his head is elongated, almost pointed. Doctor Red-face said it's because he was in the birth canal for so long. He assured me that Daniel's head would regain its intended shape in time. At least the yellow pallor that he had in the NICU has turned to a healthy, deep brown. He takes his color from me.

I almost smile but I feel another round of tears coming on. You always hear about new parents who proclaim the beauty of their child. I've been standing here just staring at Daniel, waiting for it to hit me, his beauty. So far it hasn't. I'm not sure what I feel when I look at him. I'm not sure what I'm supposed to feel.

He stirs, squirms, and fusses himself into a meow, then a whimper, then a scream. He is sounding distressed, almost desperate. Now I know exactly what I feel . . . panic.

At fourteen days old, Daniel is back in the NICU of Bronx Lebanon hospital. Three days ago, when I went to change his diaper, I thought his bowels looked a little loose. I called the hospital clinic and managed to get Doctor Red-face on the line.

"Aren't you that young girl that I discharged a couple of days ago?"

"Yeah?"

"Do you even know what baby stool is supposed to look like?

"Green water?"

"Listen, you're just a little hyper-vigilant. New moms usually are. I'm sure she's fine."

"*He*, doctor. It's a boy."

"Yeah, well boy or girl, it'll be fine." And he hung up.

Last night Daniel wailed incessantly. I tried everything. I walked the floor. I rocked him in the baby chair that Chandra bought for me. I sang every lullaby I knew and some that I didn't know. I tried giving him formula, but he wouldn't take the bottle. When I held him to my shoulder his little mouth would root around like he was seeking the breast. I regretted letting that nurse talk me into the damn shot. First thing in the morning, I call the doctor again.

"Didn't I just talk to you yesterday?" he asks.

"Yes, but the baby has diarrhea. He screamed all night."

"He was born early in the morning, right?"

"Yeah?"

"That's not unusual for morning babies. They are exhausted after birth. They sleep all that first day and are awake all night. This can become a pattern if you don't work to change it. You just need to work on breaking the pattern. This is how it works with a morning baby."

"Morning baby? But doctor . . ."

"I have to go now. I'm sure she'll, he'll be fine. Call me tomorrow if things don't improve."

I call Max.

I walk into Max's office. He takes one look at Daniel and calls for an ambulance. My heart drops straight into my stomach. It turns out that diarrhea is the biggest cause of infant mortality in this country. Daniel is badly dehydrated. Max said if I had waited one more day, I might've lost him. Then, so that I don't end up in jail for killing Doctor Red-face, Max arranges for another MD to take my case.

At twenty days old, Daniel is still in the NICU. I sit and watch as he sleeps, well, like a baby. Suddenly, I sense a presence and I look up to find Danny standing there staring at the baby. His stare is intense. I can't decide if I'm happy and relieved that he's here with me and I don't have to do this alone or pissed off that he hasn't shown up sooner. I say nothing. I turn my gaze back to Daniel. For a long while we are silent, both of us just staring at the baby.

"He's dark," I hear Danny utter.

Then, Daddy's lethal song buoys to the surface. It floats in, riding on a wave of time. *You named her Dawn. You shudda named her Midnight!* The first time Danny has laid eyes on his son and all he has to say is "he's dark?" Those words, those lyrics, should evoke in me some kind of reaction. Those words should send me spiraling back into my five-year-old life, into a home of dissonance. They should spark outrage. I should lash out. They should evoke despair. I should collapse to the floor in a sniveling heap. But I am exhausted, empty . . . numb. I have no highs, no lows, no emotions. The words wash over me and ebb away.

"His mother is dark," I say. Then I think about it, take a breath before I add, "*Your* mother is dark." The idea that these are simple facts and not comebacks or rationalizations, settles in my chest as I speak the words. He just nods almost imperceptibly, and we again fall silent, our eyes on Daniel.

"The doctor says he's going home today," Danny says, never taking his eyes off Little Daniel.

"You spoke to the doctor?"

"I'm his father." The numbness is creeping over me. I'm having trouble grasping exactly what Danny is saying, or not so much what he's saying as what he is meaning. Any anger I had because of his here-to-fore absence has resolved itself into an absolute brain haze.

"I'd like to go with you. I mean to take him home with you. If that's okay."

I can only manage a nod.

Daddy's Home

At thirty-one days old, Daniel is soundly asleep on his father's lap. Danny has come by every day since the baby was discharged from the hospital. He spends hours holding his son, just staring at him. As is our pattern, we haven't spoken about the last time we were together. There's been no mention of the "she," who is actually Outside Me, or The Duckling. There's been no explanations, no clarifications of any of the things that are clearly wrong with me. And neither The Duckling nor Outside Me have been around since then, which I think is a good thing.

Last night Danny didn't leave. He slept on the futon. It was all I could do to resist going to him and snuggling my way into his arms and letting him hold me. I wanted so much to just be held.

This evening he has come in with a small overnight bag.

"I hope this is okay," he says when he notes how I'm looking at the bag.

"Yeah, fine," is all I can manage. I am thinking maybe Danny will stay with us, make us a family, let me love him. Maybe he *can* love, at least his son, maybe even me. Maybe The Duckling was right. This was the only way. I want to applaud and cheer and do a little jig. I watch as he reaches on the wall and takes possession of the spare keys that have been hanging there on that ornate hook . . . waiting for him.

At eight weeks old, I watch as Little Daniel lifts his head, holds it steady and takes a good look around. I wonder if he knows he's home. I wonder this because he has been back to the NICU twice more. All told, he's been hospitalized three times in his short life. Each time he was dehydrated due to diarrhea. To Danny's credit, he has run to the hospital with me every time. The last time we didn't take the baby back to Bronx Lebanon. We brought him to Columbia Presbyterian instead. Max says the nursery in Bronx Lebanon is closing due to some kind of infection and this is why Daniel is so sick.

Now from little Daniel's vantage point, lying on his stomach in the small playpen that serves as his crib, I am wondering what home looks like to him. Does he know that the handsome man sitting on the futon, watching the basketball game on the little TV that he bought here for that purpose, is his father? Does he see how much smaller the place has gotten since that man removed the milk crates and replaced them with two chests of drawers and a dresser? What used to be a tiny bedroom is now a tiny dining room. Danny got rid of the single bed in the little room and replaced it with a small oval shaped table and four folding chairs. Now he and I sleep together on the futon that opens into a double bed.

And then there's that mirror. It is large and oval and framed in brass. Danny brought it here and hung it on the living room wall. I've come to think of that mirror as The Duckling's mirror—its permanent residence. In that mirror, The Duckling has re-emerged. Whenever I look into *that* mirror, The Duckling is always there silently staring back at me. *My* mirror, the full-length one that's missing a chunk from its lower left corner, still leans precariously on the wall in the little dining room. It has been spared. Danny has not gotten rid of it, at least not yet, and The Duckling has not invaded it . . . not so far, anyway. I sigh and push these thoughts from my mind.

Danny is here. He's staying with us. We're a family. It's what I've always wanted. And yes, the place has never been neater. A place for everything and everything in its place. This is a good thing. This, after all, is who Danny is. It's what I planned and plotted for, isn't it? Danny brings order, routine. He brings almost everything I have been craving. Yet, there is no music. Even though he brought a brand-new component set and put it here, even though the better part of his meticulously catalogued record collection is here, there is no music. I don't understand it. There's just this uneasy silence.

"The baby's awake," I say. "I'm going to take a shower. If he cries, be sure to check his diaper, okay?" The fact is, I hold my breath every time I check the baby's diaper, fearing the dreaded green water that will send us flying back to the hospital.

"Okay," he says, never taking his eyes off the TV screen. "Oh Dawn," he says. "Wait." He rises, goes into the other room, and comes back with the packet containing my birth control pills. Then he takes me by the hand and leads me to the kitchen, hands me a glass of water and watches until I swallow it. This is a recent new ritual. On some level, I suppose I can understand it. After all, Danny thinks that the diaphragm method failed.

On the other hand, it all seems academic because we haven't been intimate since before the baby was born. He hasn't shown any interest, which is just as well because I've been exhausted. But this *is* a hopeful ritual, I think. It speaks of steamy prospects in the future, of us being together the way we used to, maybe soon. I smile weakly and lift my face, my lips pursed. He plants a quick perfunctory peck on my mouth and turns away.

I enter the bathroom and am assailed by the smell of Life Buoy soap, a smell that used to delight me. Now I look in *my* soap dish for *my* soap. It's not there.

"Hey, Danny, did you see a bar of Dove soap I had in here?" I call from the bathroom.

"Yeah, I got rid of it."

"You what?"

"I think it just makes life simpler if we both use the same soap."

"Really? So why don't we both just use *my* soap."

"Dawn, don't be petty."

Petty? I think about that. Am I being petty? After all, it's only soap, right? And Danny replacing my crates with dressers and chests is only furniture, right? At first, I was touched, thinking he wanted to surprise me with the changes—the TV and stereo and all. It shows that he's invested, he's making this our home. But there's something about the way he does things, never consulting me. Like the time when I walked into the bedroom and found Bernadette tossed in a corner on the floor. In her place sat this big ornamental Afro-pick cast in brass—Danny's idea of art, no doubt. I didn't say anything. I just picked her up, dusted her off, consoled her, and moving Afro-Pick-Zilla to one side, I put her back in her rightful place on the dresser. Then I reminded myself to breathe.

Something here is beginning to feel different, something I can't quite put into words or even into thoughts . . . something.

I spoke to Lee about it yesterday. I held the phone between my chin and shoulder as I bathed Daniel in the kitchen sink.

"Really?" Lee had said. "The thing that bothered you most was the stuff about the doll?"

"Yeah, funny but that *is* what really bothered me. He had replaced her with this big, ugly Afro-pick. It's brass. The thing must weigh a ton."

"So did you tell him how you feel?"

"No. I just pushed that thing to the side and put Bernadette back, front and center, where she belongs. I guess he got the message because he hasn't moved her again."

"You didn't say anything, even about the furniture?"

"No. I guess it isn't so bad. Now that I think about it, it was mostly junk, just a bunch of milk crates."

"That's not the point," Lee said. "The point is that it was *your* junk. Your junk that he threw out without even asking you." I lifted a dripping Daniel out of the sink and wrapped him in a towel. I could sense Lee getting agitated on the other end of the line. She heaved a heavy sigh and said, "Remember when we talked about how Gina and Danny are the same spirit-sucking creatures?" I did remember but I didn't comment. Lee continued, "I might be overstepping here but I think you're like, I dunno, slipping away . . . again. You can't even speak up and object, tell him how you feel!? Where is the girl who survived out there on her own at sixteen years old? The girl who recognized leaving time when it came around?"

"Whoa! Slow down. Leaving time? It's not that deep. It's just little things. And think about it, he's actually taken over all the bills. I didn't ask him to do that. I guess he's really stepping up. I have no real reason to complain. I'm sure he and I will work it out . . . together."

"I hope so. I really do. But maybe you should . . . "

The memory of that conversation trails off in my mind. I find myself staring at the soap.

"No, seriously," I call to Danny from the bathroom. "Why can't you just use whatever soap you like, and I'll use whatever soap I like." Lee would be proud. I am taking a stand in what apparently is turning into the soap wars. Suddenly, Danny is in the bathroom. I'm taken aback. He towers over me, his presence filling up the space, sucking up all the air. He looks down at me and pulls me into him, roughly. I can't catch my breath. He kisses me, hard and deep. I am dazed. A sharp intake of air invades my lungs, takes me by surprise. My breaths are suddenly long, deep, and satisfying. I feel something stir, something between my legs that has been dormant for what seems like a very long time.

"Humor me," he says and walks out of the room.

Qigong

"Are you kidding me?" Lee says. "That's what he said to you? 'Humor me'?" Descending into the dank, sunless underground that is the New York City subway system, Lee and I are on our way to the breathing class down in The Village.

"Yep, that's what he said." I drop my token into the turnstile and push my way onto the subway platform. Lee does the same. The uptown train across the platform rumbles the air.

"And did you?" she asks.

'Did I . . ?'

"Humor him."

"Oh yeah, I humored him real good."

"You're unbelievable," she laughs. The train hustles into the station. We step into the car and find seats right away. It's Saturday. "So, Daniel is with Natasha?"

"Yeah. Danny was supposed to keep him, said he would take him to the zoo. Then he said something came up and he had to go. It's not like I was surprised. Danny has yet to take care of Daniel on his own. He's never even changed a diaper. I'm not sure he knows how. What does surprise me is how crazy Little Daniel is about his father. He comes alive when Danny reaches for him, has a meltdown when Danny leaves. He doesn't even do that with me."

"Damn, but Danny's flaked like this before, right?"

"Couple of times. I should've known not to rely on him. But it'll be nice taking the class without having to worry about Daniel in the center's childcare room. Some of those attendants look like they're twelve. I'm lucky Natasha was available. She's so good with him."

"Are you kidding? Natasha loves Daniel. He's like her only grandchild. I wonder why she and Eli never had any kids."

"I wonder too. But anyway, she said I should take my time. She has no plans for today, might take Daniel to the playground. She said she'll drop him home this evening."

"So Danny doesn't mind that you're going with me to qigong? I thought he didn't like the idea that I get you to come to this class with me. I'm the bad influence that makes you neglect your motherly duties, right?"

"That's not true. He never said that about you. He just thinks, I dunno, we spend too much time together or something. Which is ridiculous because Daniel is always with us."

Looking frustrated, Lee rolls her big round eyes upward, like there might be some answers floating around in the train's ceiling.

"Anyway," I say. "Danny doesn't actually know what I'm doing today. He's, ah . . . working. He'll be gone all day. So that gives us plenty of time for the class and a nice leisurely lunch."

"Do you hear yourself? You sound like some delinquent kid sneaking around to hang out with your friends." I bristle and turn away. My eyes land on a small, white man seated in the far end of the car. Apparently sensing my stare, he fends off my intrusion by slipping behind his New York Times. I turn back to Lee. I don't want to get into a throw down with her, not today. I want us to enjoy this time we have together. I don't like when she releases those words into the universe—negative words that I don't want to hear, don't want to think about.

We fall silent for a while, Lee studying her shoes, me staring at that guy's newspaper wall, the train shaking, rattling, and rolling along.

"I got into the pre-med program," Lee says matter-of-factly, as though this isn't a mind blowing, life changing revelation.

A quick jolt zaps through my chest. I take a beat and a breath before I allow myself to react. I don't want my response to sound a little green around the edges. I'm happy for Lee. I am. She's worked hard. She's earned this dream. She'll be graduating this year. I'll be lucky if I can get out next year.

"Oh my God, Lee!" I say, mustering as much enthusiasm as I can. "Why didn't you tell me?!"

"I *am* telling you."

343

"This is great, Lee!" I pull her into an embrace. "I'm so happy for you," I say. Then a question pops into my head and escapes my lips before I can stop it. "Lee," I say. "Do you ever regret it?"

"Regret . . .?" She swallows hard. Her eyes widen as they meet mine, and the realization of what I'm asking registers. She sighs as her hands slowly find their way to her chest like she's trying to hold in something that threatens to escape right through her skin.

We've never spoken about our choices—the abortion, the birth. Those subjects had somehow slipped between us into a shadowy place that neither one of us could easily access.

"No, it's not about regret," she says, choosing her words carefully. "I think it's more like a postponement than a regret. There's time, you know. Who's to say what happens, when? Life is erratic. It doesn't always conform to a timetable. I don't subscribe to first things first. Do you?"

"What, believe in first things first?"

"No. Do you regret it, you know, your choice?"

I have to take a moment before I can put together an answer. I have been thinking about this a lot lately. Regret it? No. I certainly don't regret having Daniel in my life. And Danny? We are together. It's what I wanted. But I'm not sure he loves me. And there's no music, not yet. Still, to Lee I say, "No, no regrets. It looks like we've both got what we wished for."

"Yeah, I guess," she says. "But what about *your* postponement? What about your other wish, about school? Didn't

344

you say that your playwriting professor was recommending you for that MFA program? You used to be so excited about that. And everyone knows if Professor Israel recommends you, you're in."

I had forgotten about that. I guess I put it out of my mind. Last time I even entertained the idea, The Duckling had rumbled to life, put a vice grip on my lungs and shot virtual pain through my head. But it's true. Professor Israel said that with his recommendation I was sure to get in. "That was last year," I say. "I already blew that. They won't be taking new applicants until next year."

"Perfect! Since you won't be getting *out* until next year. You should apply."

Even when Lee is being positive, she manages to get on my last nerve. "Lee . . ." I begin.

"Promise. Promise me you'll apply."

"Okay, I promise," I say, hoping that it's not a lie, hoping that somehow I'll be able to handle whatever The Duckling dishes out later.

I am in Lotus position, my feet resting on my thighs, my hands resting lightly on my knees, my forefingers touching my thumbs. My chin is tipped slightly upward. My eyes are closed. At least they are supposed to be closed. I sneak a peek at Lee who seems to be totally engulfed, her face a mask of bliss. She is so easily carried into the sifu's mellow voice. I, on the other hand, find it hard to relax, to left myself go.

"Inhale slowly. In through the nose, filling your stomach with life," he coos and I can't help thinking about the last time I had life in my stomach. "Hold," he says. "Out through the mouth. Feel the energy of the breath swoosh as you exhale. Imagine a straw from your nose to your stomach, bringing the energy of life. Relax, feel your chi."

Then Momma comes through. *Jus breathe*, she says, sounding impatient, like I should have this by now. I double my efforts to contact my chi. It must be in here someplace. I close my eyes. I let myself fall into the soft music that is tumbling lightly through the room. It is the song of the ocean and the wind, punctuated with the gentle chiming of bells.

"Let the relaxation guide your chi. Let it travel up through you," the sifu says. "Feel your toes relaxing, your feet, your ankles." I concentrate on his voice. It's becoming a melody. "The relaxation is moving through you, your calves, your thighs." Finally, I am actually feeling myself relax. I am losing myself in his hypnotic song. "Inhale," he says. "Hold, and with each exhalation release your tension. Feel your chi. Let calm and relaxation move upward through your body . . .breathe." As the relaxation eases its way into my chest, the weight of The Duckling is lifted. My lungs feel spacious as the chi, or at least I think it is the chi, rushes in. "Exhale, releasing all concerns imprisoned in your heart." As an eerie calm comes over me, it's like the maybes are turning to mist and drifting away. Now the sifu's voice seems to be coming through an echo chamber. "Inhale, let the chi flow up into your head, exhale. I am feeling the strangest sensation, like I am releasing my body, or more like my body is releasing me. "Inhale, embrace your chi, let it relax and calm your brain. Let it take you on a journey, exhale." Yes, I am so ready for a

346

journey. "Inhale, traveling, send yourself back in time or forward in time to a place real or imagined, a place of happiness. Let the chi guide you. Exhale, release all apprehensions attached to this journey."

Transported, I am sitting in Central Park with Danny. A shimmering sun is emerging through wispy clouds in a blue iridescent sky. It is rising to the music of the wind and the ocean and the tinkling bells. I lean my head on his shoulder and place my hand in his. I inhale, hold. The words "Danny, I love You" escape with the exhalation. Those words drift with the air, sway with the wind and the bells, roll with the ocean.

Suddenly, I let out a yelp. I am yanked abruptly from my trance, am tumbling back into reality. I realize that I've yelped aloud, interrupted all the cosmic travelers in the room. The sifu turns, Lee turns, they all turn and stare at me. There in my journey, Danny had squeezed my hand, had squeezed it really hard.

Momma said . . .

I turn the key, open my mighty steel door, and start down the long narrow hallway. The sound of the basketball game announces that Danny is already home. Shocked, I stop short before entering the living room. Danny is holding the baby, feeding him a bottle.

"Oh, there you are," he says. Although his words are casual, there is an undertone in his voice that causes a slight shiver to run through me. My mind flashes to the trance, to the squeezing of my hand.

"Why is Daniel here? What happened to Natasha?"

"Natasha? Oh she called a couple of hours ago, needed me to go pick Daniel up. Seems there was an emergency in the shop, something about a busted pipe. She needed to go help Eli clean up or something. Of course you would know this if you were home to get the call." And I'm wondering why *he* was home to get the call. He said he'd be gone all day. Then, with his usual mind reading skills, he says, "Yeah, I canceled everything, thought I'd come home and spend some time with you and the kid." I don't believe this for a minute. I'm sure there's something else, something he's not telling me. But I don't pursue it.

"Well, it's a good thing you were here to take the call," I say, sounding as casual as I can manage. I hang my key on the hook, walk into the little dining room, place my bag on the bureau and check that Bernadette is still seated there where she belongs. She is.

"Yeah, it's a good thing," he says. "Thing is, what if I wasn't here? What then?"

"Then Natasha would've taken Daniel with her. It might have been a little inconvenient for her but I'm sure she would've handled it." My ears are suddenly feeling hot, and a small furnace is starting up in my stomach.

"And why should some stranger be responsible for our son?!"

"Natasha? Some stranger?!" I say, feeling the gloves peeling off. "Natasha has actually known your son longer than you have! She's taken care of him; have you? She was here when I brought Daniel home from the hospital. Where were you?!"

"Dawn, let's not confuse the issues."

"No, let's. Let's confuse the hell out of them!" I say, thinking that Lee would be so proud of me. I wait for some angry, emotional come back. Instead, his face slips into cool, neutral, unreadable. There is only a slight lowering in the tone of his voice. Sweat dots my forehead and my windpipe is beginning to constrict. I push on. "I was all alone, Danny. I was scared. He screamed all night. Where were you!"

"That's not the question. Let's just deal with the here and now," he says, starting out calmly. Then, with his voice rising, "The question is: where have you been?" And finally, he bursts into a roar, "The question is: where the fuck did you go?!" Then in a sudden fit of rage, Daniel still in his arms, he stands and kicks over the little coffee table, sending the two glass ashtrays filled with joint roaches crashing to the floor, shattering into a million little slivers and shards, and stoking the furnace in my stomach.

A screech escapes me. I flinch and jump back as the furnace erupts, shoots hot liquid up into my ears. Little Daniel shrieks. The Duckling, having been disturbed, takes possession of my lungs. I bend over, trying to breathe. Fighting my fear and gasping for air, I stumble towards Danny. I repossess the baby, pull him into me and back away, both of us near hysterics. I try to sooth Daniel, knowing I need to calm myself for his sake.

Danny closes in and reaches for me. I wince and try to duck away. "Don't touch me!" I protest, but he puts his arms around us anyway and pulls us in. I struggle for release, but he holds fast. Suddenly I'm exhausted. I find myself sobbing into his chest, sniffling, and breathing, entrapped in his embrace. Then, when I am all cried out, he releases me. He takes Daniel and places him in his playpen. Daniel is surprisingly quiet. He sits up, eyes large, watching.

Danny returns to me. I back away. "Don't touch me," I say again, a low, deadly, hiss in my voice.

"Okay, I won't touch you," he says, lifting both hands in resignation. "I'm sorry. I get a little agitated, you know. I didn't know where you were. I was worried. Can we just sit down?" It strikes me how quickly his demeanor can flip. He reaches for my hand. I pull away. He motions towards the futon. I seat myself on the furthest end, which is not very far on this little futon. "I'm sorry," he says again. "I didn't know you were going anywhere." Then he waits and I feel compelled to tell him.

"I went down to the Village with Lee, you know, to the qigong class," I say, sniffling, trying to regulate my breathing.

"Oh," he says, looking pensive. "So did your friend Ralfie go too?"

"What?! Ralfie?"

"It's just a question."

"No," I say. He waits for me to say more. "It's just an answer," I say.

He shakes his head and smiles that smile. Suddenly sober, he says, "I didn't know." It's an abrupt change of subject but I know exactly what he's talking about. "I never got a message. If your roommate knew, she never told me. No one told me. It wasn't until I got a call from that guy, your good friend Ralfie. He told me you had given birth and that the baby was in the hospital." I nod, knowing this is true, remembering how happy and relieved I was when he did finally show up. And we are silent for a long while before he says, "You didn't tell me that you were going to that class with Lee."

"I didn't know I had to tell you where I'm going. I mean, especially when you weren't going to be here anyway."

"That's not the point."

351

"So what's the point?"

"The point is we should communicate with each other, agree about certain things, like where you're going and who you're going with and who's taking care of Daniel."

I am trying to wrap my head around this. Open communication, what a concept. Does that mean he'll tell me where he's going and what he's doing as well? Will he be telling me who he's going with? I decide not to go there, not now. I'm not up for another throw down with him tonight.

Instead, in the tradition of open communication and abrupt changes of subjects, I say, "So I promised Lee that I'd apply to the MFA program." That promise becoming bonded in truth the moment I speak the words. I hesitate, brace myself, but there is no rumbling from The Duckling. "Professor Israel is recommending me, which makes me a shoo-in," I say. "It's a great opportunity." My news is greeted with a blank stare.

"Oh, you promised Lee."

"Yes, I promised Lee. What's wrong with that?"

"I didn't say anything was wrong with that, did I?" He takes a breath, turns, and looks in Daniel's direction. Then turning back to me he says, "Look Dawn, I'm going to be making a lot of money soon. Enough to take care of all our needs. You won't need school or programs, or Lee, or anything else. All you'll need to do is stay home and take care of Daniel."

Grey fog is pushing its way into my head and I'm having trouble hearing. "What?" I ask. "A lot of money? What, from dealing drugs?!"

"It's just a little weed."

"A lot of money . . . with a little weed."

"Okay I'm going to be moving weight. Just this one time," he says. I just stare at him like he's speaking some weird language that I don't understand. "Okay," he says. "Maybe a few times, but it won't be forever. This is a good thing. So yeah, I was waiting until it was for sure to tell you. And we can get out of this dump. I've been looking at houses in Jersey just south of Atlantic City. I'm going to put a bid on this one in particular. You'll love it. We'll have a real home. We'll be a real family."

Fog is closing in on my mind. I think I hear Momma's voice—a caution, something about making wishes and being careful . . . being very careful.

The Debate

"Dawn, you go check on Luiscita and I'll go see if I can get Joaquin to settle down for his nap," Lee says. We are at our work-study job in the daycare center just off campus. I approach Luiscita to find her whimpering on her cot.

"Cita? What's wrong honey?"

"She wants her blanky," Roxanne, ever the group spokes-kid, says from her napping cot in the next row. I notice that the tiny weather-beaten blanket is right at the foot of Luiscita's cot.

"Cita, here honey, your blanky is right here," I say, handing it to her. She withdraws, covers her face with her little hands and weeps louder.

"She can't. She not allowed," Roxanne says. "Mrs. Clune said she had to learn to sleep without it. She so mean."

Heat bristles through me. I take a breath, muster a smile, and say, "I'm sure Mrs. Clune won't mind. I'll talk to her. Here honey, it's okay." I hand her the blanket. She reaches for it, tentatively at first. Then she grabs it, tucks it under her chin, and placing her thumb in her mouth, she falls into an instant sleep.

"What was up with Luiscita?" Lee asks.

"Clune being a bitch wouldn't let her have her blanky."

"Yeah, she does shit like that sometimes. Luckily, she's retiring next month. I met the new teacher. She seems cool." Then she pauses before she says, "So what's up with you?"

I have been expecting this question. I've given it a lot of thought. The fact is, I am having a lot of trouble trying to figure out what's up with me. "What makes you think there's something up with me?"

"Well for one thing, Roxanne said . . ."

"That I'm sad?"

"Yep, there's that. But you've been acting weird since Saturday. I don't need Roxanne to tell me something's up."

The events of Saturday evening push their way in and out of my mind. I haven't talked to Lee about it because I'm not exactly sure what happened, what it means, and how I feel about it.

I remind myself to take a breath. Then avoiding Lee's eyes, I look across the room at Mrs. Clune sitting at her desk thumbing through a magazine, seeming so detached from everything around her. And for a flash of a moment, I fear that could be me. I fear that I may be slipping further and further away too. It's like I'm slipping in and out of me.

"Danny went off on me," I say. "He was worried, you know. He didn't know where I was."

"Went off on you how? He didn't hit you, did he?"

"No, no, nothing like that. He was, like, agitated, yelling, stuff like that." I didn't tell Lee that he kicked over the coffee table. She'd make too much of it.

"Oh okay," she says. "Because I'd like to think you'd draw the line at being attacked physically." The specter of a meaty fist coming down across my face invades my mind. Lee must see it, that image reflected in my eyes because she hastens to add, "Of course you would. I know you'd never stand for that, not you. You'd never let a guy hit you." Silence wraps around us as I am thinking that I'm not so sure, not anymore. I'm not so sure of anything.

My mind drifts back to last Saturday. I'd been trying to get my head around Danny's plans for us. He said he wanted to move us to Jersey, all the way to Atlantic City. I was horrified. "No way," that's what I should've said. "No way," those were the words rattling around in my head, trying to find their way to my mouth. But that damned duckling barged in, held my breath hostage, sent thoughts into my head, and much to the chagrin of Outside Me, who was standing there, those thoughts actually started making sense to me. Outside Me? I bristled. Where had she come from? Where had she been? She hadn't shown her red-boned face since the day she "did it." Her presence was confusing. I didn't know how to feel about her. *Who is who?* Was she a friend?

This is a good thing. This is what we wanted, what we planned. The Duckling thought at me. I grabbed my head with both hands trying to block that horrid voice that grated on my teeth. I ran to the bathroom and locked myself in, ignored Danny mumbling on the other side of the door, some-thing about my being all right.

"Turn away!" Outside Me urged. "Don't engage," she said. "Don't listen. Plunge your fingers deep into your ears!" I ignored her. Her and her light-skinned privilege never worked for me. No. I couldn't trust her anymore. She was so unreliable, just popped in when it suited her. Instead, I aban-doned my practice of non-engagement. There, locked in the bathroom, I resolved to confront The Duckling head on. Out-side Me stepped away as I shot thoughts back at Duckling.

Lee's right. He's beginning to act like he's the father and I'm the child, I thought at it.

He worries about us. He's just being protective.

Protective? He's menacing. He likes scaring me.

He's under a lot of pressure. He just lets off steam. He's not his father. He'd never hurt us. He said as much.

He's dealing drugs, I persisted, steadily projecting thoughts right back at it.

He needs to provide for us. It's our fault. We made him a father. He didn't ask for any of this. But look how he's stepped up, pays all the bills. Anyway, it's just grass. It's not like he's addicting people.

But this house in Jersey . . . he's planning on buying it with no input from me. I've never even seen it.

He's a man. Men like to take the lead. Why can't we let him? A house is a house. As long as we're together, that's all that matters.

Yeah, but this house is all the way down in south Jersey. I'd have to give up my friends. Lee, how can I give up Lee?

357

We're being overdramatic. We can visit. There are phones.

Eli, Natasha—they're like family to me.

More drama!

Ralfie, oh my God he's always wanted to make me cut ties with Ralfie.

He's jealous. It's sweet. It shows how much he loves us.

But he tries to keep me away from Lee too. They are the best people in the world! They are my very best friends.

More drama! Do we want Danny? Do we want the music? Do we want the breath? Or would we prefer our friends?!

I had to pause for a second. The flip-flopping in my mind was making me queasy. I looked at Outside Me, saw her disapproval. I knew I needed to stop engaging The Duckling. I needed to get in contact with my thoughts—my own thoughts, my own feelings. But The Duckling's arguments were morphing from compelling to convincing. Still, there was this other thing that hung in the air, this other concern,

What about school, the program? I think at it. *What about this opportunity that I stumbled into? It's a real chance to be a college graduate. Getting into C.C.N.Y., meeting Danny, those things are intertwined. My grandma always said there are no coincidences. I think I'm meant to finish school. I think I'm meant to be somebody. I mean, not just Danny's baby momma. Why can't I just tell Danny no? He can sell pot anywhere. Why can't we just stay in the city? Why can't I have it all? And now that I think about it, why should I listen to you? You've never been on my side.*

Why listen to us? Because we are one, you and me. Because we were right. It worked. Because we remember, don't we? We said, Do it! Then we did it.

My head was whirling as I realized that The Duckling was right . . . again. It did work. Danny is here with us. And how would I manage financially without him? We are a family. And he would never hurt us. He did say as much. We love him. He loves us—he must. Outside Me stepped forward. She opened her mouth like she was about to speak but closed it again and shrugged her shoulders. I watched her turn and disappear into the shadows.

Danny was standing outside the bathroom door, waiting for me to emerge. When I did, he pulled me into his hard body, his very hard body . . . and I let him.

"You okay?"

"Fine," I'd said, wrapping my arms around him, leaning my head on his chest, listening to his heartbeat, inhaling him with deep, easy breaths. All my previous concerns were draining away. I looked up, then, into those wolf eyes. They were bright with desire as he brought those lips down on mine . . . What is it about make-up sex?

I avoid Lee's eyes. I'm not so sure what I would do if Danny ever actually hit me. I'm not sure that I'm that same girl who would not be treated that way. What I *am* sure of today is that I won't be telling Lee everything that happened on Saturday. I definitely won't tell her about The Duckling. I won't say anything about the make-up sex either—about how amazing it was. I'd be too embarrassed to admit that Danny can bring me under his spell so easily. Instead, I try to ease into the news about the house.

While gathering my thoughts, I glance over at Mrs. Clune who is still absorbed in her magazine. The children are still asleep. I take a breath, and without looking directly at Lee I say, "So, you know how I always talk about wanting a nice home for my family."

"Yeah?" she says, like she somehow knows I'm about to tell her something disturbing.

"It's the funniest thing," I say.

"Yeah?" she says again.

"Seems Danny has been house shopping."

"Danny what! First of all, where would Danny get enough money to buy a house?"

My answer is a stare, no words required.

"Oh," Lee says. "And you're okay with this?"

"It's only grass."

"Must be a hell of a lot of grass."

"He'll be moving weight for a bit, just until he's straight with the funds."

"You sound like you're all up in the life. Again, I ask, you're okay with this?"

"Moving weight isn't really the part that I'm not okay with."

"There's more?"

"It seems the house that he's looking to buy is in Jersey."

"Jersey? Where in Jersey?"

"Oh, just a little south of Atlantic City."

"And it begins!" she says, throwing her arms in the air. Some of the sleeping kids stir.

I lower my voice and ask, "What begins? What are you talking about?"

"This is what they do. This is how they control you. It's what my ex did, remember? I told you. That's how I ended up in Connecticut, away from my friends and family. I followed him there," she says, heaving a breath before she continues. "The beatings began when I started confronting him about all those other women he was dealing with. I had to realize I'd never finish school, that I might not even survive," she pauses and looks me directly in the eyes. "I had to decide who I loved more, him . . . or me." She blows a breath through tight lips, deciding what to say. "It was my cousin, Rosa, that helped me come to my senses. She understood the situation after one visit. Thank God her mother, my titi Pilar, had connections in the SEEK program. That's how I got in," she explains. Then smiling sheepishly, she adds, "It's always who you know."

My response comes directly from The Duckling. **"Our Danny isn't like that! Our Danny would never do those things. We need to give our Danny the benefit of the doubt."** These are the exact words that spring from my mouth. I am horrified. Am I losing control? Has the damned Duckling evolved to the point that it can literally put words in my mouth?

"Our Danny? As in yours and mine? Really? Cause he's definitely not my Danny!"

"You know what I mean. I mean Danny, my Danny." Then coming directly from The Duckling's playbook, I hear myself say, "South Jersey isn't that far. We can talk on the phone every day. I don't think it's long distance. And Danny has a car now. I'm sure he'll bring me to visit whenever I want." I realize that I agree with what I just said. I *am* actually "down" with The Duckling! Lee drops her eyes and turns away from me. I touch her arm gently, trying to keep her with me. "Lee this *is* my dream. This is what I've wished for. Please be happy for me. I need you to be happy for me."

Some of the children are sitting up on their cots. Nap time is over.

"I'll help you get them up and put out the snacks," Lee says. "Then I have a class."

"Lee . . ." I call. If she hears me, she doesn't react. Avoiding my eyes, she goes about the tasks she's laid out.

Then she grabs her book bag, goes to the door, and turns back to me. "An apartment," Lee says. "A studio is being renovated in my building. It won't be ready for a few months, but when it is, the rent will be less than you're paying now. Jamal knows the landlord and I'm sure he can swing something for you. It's a really nice building." I've never seen Lee look like she's looking now, so drained, extremely un-Lee.

"A studio?" I ask. "A studio isn't big enough for . . ." I stop short as her meaning seeps through.

"Um jus sayin'," she says and walks out the door.

Many Milestones

At eight months old, Little Daniel is sitting up in his highchair. He and I are sitting at the table. We are waiting for Danny to get home so we can eat dinner. We eat dinner together every night at seven sharp, another ritual.

While I'm waiting, my mind drifts back to the last real conversation I had with Lee. The words *controlling* and *beatings* hover around me like spirits. I shoo them away with a sweep of my arms. More words float in. *Studio apartment.* I picture it in my mind: a neat little place with parquet floors like in Lee's apartment, the sun streaming through a picture window, a little nook for my bed and Daniel's playpen . . . the music? I am suddenly doubled over with a sharp ache that rips through my head, followed by The Ducklings grating voice. *That's not part of the plan. It's not what we wished for. We've gotten what we wished for, and we should be happy.* It punctuates its sentiments by seizing my windpipe. I wheeze a strained breath. When The Duckling releases me, I stumble backwards, gasping, and terrified. The Duckling's attacks are becoming increasingly harsh. But on some intangible level I am thinking maybe The Duckling is right. Maybe The Duckling is always right. Maybe it punishes me for my own good. I *do* have what I wished for, don't I? Maybe I should be grateful.

It's 7:10 and Danny is not here yet. I've already started trying to feed the baby, but he is fussy and whiny and refuses to eat. I'm hoping maybe he'll eat for his father. I'm starting to worry about Danny because he is rarely late, especially not for dinner. At 7:12 I hear his key in the door. The dinner is cold, and I prepare myself. Danny can't possibly have something to say when he's the one that's late. He walks into the room. Daniel goes incandescent. He giggles his happy giggle, the one that springs from him every time his father walks through the door. He claps his hands, wiggling his fingers; he reaches out his little arms for Danny to pick him up.

I expect the usual whiff of Life Buoy soap to follow Danny in. Instead, there is another smell, something different but familiar. I've always had a keen sense of smell, but since the pregnancy, my nose can rival that of a bloodhound. It's soft, feminine . . . Dove. At first, I think that Danny has relented and brought me back my favorite soap. Then I realize that the smell is actually on him, on his body, in his clothes. I don't understand. Has Danny strayed from his ritual? Has he abandoned his Life buoy soap? It occurs to me that I am being silly, though I'm not really sure the notion is mine. It's just a smell, right? It means nothing. Actually, I'm probably imagining the whole thing. Then I catch the look in his eyes.

They quickly skip past me and focus on Daniel. And just like that, I know. I'm not sure if it's betrayal or indifference, but I know. He hasn't bathed with Dove soap. He has been very close, intimately close, to someone who has.

"There's my little man," he says as he whips Daniel from the chair, swings him high into the air. Daniel squeals with delight. When he is lowered to his father's chest, he wraps his arms around his neck and rests his head on his shoulder. I stare at their tender embrace, marveling at the bond between them, and despite being upset about the smell of Dove, a warm feeling radiates out from my stomach.

Turning to me Danny says, "Sorry I'm late. My father was rushed to the hospital, so I went to Brooklyn to help my mother."

"Oh my God! Is he okay?"

"He'll live," he says, a touch of ice in his tone. "So anyway, I can't stay," he says. "I'm going to be staying at the dorms tonight and for a few days—business." I fix him with a doubtful stare. "What!? I need to handle things in order to do the deal I told you about. It looks like it's going to take more time than I thought to hook up the house. I'm still working on it. We might have to shelf it for a few months," he says before adding emphatically, "But it is going to happen."

I'm conflicted; I can't figure out whether I'm happy or sad about the house. But a feeling of relief is easing over me. As I think that this gives me some time to convince Danny to stay in New York, I brace myself for a rebuke from The Duckling. Nothing.

Danny is high. I don't know why this should surprise me except that since he's been staying here, neither one of us have been getting high. I stopped smoking altogether during the pregnancy, and since we started sleeping together again, things have been good, no grass required.

Something about the way he's been holding me, the way we curl into each other like we are one; something about the way he whispers that word, like a prayer, into my ear. *"Dawn . . ."* Something. I can feel it. I've been feeling so intensely in love with him lately . . . and he's been letting me. I think he's feeling it too, even though he hasn't said it—probably never will.

I take Little Daniel to the futon to change his diaper. Danny would have a heart attack if I put the changing pad on the table and changed him there. I pull down the rubber pants, undo the safety pins and open the diaper. My heart jerks, my breath catches in my chest . . . green water. Danny has grabbed his overnight bag and is heading for the door.

"Danny, he's sick again!" Danny stops abruptly, turns, walks back to me, wavers, avoids the baby's beseeching eyes. Calculations and considerations flash across his face. Then he takes out his wallet and throws several bills onto the futon.

"You can handle this. Take a cab. I gotta go."

"What? You're not coming with me?"

"Dawn, I have business. This thing is about to take off. I'll call you later to see how he is." He turns to leave but I grab his arm. It feels like steel. I'm holding on to him with two hands. I am a cat, my claws digging into his flesh, tears erupting in my eyes, the smell of Dove soap wafting through the air.

"I hope she's worth it," I hiss, waiting for denials, explanations, or at least excuses. Instead, he glares at me. His eyes are hard, scary hard. I am frightened but I don't let go. I cling, dig my nails in deeper. I can't let go. We've come such a long way. We are so close, a house, a real home. How could I possibly let go?

In a growl at least two octaves lower than normal, he says, "She is!"

He rips away from my grip, then. A trail of angry red scratches color his arm. He palms my face like a basketball and shoves me back onto the futon, hard. I fall backwards, barely miss landing on the baby who begins to wail.

I watch Danny make his way down the long narrow hallway. It's as though he's moving in slow motion. His body heaves with every step he takes. He glances back, and his head appears to ripple. He hesitates, taking a long deep breath as concern flitters across his eyes and eases away. Then lifting his chin, he fixes his face into a cold, indifferent glare before he turns away and disappears through the door.

Dazed and dry-eyed, I sit hearing Lee's words in my head. *"An apartment, a studio apartment, affordable . . . Where is the girl who recognized leaving time when it came around?"* I realize I don't know where that girl has gone. I only know she's gone. She left some time ago. It seems like eons since I was that girl. I just know that I'm not going to give up on us, not now. How can I? I can only breathe—really breathe—when I'm in his arms. We are a family. This is just what Danny

367

does, isn't it? He pulls away just when we are on the verge of the music? Yes. That's why he always plays Smokey's "You've Really Got a Hold on Me." Suddenly, I get it. I hear those words, the real lyrics, the ones that express resistance and fear of being trapped by love. That's what he feels. It scares him. I scare him. Lee is wrong. We just need more time.

I am hearing the echo of the slamming door as Danny leaves. It vibrates the walls, sends fear and shivers through my body.

I pack up the baby and hurriedly make my way to the hospital . . . alone.

368

Game On

At eight months and nineteen days old, Little Daniel lies helplessly in a crib in the Columbia Presbyterian's Pediatric ICU. His hands are tethered so that he can't pull out the tubes that they've forced into the sides of his tiny head. This is his ninth day in the ICU. When he first arrived, he used to howl his outrage at being confined in this way, demanding release. After a few days his howls became pleads, then whimpers. His big eyes searched for me, for Danny, not understanding, asking how we could abandon him like this. My heart is collapsing.

The day that Daniel was admitted, I didn't go home. I stayed in the hospital, dozing in a chair in the emergency room. No one even noticed me, and I'd certainly slept in worse places. I thought I could probably pull that off for a few more days until Daniel was released. I went home, showered, packed a small bag, and returned to the hospital. That's when an attendant noticed me. For some reason the idea of leaving the hospital without Daniel this time was ter-

369

rifying. I broke into hysterics when he tried to make me leave without my baby. But a nurse interceded, and they actually put a cot for me in Daniel's room. I was so grateful. She said it was some kind of program. The hospital did this in the case of gravely ill children . . . gravely ill, my Little Daniel. The words got snagged on a rusty nail in my brain.

I tried to reach Danny. I called the house several times, no answer. I haven't been able to reach him at the dorms. Either no one picks up the lounge phone or they say they've slipped messages under his door. I'm told there are a growing stack there.

For the past few days, Little Daniel has been lying quiet, resigned. Am I losing him? I have lowered the side of the crib. I am bent over for hours on end, my face next to his so that he knows I'm here. He's not alone. The mask they make me wear prevents my skin from touching his. His eyes have slipped away and I'm so scared that he may do the same.

The doctors say that they can keep hydrating him, but the infection is viral and not responding to anything they've tried so far. They are speaking to me in "doctorese." They are uttering unintelligible phonemes and nonsense syllables. I can't grasp any of it. Not with all the noise, the beeps, and buzzes from all the machines and monitors and that damn high-pitched squeal that keeps blaring through my brain. The only utterances that have made their way past the ruckus are, "We're trying something that we hope will boost his immune reaction. Now we'll just have to wait and see if he can fight it off." And even this I'm not sure I understand . . . or actually heard.

370

I call Max.

It takes a while for him to respond. He has patients. But when he finally arrives, he looks at the charts and talks to the doctors and turns to me.

In clear and brutal terms, he says, "You should prepare yourself. The next few hours will be pivotal."

I lean over the crib, oblivious to the growing ache in my back, when I feel the hand on my shoulder. I look up into Lee's tear-filled eyes. We embrace and cry. Ralfie, Chandra, and Natasha follow her in; my eyes fix on the door.

"Jamal has classes," Lee says.

"Eli can't close the shop. He sends his prayers," Natasha says. I acknowledge with a nod, still watching the door.

"He's not with us," Ralfie says. "I called the lounge phone in the dorms; that girl Angel picked up. She said she'd give him the message." I have a different question in my mouth but am unable to push it out.

"Max called me," Lee says, explaining how she got word about Daniel being so sick.

I nod, but that is not the question I want to ask. I want to ask, "Why isn't Danny here?" But the question has no energy behind it. Its importance is slowly fading into a remote, minor chamber of my heart. How would Lee know, anyway? How would anyone? What does it matter?

"She needs some rest," Max says. "They told me she hasn't eaten all day. There's a cafeteria next to the nurse's station. I'll stay here with Daniel. I'll call over there if there's any change."

371

I resist. "No! No! I can't leave him! He shouldn't be alone," I cry.

"Dawn, he's not alone. Max is with him. You know Max will take care of him, don't you?" It is Ralfie's soothing voice.

"Yes," I say, feeling dazed, my voice a shadow of a whisper. Gently, Lee puts her arm around me. I allow her to lead me out of the ICU. My brain is filling up with tiny indiscernible voices, murmurs.

I find myself sitting at a table with my friends, contemplating French fries, poking at them with my fork. Aside from the murmurs in my head, no one is speaking.

"You know, I connived for this child," I whisper. "I plotted and planned for him. I took their advice, you know. I thought I knew what I was doing but I wasn't prepared." I am mumbling, not addressing any one in particular, talking to French fries and murmuring entities. "But I didn't think things through, you know. He was supposed to be the means to an end, the cement." Ralfie moves to my side, places his hand on my shoulder.

"Dawn . . . "

"He was supposed to be the bond," I cry, the murmurs in my head resolving themselves into words that come pouring out of me. "He was supposed to bridge the gap where I knew, deep down, no connection ever really existed. But it turns out he's a person, an actual person. He's not a doll. He's not Bernadette, not here to be my companion. It's not his job to love me, to bring me love. That's not why he's here. It's my job to love him. He's here for *me* to love." Then addressing Ralfie, I wail, "Oh God Ralfie! What have I done?" Then I am surrounded; they are all at my side. And I'm feeling embarrassed at blubbering the way that I am . . . again. But I can't stop myself. "I guess I was naive, you know. And I know that's no excuse. I listened to them, the other me—The Duckling, that Midnight Duckling."

"What?" Lee says. "The Duckling? What does any of this have to do with The Duckling? I thought we retired that damned Duckling."

I continue to address Ralfie. "It was like a bet, you know; yeah, a bet. I know now. I get it. People shouldn't make wagers with God, especially if He doesn't really know you like that, right? He must have been watching. That's what Momma always said. 'He's always watching.' Is that true Ralfie? Was he watching?" I am sobbing. "Did he see what I did?" I use my sleeve to wipe the tears rolling down my face. Ralfie hands me a napkin from the table. I don't wait for his answer to my questions. "I'm the one who took the gamble, bet on the game, but it's Little Daniel who is taking the loss."

Now Chandra steps in closer. "Dawn," she says. "It's not your fault that the baby's sick."

"But it's my fault that the baby's here," I cry. "He fought hard, you know. It's like he was refusing to participate, resisting the light. It's like he knew. It's like he never wanted to be in the game; the game that I was playing. Like he wanted to stay where it was warm and safe, somewhere off on the sideline." I fall silent, think about how he's suffering, his tiny fists clenched, restrained to the crib, tubes in the delicate skin of his little head. "But they clamped those steely forceps on his tiny skull and forced him into play," I sniffle, " . . . and I let them!"

A nurse rushes in and says that Max wants us back in the ICU.

"It may not be long now," Max says, placing his hand on my shoulder as he checks Daniels vital signs on the screens and monitors.

"Isn't there anything we can do?"

"All we can do now is pray," Max says.

I turn to Ralfie, the God-guy. "Ralfie . . . "

"I could lead us in a prayer, but I think that it might be better if you just talk to him. Tell him how you feel while he's still here to hear you. Confess. Make it a wish, not a prayer."

I turn to Daniel. I take his tiny hand in mine. It feels limp and listless. His eyes are closed. His breathing is shallow.

"Daniel," I say. "My dear sweet Daniel, you have a decision to make. I wish . . . I wish you would stay. I just want you to know that if you stay it would be on your own terms. It will be a do-over, our do-over. I know that you have been teetering between two worlds for so long, in and out of hospitals, hit and miss." I pause, my voice hitching in my chest. "And faced with the idea of losing you, I'm heartbroken. I'm so afraid you're about to call time-out and slip away." I look up at Ralfie who nods his encouragement. "Just being here you've taught me so much already," I say. "Please, Daniel, stay. Stay because I have so much more to learn, and you have so much more to teach." I pause, trying to collect the thoughts that are rampaging through my brain. "And I want you to know that I want you . . . for you . . . not for him. Please, Daniel, stay," I sob, ". . . for me."

The Throw Down

It is a Sunday. Daniel has been discharged from the hospital. Though he's slightly underweight, he's made a good recovery. As Daniel, Ralfie, and I enter the apartment, Little Daniel is his bubbly, rambunctious self.

We walk in to find Danny seated on the futon watching the game. I am surprised. I am relieved . . . I am pissed. I've called the apartment over and over, but Danny never answered. Ralfie is the one who picked us up from the hospital and lugged the heavy case of special formula that was prescribed for Daniel up five flights of stairs.

"Oh hey," Danny says. As he looks up from the TV screen, I think I see a touch of relief push its way across his face. Then he smiles, but it isn't "that smile." It's a tight, uneasy smile—a plastic smile. It's a short-lived smile that fades the moment it registers Ralfie walking in right behind me. "And if it isn't the knight in shining armor," Danny says, wolf eyes fixed on Ralfie.

"Hey Danny," Ralfie says, placing the box on the floor and extending his hand to shake. Danny doesn't stand. I suffer an anxious moment fearing that Danny might do something stupid like squeeze Ralfie's hand, or worse.

"Or is it the comic sidekick?" Danny says as he shakes Ralfie's hand uneventfully.

"I'll cop to that," Ralfie says, not missing a beat. Then Ralfie turns to me. "You gonna be okay?"

Now Danny stands, slowly pulls himself up to full stature and says, "Why the fuck wouldn't she be okay?"

"Danny," I say, placing my hand on his chest.

"Yo dude, it's just a question," Ralfie says, and although his hands say peace, his eyes are dark and intense . . . no puppy dog here.

"Ralfie," I say. "I'm fine. Thanks for everything." I place a kiss on his cheek. Ralfie probes my eyes for affirmation. I nod. "Fine," I say again. Then nodding a goodbye to Danny, that comes off like a warning, he exits.

I turn to Danny, not knowing what to expect. He has shifted into neutral, his face unreadable. A light sweat is basting my forehead. This is the cool that always precedes the storm. He stands up, reaches for Daniel. I flinch, step back, angle my body away from him, denying him access to the baby. Over my shoulder, Daniel is reaching out to his father, squealing, his little fingers wriggling. I ignore both of them and put Daniel in his playpen.

"What, I can't hold my son now?"

"Really? You have a son?"

"That's what you told me."

"Yeah well, maybe I lied."

"Dawn, I'm trying to hold it together here. Don't start."

Don't start, I hear the words like an echo in my head. Then I realize that it's that damned duckling shooting thoughts at me, its voice searing my brain. Determined not to engage, I ignore it.

To Danny I say, "Oh, I'm gonna start. I'm gonna start right now by asking where were you!" Something is sparking in my stomach—annoyance.

"You see," he says, his voice like ice water. "That's your problem. You always ask the wrong question. The real question. The question that matters is, where were *you*? All this time, all these days, where have you been?" He does not scream or roar or raise his voice at all. Surprisingly, this icy whisper frightens me more than a roar. He is an animal quietly stalking . . . and I am the prey.

"Our son was in the hospital, Danny. Where do you think I've been?" I try to mimic his cool. The spark of annoyance in my stomach is mixing with fear and turning to irritation. ***Don't start!*** The Duckling screeches.

"So . . . what? You're saying that for over two weeks you were in the hospital? Let me get this straight. You're saying that you ate there, that you slept there—for over two weeks. Is that what you're saying?"

"Yes," is all I say, the irritation and fear in my stomach turning into a warm, comfortable anger. Why should I have to explain myself?

Don't start!

I ignore The Duckling. I set my face and meet Danny's glare head-on. He takes a step towards me. Despite my resolve, I take a step back. But I do manage to hold my eyes steady. Little Daniel has pulled himself up on the side of the playpen. He is standing there bouncing with excitement, clambering for Danny's attention. Danny looks from me to Daniel and back again, like he's asking permission. "Don't touch him!" I shout.

Don't start! from The Duckling.

That's when something totally unexpected happens. Danny caves. He just collapses into himself. He plops back onto the futon, reaches for a half-smoked joint that is in the new ashtray that he bought, lights it, and takes a long noisy drag.

"I've been in Jersey. That's where everything is going down. I had to be there to protect my interests, our interests. My total investment was at stake. I had to be there. I called every night, but you never picked up. You weren't here. That meant Daniel wasn't here. That meant . . ."

"That is such bullshit, Danny! You could have called someone! Lee, Jamal . . ."

The Duckling screeches, *We push him. This is why he goes off.*

"Your friends; I dunno your friends like that. I don't have their numbers."

"Max, he's a doctor. He's definitely listed."

"What, under Max? I dunno his last name. You never use his last name."

"I can't believe that you couldn't take a couple of hours to come and see about us. There must have been another distraction, a distraction that bathes with Dove soap."

Why must we go there?!

"Dawn, there is no one." Our eyes meet. I'm sure he sees his lie in my eyes. "Okay, there was no one this time. And there is no one that means anything, any time."

I let that comment fly right past me, but The Duckling doesn't. *None of those hoes mean shit to him. Men need their side action. Why can't we just let him have that? He'll always come home to us.*

"The hospital. Why didn't you call the hospital? You could've reached me at the hospital. They would've gotten a message to me. There's . . ."

"Daawn!!" he screams. The boom in his voice causes me to almost jump out of my skin. The baby starts to wail. Danny is on his feet. "I did call!" he says. And I think I hear water in his voice. "I called every day. In fact, I went there. I saw you standing there. I saw him lying there in that ICU, all those tubes and machines. I couldn't bring myself to go in. So I introduced myself to one of the nurses—that little Asian chick—told her I was his father, asked if I could call for updates." I picture Danny smiling at the nurse, bringing her under his spell. "So every day she told me how he was doing. I knew it was hit or miss, that we might lose him. I knew!" he says as he slowly sits back down. With his elbows on his knees, he places his head in his hands and says, "My father died, seven days ago. Yeah, and I can't believe how hard it hit me. I guess I always thought that his kind of evil asshole never dies. I just, I couldn't face another death. I couldn't deal, you know, with the idea of losing Daniel too. So the thing is, I had this weird idea that if Dad knew how I feel about my son, his spirit could follow me. I know how this sounds. I was afraid that I would lead him to Daniel. I was afraid he might take Daniel with him, you know, just to punish me."

I am petrified, not in the sense that I'm frightened, more in the sense that I'm made of stone. I am a statue. Danny fears his father even after death. The digestive acids in my stomach have extinguished the angry fire that was flaring there, and I am suddenly empty of words. That's when The Duckling stretches out in my lungs and puts a clamp on my windpipe.

Knew it! Knew it! We shouldn't start. We should never start! What can we possibly say to him now?

I am doubled over, gasping and wheezing, straining to breathe. Danny is suddenly by my side.

"You okay?"

I can only cough in response. The room is spinning out of control. I stagger, strain; darkness encroaches, is poised to absorb me. Then Momma comes through. *"Be the master of your own mind, Lil Girl. Jus breathe."* I need to relax. I must not blackout! I visualize a straw bringing the chi in through my nose, down into my stomach and out through my mouth. I visualize my chest opening up. I manage a breath, then another. I am the master of my own mind.

What are you doing? Stop! We need to apologize. We need to have make-up sex.

I turn towards The Duckling's mirror. The hideous hybrid—part beast, part me—was there, staring, as mute as ever. Clearly it prefers to torture me with its horrid voice beamed directly into my mind. I pull myself upright. I stand before it—defiant, erect, and breathing. I've done it. It's possible! I've confronted The Duckling.

Stop! It shoots caustic thoughts at me. *We have to apologize, have make-up sex. Or we will drive him away!* It adds in a low but deadly croak, *It may be the last thing we ever do!*

It is a threat. It settles in my gut. There, it mixes with adrenaline and light-skinned indignation. The combination ignites, flares up inside me, and emerges as a scream.

"Shut up! Shut up! Get out of my head and leave me the fuck alone!"

Danny is staring at me now, his mouth open, his expression as blank and clueless as The Duckling in the mirror.

Game Over

I used to sleep. Even when there was nowhere that I could call home, I used to lay my head down in any number of frightful, unfamiliar places . . . and sleep.

Now I doze in a semi sleep-like state. Any little squirm or rustle from Daniel and I'm on full alert, listening. It's been six months since I've heard those cries from him, those cries of distress. It's been six months of not unpinning a diaper to see green water, six months, no emergency room. Daniel has gained weight. He's started walking. I'm pretty sure we're out of the woods. I'm pretty sure he's chosen to stay.

So, I should be able to sleep. I should be able to close my eyes and rest assured, without having to listen for disturbing sounds. But Daniel's murmurs are not the only noises that rattle me these days. It's six a.m. And despite my mixed feelings, I still find myself listening for the sound of Danny's key in the door.

I remember the six a.m.'s . . . our six a.m.'s, when Danny would come for me, when we would sit in Central Park and watch the sunrise. It seems like a million years ago, but I remember. Now, early mornings with Danny usually consist of him coming in high, a myriad of aromas wafting in with him, all of which assault my senses, insult my intelligence. I don't ask questions anymore. I don't "start." I don't want another scene. And The Duckling's threat lingers in the air. I don't need another confrontation with that evil black thing

Today, for some reason, Lee's words about the studio apartment and the MFA have been stomping across my mind. *"Where is that girl who survived out there on her own at sixteen years old?"* she'd asked. *"Where is that girl who recognized leaving time when it came around?"*

I consider that question. When did that girl leave? If I had to pick a day, I think it was that day in the dorms, the day when I all but moved into Danny's room. I was leaving. I was going for the door, my head held high. I was giving into the tug, the familiar, the comfortable, the craving for closure that always set me free. I was channeling my inner gypsy woman. Then there was music, a song: "Please Won't You Stay." He played me that song. I betrayed my inner gypsy for a song.

I let Lee's words march across my mind. I allow the sound of their trampling footfalls to diminish and dissipate into thin air.

Lately, Danny's become more and more erratic, having abandoned all pretense of ritual. I never know when he'll show up or how long he'll stay.

So I have actually taken some of Lee's advice. On the days when Danny's here—when he spends hours on the floor playing with Daniel, when we eat dinner together and sit on the futon watching TV, my head on his shoulder, his arm around me, when we are a family—on those days, I've learned to lower my expectations. I just take it easy. I keep in mind what's really important: Little Daniel. Even this has me conflicted. I know I need to do what's best for Daniel. He comes first. I promised him. And Little Daniel loves his father. Even though Danny may not be able to love me, he clearly loves his son. It's probably best for Daniel to have the father that he adores in his life, right? I can't deny Daniel a father, can I? It's best for all of us. Together, a family—it's probably the only way we can find the real music.

This is not to say that on the days when Danny slips into bed with me, when the only smell his body bears is Life Buoy soap and essence of Danny, that I'm not happy to be in his arms. I am. But afterwards—when he pulls me in close, when we curl into that fetal position, when we are one entity and he speaks my name in a husky whisper that sounds like an aria—I don't let myself feel it, not like before. It's like I have lowered the volume on those feelings, though they have not been entirely muted.

It's eight a.m.

Gazing into the oval mirror, The Duckling's mirror, I am captive. These words tiptoe across my mind: *Who is who? Who are you?* The Duckling stares back at me. As always, it just lurks there, silent, like the connections between its brain and its vocal cords have been severed. Its expression is vacant. It hasn't actually spoken aloud since . . . the diaphragm business. And it hasn't sent thoughts into my head since that day when I stood erect and showed it that I could master my own mind. I'm still not sure how I managed that, but I did. Still, it's there, always there, staring back at me with my own eyes. Today it seems subdued; it looks small and drab, Midnight black . . . and ugly.

I hear the rattle of Danny's key turning the cylinder in the door lock. The Duckling and I part ways. It releases me. I, in turn, dismiss it.

I am dressed and ready to go. I reach up and grab my keys from the ornate hook on the wall. I'm relieved that Danny has kept his word. He has come to take care of Daniel today while I go to class. Natasha, who usually keeps him for me when I'm in school, is under the weather. Aside from relief that he's here on time, I'm not sure what I feel. These days my feelings about Danny, about "us," run the spectrum.

He walks into the room, parks his keys on the ornate hook, goes over to the stereo, places a single forty-five on the turntable and sets it to repeat. I expect him to go and check on Daniel. That's usually the first thing he does when he arrives. Instead, he reaches for me. The sound of the singer's mellow baritone begging his woman to stay by his side, weaves ribbons of soulful sound throughout the room. Then with an audible sigh, he pulls me in. He wraps his arms around me, rests his chin on my head and just holds me, swaying ever so slightly to the music. I'm confused. I'm wary. This is not part of any routine that I'm aware of. It takes a while for me to return his embrace. With my keys in hand, my arms slowly find their way around him despite the variety of aromas that are wafting off him. He's high. I don't know how long we stand here holding each other, but I know it is long enough that it starts feeling awkward to me. I am impatient. Instead of the sensations that usually entrap my brain when Danny touches me, I'm thinking that I don't have time to be held right now. I need to get out of here or I'll be late for class. Ms. T arranged for me to take incompletes instead of F's in my classes. I'm not being dropped from the program. I'm taking a double load so I can get out next year. And on top of all this, I just got the acceptance letter for the MFA program. I've been granted a do-over. And I don't plan to blow it.

Danny releases me, then takes my hand and leads me into the little dining room. Does he want to do it on the pristine table?

"Danny, I need to leave. I don't want to be late for class." He has firm possession of my hand as he retrieves my birth control pills and leads me into the kitchen. Annoyed, I toss the keys on the coffee table. The music plays. The mellow lyrics are clearly aimed at me, begging me to stay.

"Danny, I really need to go. I . . ."

"Stay with me," he says. "I have great news, baby." Baby? He never calls me baby. "It went down, the deal. It was flawless. I wish you could've seen me. I was so cool. I was dealing with some big-time heavy dudes. I mean, these guys really know what they're doing," he says. I think these are the most words he's spoken to me in quite a while. "So that house is all but ours. I put a bid on it. I want you to come out and see it. Pack up the kid and we can go right now." Then he adds, "That is, after we're done." His voice is husky with desire. He pulls me into him, kisses my forehead, my nose, my lips. Having been set to repeat, the song plays on. *Please won't you stay . . .*

It is in this moment that I acknowledge something in me has shifted. These things—the holding, the kissing, the urgency in his voice—could easily bring me under his spell . . . before.

Who is who? Who are you?

I am someone who is supposed to be a college graduate. I know that now. I am someone who may have made mistakes. It's true they were not always honest mistakes, but I think they were mistakes none the less. I did it for the love. I did it for the music. I did it for the deep, easy breaths. And something good came of it: Daniel. So now I've been granted a do-over. How many people get do-overs? I love Danny. I do. Little Daniel loves Danny. I can't separate Daniel from his father, can I? But I also can't go live in some house in Jersey with a big-time drug dealer, can I?

"Danny," I say. "I don't want to be late for class. Can we talk about all this later?"

"Class? After what I just told you? Dawn, you don't get it. You don't need a class. You want a diploma, what, one of those MFA's? I'll buy you one. I'll give it to you in a solid gold picture frame and no one will question its validity. You want friends? I'll buy you some of those too. Everyone has a price." I'm not sure if it's the pot talking or if he's actually serious.

I sigh and say, "I gotta go." As I try to push away from him, he grabs me by the wrist, hard. "You're hurting me," I say.

"No," he says. "What you gotta do is take this pill, climb your black ass into that bed, spread those legs, and lay there while I give you the ride of your life. Then," he says, emphatically drawing out the words, "we're going to see our new home." The song's sweet pleading refrain is in direct contrast with the look in Danny's eyes.

"You're hurting me," I say again, my voice low and deadly. I glare at him.

"Dawn," he says, now sounding like he's talking to a petulant child. "Don't be difficult."

Lee's words flood my mind, *This is what they do. This is how they control you.*

Danny hands me a pill and a glass of water. Suddenly an irritation that has no name is morphing into an equally anonymous anger. Something that has been neatly folded and tucked away deep in my chest along with my self-respect, rises up. It works its way into my brain, which in turn sends a signal to my arm, my hand. I slap the pill away. It falls to the floor and rolls under the stove.

"What the hell?! You are one crazy bitch, first screaming into the mirror, now this shit! What the fuck is wrong with you?!" he yells.

Surprised by my own actions, I stop to consider his question. What *is* wrong with me? Maybe everything? Maybe nothing? I don't know, never did figure that out. And right now, I don't really care. What I do know is that I'm absolutely loving the dumb open-mouthed expression of shock on his handsome face. And for some reason I'm not afraid. It occurs to me that when you're a crazy bitch no one messes with you.

"I've decided that I'm not taking any more damned pills," I say, looking him directly in the eye, sounding fairly matter-of-fact. My resolve is taking form as I speak the words. "Those pills aren't good for me. I don't think I should do things that aren't good for me."

Who is who? Who are you?

Stay, stay . . . The begging, pleading song drones on.

"Wha?"

"Yeah, and your game, it's not good for me either. I don't think I want to play your game anymore. You know, the yo-yo game. You push me away, you pull me back," I say, warming to my outrage.

"You're not making any sense."

"I'm not a yo-yo, Danny. You don't control me. I won't play your game and I promise to never again make you play mine."

"My game? Your game? What's this all about? Where's all this coming from? Are you okay?"

I want to tell him. I want to confess. But I'm not ready. What if he hates me, rejects his son? "Nothing, nowhere," I say, wavering. "I'm just going back to the diaphragm. That's all."

"That doesn't make any sense. We already know that doesn't work. That's how you got pregnant in the first place. How would having another kid be good for you? For either of us?"

My mind swings back to what Ralfie said in the hospital. He said that I should confess to Little Daniel. And it strikes me now that my confessions will only be absolute when I confess to Danny as well. And maybe it's that secret, that big lie lurking between us that prevents the music from entering our lives . . . maybe. My hands begin to tremble. I hold them up and stare at them, willing them to stop. He clasps my hands in his and holds tight. He's looking at me like he really fears I'm losing my mind.

"You're a good man, Danny. I've seen it in you. You can be *my* good man. You can be a good father to Daniel. He loves you. You can be the Papa to my Momma. That's why I did it," I say as that sound, that *pop* of the needle, assaults my mind. "So we can be a family. In time we can have a home, the right home, the home both of us want. That's the only way we will have the music."

He drops my hands and steps back from me with wide-eyed apprehension. "What the hell are you saying?"

"I did it, Danny. I poked a hole in the diaphragm. It was me. I know it was me—not that duckling or Outside Me, that imposter. I know now that Outside Me is not me . . . not *all* of me."

"You what?!"

"You're not your father, Danny. You don't have to be your father! You don't! That's not who you really are! I can help. I can pull you back. I've done it before," I sob. "I did it for us. I know now that I was . . . "

I am purging, feeling strong, unburdened, unafraid. That is, until it happens, and I realize I have over-played my hand. It happens so fast I don't see it coming. I miss the signs—his fingers, one by one, slowly curling into fists and his tone dropping two octaves.

One blow . . . I'm seeing stars. I'm literally seeing stars . . . again.

A sharp pain spikes in my left eye as the glass contact lens scrapes across my cornea. For the slightest of seconds, I look around for an avenging Siegfried to come to my defense. There is no Siegfried. There is just me. Me . . . my head snapping back ever so slowly as I spy the utensils hanging on the wall, the shiny stainless-steel rack that Danny put there so that all things have a proper place. There is a spatula, a potato masher, a big mixing spoon and a large sharp . . . knife. With my eyes rolling back in my head, I reach for the knife.

Stay . . . The pathetic song persists.

I feel the knife's smooth, cool handle in my hand. I swing it hard at Danny's face. But someone—maybe Momma, Outside Me, maybe even God, assuming he actually knows my name—put the spoon, not the knife, in my hand. I think we are both shocked when the spoon actually makes contact with his face, its blunt metal edge opening a small rough gash on his cheek. A drop of blood trickles down his chin.

I am about to die. Danny can snap me out with two little fingers. I think about my expiration date, imagine the headlines: Man kills his Baby Momma in . . . what, a jealous rage? No, just a rage, rage. I think about my baby. Oh God, if you know me at all, please don't let him grow up with my mother and her husband. Please let Lee and Jamal, or even Eli and Natasha raise him. Please!

I resolve to fight for my life, for Daniel's life. I am picturing the kind of life Little Daniel will have living with Danny, living with *this* Danny. Love is not enough. Fight! I swing the spoon around for another strike. My only hope is to somehow get away. He catches my hand in his vice-like grip and forces me to drop the spoon. With one hand he grabs me by the throat and pushes me up against the wall. I am gasping for air, my nails ripping at his clutch. There is a crazy person in his eyes glaring out at me. Terrified, I realize this must be that person, that person who was so full of rage, that person who could not be restrained, that rage which could not be extinguished. This is that person, the one who kicked his father as he lay helpless on the floor, kicked him over and over again.

I don't know where the resolve comes from. Perhaps it's because I'm accustomed to surviving on so little air. Perhaps this is just how it goes when you know it's your time. I relax. I drop my hands, glare back at him, defiance in my eyes. *Do it!*

We are locked in a deadly stare. His hand is on my throat, but he is no longer squeezing. His face is so close to mine that I can feel his panting breath, and I'm sure he can feel mine. Something static rips between us. It sparks, crackling the dry air before it flits away. I watch as that crazy person recedes, as he slowly returns back to wherever it is that he resides. I watch as he is replaced by a person whose eyes look horrified and truly remorseful.

It is not enough.

Now, I can no longer hear the record's refrain. I can only hear the sounds of our hearts pounding in our chests, our heavy panting and . . . Little Daniel, ripped from a deep sleep, shrieking in the next room. Danny releases me. Gasping and coughing, I push past him. I stumble to Daniel's playpen. I snatch him up. And working to catch my breath, I strap him into the baby sling and position him on my hip. Mollified, he wraps his chubby arms around my neck and rests his sleepy head on my shoulder. I stomp into the little room and locate my oversized pillowcase. I rummage through the drawers, throwing things on the floor. Danny stands in the doorway.

"What the hell do you think you're doing?"

I'm sure he's more concerned about the mess on the floor than he is about what I'm doing. I begin tossing things into my oversized pillowcase. That's when I catch my reflection in the full-length mirror—*my* mirror. Only it's not my reflection at all. The Duckling has broken our uncodified truce. It has invaded *my* mirror. And speaking aloud, its caustic voice scrapes razor blades across my brain . . . again.

What the hell do we think we're doing? it cackles, paraphrasing Danny's menacing tone. A thread of terror is weaving its way into my heart. I don't engage, ignore both of them, toss clothes into the pillowcase. *We can't do this!*

"*We* can't," I say, speaking aloud, tossing books into the bag, trying to keep a tremor out of my voice. I never look in its direction. "But *I* can."

"What?" Danny asks.

We love him. He's buying us a house, a home. What about the music?

"Yes, the music. I wanted it so badly. I still want it, but I won't find it here, not now," I say aloud, looking around for more possessions. "Danny has his music and I have mine." Biting back fear, I turn to confront the Duckling's ugly face. "His music, it's not in my key, never will be. I know that now. I can't subject Little Daniel to a life of dissonance."

"Who the hell are you talking to?" Danny says.

But Daniel loves his father. We're driving him away. We're ruining our life, but it was you alone who ruined Mommy's. It was your Midnight face that drove Daddy away!! it says and breaks into a cruel ear-piercing guffaw.

I know for sure that a physical attack from The Duckling is coming. I have been trying to prepare myself for it. But what I should've known is not to engage The Duckling emotionally. I should've known that eventually it would go there, find a way to stab at my heart—that it would find a way to get inside me, to poke a feathery finger into my open, bleeding scab . . . my Daddy, my shame . . . my guilt.

With both fear and anger spiking, I am trembling and trying not to erupt. I want to scream, but Daniel has fallen asleep in the sling. Still, the need to react is building. The solution eases into my mind like it's been there all along.

I have to kill The Duckling.

I have to kill The Duckling, or this time it will surely kill me. It is the only way I'll ever be free . . . be me. The Duckling is a liar. Suddenly, I know that. We are not one and the same. I will not die if it dies. It will die alone, and I will live on for

Daniel. I have to live on . . . for Daniel. My brain is working overtime. I need to come up with a plan before it . . .

Oh, but we are! it rails, all up in my head, in my thoughts. **We *are* one and the same. And now . . . we are no more!** It grabs my windpipe. As it squeezes, gradually increasing the pressure, I can only manage strained, wheezing breaths. It puffs itself up into full stature, filling the space in my lungs. I sputter, cough, wheeze, grab at my chest, and reach for Daniel who has fallen asleep in the sling attached to my side. The pressure is growing. I am drifting in and out of ominous spikes of light and dark shadows. I sense Danny near me. I think he is talking at me. I think he is mocking me. I think, maybe, he has allied with The Duckling. Maybe I feel his hands around my neck. Maybe it is Danny who is squeezing the life out of me.

My legs are failing. I slump; grab on to the bureau. Through heavy fog and dark clouds, I see Bernadette. She is sitting there, impassive. I reach for her, but she is beyond my grasp. Instead, my fingers brush past something cold, something metal, something heavy.

And I know.

My fingers wrap around Afro-Pick-Zilla. Still slumped over the bureau, I manage to lift it, its hefty weight comforting and reassuring in my hand. Then, with a strength and determination that comes from somewhere outside of me, as well as something inside of me, I pull myself upright, steady myself, rear back and heave the pick like a spear into the mirror with everything I have. The impact is jolting. The mirror explodes into a thousand sparkly shards. Danny who, as it turns out, has only been ineffectually patting me on my back, now moves to restrain me.

"What the hell?!!" he shouts.

Daniel starts, wriggles, opens his sleepy eyes but amazingly does not burst into tears. The Duckling's ugly midnight face is splitting into faults and fissures as it slowly crashes to the floor. *What*, it shrieks . . . *have*, it screeches . . . *you*, it squeals . . . *done?!* it squawks.

My windpipe spasms, squeezes, then opens wide. I am coughing, wheezing, breathing . . . laughing. I have done it! I have poured water on the Wicked Witch of the West, and I am free. Revived, I inhale a deep, satisfying breath, hold, release, release, repeat, stand erect.

"Get off me!" I hiss, shaking off Danny's grip.

He releases me, face in shock, hands in surrender. Clearly perplexed, he steps back. I retrieve Bernadette from the bureau and gingerly place her into the bag.

I push past Danny, stomp and stumble back into the living room. He follows. *Stay, stay, stay* . . . That pitiful, pleading song is still whining and wailing through the room . . . so damn annoying.

I am on a tear. On autopilot, I smack the arm of the record player. The needle caterwauls across the grooves. Danny grabs my arm. Now steady on my feet, I jerk myself free. Our eyes lock. We are in a stare-down. I have no intention of blinking first. I am steel. He must see it. He drops his eyes.

I grab my keys from the coffee table, start down the long narrow hallway, and avoid looking into that other mirror, The Duckling's mirror. I'm afraid it will be there, resurrected like the Phoenix. I'm afraid it can't be killed, that I'll never be free of it. But I do look. I must look. I have to know.

It's me! No mute, hapless duckling. I am actually seeing me. Yes, it's the me I've always been—no disguise, no Outside Me, none needed. It's me, my flawless black skin, my pretty face, my large expressive eyes. I smile. Yes, it's the me that I always was. I take a reviving full-chested breath. There's no ugly black obstruction!

I stop in front of the key hook on the wall. I hesitate. Something is working its way into my chest—something old, familiar, and comfortable, something I crave . . . closure. I reach up and place my keys back on that hook. I stare at them for a while. My eyes tear up as they hang there, swaying themselves into place.

"What, you're not coming back? Bitch! You can't take my son from me!"

"I have no intention of separating you and your son, Danny. You can see him whenever you swing into town." I turn to face him. He is standing there staring at me, a confused, helpless expression on his very beautiful face. But Danny is not what I'm focused on right now.

Something new and alien is moving through me. In my mind's eye, I am seeing the little apartment that was my sanctuary, my home . . . finally, a home. I am looking at the little square living room, its gleaming hardwood floors, paid for with work-study money, the little coffee table Natasha and I stripped and refurbished by hand. I'm remembering the little single bed that Lee and I found at a used furniture shop, remembering the sound of the gumbo pot, hearing the dripping water strum it like an instrument.

"Go on then!" Danny says. "Run! That's all you ever do. You run away from your life!"

"No, Danny, not this time. This time I'm running *towards* my life," I say. But I'm wavering, not sure I believe it. There's something, some different kind of closure is slowly tugging at me.

I am putting one foot in front of the other, making my way down the long narrow hallway, heading for the door, heading for . . . what?

Danny is talking at me, but his voice has faded to background noise as Little Daniel emits a soft murmur into my ear. It has a melody. I am feeling the rhythms, hearing the song . . . the music! It is surrounding me. It is inside of me. It is vibrating through every cell in my body, blasting out through every pore. And I think it might've been here all along. Yes! It's been right here in the home that I've made for us, for Daniel and me. I just had to learn how to hear it.

"You're crazy. You know that?! You have lost your fucking mind!"

With that, I turn on my heels, rapidly close the space between us.

"Wrong again," I hiss, all up in his face. "I've found my fucking mind. And I plan to hold on to it."

"Well, bitch," he says. "If you're going, then go ahead . . . go."

I look up at the two sets of keys hanging on their hooks. I take possession of one, hesitate, then grab the other. My eyes are fierce. My intent is clear. A mixture of disbelief and comprehension move across his face.

"No . . . you go," I say, resurrecting the cruel words he said to me so long ago.

"What?!" he asks, so cute when he's perplexed.

In a cool, even voice I say, "Get out, Danny. Pack your shit and get out."

"Daawn . . ." he coos. And I realize that he can do it at will, speak my name in a tone that sounds like an aria, like it's being carried in on the wind—that same tone that used to reach in and touch me in all my warm, intimate places. Nothing.

"Leave!" I roar. Then, my heart pulls into a quiver as the "daddy kicking" crazy guy flashes in his eyes.

I am a badass.

I hold steady, repress my fear, repress my relief when the crazy guy flitters and peters away, replaced by a Danny who looks full of regret, truly sorry, resigned, and maybe even ashamed.

The sight of Danny's fine brown frame carrying its luggage down that long narrow hallway is shaking. With his head hanging low and his shoulders slumped, he looks so small. As I watch him go, I inhale long satisfying breaths and release a riot of feelings with each exhalation. On this day, there has been too many rollercoaster emotions in too short a time.

I square my shoulders. Little Daniel's head is resting there. His breathing is like an R&B concert in my ear. My

heart, strong and steady, is marking time with the melody—
no flutters, no palpitations. A feeling that had abandoned me
for so long is flooding in and filling-up the void in my chest.
It's my self-respect! Now I know; I'm hearing the music that
will make this place a home; it's Aretha! Her song, like an
anthem, is blaring out inspiration

... "Respect."

ACKNOWLEDEMENTS

How does one write a book acknowledgement? I wondered. Then, for some reason, it occurred to me that acknowledgements, like charity, should begin at home. And for me home is wherever my husband is. My husband, Jose Alfaro, is the best person I know. Jose who puts up with me when I'm on a writing binge, who never has a negative remark. Jose whose positivity sometimes drives me up the walls. Jose who cooks while I write. Thank you, Jose, for always being there for me. You sustain me in ways that I've yet to find words for. I'm sure there would be no book without your patient support.

I want to thank my editor, author Misty Mount, whose professional insights were invaluable in guiding the work. Misty, thank you for going the nine rounds with me, for giving me my space, and teaching me the art of a working partnership.

Author Elaine Auerbach is my cousin-in-law, a gifted writer, and experienced editor. It never hurts to have a gifted, experienced editor in the family, and in this case, it's a blessing. Elaine, thank you for reading and rereading the earliest drafts of this story. Thank you for pointing out, (to use your words) that "the story had beautiful smooth skin and bones; but it was lacking the muscle tissue needed to hold the skin and bones together." I've never forgotten that metaphor. It helped to shape this novel and all the others that I've written since. Thank you, Elaine, for the time and effort you invested in my work, and for your amazing sense of story that helped bring this book to life.

"BOW" (Banquet of Words)—this is what we call the little writing group that I'm privileged to be a part of. Bob Sickles, Jennifer Tulchin, and Laura Martin are all extraordinary, caring people and talented writers. I trust them. I trust their friendship. I trust their honest, straightforward, spot-on critiques. Guys, thank you for the warm support and encouragement that you've given me over the years. It's kept me going.

I also want to thank all my teachers at Sarah Lawrence College's Writing Institute. They've encouraged me and taught me so much about the craft of writing.

Bill Berry was the CEO/publisher at aaduna magazine. His penchant and passion for supporting all phases of art and culture is prolific. Thank you, Bill, for not only choosing to publish one of my early short stories, but for nominating it for the Pushcart Award. I'm not sure you knew, but that affirmation of my work gave me the confidence to go on and pursue longer form writing projects. It made me believe I could actually write books.

Last, but extremely significant, and the hardest acknowledgement to write, I'd like to express my profound gratitude to my best friend, the late Alice Meyerson. For over ten years, Alice and I were a little writing group of two. Although she was an extremely gifted writer in her own right,

Alice poured a lot of time and effort into the shaping of *my* book. When I'd suggest that we get back to *her* work, she'd smile, her smile, and sounding like a giddy child she'd say, "No, this is fun. Where do you plan to take it next?" Alice, I thank you for your genuine interest in my work and your generosity, which is unprecedented in writing circles. I thank you for sharing with me your magical words and the unique stories that you had to tell. I'm pretty sure that I would never have completed three novels in eight years if I wasn't hustling to finish a chapter, to share with you each week; pretty sure I wouldn't be celebrating the publishing of one of those books if, right before you departed, you hadn't made me promise to start sending out my work. Alice . . . thank you.

Born and raised in the Bronx NYC B. Lynn Carter graduated The City College of New York with a degree in creative writing. More recently, she's been studying creative writing at Sarah Lawrence College's writing Institute.

Lynn's short story "One Wild Ride," published in Aaduna magazine, was nominated for the Pushcart Award in 2014. She's had short stories and poetry published in the Blue Lake Review, Drunk Monkeys, Ascent Aspirations, Enhance Magazine, The Story Shack and the Bronx Memoir Project, among others and is listed in Poets & Writers directory of writers.